Danielle Thomas was born in Zambia, of British and Welsh/Irish parents. She graduated from the University of Cape Town and then went on to teach for fifteen years, showing a special interest in the education of 'difficult' children. For the past twenty-seven years she has been doing research for her author husband, Wilbur Smith. Her first three novels, *Children of Darkness*, *Voices in the Wind* and *Cry of Silence*, were huge successes and are all available in Pan paperback.

DANIELLE THOMAS

Drumbeat

PAN BOOKS

First published 1997 by Macmillan

This edition published 1998 by Pan Books
an imprint of Macmillan Publishers Ltd
25 Eccleston Place, London SW1W 9NF
and Basingstoke

Associated companies throughout the world

ISBN 0 330 36790 0

3 5 7 9 8 6 4 2

A CIP catalogue record for this book is available from
the British Library.

Typeset by CentraCet, Cambridge
Printed by Mackays of Chatham plc, Chatham, Kent

Chapter One

THE AFRICAN sky seemed colourless and clear as glass in the early dawn. Gradually the eastern horizon stained to lemon, as pale as the delicate petals of the ipomoeas growing wild in the Zimbabwe bush. The early morning translucency was marred only by a skein of flighting duck. They formed a wavering line of black specks against the soft light as they followed the drake.

It was April and the early mornings and evenings were cool and pleasant.

The sky would soon grow golden as the sun rose hot and high in the heavens and drummed down on the land, quivering trees and shrubs in the valleys into a shimmering heat haze.

Pat Gifford walked barefoot on to the cement verandah surrounding his home. He lifted his head and breathed in great lungfuls of the crisp air.

Pat had seen his two score years and ten. Even though age had added girth to his once slim body, he was immensely powerful. He walked with the stride and purpose of a man half his age.

Suddenly something hit him hard and swift behind his knees, almost knocking him over. He swung round, always wary of snakes coiling down from the thick purple bougainvillaeas hanging over the verandah.

'Sheeba,' he roared. His red Rhodesian ridgeback bitch lifted her lips in an ingratiating grin and every inch of her lean body wriggled as she spun around him in greeting. 'All right, girl, calm down,' he soothed, as he fondled her silky ears. 'I know you're pleased to see me. You know that I love you. Now, let's stop this nonsense.'

Sheeba licked his toes then lay across his feet, happy to be with him.

Pat stroked his square chin, then rubbed the top of his head, now bald and shiny and fringed with thick hair. He knew that these gestures were becoming a habit, but he found them reassuring.

He looked to the north as he did every morning, to where a great white cloud of mist, the Mosi-a-Tunya, the smoke that thunders, hung over the land.

At times he believed that he could hear a dull roar as the full breadth of the mighty Zambezi River plunged through separate falls and cataracts to drop one hundred and eight metres sheer into the gorge below. At this time of the year, when the waters were at their peak, the force and fury of the river plunging over the Victoria Falls threw up a spray which could be seen seventy kilometres away.

Pat owned two ranches, Kame and Ganyani, both within an easy hour's drive of the Falls. He used them as private hunting ranches, making money from wealthy overseas hunters who came for the buffalo, the antelope, including the magnificent sable and roan, and the occasional elephant. He also leased the hunting rights to the land between his ranches, thus increasing the safari area he could offer clients. He and his son Erin lived on Kame, named after the famous Great Zimbabwe ruins, now a World Heritage site.

Kame was a beautiful place with outcrops of granite

2

rocks, teak forests and stands of mopane trees. Their butterfly-like leaves and turpentine scent in spring seemed irresistible to elephants. The rocky outcrops were dotted with the contorted trunks of giant baobabs. Along the river wild date palms clustered.

Ganyani, meaning the Wild Dog, was by contrast a dry, desolate-looking ranch. Yet varied with the dry areas were grass plains where the teak and magnificent *mukwa* trees grew. It had no perennial stream but relied on pans and boreholes for water.

Pat had listed more than four hundred species of birds on this ranch and his son happily watched over the ever-increasing herds of antelope, buffalo and zebra. The resident lions and leopards seemed to make little difference to the large numbers of game.

Both men firmly believed that it was their duty to protect the game and habitat in this area. They felt that the exploding population in Africa was endangering the wild animals and the unspoiled bush, things which made Africa special and different from any other continent. It was the cradle of mankind and held its heartbeat. It must not be destroyed.

Pat hoped that when Erin married he would make Ganyani his home. He would then have the freedom to run his own ranch, yet stay close to his father.

Pat and Erin loved their land with a passion men usually reserve for women. Pat's family had marched to the drums of war, fighting in the Matabele uprising, in the late 1800s, as well as in the recent fifteen-year-long Bush War.

Pat had lost two sons in this bloody war which had torn the small nation apart. Erin was his youngest. Now a tall, wiry twenty-five-year-old, he was bronzed by the sun and in some respects mature beyond his years. The boy was still trying to accept what he saw as the needless deaths of his twin brothers.

The country was finally settling down. Former enemies were now friends and the horrors of war were beginning to fade. But his brothers were lost to him for ever.

Occasionally the Marxist ideology which had brought the ruling party to power would come to the fore again and there would be talk of nationalizing industry and private land. It was a subject which made Pat Gifford turn pale with rage and frustration. He would sit on the verandah with a whisky in his hand damning everyone who he considered was ruining this wonderful country.

Only when the moon lost its light would he stumble off to bed, still shaking his head and muttering about money and power-hungry idiots.

The Giffords' roots were deeply entrenched in the rich, red soil of their private game ranches where Erin acted as a hunter-cum-guide. He was fearless, an excellent shot and knew the land intimately. Both Giffords had drunk deeply of the waters of the Zambezi and according to the legend of the Shona tribe, they would now never leave the country.

Pat turned away from the spray hanging over the Falls and shaded his eyes as he caught sight of the wavering line of black specks to the east. He watched them for a few moments then turned to accept a mug of coffee from his son who had come to join him.

The two men stretched themselves out in the old cane chairs which creaked beneath their weight.

'Another day of fence patrol with my Swiss "Elephant Man",' said Erin, blowing on his coffee to cool it. He flinched as a few drops flew over the rim and landed on his bare leg.

He was referring to a Swiss hunter who came out every year. When attacked by critics because he shot elephant, the gentleman declared that it was impossible for a breeding population in excess of half a million to be endangered. He agreed that the elephants were not in one group but thinly scattered across the African countries. But, with the logic of a banker, he pointed out that the countries which carefully culled and managed their herds had an increasing elephant population. Countries which had banned hunting opened the doors to poachers and had depleted their herds to the point of extinction.

He paid his £950 per day for fifteen days and went home happy with his trophy tusks. He had shot on Kame every year for the last decade, thus earning him the nickname Elephant Man.

Pat had reached the age where he disliked elephant shoots. He felt that, like himself, elephants deserved to live out their lives in peace. But the revenue paid for the trackers, skinners, camp staff and upkeep of the Cessna plane which he used to collect clients from Bulawayo or the Falls airport and fly them straight to the ranch. He knew that Zimbabwe had to cull almost six thousand elephant each year to protect the habitat. It was a necessary part of the new game management. The money from the sale of meat, ivory and skins could be used to help the Game Department, who were always desperately short of funds to train rangers and buy vehicles to combat poachers, who came not only for the ivory, but also for rhino horn.

But it seemed impossible to separate emotion from the word 'elephant' and Pat had no answers to the problem.

He watched his son flick hot liquid from the sun-bleached hair on his leg. Erin was as fair as his brothers had been dark. He took after his mother, generally acknowledged as the most beautiful woman in the area. She had died when Erin was a teenager. The doctor said it was malaria, but Pat knew that she had lost the will to live after the death of her sons and the massacre of her family in the remote Vumba Mountains.

The Bush War had taken its toll of women, as well as the men who fought for their beliefs and ideals.

Pat adored his remaining son but made him work as hard as any member of his staff. He knew that to exist peacefully in the new country the boy would have to learn to be hard yet just. He would not allow sentiment to cloud his judgement as he tried to be both father and mother to the young man. Looking at Erin now, Pat was proud of his son.

'I know it's boring work to patrol the fence, hoping that some big bull has stepped on it and come on to our land, but keep your client interested in the possibility of lion spoor. Jacob tells me he heard one roar down in the south-east near Sina Pan,' said Pat. 'Try Kame today. Give Ganyani a rest.'

Erin nodded, then smiled. He and Jacob had been friends since Erin was a child. Jacob had followed spoor for Pat before Erin was even born.

'I swear that Jacob hears lions in his sleep every night. He's only happy when we're tracking lion or buffalo. He says that shooting elephants is like shooting the Matobo Rocks, the bald heads. They remind him of his tribal elders.'

'Enough about bald heads, young pup,' growled Pat.

'Get that tracker of yours and collect your client, who'll be up and waiting if I know him.'

Erin glanced up at the sky, drained his mug and jumped down from the verandah shouting for Jacob and his back-up, Jonas.

'Did you hear the drums last night, Dad?' he asked as he swung into his open-topped Toyota. 'Wonder what's up? They kept at it until dawn.'

'We'll know soon enough,' replied Pat, wiggling his bare toes on the cool concrete.

He only wore shoes if he had to go into Harare on business, usually to visit some government minister.

Erin had tried hunting barefoot like his father but after an hour of pulling out thorns and wincing as stones cut into his insteps he returned to wearing his 'veldskoen', shoes made from the tanned hide of the kudu with thick flexible soles. He teased his father, saying that there was very little difference between the bracelet made from the deeply cracked sole of an elephant pad which Pat wore on his arm and Pat's own feet.

As Erin gunned the Toyota, Pat shouted to him, 'I may be home late. You know how people waffle at these ministerial meetings, especially in Harare.'

He loved the Matabele, known as N'debele, an offshoot of the Zulu nation. He was still a little distrustful of the Shona who were the dominant people in both government and the Harare area.

Suddenly Erin switched off the engine and all was quiet.

'Be careful, Dad. Don't tell them what you think of the system. Those drums were not singing last night. They worry me.'

'Don't fuss. Off you go while you still have a client.'

Pat watched his son until a cloud of red dust obscured the truck. He then stood up and flung his arms out as if to embrace the whole of Kame and Ganyani.

I'll die rather than give up an inch of my land, he pledged silently.

Before going indoors to dress for the meeting, he looked once again to the east and frowned. The skein of duck was still flying, but there was something wrong with the formation. He shook his head, unable to waste time pondering the flying habits of wild duck. He was already late.

'Rudo, see if the phone is working,' he shouted to the N'debele woman who now looked after the house. 'Tell Mr Hanley that I'll be at his place in fifteen minutes. No, make it ten.'

He ran into his room and pulled on the freshly pressed khaki slacks and safari jacket which he considered formal dress. He then eased his feet into a pair of soft beige veldskoen and groaned.

'I polished these,' said Rudo, handing him a pair of leather moccasins.

'No, these things are bad enough,' he said, lacing the velskoen as loosely as possible.

'Where is your tie?' Rudo opened the door of the old teak wardrobe and shook out a navy and red striped one.

'I'm going to meet two members of the Department of National Parks, not the Prime Minister, Rudo. It's only Matamba and Tigera today, not important enough for a tie.'

Not important, he mocked himself silently. They only head the committee for designating hunting concessions and conservation areas. These men are only my future. If I am to retain hunting rights on the land I lease between

Kame and Ganyani I have to like and work with these men.

Kumgirai Matamba, a good name – meaning to beg for – and that's just what I have to do today. Beg for the land. Land we have loved and nurtured all our lives. Land which gives a good living to all my people, employment and food to those who would otherwise be a burden to the already overburdened government. But how do I take off their blinkers and make them see that we are essential to the country's economy?

'But Matamba and Tigera are important men,' said Rudo. 'The drums say so, they . . .' She stopped, unwilling to repeat the message carried on the soft wind of the night.

'Say what?' Pat felt a chill through his shirt. There were so many things in this land which were still dark and dangerous. Though he had said nothing to Erin, he had lain awake the night before, fruitlessly trying to read the message the drums had beaten out so monotonously.

Looking at Rudo's closed face and downcast eyes, he realized that it would be a waste of time trying to persuade her to reveal what she had read in the drumbeats.

'Make some of your best kudu stew tonight, Rudo,' he said with a thin smile. 'Erin is bringing his elephant hunter up to the house for dinner. It is the last day of the hunt and they have not found *nzou* yet. I've told them not to hunt on Ganyani today but to try Kame. Perhaps they will be lucky.'

He thought he saw a flicker of relief cross her face, but decided it was only the play of light through the wooden blinds on the windows.

'They will find one this afternoon, a good one,' she answered, putting away the only tie he possessed.

He laid down the ivory-backed hairbrush with which he was smoothing his hair.

'Oh, and is your Jacob a witch doctor too? Can he talk to the spirits and find out where the big bulls eat and sleep? Perhaps Salugazana came to him in a dream, or put her voice into the drums last night . . .'

Rudo smoothed her apron over her broad hips and compressed her lips, a sign that she was upset.

'Mr Pat, it is not good to talk like that. Salugazana was our greatest *nganga*. You know that even Lobengula went to hear her words of wisdom.'

Yes, thought Pat, and look what happened to your Matabele king. In the Moffat Treaty he agreed not to sign any contracts without British approval. He then signed a concession for Charles Rudd, one of Cecil Rhodes's agents, giving away exclusive rights to all metals and minerals in his kingdom. Rhodes used this to form the British South African Company under Royal Charter. He brought in hardy pioneer stock and eventually took over all of Lobengula's land.

On advice of the great Salugazana, Lobengula had decided to fight the new pioneers who came to settle in Rhodesia and regain his land. He failed and died on his retreat northwards.

'If our Swiss hunter has to rely on Jacob's messages from the *ngangas*, then this will be the first time he will return to Zurich without a pair of ivory tusks for his trophy room,' he said instead. 'That means no money from him next year. He will be an unhappy man, Rudo, and an unhappy hunter.'

Rudo sighed. The ways of these men were strange. She handed him his briefcase. It was old and battered, but polished to a deep glow by her loving hands.

'You are right about the *ngangas*, Rudo,' agreed Pat, sorry that he had upset the woman who had done so much to ease Erin's pain when his mother died. 'Salugazana was a great one and the *ngangas* are most important.'

Rudo smiled and her teeth gleamed white and lovely against her chocolate skin.

'Is Jacob treating you well?' he asked, worried that the tracker would soon find another woman to join him.

'Oh yes, Mr Pat. He is a good man.'

Pat grinned and wondered how many women in Bulawayo said the same about his good-looking N'debele tracker. Pat knew that Jacob had sired three sons with Rudo. Looking at her gentle face, he made up his mind to keep Jacob away from Harare. The ladies there were more sophisticated than those of the quieter Matabeland and he certainly did not want to lose his superb tracker. Jacob had stood shoulder to shoulder with him on many a lion and buffalo charge. The man was fearless. He knew that Erin was safe with Jacob.

Pat looked at the large enamel clock on the dressing table. He had five minutes to be at his friend Fred Hanley's ranch.

'Fly safely, Mr Pat,' whispered Rudo as she watched him open the door of his yellow Cessna and wait for his ridgeback bitch to jump into the back seat.

'Down, Sheeba,' he commanded and shook his head as the dog licked his face in happiness. Her ears drooped and she trampled the seat as she turned in circles until satisfied that she had found the most comfortable position. She curled up with a sigh, ready to endure the flight.

It was only the ridgeback's devotion to Pat which made her go in the plane. The dog followed him everywhere. His ranch labourers always knew when he was about to appear. They boasted that he could never surprise them, as the 'red devil dog with the yellow eyes of a leopard' always preceded him, giving away his whereabouts.

They treated Sheeba with great respect. Those who had come too close to Pat and felt her teeth now kept their distance. She was courageous, one of the few breeds of dog who would not turn from the smell of a lion. Pat knew that she would kill anyone who tried to harm him, even if she died in the attempt.

'Good girl,' he said as he taxied on to the hard dirt strip which served as a runway. Busy with pre-flight checks, he did not notice that the loose V formation of ducks from the east was rapidly changing shape.

He swung the Cessna around, put the wing flaps up, checked that the carburetter gauge read cold, applied the brakes, then opened the throttle to full. The Cessna shuddered as it strained for take-off. Yet still Pat did not release the brakes. He needed a maximum performance take-off to clear the mopane trees at the end of the runway. He terrified his friends with this short-field take-off, but his wife had loved the tall mopanes and he refused to cut them down.

Sheeba moaned softly, hating the noise and shaking of the plane.

'All right, girl, here we go,' Pat said as he finally released the brakes. The plane flew forward as if shot from a catapult and Pat smiled as the tops of the trees bent to the wind as the Cessna skimmed them. Hoping to pick up Erin's truck and give him a low fly-past, he turned south but no cloud of dust marked the Toyota's progress.

Perhaps Jacob found the right *nganga*, he thought, and they are following the dinner-plate pads of an elephant. He could visualize the deep ridges on the soles of the footprints and feel the excitement of finding spoor. Unconsciously he crossed his fingers.

After a few moments he swung on to a south-westerly heading which would take him over the Hwange National Park, fifteen thousand square kilometres of burning Kalahari sands, grassy plains and extensive forests – a wonderland, reported to have a greater density of wildlife than any other park in the world. Pat could never resist flying over Hwange to spot buffalo and elephant.

Fred Hanley's ranch shared part of the south-western boundary of Hwange. Fred, like Pat, was an old-timer. Zimbabwe was his love and his home and he could envisage living nowhere else.

The Lancaster House talks, masterminded by Margaret Thatcher and chaired by Lord Carrington, had brought into being in 1980 an agreement to end the squabbles for power after the Bush War. The agreement had contained a clause which guaranteed the white electorate twenty seats in the House of Assembly and ten in the Senate. Fred Hanley had been one of the members of the Senate.

Though the clause was intended to be inviolate for ten years, the President was still firmly committed to a one-party state. After seven years the guaranteed white seats in the House of Assembly were abolished and two years later the Senate followed the same pattern.

Disillusioned, Fred's sons left Zimbabwe for New Zealand taking his beloved grandchildren with them. They had lost all faith in the new country, but Fred Hanley decided that 'adapt or die' would have to be his new motto.

Though he and his wife Blanche missed their sons and grandchildren constantly, they now showered all their love on Briar, their eldest daughter, who was unmarried and lived with them.

Fred was sitting in his open-sided Land Rover at the edge of his airstrip looking up at the sky. Briar was in the driver's seat beside him wearing khaki shorts, a long-sleeved shirt and canvas shoes. Her floppy bush hat was pulled well down on her head and her eyes, blue and trusting like her father's, were shielded from the glare by dark sunglasses.

Suddenly Fred leaned over the seat and picked up his briefcase, beautifully crafted from elephant skin, bought at one of the curio stores in Harare.

'He's here.' His pale blue eyes were mere slits against the sun but he refused to wear sunglasses, declaring that they ruined his eyesight.

Briar stared up at the sky, now a bright burnished blur, and saw nothing. Her father's extraordinary eyesight belied his age. She wished that she had his vision.

'He couldn't resist flying over Hwange,' said Fred, looking at his watch.

'You'll never teach Pat that people, especially government officials, are more important than animals,' laughed Briar.

'Unfortunately we need the officials to give us the stamped papers to keep the land for the game,' Fred grunted.

He climbed down from the Land Rover favouring his weak leg, a reminder of the Bush War. A war he should have left to younger men, as Blanche and Briar kept reminding him.

The wind picked up his thick mane of white hair and whipped it over his forehead. He quickly smoothed it down with his fingers, knowing that Pat would mock him for sporting a pop star look. Pat was secretly envious of Fred's luxuriant head of hair. Fred in turn was embarrassed by hair which he felt should belong to a woman.

Sheeba stood up on the back seat panting with excitement as the Cessna bumped down in a cloud of brown dust. Briar and Fred turned their faces away until the plane had come to a stop and Pat opened the door.

Sheeba was the first out. She squatted quickly in the sand. By the time she turned round to smell the urine, it had vanished into the dry ground. She looked puzzled for a moment, then ran to greet Briar who usually had a piece of dried sausage in her pocket. She was not disappointed. Sheeba swallowed the last piece in a great gulp as she heard Pat whistle. She ran to the plane, gave his hand a quick lick of apology and jumped on to the back seat.

Fred clapped Pat on the shoulder in greeting and watched as he bent to kiss Briar. There was a time when the two men had hoped that Briar would marry Scott, Pat's oldest son, born a few minutes before his brother. Fred shook his head. That could never happen now and it seemed as if Briar had lost interest in men.

'I see you're all dressed up for the meeting,' Fred mocked gently, looking at Pat's khaki safari suit.

'He has shoes on,' shouted Briar from the Land Rover.

Pat grinned. 'Your suit and tie will have to do for both of us,' he said. 'Come on, let's get this over with. I'll buy you a drink at Meikles Hotel after this indaba.'

Fred nodded, wishing that they were indeed going to an indaba, a gathering where they would sit in the shade of a tree and talk to the grey-haired elders of the tribe.

That was the Africa he loved and understood, not this

new one, where most men were in their positions for personal gain. The welfare of the people, animals and care of the land came low down on their list of priorities.

Don't be small-minded, he chided himself mentally. There are some good and well-intentioned men in the government. Remember the odds they have to battle against.

'Dreaming again, Fred,' said Pat as he dipped one of the plane's wings in salute to Briar. She sat motionless in the Land Rover with her hands draped over the wheel until the plane vanished to the west.

Every time she saw Pat Gifford a vivid mental image of Scott returned to remind her of what might have been. Unbeknown to their parents, he and Briar had decided to marry when the Bush War was over. They loved with all the innocence of youth. Briar felt that it made his death harder to bear. If only they had made love . . .

Stop it, Briar Hanley, she reprimanded herself. You are over thirty years of age and should not still be hankering after love trysts held at a waterhole, where you watched game come down to drink in the moonlight.

But even as she scolded herself, she saw once again the still pool bleached silver by the moon and the droplets sparkling bright as fireworks as the great elephants tossed the water high into the air, letting it cascade down over their dusty backs.

She closed her eyes and felt Scott's lips on hers, felt the strength of his body as he held her in his arms. She heard him pleading, 'I may not come back, Briar. Let's make our memories now.'

She thumped her hands down on the steering wheel, almost delighting in the pain as it tingled up her arms.

'Fool,' she said out loud. 'Stupid, stupid little fool. Your precious virginity was so important to you, now that's all you have left.'

Angrily she turned the key in the ignition and listened as the engine coughed and spluttered before taking hold. This was a new Land Rover but it behaved like a second-hand one. Pat and Erin made a good living out of hunting on Kame and Ganyani but the Hanleys lived comfortably on money from Fred's inheritance, some of which he had invested in lucrative business ventures.

Her father had frequently been offered a good price for Inyati Ranch because of its position to the west of Hwange Park. But the thought of leaving the ranch horrified them. Granted to their family by Mizilikazi, Lobengula's father, in 1859 when the first missionary station was allowed to open, it had been their home for several generations.

Fred secretly hoped that one day the rest of the family would return with their children and forge a future in the new nation. He dreamed of Inyati Ranch remaining in Hanley hands for many generations to come.

Briar swung the Land Rover on to the track leading back to the thatch-roofed ranch house. There her mother would be waiting for her to help make melon and ginger jam, using up the few melons which the baboons had not stolen.

Briar caught sight of the house nestling amid bright red and white bougainvillaeas and poinsettia trees. On the spur of the moment she swung the Land Rover round in a tight circle and hurtled back down the track.

Blanche watched the dust hanging in the still air and wiped her hands on her apron. She knew that Briar would not be back for hours.

If only that waterhole would dry up, she thought. Briar

makes it a shrine to her memories. It's worse than having a grave to visit. Scott is still so alive at the waterhole.

As she approached the pan of water, Briar pulled off the track and parked under a mopane tree.

The point three-seven-five felt heavy in her hands as she lifted it from the gun rack. She always carried a gun when alone at the pan. Lion often lay in wait for the game as they came down to drink and a family of elephants would usually come to play in the cool water which bubbled up from an underground spring.

She knew that her mother thought these visits to the pan were morbid, but she always drew strength and peace from the place where she had once known love.

The pan was devoid of life as she settled down with her back against a large teak tree, aware that if she sat absolutely still the animals would filter back to drink. She closed her eyes and let the sounds and smells of the bush she loved seep into her.

She knew that her father had been warned about impending trouble and was worried. He tried to hide it, but she had detected a false note in his laughter lately and in the over-emphasis of his assurances as to how secure was their claim to Inyati Ranch.

Please let everything go well at Dad's meeting today, she prayed. Let us keep Inyati.

Chapter Two

'JONAS, YOU are jumping around like a monkey with fleas,' said Jacob to the tracker seated beside him. 'And your eyes search the skies like the *mbila*. You too are looking straight into the sun, just as the rock rabbit does.'

Jonas seemed deaf to Jacob's admonitions and continued to scan the heavens.

'Elephants and lion do not walk in the sky. Their spoor is found in the soil,' said Jacob. He kept his voice low so that Erin and the Swiss hunter would not hear.

'Before the Big One left Kame,' said Jonas, referring to Pat, 'just as the sun was lighting the heavens, I saw many black duck against the sun, only they did not fly like duck.'

Jacob nodded. He too had seen the wavering skein black against the rising sun but had paid them no attention. He was checking that the vehicle had its tool kit, spades to dig them out of sand or mud, fresh water in the water bottles, food packed by Rudo, the medicine chest ready and clean, and extra ammunition. He knew that Erin, like his father, expected everything in the Toyota to be in perfect order before each hunt. Erin was young but was a hard taskmaster. That was part of what made him a good hunter.

'What of these duck, Jonas?' Jacob asked in Sindebele,

the language of the N'debele people, so that the Swiss hunter could not understand.

'They were flying straight for Kame and suddenly turned and flew back to the fence line. They were a long way from me but I knew them. You know them too, Jacob. We both saw many during the war.'

'Helicopters, Alouette 3s,' breathed Jacob. 'But why here?'

'I think these are the birds of death of which the drums spoke last night,' whispered Jonas. He glanced at Erin, well aware that the young man was fluent in Sindebele and Shona. But Erin was concentrating on keeping his client content.

Fortunately the Swiss banker enjoyed spotting birds so Erin was pointing out bateleur eagles, red-headed weavers and three-streaked tchagras, while trying to study the soft sand for elephant spoor.

Jacob and Jonas had both fought in the Bush War, though on different sides, and they were well acquainted with helicopters. Jonas had fought in ZIPRA, the military wing of ZANU – the Zimbabwe African National Union – whereas Jacob had fought with Erin's two brothers, believing that the rural population was better cared for under an experienced white government.

'Yes, the drums,' said Jacob soberly. His loyalty lay with the Giffords, but in Africa certain things were secret and the answers open only to the black man who did not share with others the language of the drums.

The drums were theirs. Carved from a single tree trunk with animal hide stretched tightly across the top, the drums were part of Africa. They were beaten only by men.

Erin caught the word drums and strained to hear what

Jacob and Jonas were saying. He knew that they would lapse into silence if they thought he was listening, so he hung his head over the side of the Toyota pretending to study the ground intently.

He had learned that in Africa silence gains more answers than questions. He hoped that his Swiss client would look for birds quietly, allowing him to concentrate on the whispered conversation in the back of the Toyota.

Erin still shivered or thrilled to the insistent beat of drums shattering the velvet stillness of the night. He was in awe of the uncanny sense of rhythm and the power of the synchronized sounds which seemed to shake the land and make the stars tremble.

'The drums could not have meant death on our lands,' whispered Jacob.

'Then why were the birds of death flying to Ganyani today? For that was the direction of their flight,' argued Jonas. He was rather proud of himself; for once he knew something Jacob had not noticed. 'Perhaps the Big One too read the message last night and that is why he told us to hunt on Kame today,' he continued, his voice rising a little, as the enormity of what he was saying registered.

'Quiet,' commanded Jacob, glancing at Erin. 'You know that the Big One would have been there to greet them with his gun if he thought they were going to Ganyani. He would never allow birds of death on his land.'

'But what do they seek on Ganyani?' asked Jonas, scratching his neck, in perplexity. 'There is nothing of value on that land.'

Jacob shook his head. His sharp eyes looked ahead and through the heat haze he saw a trampled cable. He leaned forward and tapped Erin on the shoulder. '*Nzou,*' he said.

The Swiss banker sat up straight and alert, as if splashed with cold water. *Nzou* was the one word he knew in Sindebele.

The joy of finding signs of elephant at last was lost on Erin. His mind kept repeating the conversation he had overheard. It frightened him. He knew that private ranch owners were always at risk of losing their land as the government desperately sought to placate the landless and to fulfil their election promises.

But he could not believe that they would fly in a military detachment and take it by force.

They would never do that, he comforted himself silently as the Toyota rolled closer to where the fence looked as if a steamroller had run over it.

Strange to find so much of the cable down, he thought. A cow must have flattened it to let her young calf cross. Then his thoughts returned to the conversation he had overheard.

Dad is in Harare now talking to Matamba. Tigera was here recently having dinner with us. They could not take our land, he told himself. Erin forced himself to concentrate on the hunt, but the look of greed in Tigera's dark eyes when he saw the herds of antelope on Ganyani danced in front of Erin even as he turned to banter with his trackers.

'Your eyes are still good even though you are now an old man with a wife and three sons,' he teased Jacob. Jonas crowed with delight. He was always subservient to Jacob and enjoyed it when Jacob was discomfited.

'And tell me, old Jacob,' continued Erin, 'how did you not see that those duck were Alouette 3s, our old helicopters from the War days?'

Jonas's laughter died and he stared at Jacob aghast.

22

'My eyes were on the ground, Erin. I am a tracker not a watcher of birds like Jonas,' Jacob answered quietly.

'Not *a* tracker. The best,' smiled Erin. 'But tell me, where do you think they are going and why?'

'A lion is a lion is a lion,' answered Jacob.

'True, there is no way one can foretell or explain why lions act the way they do.'

The Swiss banker had sat patiently while Erin spoke to Jacob and Jonas. He presumed that they were discussing the elephants. Now he started agitating, eager for action.

'Do we have spoor to follow?' he asked.

'Oh yes,' answered Jacob as he jumped down lightly from the spotting seat, set high on the back of the Toyota.

'A good one,' continued Erin as he saw the size of the spoor deeply embedded in the soft sand. For the next few minutes the helicopters were forgotten as guns and ammunition were checked. Water bottles were handed out and the small first-aid box was tucked into a rucksack and strapped on to Jonas's back.

Just before leaving the truck Erin took a wide crepe bandage from the cubby-hole and put it into his back pocket.

Jacob watched and grinned. How could a bandage cure a snakebite? Everyone knew that if a puff-adder bit you, you would either die of the pain and poison or you would lose that part of your body. It turned black and rotted away. Even children knew that.

Erin parked the Toyota in the shade of a mopane tree and made sure that there was nothing lying out of the tin trunks which the monkeys or baboons could steal. He then moved into place in the single file behind Jacob. Jacob carried the client's gun, a precaution he always took to avoid being shot in the foot or back by an over-excited hunter. The Swiss banker was behind Erin. Jonas brought up the rear.

They moved silently in the bush, both the hunters and the hunted. As they walked the heat intensified and sweat plastered their shirts to their bodies. The heavy silence found only in the deep African bush seemed to suffocate them. Their breathing was quick and shallow.

Suddenly the sickening sound of rapid machine-gun fire broke the stillness. It was faint but unmistakable to those who had fought in the Bush War.

Someone was shooting twin MAG machine-guns. The 7.62 calibre gun was standard equipment on all operational helicopters.

They are on Ganyani, Erin thought silently. As quickly as the thought entered his mind he threw it out. It was too dreadful to contemplate.

'The drums,' Erin whispered urgently to Jonas. 'What did the drums say last night?'

Jonas turned to Jacob for help, but Jacob was studying the ground, drawing circles in the sand with the toe of his shoe. Realizing that he was trapped and terrified in case the helicopters came to Kame on their return, Jonas whispered in reply: 'They spoke only of birds of death which would fly today. None were to say that they knew of them. All were promised land soon.' He swallowed and looked again at Jacob, but Jacob had turned back to the spoor. He was a man of Africa. He had seen nothing, neither had he heard anything.

Erin squeezed Jonas's arm and then said loudly, 'I understand, Jonas. The drums talk only of men's secrets and it is not right of me to question you.'

Jonas smiled at him in gratitude.

'What were those shots?' asked the Swiss hunter as they stopped.

'Only some other hunters on a neighbour's ranch,' answered Erin, swallowing down the bile of fear which rose and flooded his throat.

'It sounds as if they are having a war not a hunt,' grinned the banker.

Erin merely nodded. Whatever was happening on Ganyani – if it was Ganyani, as sounds were deceptive in the bush – was happening on a very large scale. It sounded like a fire-fight during the Bush War.

The chatter of choppers and automatic fire dogged their footsteps. By late afternoon even the little banker was looking apprehensive.

'Are you sure they're not fighting?' he asked Erin. Hunting elephants was dangerous but enjoyable. He certainly had not paid £950 a day to land in the middle of a war.

'No, no, I assure you it's nothing to worry about. Occasionally our neighbours hire helicopters to count and cull game. That is probably what is happening now. The only danger we are in here is that when you see your big bull you won't be ready for him, as your mind is on someone else's gunfire. Now let's hunt.'

Satisfied, the banker turned his attention back to the spoor.

The great African sun was setting in the west. It shone a rich red through the thick clouds of dust thrown up by the convoy of lorries grinding their way through the sand on Ganyani.

'Ah,' sighed the Swiss hunter as he looked up at the teak and mopane trees etched starkly black against the setting sun. 'This Africa is so very beautiful. Beautiful and peaceful.'

He was a happy man. The gunfire had ceased in the late afternoon. He had two ivory tusks lying in the back of the Land Rover. They were sixty and seventy pounds, a respectable weight. The days when hunters regularly took hundred-pound tusks were in the past.

The bull elephant had been tracked so skilfully that it ambled along at an easy four miles an hour, rather than breaking in alarm into its shuffling stride of some ten miles an hour which none but the very fit could follow for long. This had been a good and easy hunt.

Jacob and Jonas hung on to the roll bar in front of their high bench, as the Toyota jolted and swayed over the rutted track. Erin was desperate to reach home and contact his father, hoping he would know what had taken place on Ganyani that day.

Chapter Three

THE ROOM was stuffy and Fred surreptitiously loosened his tie. He drained the glass of water standing on the polished table beside him in the conference room. He once again admired the furniture made from the hard wood of the *mukwa* tree. *Kiaat* the wood was now called, he reminded himself. It was becoming scarce as the local people felled the large trees and burned them to produce charcoal which they could sell.

Fred saw Pat glance at his watch. They had been sitting here since midday and it was now late afternoon.

Time had passed fairly rapidly as the two men waited. When people heard that Fred Hanley was in the building, the room quickly filled with those who had known him when he served in the Senate. He was both liked and respected.

He and Pat took the opportunity to question the staff about their feelings towards the new government. Most of them, mindful of their jobs, had little to say. But a few were more forthcoming and they bemoaned the passing of the UDI era, under the ex-Royal Air Force pilot Ian Douglas Smith.

'Smithy wasn't too bad, though we wanted him dead at the time,' said one of the secretaries. 'At least money did not have to change hands before papers were signed. Now, unless they see your money, their pens remain deep in their pockets.'

Fred and Pat laughed and chatted with the staff about earlier days, until, in the same uncanny manner of elephant sensing danger and vanishing soundlessly into the bush, the room emptied of people.

The imposing double doors swung open. Preceded by two secretaries and what Pat later described as three heavies, Tsvakai Tigera and Kumgirai Matamba appeared. They took their places at the table, citing important government business as the reason for their late arrival.

Pat and Fred had the highest regard for the Department of National Parks and Wildlife Management. The parks were well managed and their conservation techniques advanced, but Pat was wary of Tigera and Matamba. The granting of hunting concessions and the designation of conservation areas gave them great power, as companies were willing to pay well for these concessions.

'Ah my friend,' said Matamba, clasping both Fred's hands in his own large, fleshy ones. 'It is good to see you again.'

Fred looked up at the jovial man and mentally calculated his weight. Matamba's coat strained at the buttons and his thighs rubbed together as he walked.

'I see you are still well,' Fred answered with a smile.

'Yes, and as you also see I am no thinner.' Matamba roared with laughter at his own joke. The tears rolled down his cheeks and his jowls quivered. He held out his hand and one of the secretaries placed a large white handkerchief into his palm. As he mopped his eyes he stopped laughing and studied Pat.

Tigera greeted Fred and deliberately ignored Pat, who was waiting to shake hands with the two men.

Matamba looked at Tigera who motioned imperiously to a chair beside him. Matamba shook his head and held out his hand to Pat. He then joined Tigera at the table. Tigera continued to ignore Pat and began to shuffle his papers.

Fred, infuriated by the slight to his friend, pushed back his chair from the table. The sudden noise made both Matamba and Tigera look up.

'You, Mr Tigera, of course know Mr Pat Gifford,' he said icily. His voice matched his eyes, both hard and cold as steel.

'But of course,' said Tigera, leaning across the table. 'Mr Gifford kindly invited me to his beautiful ranches a few months ago.' He held out his hand to Pat. Pat hesitated a moment before taking it. He was certain that there was a reason for Tigera's rudeness, but was at a loss to know what to do about it.

'You are such a busy man that I thought you must have forgotten the occasion,' answered Pat graciously, though he would have liked to pull the gold-rimmed glasses from Tigera's face and punch him.

'No, no, Mr Gifford. I could not forget Ganyani. All that land and all that game.' He paused and lit a cigar. 'And only the occasional hunter to enjoy it.'

Pat felt winded as if someone had kicked him in the stomach.

'But well managed, and because of the hunting and culling the families in the area all have employment,' broke in Fred. 'That is one thing we must remember, Mr Tigera. Hunting is an important part of conservation in Zimbabwe. We also have some of Africa's last great wilderness areas here. They must be preserved by men with Mr Gifford's dedication and love for the people and the country.'

29

'Our animals and the wildness of our country draw in the tourists. With the tourists comes our much needed foreign exchange,' added Pat quietly and persuasively.

'Yes, yes,' Tigera agreed irritably. 'We also need land for our people.'

Matamba said something to him in a low voice and Tigera's whole demeanour changed.

'We can talk of business later. First let us be sociable and have tea. You see, I too have picked up colonial habits.' He chuckled and clapped his hands. 'Tea for four.'

Both secretaries left the room hurriedly.

'You were talking of Ganyani, Mr Gifford's ranch,' said Matamba.

'One of Mr Gifford's ranches,' interjected Tigera.

'I have not had the pleasure of seeing it,' said Matamba.

He waited for the expected invitation but Pat was regretting ever having invited Tigera to visit Kame and Ganyani. At the time it had seemed a good idea to make friends with those in power. Now he realized that it had only excited envy and a desire to possess the land.

'Has your department decided whether to grant new hunting concessions in the Chizarira area, or are you going to extend the Chizarira National Park down to Chete safari area?' asked Fred, changing the subject. Tigera looked stunned; only one or two people knew of a proposed change in these areas. 'I hear that there is an American billionaire,' Fred continued, 'who wants to spend millions on conservation in Africa. Apparently his great-grandfather used to hunt here and he now wants to do something for our country.'

'The drums must have been talking again,' said Matamba softly to Tigera. 'None should know of the man or his offer.'

30

'South Africa does,' said Tigera. 'They wish him to spend his money to make a migratory elephant corridor from N'dumu up to the north of Mozambique.' He tapped his pencil on the table at the thought of all the money going to South Africa and Mozambique. 'The South Africans have been talking to this man, but I feel the money will rest safely in Zimbabwe.'

Tigera smiled at the thought of all the favours he could demand with the promise of some of the money. It would mean more trips to Europe to consult with management experts. Over the years he had acquired a taste for the ladies of the night who patrolled the Rue St Denis in Paris.

The men spent the next hour sipping tea, crumbling dry biscuits and discussing the possibility of extending the Chizarira National Park, set high on the Zambezi Plateau with magnificent mountains and deep ravines, down to the lowlands of Kariba.

Fred suggested that they could consider including the land between Chete and Matusadona National Park as well. Pat lost interest in the conversation. He had a feeling that Tigera was merely filling in time. In Pat's experience government officials did not discuss future plans for land usage with owners of private ranches. They usually treated them with suspicion and dislike. Tigera was waiting for something.

Pat studied Tigera carefully as he and Matamba listened to Fred, and observed his excitement at the thought of having almost another million acres of pristine bush shared by only two companies. One company would be granted a concession for hunting and the second company one for walking and photographic safaris.

Tigera was a lean dyspeptic looking man who walked with a slight stoop. His eyesight was poor and the glasses he wore gave him the air of an interrogator. No one knew how he had obtained the enormous power he wielded, but it was rumoured that he had arranged for the timely disappearance of people disliked by certain ministers shortly after the Lancaster House Agreement.

Pat thought that Tigera might be suffering from either tuberculosis or Aids, both of which were rife in the country.

As Fred and Matamba studied the large scale aerial map of the area in question, Tigera kept fiddling with papers on the table. His slender fingers slid paper clips in and out of pages as he pretended to read them. Every now and then he said a few words to Fred or Matamba but he was obviously distracted.

He kept looking at the large black and white clock on the wall above Pat's head. Pat resisted the impulse to turn around and check the time. Instead he scratched his arm and kept an eye on his own wristwatch.

They were waiting. But why?

Pat stared out of the window at the jacaranda trees. In spring they were clouded in blue and mauve bell-shaped flowers, which drifted down in the heat, soft as silk scarves, to lie at the grey base of the trees.

The loud beep of the phone beside Tigera shook Pat from his reverie.

Tigera snatched up the phone and held it to his ear. As he listened, his eyes hooded and a small smile stretched his lips.

'Good. Make certain none remain.' He stopped talking and glanced at Matamba who was leaning towards him and listening to the conversation.

'Yes, even the young. Do you understand nothing, you donkey? I said everything. Everything!' he shouted. 'Of course it gets dark when the sun goes down. Mount searchlights and continue.'

Pat and Fred stared at him. Neither was fluent in Shona but they understood a little. Tigera lowered his voice and smiled, but the anger did not leave his eyes. He nodded at Matamba.

'It is done. Within three days the lorries will have left. The people will eat.' He did not add, 'And our bank accounts will be fat.' That was unnecessary, it was understood. It was the way of Africa.

Matamba leaned across to him and whispered in Shona. 'Are you going to tell them now or let him see for himself?'

Tigera licked his lips. The moment he had waited for since he saw Ganyani had arrived.

'Only a small warning, enough to keep them away for three days until the trucks have left,' he answered.

'Make it good,' cautioned Matamba. 'This Gifford is no fool. I hear his son is a man among men. I have no wish to feel a bullet in my back one night.'

Tigera smiled. 'I have met the son. You need have no fear. The bullet would not be in your back at night, but in your front by day.'

He patted Matamba on the shoulder and walked across to one of the windows. Tigera let the silence grow as he stood with his back to the room looking down at the tree-lined street.

When he turned to face Pat and Fred, the smile had vanished. His face was composed and grave.

'Gentlemen,' he said, 'I have news which it is my sad duty to impart to you.'

Fred looked at Pat. Both men sat up straighter in the high-backed chairs.

'A few weeks ago we were advised that a strong and

well-armed band of poachers had entered Zimbabwe and were operating somewhere in the Hwange Park area.'

He clicked his fingers and one of the secretaries hurried to refill his teacup. Tigera sipped the tea, enjoying the tension he had created.

'I of course approached our air force commander and asked for an anti-poaching unit. The military are always ready to assist us. When they heard our estimate of the numbers of poachers we were given choppers, LMGs and AK-47s. You gentlemen will understand that the utmost force must be used to combat and eradicate poaching.'

Tigera paused again and stared at Pat. The light played across the thick glass in his spectacles, veiling his eyes. His voice was thin and high.

'We will follow and wipe out poachers, no matter where we find them. State or private land.' Slowly the import of what Tigera was saying hit Pat, but he refused to believe it.

'Mr Gifford,' he said, 'I have to tell you that neither you nor any member of your staff or family may enter Ganyani until you receive permission. At the moment an anti-poaching campaign is being carried out on the ranch. It would be extremely dangerous to enter the area. The anti-poaching unit have orders to shoot anyone on sight.'

He paused and sipped his tea delicately.

'You have only one son. Is it worth losing him too?' He allowed himself a small smile as he saw anger tighten Pat's face and outline his lips in white. Pat's knuckles stretched the skin as they clenched the arms of his chair. Fred was sure that if *kiaat* was not such hard wood the arms would have broken.

'Don't,' he warned in a whisper. 'They hold the whip.'

For the moment, but only for the moment, vowed Pat.

'My animals?' he spat out, the words venomous as snake's poison. 'What's happening to my animals in this rodeo round-up of supposed poachers?'

Fred shook his head in mute warning. Aggression was not the answer in this situation.

'Animals, Mr Gifford?' sneered Tigera, affecting surprise. 'Our main concern is poachers. But animals do tend to panic with noise. I'm afraid that the gunners cannot be held responsible for any bullets which stray from a bucking chopper.'

He turned back to the window. Matamba kept his head down pretending to study the map. He did not want to see the look of disgust on Fred's face.

'When do you expect the operation to be over?' asked Fred, mouthing the words as if they were as bitter as aloe juice.

'Three days,' said Matamba quickly.

'It has to be four,' corrected Tigera in Shona. 'There must be no traces of meat being dried when they go back. It has to look like a genuine anti-poaching campaign. No one will know where the animals are. It will seem that they have fled in terror, probably into Hwange which is National Parks property.'

Matamba watched in silence as Tigera lit a cigar, threw back his head and blew smoke rings which rose round and perfect, until the slow-moving air from the punka fan shredded them and they vanished.

Those who sleep with a snake often die of its poison, he told himself silently. Tigera was clever, but too hungry for money and power. He would do well to distance himself from Tsvakai Tigera before he himself was ensnared and unable to move away.

The disdain and horror mirrored in Fred Hanley's face

had affected him more than he wanted to admit. He had always enjoyed a good relationship with Fred and realized that in Fred's eyes he was now as tainted as Tigera. But money is a powerful aphrodisiac and he, like most men, had fallen prey to its promises.

This will be my last venture with Tigera, Matamba promised himself.

'Four days at least,' said Tigera in English. Matamba remained silent. He tried to smile at Fred as if to apologize but Fred refused to look at him.

Pat pushed back his chair and glared at the two men.

'Remember that just as the hyena cannot escape its own stench, so evil always follows those who do evil.'

He was rewarded with flickers of fear in their eyes. Pat had lived in Africa long enough to know that superstition still lurked beneath the veneer of sophistication and that drums still spoke louder than reason.

'Let's go,' he said to Fred.

The two men heard the secretaries twittering around Tigera and Matamba as the doors slammed behind them.

Tigera stubbed out his cigar in the large copper ashtray. He continued to grind it until the tobacco escaped from the tight casing and spilled over onto the table.

The slamming of the large doors and the look of contempt on Fred's face sat sour and heavy in his stomach.

He had no compunction for the slaughter he had ordered on Ganyani. In Africa the spoils always went to the strong. He intended to take all he could, before there was a change of government, a rebellion or a coup, all commonplace occurrences nowadays.

'They have enjoyed the beauty of the land long enough.

Now it is our turn,' said Tigera. Matamba was silent. He merely shuffled the papers into neat piles on the table.

'Next Kame,' gloated Tigera, taking Matamba's silence for acquiescence.

No, no, Matamba wanted to shout. You have Ganyani, leave him Kame. But he remained quiet, merely mopping his face and stuffing the damp handkerchief back into his pocket.

It is a wise man who listens before he answers, he cautioned himself.

'Next week I'll let Gifford know that we have regrettably found tracks of poachers on Kame and they'll have to leave for their own safety.' Tigera paced up and down the long room as he spoke.

'Pat Gifford will never give up Kame.' Matamba broke his silence. Sitting hunched over the papers he looked like one of the great chiefs of the Zulu nation.

Good living had poured fat over his once tall and imposing body, but he still had an almost regal presence.

Tigera removed his glasses and peered at Matamba as if he were a strange insect.

N'debele dog, he thought. You have the pale belly of the jackal. You, like the jackal, are happy with scraps after the Shona lion has fed.

'All men have a weakness,' he replied coldly. 'Find the weakness and you have the man.' He let the silence grow and fill the conference room.

'You mean Erin,' said Matamba. 'His son.'

Tigera smiled. 'I see we are still brothers in thought. Gifford will never risk the life of his last-born. He has no wife. He will have no ranches. No, my good friend, we have Gifford. By winter we will have Kame and Ganyani.' Matamba shook his head.

'Don't worry, it will all be legal. We will make him an offer for the useless land. He will accept. There will be none to point a finger in our direction.'

Tigera chuckled, a mirthless sound and it chilled Matamba.

Matamba's sister had a son who was a skinner and lived on Kame. The boy always came home with stories of Pat and Erin. Calling them the 'White N'debele', he had said, 'They understand and respect our language and our customs. They are good men and look after us well. The young one, Erin, has the heart of a lion. His father is like an old *nyati*. If left in peace he will stay alone and quiet like the old mud bull, but if angry there is none more dangerous or cunning.'

The boy's description of Pat Gifford slipped into the memory banks of Matamba's mind as he listened to Tigera.

'What will happen to Gifford?' he asked. 'You know that his friend Hanley still has many contacts. They are powerful and listen when he speaks. Believe me, he will speak to them in private with a tongue of honey.'

Tigera stopped pacing, sat down at the table, selected a new cigar from the wooden box and carefully clipped and lit it. He inhaled deeply before answering.

'The billionaire who wishes to invest money in conservation?'

Matamba nodded, a little bemused at the change of tack.

'I did not wish Gifford and Hanley to hear what only a few know. Papers were signed yesterday. South Africa and the elephants will have to wait for their migratory corridor through Mozambique. The money is ours.'

Tigera inhaled again and spoke before Matamba could comment.

'This American is as cunning as a bull buffalo. He actually wishes to see his money put to good use. He will remain here until he is satisfied that we have set up and staffed a conservation area. He will pay for us to set up the area. But only when everything pleases him will he give us the money to run the place.'

'What has been decided?' asked Matamba.

'We have given away one million acres of land for conservation,' Tigera answered. 'Part will adjoin the Chirisa safari area, part the Chizarira National Park. There will also be a tongue running past the Chete safari area to Kariba.' Tigera sighed. 'To have the money we had to agree to his terms. He demands to have part of Kariba in the new conservation area.'

'Kariba?' queried Matamba. 'Why Kariba?'

'The man has strange ideas, but good money, so we humoured him. He has this American sentiment for the Tonga people who were moved when the dam flooded their land. He also believes in Nyaminyani, their River God, who they said would never allow the Zambezi to be dammed. He seems to believe in the nonsense that Nyaminyani will one day rise from Kariwe, his rock fortress, and the dam will burst.'

Tigera laughed but Matamba was grave. He contemplated the catastrophe of almost one hundred and eighty billion tons of water, dammed in an area the size of Wales, bursting out and raging across the country.

'Like most rich men he is a little mad,' said Tigera, 'so we agreed. Who knows what will happen in a few years? Boundaries can and do change.'

Tigera pressed a bell concealed beneath the table.

The two secretaries came in carrying trays with square cut glasses, a crystal whisky decanter and small dishes filled with sardine-like *kapenta*. The sun-dried fish from Kariba was a delicacy which Tigera enjoyed with his whisky at the end of a working day.

'Another dreadful habit we have kept from colonial days,' said Tigera, raising his glass to Matamba.

Matamba stuffed a handful of the strong-smelling fish into his mouth and nodded. He would have preferred a mug of home-brewed beer, and gulped down the whisky as if it was gall. His mind, like a hooked tiger fish, had been racing round and leaping from one idea to another while Tigera was talking.

'This million-acre hunting safari and photographic safari area which is to be proclaimed,' he said nonchalantly as if the subject was of little concern to him.

'Yes?'

'Who will be appointed to run the new hunting area?' He crammed another handful of fish into his mouth and chewed them slowly as he waited for Tigera to answer.

Tigera refilled his glass.

'Kirk Madden had the adjoining concession,' he said, toying nervously with his glass.

Too quickly, thought Matamba. Tigera never answers quickly. He is like the adder sleeping in the sun who does not move until stepped on. 'Kirk Madden.' He rolled the name around. Why was it familiar? He looked deep into his glass as he remembered. He did not want Tigera to see the recognition in his eyes.

Of course, he thought. My brain must be growing old and fat like my body.

Kirk Madden fought for the forces who were against us, but he was also our undercover agent. He did some excellent work and gave us invaluable information. He was given the hunting concession as a reward. It caused a furore at the time as everyone knew Madden had very little money, certainly not enough to buy a prime hunting concession.

With pain sharp as shrapnel exploding in his face, Matamba remembered a confidential report he had seen. It was information from Madden which had led the Gifford boys' patrol into a carefully laid ambush. The two young men had died in the ensuing fire-fight. It had been during the early stages of the war when barbaric acts were perpetrated to instil fear into the opposing troops. The boys' bodies had been dismembered and hung on trees as a warning.

Pat's wife had woken screaming for months after she heard the news. Her nightmare was always the same: that her sons had still been alive when their bodies were butchered. Pat could offer her little comfort as the complete patrol had been killed. There was no one to assure her that the boys had died in a storm of bullets and knew nothing of what was done to their bodies.

'Have you thought of anyone for the new concession?' asked Matamba, pushing the unpleasant thoughts away.

Tigera sipped his whisky delicately.

'No, but it will bring us a very good sum of money,' he said. 'It will not be sold cheaply. Fable says that Zimbabwe is the ancient land of Ophir, which enriched Solomon and Sheba with ivory and gold. Let it also be our modern day Ophir. It will enrich us in foreign currency.' He coughed and rested his cigar on the edge of the copper ashtray. 'That will be our gold and ivory,' he laughed.

Chapter Four

WHEN PAT radioed from the plane to say that Fred would be spending the night with him at Kame, Blanche and Briar drove over to join them.

Briar was pale and withdrawn on the drive and kept her concentration on the road. She answered her mother's questions in monosyllables. Blanche eventually lapsed into silence, believing that her daughter was worried about the outcome of the meeting in Harare. The news had to be bad, or Fred would have returned home.

But Briar was trying to decide how to tell her parents that she would be leaving them. She knew how much they relied on her, but sitting at the waterhole that day had strengthened her resolve to forge a new life for herself. She had to keep her dead love as only a tender memory, to be taken out and examined as carefully as a sepia photograph, then locked away in the dark drawers of her mind.

Kirk Madden had phoned her again. He was at the Victoria Falls with a party of hunters who had decided to visit the Falls before beginning their safari.

'Come up, Briar,' he had pleaded. 'I need someone like you to run the camp and smooth prickly tempers when the game doesn't materialize. It's only a three-week safari and they're a great family of Italians. I've been here with the Andrettis for a few days. You'll love them.'

There was a long silence. Kirk renewed his exhortations.

'If you don't like the job or can't bearing working with me, you can go back to Inyati and I'll start looking for someone else. Please, Briar. Please say yes.'

Briar had met Kirk Madden at a wedding on a neighbour's farm during the Bush War. The party afterwards had degenerated into a hysterical bout of drinking, shouting, fighting and laughter. Pent-up tensions were relieved and everyone went a little mad.

Briar was dancing with Scott Gifford when Kirk, a short, heavily muscled man, cut in and tried to claim the dance. Pat's son lifted Kirk by the lapels of his coat as easily as picking up a puppy by the scruff of its neck and carried him on to the verandah. At the top of the steps he threw him out onto the ground.

'Briar is mine,' he had said. 'Find your own.'

The wedding guests streamed out into the night and cheered wildly.

Kirk, like many small men, had an overwhelming ego and was unforgiving. He had never forgotten the humiliation. After Scott's death he had tried to court Briar, but she was numb to all emotion and made no response to his overtures. He now contented himself with the ladies for sale in the bars of Bulawayo and Harare, plus the occasional bored wife or daughter of a hunter.

Briar did not like Kirk, but the invitation to work on the hunt seemed the perfect opportunity to leave home.

When Blanche and Briar reached Kame and heard the news from Fred, Briar put all her problems aside. She helped Rudo as she scurried around preparing dinner and putting fresh linen in the guest rooms.

Rudo realized that something serious had taken place. The home had the same cold feeling as when Pat's wife had died. Even Sheeba walked behind Pat with her tail between her legs, as if uncertain as to whether she was the cause of her master's anger.

The drums started beating out their message in the late afternoon and had grown more insistent as darkness fell. The Giffords and the Hanleys sat up all night discussing the implications of the meeting in Harare. They were listlessly picking at the chicken Rudo had prepared for dinner, when the familiar clatter of choppers passed over the house.

'That's what that swine Tigera meant by lights,' shouted Pat. He pushed his plate away and gravy splashed on to the starched white tablecloth.

'Pat, Pat,' reasoned Fred, 'we don't even know that they have killed the game. Perhaps it *is* a genuine anti-poaching campaign.'

Pat shook his head in mute denial.

'The army are convinced that their choppers have gone out after poachers,' insisted Fred. 'I still have friends who are high up in the military. They are Sandhurst trained and honourable. They would not lie to me.'

'Tigera and others like him have influence over the ones who don't know the meaning of the word honour,' said Erin, joining in the conversation.

His hair, bleached silver blond by the sun, flopped over his forehead. Irritably he swept it away only to have it fall back. Briar studied him across the table. He looked so much like Scott. He, too, used to keep combing his hair away from his face with his fingers. She felt tears of self-pity burn her eyes.

Stop it, she commanded herself. Your family's closest

friends are facing ruin and the loss of everything they love and all you can do is feel sorry for yourself.

'I agree with Dad. The country is desperate for meat. It fetches high prices. Ganyani is full of meat,' Erin continued, pushing his plate away. He had not eaten anything. 'Tigera saw the opportunity when he was here. If he clears all the game, the land is worthless. Then, in the name of the government, he can make us an offer for a barren area. It'll be low. If we don't take it . . .' Erin paused as he saw the warning in Fred's eyes.

He followed Fred's glance and was shocked at the sickly pallor of his father's face. Pat Gifford seemed to have aged twenty years in that one day and his hand shook as he lifted a mug of beer. He put it down untasted.

'Tigera will not be satisfied with only Ganyani,' said Pat heavily, as if he was having difficulty forming the words. 'Kame will be next. Our beautiful Kame.'

'Come, Pat. This is all supposition. We'll go to Ganyani in a few days and find it unchanged. Perhaps a few animals dead but the rest will be there. Jacob and Jonas can show us how skilful they are at tracking. I haven't seen your herd of sable for ages.' Fred smiled at Erin, hoping to change the subject. 'Young Erin has been boasting that he now has forty in the herd. I want to see them myself.'

'You will,' answered Erin, realizing what Fred was trying to do.

'No!' roared Pat, suddenly sitting up straight in his chair at the head of the table. 'Don't treat me like a child. There are no animals left. We all know it.' He glared at Erin and at his friends, as if they were strangers. 'They have done this sort of thing before and will do it again.'

Fred Hanley studied his friend then pushed back his chair. 'I have a call to make,' he said as he excused himself from the table. Matamba, he thought. I'll have to get to him.

Blanche held up her hand as if to stop him, but he ignored her. All were silent. The faint rising wail of hyenas and the thrilling quavering chorus of jackals filtered into the room. The irresistible call of Africa. Briar shivered. This land she loved, which continued to feed on blood. Would it never be satiated?

Chapter Five

ON GANYANI three sable antelope calves, their coats still fawn in colour but showing signs of turning dark, were stepping delicately over the rough terrain. The scattered rocks were stained red by the swiftly setting sun and by another substance they could not identify, but the smell frightened them.

The oldest calf found his mother. He stopped in consternation as the silky black body with the startling white underparts did not respond to his nuzzling. The white tufts in front of her eyes which lengthened into streaks along either side of her muzzle looked like dried tears in the dying light. Her eyes stared sightlessly up into her calf's face.

He gave a small snort of alarm and the other calves joined him. Carefully they picked their way around the bodies. This magnificent herd of forty proud and defiant buck had once been Erin's delight on Ganyani. Now they lay scattered across the rocky slope, like black and white dominoes, their stiffening bodies ugly in the rictus of death.

The great five-hundred-pound bull lay at the foot of the slope where he had taken his final stand to protect his herd. His widely curved horns, heavily ridged in front, were almost four feet in length. Many a lion had given way to the sudden vicious sideways thrust made by the scythe-like horns. The points of those horns were now wedged into the ground, pinned there when his neck was broken by a ragged hail of bullets.

Ganyani, the place of the Wild Dog, a haven for animals, was now a place of death and terror.

The few animals which had escaped and hidden deep in the forested areas or found refuge among the rocks now crept tentatively out of their hiding places, believing that darkness would protect them. Their eyes were dull with fear and their nostrils stretched wide to the acrid smell of cordite and the sickening sweetness of blood.

In the distance hyenas howled and chattered, excited by the blood. They would soon arrive to begin a macabre feast.

The oldest sable calf shivered, folded his spindly legs beneath his belly and lay down beside his mother. As her body cooled in death, he again grunted softly. Bewildered and afraid, the young calves huddled together as the night became colder and the maniacal howls of the hyenas grew close.

Shredded clouds streaked across the face of the moon, letting the silver light fall fitfully across Ganyani. Nervously the animals called to one another. They found comfort in the soft lowing of their kind. A herd of buffalo milled restlessly on the grassy plain in front of the hill where the sable calves shivered and tried to sleep.

The buffalo walked ponderously in circles, their massive heads held well below their shoulders, their muzzles thrust up, scenting blood and death and fear. A few solitary and usually evil-tempered old mud bulls joined the growing herd.

The calving season had just ended. The young buffaloes pushed their way unsteadily through the jostling herd.

Their nostrils twitched as they tried to locate their mothers, their plaintive calls lost in the deep bellows and lowing.

A heavy bank of cloud reared up and hid the moon, turning Ganyani into a black and sinister place. Eerie wailing cries heralded the arrival of the hyenas. Instinctively the buffalo, the most formidable of all African big game, formed a circle. The bulls snorted with rage as they herded the cows and calves inside the protective ring.

The unearthly wailing turned to the shrieks and cackles of lunatic laughter as the hyenas found the first carcass. Jaws more powerful than those of any living mammal crushed the largest bones with ease. As the excitement of these slope-backed creatures mounted so did the ear-splitting noise.

The buffalo were aware of the danger these scavengers posed to the surviving herd. Soon they would scent and kill any young calves who had wandered away in the darkness. They snorted and tossed their horns, daring the hyenas to approach.

Suddenly a noise even more terrifying shattered the night. The clatter of helicopters. Before the animals could turn to run for cover they were blinded by daggers of sharp white light beaming down on them.

'We've got them,' shouted the 'tech' manning the light machine-gun on board the helicopter.

'Orbit them,' he screamed as bullets hailed down on the herd. 'Keep orbiting. Keep them in a tight circle and we'll have the lot.'

The door had been removed from the bull-nosed Alouette 3 to facilitate rapid entrance and exit. In the frenzy of killing, two other men wedged themselves into the open door with their AK-47s.

The clashing of chopper blades and chatter of the guns,

magnified in the confined cabin, created an orchestra of noise and light. It heightened the crew's senses and filled them with excitement. These men were fighters. They had been trained to kill.

The sight of dying creatures crazed them, as easily as intense heat turns placid bees into berserk killers. A second helicopter joined the first. When they saw that the buffalo were helpless in the tight circle of noise and dazzling light they flew on to fulfil their orders: '*Find and kill every animal on Ganyani by daybreak.*'

'There,' shouted one of the gunners. 'They're mine. The three on the top of the hill.'

The sable calves were too exhausted and terrified to flee. The oldest one tried to stagger to his feet, but his knees buckled. He lay with his nose pressed deep into his mother's flesh as bullets streamed into him.

The hyenas lay strewn around the carcass of a large kudu cow, their mouths open to reveal their great blood-stained carnassial teeth. These creatures had been screaming their hideous laughter at the chopper as they died.

Their work completed, the pair of drab, camouflaged Alouette 3s turned away. They hovered over the lines of lorries for a few minutes, letting the men below know that they could move in and start skinning animals and cutting the meat into strips to dry.

The choppers then flew towards the dawn, rising fresh and beautiful in the east.

The skinners squatted round tiny fires which they had built on the ground to fend off the chill of dawn. They watched the helicopters until they were swallowed up in the brightness of the rising sun.

The sun brought with it a blemished sky. It seemed as if dark ash motes from a bush fire were pock-marking the heavens.

Chattering broke out among the men and soon dozens of children armed with stones and long sticks were sent out to keep the vultures from the carcasses.

The skins, horns and meat butchered on Ganyani would be packed into the tarpaulin-covered trucks and driven back to Harare. Once in Harare others would take charge of the trucks. The skinners would be paid off and left to return to their homes.

The drums had demanded silence. None would speak of what they had seen or done. The order of the drums would be respected.

Jacob and Jonas spooned the last of the stiff maize porridge from their enamel plates in silence. They washed their breakfast down with a large jug of soured milk. Both trackers looked up at the sky as two 'birds of death' flew overhead. Neither spoke, but they studied the ground as if they were personally responsible for the slaughter which the drums had predicted.

'We could have warned them,' said Jonas softly.

'So they could use rifles against choppers and AKs?' scoffed Jacob. 'What is done is done.'

'But this will not end. The drums spoke of Kame. Our wives, our children. Why must they do this to us?' whispered Jonas.

'The elephant is large and powerful. In the bush all fear him. They run from the waterhole and leave the sweetest grass to him,' reasoned Jacob.

He called out to Jonas's wife and asked for more milk.

She hurried to obey. She had given both men breakfast this morning, as Rudo had gone up to Pat's house before daybreak saying that there were many for breakfast and she knew Pat and Erin would need her.

Jacob was sickened by what he knew had happened and terrified that his family would soon be killed, but he kept his voice low and calm. He did not want Jonas spreading alarm through the little village on Kame where they all lived. Perhaps, he thought, the killers will be satisfied with Ganyani?

Jacob had read the greed in Tigera's eyes when Pat proudly showed him the herds they had nurtured on Kame and Ganyani and he knew in his heart that Kame would not be spared.

Chapter Six

ERIN FLIPPED his blond fringe back from his wide forehead and carefully smeared black camouflage grease across his face. He felt his gut tighten as the familiar smell brought back images of a war he was trying to forget.

He caught the sound of soft footfalls in the room, but before he could turn around Pat clapped him on the shoulder. His father's hand was hard and heavy, but it felt comforting.

The two men turned to study their blackened faces in the mirror. Erin had the same wide shoulders as Pat and they both topped six foot two inches in height. If it wasn't for Pat's bald dome and greying friar's fringe they could be mistaken for brothers. Their clear blue eyes looked odd in their black faces.

'Have you done your hands?' asked Pat. Erin nodded. 'Then let's go.'

At the command Sheeba wormed herself out from under the bed and stood wagging her tail hopefully. She gave a small whimper to let Pat know she was ready.

'Quiet!' he hissed. 'You stay here. Guard, Sheeba, on guard.'

The ridgeback's ears drooped and she looked as miserable as she possibly could, but Pat was adamant.

'Stay.'

She lay down and rested her head on her paws. Her bright yellow eyes followed the men as they left the room.

They crept from the house as stealthily as if on night patrol. The Hanleys were still staying at Kame. They had refused to leave Pat and Erin alone until they were sure that Pat had accepted the situation at Ganyani and would do nothing foolish.

The two men breathed a sigh of relief as they passed the guest rooms where the Hanleys slept. Like shadows they slipped through the garden to where they had hidden their rifles, water bottles and hunting lamps.

Suddenly they froze. In the distance they spotted a figure with a rifle slung over each shoulder blocking the way. Automatically they split into the once-familiar encircling and attack movement.

'You would not visit the hyenas on Ganyani without me?' said Jacob softly as they drew near.

Pat and Erin breathed out long shuddering sighs. Both men had been holding their breath, intent only on ridding themselves of the figure who threatened to thwart their plans.

'You cannot come, Jacob. It's dangerous,' said Pat. 'They will shoot anyone they see on Ganyani.'

'You are right, Mr Pat,' answered Jacob and they could sense him smiling. 'You track well, you talk Sindebele well, but those pale eyes will make very good targets for their AKs. They shine in the moonlight like the white circle around the tail of the waterbuck.' He spat on to the ground at his feet. 'You need me. I will not let you go to Ganyani alone, as I know what you will find. For three nights I have listened to the drumbeats. It is enough. Either I lead you, or I follow you.'

Pat and Erin exchanged glances.

'Lead, Jacob,' said Pat. He and Erin collected the lights and water bottles.

The little group moved cautiously into the bush, a place which at nightfall becomes the domain of predators. Animals which, unlike humans, have extraordinary nocturnal vision, hearing and smell.

The moon stood high above the treetops, yet still the three men walked, unaware of the beauty of the night sky where stars played hide and seek in the clouds. Jacob stopped twice, so abruptly that Erin almost careened into Pat.

'*Nzou*,' Jacob whispered.

Both men strained their eyes until they watered but neither could see anything. It still mystified Erin how something as enormous as an elephant – about eleven feet high and weighing six tons – could stand so motionless that it melted into the bush and became invisible at night. He could not see the beast, but he could smell the fresh droppings on the sandy animal pathway which they were following. As they stood waiting for the elephant to move away, they heard the rasping cough of a leopard close behind them.

Jacob hissed. They turned to face the sound. The grunts, followed by a husky intake of air, sounded like someone sawing wood. Pat felt the hairs stand up on his arms. He had a healthy respect for the solitary leopard, the *mbada*, a hunter adroit at scalping its prey, but he was not happy to have one following them.

The sawing stopped. They heard the animal cough softly to the right of the track. Jacob motioned to them to continue. The moon had started sliding down the sky when Jacob finally held up his hand.

'We are on Ganyani now.' Erin looked around at the

anthills and mopane trees. Nothing was familiar. He shrugged. He no longer argued with Jacob and Jonas as to their whereabouts. He was accustomed to his trackers knowing exactly where they were and trusted them completely.

'We no longer fear *nzou* or the *mbada*. Now watch for the two-legged hyenas.'

They all checked their rifles, making sure that the magazines were full, with a round chambered and the safety catch on.

'Rifles against AKs,' snorted Erin.

'That's equality,' answered Pat softly. 'Some are allowed to have automatic weapons, some not. These are the rules after a war, my son.'

'And the rules are made by the politicians,' said Erin.

'Right. They are the new victors.'

Jacob now seemed to change into a creature of the night, a predator, his senses finely tuned to all the smells and noises. They could almost feel an electric charge surround him.

Imperiously he gave them a hand signal. They flattened themselves on the ground. Slowly Jacob began a laborious 'leopard crawl' towards a rocky outcrop. He did not seem to feel the sharp stones and thorns as he slid along on his belly. He moved alternate arms and legs forward in a slow rhythm, slithering over the ground with the ease of a snake.

Pat and Erin followed, careful not to dislodge any loose stones. Suddenly Jacob froze. Erin cracked his mouth against the sole of Pat's foot. He had been keeping his head so low that he did not realize that Jacob had stopped crawling. He sucked his bottom lip which was bleeding. The blood dribbled into his mouth leaving a taste of iron. He swallowed hard, not wanting to spit in case the sound alerted the skinners and the guards who had probably been posted.

Slowly Pat and Erin crawled level with Jacob and lay one on either side of him.

'Oh my God,' breathed Erin.

Pat shook his head at him. Erin could still hear his mother say, 'Do not take in vain the name of the One who made, and is part of, all this beauty around us. If you must swear, find other words to use.'

Since her death Pat allowed no one to blaspheme near him. A few of the hunters had been surprised when they too were admonished.

The sight which greeted the three men as they peered cautiously between the rocks had made Erin forget for a moment his promise not to resort to profanity when angry.

He felt the sting of tears as he looked at his once graceful sable antelope. Smashed by bullets, their limbs, necks and sweeping horns were broken and contorted. Their white bellies were ugly and swollen with the gases of death.

'Bastards,' breathed Pat, as he studied the three calves tucked tightly into the adults' flanks.

As if sensing that they were watching, one of the calves twitched its legs and tried to lift its head. It had not enjoyed a quick death. Instinctively Erin raised the rifle. Instantly Jacob pinned his arms to the ground, immobilizing him in a grip which closed like the jaws of a hyena. Within a few seconds Erin's fingers were numb. Jacob snatched the rifle before it fell.

'One shot and they'll be here in minutes,' he warned, angry at Erin's loss of control.

Pat handed Erin his binoculars.

'See if you can spot anyone,' he said. His hands were

shaking with how close they had come to revealing their presence, yet he sympathized with his son. His fingers, too, had longed to pull the trigger and put the calf out of its torment.

'There is no one,' said Jacob. Neither man questioned him, as his eyesight was legendary. He never used his binoculars, yet spotted game long before they did.

Jacob handed Pat his gun and unsheathed his skinning knife, honed to shave the hairs from a man's arm and slip between ribs as if sliding into melting butter.

'No!' said Pat and Erin in unison as Jacob wormed his way over the ledge. But it was too late. All they could do was wait and pray that no guards had been set.

They won't be expecting anyone on Ganyani, Pat comforted himself. Everyone has been warned to stay away. The drums have spoken and the people will listen.

But perspiration traced pale streaks through his black camouflage paint as he watched Jacob approach the calf, inch by slow inch.

Erin eased his cramped fingers from the rocks as Jacob stretched out his arm. He plunged and twisted the knife deep into the calf's throat. It twitched feebly and lay still. Death had come at last. Jacob continued to work at its throat, making it look as if a predator had gnawed at the small animal. He then started the long crawl back to safety. Erin squeezed Jacob's shoulder as he settled down between them.

'Thank you,' he whispered.

Jacob smiled sadly. 'We must leave,' he said. 'The way back is long. Today the meat lorries will start leaving for Harare.'

Pat took a last despairing look at his land. Reedbuck

and impala lay scattered like brown autumn leaves. Gany-ani was soaked in blood and stinking with dead animals. Finally he turned away.

When the three men reached the comparative safety of the bush they stood up. Jacob studied the sky while Erin and Pat stretched their cramped limbs. The tarred black-ness of night had given way to the dull grey which tells tales of the approach of dawn. The dim light made walking through the bush easier. Jacob set off at a slow jog.

'Jacob,' called Pat softly. 'Is it wise to move so quickly?'

'We must,' answered Jacob over his shoulder, not lessening his pace. 'Look at the trees.'

Pat and Erin turned back and saw that the mopane trees were bowed beneath the weight of great hunched black birds.

'Vultures mean the men are working close,' said Jacob. 'We must be away from here before the sun is yellow.'

Black-cloaked mourners attending the wake of my animals, thought Pat fancifully. He knew that daylight would bring a cacophony of shrieking, fighting, flapping vultures as they tore into each other and the carcasses of his creatures. He hated those birds, so graceful and power-ful in flight, yet so hideously ugly when hopping and squawking around a dead body on the ground.

Jacob kept sniffing the air as he jogged. Pat was about to ask him what he was hoping to smell, when the faint sickly-sweet stench of rotting meat was carried to them on the wind.

'The blackbirds wait for the men to hang the strips of meat on the trees to dry,' said Jacob. 'The skinners will start packing the lorries at Shamba Pan today. They are losing too much meat to the birds.'

Pat paused. 'How do you know that they are losing part of the meat which is hanging out to dry? How do you know that they are at Shamba Pan today?'

'The drums were silent last night. For the first time this week they did not speak,' added Erin.

Pat thought he saw a look of pain – or anger – flash across Jacob's eyes.

'Yesterday I was an extra N'debele skinner sent to help them,' he replied.

Pat and Erin stared at Jacob, aghast.

'You were what?' exploded Pat. 'You helped butcher our animals?'

'Butcher yes, but not kill,' answered Jacob. He seemed to grow in stature as he stared into Pat's blue eyes.

'Dad,' broke in Erin, 'don't you see, Jacob went to Ganyani to find out what had happened. The only way to get in without being shot was to pretend to be one of the workers.'

Pat slammed his fist into his palm.

'Jacob, I owe you an apology for even doubting you. I am so sorry,' said Pat. 'It was a very brave act.'

Jacob grinned, a wide engaging smile.

'Mr Pat, you never have to say sorry to me. When I see what they are doing to Ganyani and to you and Erin I feel such deep shame inside, for they are my people who are doing this.'

'No, Jacob,' said Erin, 'your sort of people would not do this. They may poach a few animals, but they would never wipe out a whole game ranch. This is the work of men eaten up with greed. Most land- and power-hungry people are in governments. Not only our government, but governments everywhere.'

'If they're after meat then our predators will be spared,'

said Pat in a lighter tone. 'At least we'll keep our lions and leopards.'

'No, Mr Pat. Yesterday I skinned our big *shumba*. The lion we have often hunted, but he was old and too clever for us. You remember, the one with the black mane over his shoulders.'

Pat shook his head in silence.

'The skins and claws will fetch a good price in the curio stores, Dad. The elephant will go the same way – the meat for sale with the venison, tusks and skins for curios. What do a few animals matter when there are bank accounts to be filled and people to placate?' said Erin bitterly.

This day has changed Erin, thought Pat, probably for ever. My youngest is now a man. A hardened man.

Even as he mourned the loss of Erin's innocence, he broke into a jog behind Jacob.

'Keep close,' he warned Erin.

They will pay for this, vowed Erin silently as he closed the gap between himself and his father. If it takes me a lifetime I'll find out who ordered this massacre and he'll die.

Chapter Seven

THE HANLEYS stayed a week on Kame until they were satisfied that Pat's anger had abated. Fred had spent hours on the telephone trying to rally support for Pat, only to be assured that Tigera and Matamba had gone through the correct channels to obtain help to combat a large force of armed poachers. No crime had been committed and nothing could be done.

Fred had arranged for Matamba to meet him at Inyati, but was keeping it secret. He had no wish to raise Pat's hopes and then have to dash them if Matamba did not bend to pressure.

The time the Hanleys spent with the Giffords made Briar decide to accept Kirk Madden's offer.

It did not seem right to break the news when her parents were so upset about Pat and Erin, but she knew there never would be a good time to tell them that she was leaving. So, the evening before they were to return to Inyati, she broached the subject. Silence greeted her explanation. Neither Fred nor Blanche looked at her, though in the moonlight which forced its way through the tangled branches of the bougainvillaea, she thought she saw tears in her mother's eyes.

'I am thirty-two,' Briar said. 'I must do something with my life. It's only for three weeks. If I don't like him, or the job, I'll come home immediately.'

Still her parents were silent. They sensed that they were about to lose their daughter.

'I love you both so much,' said Briar. 'Please try to understand.'

'We do,' said Fred gruffly, 'though Inyati won't be the same without you.'

'You have our love and our blessing,' said Blanche as she stood up and crossed to where Briar was sitting.

She put her arms around her daughter and as she hugged her, images of Briar as a chubby baby, a skinny school-girl and a beautiful young woman clicked across her mind. She found it impossible to believe that more than thirty years had passed since she held the infant Briar in her arms.

'Kirk Madden,' said Pat, entering into the conversation. 'Wasn't he the one who was giving information . . .?'

'Yes,' cut in Fred warningly. 'There were some ugly rumours about him after the war. They were never proved.' He shrugged. 'The stories were probably due to jealousy because he was granted the hunting concession near Chete.'

'What did he do to earn the concession?' asked Erin. 'He could not possibly have five million to bid for the right to hunt in that area, to say nothing of the price he has to pay the National Parks for each animal in the quota they have set to be culled.' Erin paused, mentally totting up the quota value of an area so rich in game. He took a quick breath and continued. 'If he has to pay the money upfront to the National Parks before he has even sold the safaris, he will need secret backers or I don't see how he can do it.' He paused. 'I met him a few times. He was at school with my brothers, though I think he was a year or two older. I know they didn't get on.'

'His backers had better be American,' said Pat, returning to the subject of the concession. 'The powers that be now want the quotas paid in US dollars. That'll wipe out three-quarters of the old concession holders. The only profit they make is by buying the animals on the quota from the National Parks in Zimbabwe dollars and selling them to the clients for US dollars.'

'Another nail in the coffin of foreign exchange for our country,' said Fred, taking a mouthful of beer.

'It's almost as ill-advised a policy as the one saying that all animals belong to the government whether they are in reserves or on private ranches.'

Erin nodded in agreement then returned to the subject of Kirk Madden, unaware that Fred did not want Briar upset about the man who could be her future employer.

'I remember my brothers saying that after school Madden drifted from one job to another. If you believe all the stories, he collected women the way some men notch guns.'

Finally he realized what was happening. Pat leaned across.

'Won't you fetch us some more beers, son?'

'Sure, Dad.'

Fred gave a low whistle.

'Don't worry, Dad,' Briar said, knowing he did this when he was upset. 'I won't be a notch on his gun.'

He laughed and hugged his daughter.

'I'd have to kill him if he hurt you,' he said jokingly.

Erin heard the end of the conversation as he padded back on to the verandah.

'If Fred missed I'd get him,' he said. 'You were almost my sister-in-law, so I have to look after you now.'

They spoke on into the night, realizing that life had changed for all of them.

When the cocks started crowing down at Kame village, Fred and Blanche decided to drive Briar to Victoria Falls. They wanted to meet and assess this Kirk Madden for themselves.

Chapter Eight

THE LAND ROVER rolled slowly through the small town which had grown up around the Falls.

'Don't say it!' warned Blanche and Briar in unison as Fred hit the steering wheel with the palm of his hand.

'I hate these new hotels and casinos. Who needs a shopping mall and a million curio stores?' he groused, ignoring their admonition as he skirted a group of tourists standing in the middle of the road. Their arms and legs were boiled a dull red by the tropical sun. They seemed numbed by the heat and dust.

Fred hit the steering wheel again, winced and sucked his fingers until they stopped tingling, then smiled at his wife and daughter. They had seen him smile so seldom since he and Pat had flown to Kame from their meeting in Harare. The women exchanged relieved glances but were silent.

'In the good old days we had a few rest huts, a trading store and the great old Vic Falls hotel,' he said.

'It's the International Airport that has changed life here,' said Blanche, watching a steam engine pull into the small Falls station. 'If a place is easily accessible then tourists flock to it. We need foreign exchange, so the country caters for their sophisticated needs.'

'If they want sophistication let them go to Paris or London,' said Fred, swinging the Land Rover on to the dirt road leading to the Falls Hotel. Briar smiled at her mother and shook her head, as they were forced to give way to a bus from the airport which disgorged a horde of chattering tourists in front of the hotel.

The group stood and posed for photographs with the doorman. His red jacket was plastered with badges given to him over the years by visitors to the grand old hotel, which dated back to colonial times.

The doorman gave his wide smile as the Hanleys passed him. They slipped through the long entrance hall, crossed the courtyard where enormous mango trees lined the two lily ponds, and walked gratefully into the cool high-ceilinged sitting room.

Briar studied the few people lounging in the pale green and white room, but Madden was not among them. Taking a pair of sunglasses from her leather shoulder bag she went out onto the terrace. Tables bright with checked cloths were set up beneath the spreading branches of the tall mahogany trees.

The shaded area was packed with people enjoying a buffet lunch. Waiters were scurrying around like termites, fulfilling orders for drinks. The European visitors looked dehydrated. They were sweating and wilting, unaccustomed to the heat and humidity of the Zambezi Valley.

The roar of the Falls and the cloud of spray were clearly visible from where Briar stood. She felt the same thrill and sense of wonder which this place always invoked in her. It seemed as if the power and majesty of the pounding waters called to her soul and gave her strength.

'Do you see him?' Her father's voice broke into her reverie.

'Not yet, Dad. Remember he'll be with a group of people.'

As she spoke, Briar suddenly caught sight of Kirk. She studied him in silence for a while. She noticed that he still affected the same hairstyle, shaved close at the back and sides with a short bristly top. He smoothed down the sides as constantly as a woman seeking attention. His ginger hair was bleached by the sun to a strawberry blond, as were the hairs on his arms and legs. His khaki shirt was tight and open to the waist, showing off his muscular build and hairless chest to perfection. He had tilted his chair back from the table and as he rocked back and forth on it, he was the picture of arrogance.

'There he is,' said Briar, pointing him out to her parents.

Fred's eyes narrowed as he looked at the hunter. 'Let's go down and meet him,' he said.

Guido Andretti, a millionaire industrialist from Milan, glanced at his wife, Maria. He noticed that she had undone another khaki button on her thin cotton blouse and her olive skin rose high and rounded on each side of the deep cleft between her breasts. Her hair, a rich mahogany brown, swung across her face. Frequent visits to her hairdresser kept the tell-tale grey streaks at bay. A daily visit from a private fitness instructor kept her body trim and gave it the suppleness of youth.

Guido accepted the fact that his wife was becoming even more attractive with maturity. She still flirted with any personable man present. When he was younger this used to annoy him, but now he was in his late fifties he understood and accepted this weakness in his wife. He had warned her that if she stepped over the line and entered into physical intimacy he would leave her.

Maria had merely laughed at the threat. She was no

fool and would not jeopardize her position in society. In
Milan, news travelled even faster than it did by drumbeat
in Zimbabwe. In Milan, Guido would know that she had
slept with someone before she had showered and dressed
after the session.

But during the few days they had been in Zimbabwe,
she had felt wild and reckless. The raw land sang to her
and she responded. Here at the hotel the insistent beat of
the drummers, who played near the giant chessboard laid
out on the ground, throbbed through her body. She was
once again young, desirable and the most beautiful girl in
Milan. Her family had all been blessed with dark, velvet
eyes shaded by the impossibly thick, long lashes which
seem to be the prerogative of Italians.

Maria had borne Guido three children, the last of whom
was Marco, the boy he wanted and needed to perpetuate
the Andretti name and business empire. Tomasina, the
eldest, was carving a niche for herself in fashion design in
Milan. Until her brother Marco was born, she had lived
with the shame of not being a boy. Her father had named
her Tomasino when she still floated in her mother's womb.
When he realized that the new-born babe did not possess
the necessary appendages to be Tomasino he had abruptly
left his wife's bedside. She had named the little girl
Tomasina to appease him.

Tomasina grew up to be an extraordinarily beautiful
girl. She had the enviable slimness of a top model and
carried herself with grace, totally unlike the tomboy suggested by her name. That role was left to the second
daughter, Tara.

Tara barely reached her sister's shoulder. Her hair was
cut into a wild urchin tangle, unlike Tomasina's thick
mane which she swirled into a knot on top of her head to

give herself even greater height. Tara had inherited her voluptuousness from her mother. She had 'a pasta figure', Maria teased. Tara preferred to describe her shape as that of Sophia Loren.

Guido adored Tara even though they quarrelled constantly. She was as stubborn and shrewd as her father. What her mother and sister gained by feminine wiles and tears, she won in battle.

Marco, the heir to the Andretti millions, was being carefully moulded into a safe, stolid businessman. He would play no wild cards. He would not drive his father into screaming rages as Tara did. The good looks in the Andretti family had been handed out to the girls, and Guido often bemoaned the fact that his son did not have his large frame and physical presence. Marco was small and slim, with the sort of face which was instantly forgettable. He had recently grown a moustache. In the office he affected a pair of round rimless spectacles, which, Tara said, made him look like a scared mouse.

Secretly Guido felt that he had been let down badly. Tara should have been the boy. She had the necessary fire and drive to push the Andretti fortunes up, but she was showing signs of wasting her time on foolish ventures to 'save the planet'. She rushed around the world attending meetings in poverty-stricken countries about incurable diseases. Guido was terrified that his beloved daughter would fall prey to one of these diseases and be lost to him.

So he sighed and resigned himself to turning Marco into a hard businessman. The family fortunes might not increase but they would be safe in his hands.

This safari was to mark the boy's twenty-first birthday and his election to the board of Andretti and Son. When Tara threw a tantrum on hearing that it was to be a 'men only' safari, Guido had capitulated as usual. Tomasina decided to join them and gain some fashion ideas from the ethnic African dress. Maria's reason for abandoning her busy social schedule was a new collection from Krizia, one of her favourite designers, which featured leopards with glittering eyes whose bodies stole stealthily around the cotton knits. Maria could not resist them. Her set of matched leather luggage now bulged with couture safari clothes.

Guido had watched her pack and had added some thin khaki shirts of his own.

'I'm not wearing those things on safari,' sniffed Maria as she folded her new clothes and layered them between sheets of tissue paper.

'Oh, you will when we get into the thick jesse bush, or you crawl along on your belly,' grinned Guido.

Kirk had been delighted when he met the Andretti family. He immediately assessed the women. Maria was a possibility, he decided, though it was not wise to play around with the wife of a wealthy man. Wealth usually held hands with power and influence. He did not want to lose his job.

Tomasina was stunningly lovely. He undressed her mentally every time they were together. If Guido and Marco were with him, he wore his dark glasses to conceal the lust in his eyes. Tomasina seemed unaware of his attraction to her. Men had paid her attention ever since she was a teenager; now she accepted it as the norm.

But Tara noticed it and was determined to protect her elder sister. Kirk kept away from Tara. She was abrasive and questioned his decisions. He liked women to be feminine, submissive and to admire him.

Guido fell into an easy relationship with Kirk. He had

visited most parts of the world to hunt elusive game and was a good and knowledgeable hunter. They spoke of rifles, ammunition, and Ward's book of world records for trophy game.

All in all, the Andrettis were enjoying their stay at the Falls.

Fred Hanley held out an arm to each of his women. He led Blanche and Briar down the steps and on to the shaded lower terrace.

As they walked towards Kirk Madden and the Andrettis he glanced sourly at the men happily beating the tall drums.

'These are happy drums, Dad,' whispered Briar. 'They are only here to add flavour and atmosphere to the place.'

'They do have a message,' he replied. 'All drums talk. They say, "Take their money. Make us rich."'

Briar and Blanche laughed. The sound of their laughter alerted Kirk.

He swung forward in his chair and stood up to meet them. He looked at Briar appraisingly. She wore beige shorts and shirt and her tiny waist was cinched with a wide leather belt. She had pulled a dark green cap well down over her forehead and left her blond hair swinging free from the back.

'Briar,' he said, putting his arms around her as if they were old friends. 'How wonderful to see you.' When he tried to kiss her, she pulled away and his lips landed on her cheek.

'I would like you to meet my father and mother,' she said formally.

When the greetings were completed, Kirk introduced them to the Andretti family.

Fred and Blanche stood speaking to Kirk and the Italians for a while longer, then both embraced Briar and walked away, anxious to return to Inyati. Briar watched her father put his arm around her mother, his limp more pronounced than usual. Her parents were so happy and content in their love. Yet again she cried out silently for someone to cherish her.

'There's something about that young man I don't like,' said Fred as he paused at the top of the steps and looked back at the table where Briar was now seated beside Kirk.

'You'll never like any man who may take Briar away,' teased Blanche.

'You know me too well, Blanche Hanley,' he said.

Blanche stood up on tiptoe and kissed him lightly on his cheek.

'Blanche!' he whispered, glancing round the sitting room to see if anyone had noticed her open display of affection.

His wife merely smiled and tucked her arm into his. They returned the doorman's salute and huge smile. As they left the gracious hotel behind them, Blanche turned round, but the building was hidden in the haze of dust which settled on the brightly coloured bougainvillaea bushes as if to dull the splendour of their papery flowers.

By the end of lunch Briar had decided that the next three weeks promised to be very enjoyable. The Andretti family had all the exuberance and zest for life which one associates with Italians. They laughed and ate with gusto. Their hands flew as they spoke and their enthusiasm for Zimbabwe and the splendour of the Falls was infectious.

After the horror, strain and sorrow of Kame and Ganyani, Briar felt herself relaxing. She was able to laugh. She even found Kirk's stories amusing. She was certain that, if she took up a permanent position, her parents would soon settle into a new routine at Inyati without her.

Fred and Blanche climbed into the Land Rover in silence.

'I agree with you,' said Blanche suddenly as Fred pulled into the petrol station on the corner of the main road.

'What? Agree with what?' After almost fifty years of marriage to Blanche, Fred was still surprised by her swings in conversation.

'Young Madden, Fred. You said you didn't like him. Neither do I. I wouldn't buy a second-hand car from that man.'

Fred laughed and opened the door to talk to the attendant.

'He's too glib,' Blanche continued. 'There is something calculating in his greeny-yellow eyes that I don't like.'

The smell of petrol wafted into the car as a whirlwind twisted the soft sand on the road into a cone and carried it past the petrol pumps. Blanche felt nauseous. Since the deaths of Pat's two sons and of his wife, who had been her best friend, she and Briar had led lonely lives. Now Briar was gone. Blanche longed to be back at Inyati, back in her familiar home.

Suddenly deep drumbeats pulsated in the confined space of the Land Rover. The monotonous yet insistent pounding seemed to explode in Blanche's head.

She covered her ears with both hands. 'Muffle the drums. Muffle the drums, Fred,' she shouted.

Fred stared at her in alarm. This was not the brave, quiet woman he knew and loved.

'Blanche,' he soothed, putting his arm around her shoulders. 'Blanche, you're upset because we've left Briar with Madden. It's hot. You're missing your home. You hate the smell of petrol. Come, love, everything is fine.'

'No, it's the drums. They are the heartbeat of this country and someone is trying to stop the heart.'

Fred held Blanche to him and called to the petrol attendant.

'Bring a cold Coke quickly. My wife is not well.'

When the drink came, he eased the plastic straw into her mouth.

'Blanche,' reasoned Fred, 'that drum is outside the curio store. Calling the tourists. The beating attracts them and they home in, like tsetse flies to a trap.'

Blanche started sipping the ice-cold drink. As it cooled her she relaxed.

'Sorry, Fred. It's just that those drums talking in the night brought so much unhappiness to Pat and Erin. They really don't deserve it. They've had more than their share of bad luck. It's not fair.'

'Life is not fair, Blanche. It's hard and often merciless. We have a wonderful country but not everyone in it is good and honest.'

'As we have just seen,' answered Blanche bitterly. 'And the drums knew. They knew what was going to happen. They beat out their message of fear and silence, night after long night. They are being abused. They brainwash the rural people. They must be muffled.'

Fred handed the empty tin to the attendant, put the Land Rover into gear and they jolted away in a cloud of black exhaust fumes.

'Africa without the drumbeat would be as sad as an Africa without wild animals. Imagine Inyati with no elephants, no predators or buck, only sheep and cattle. The magic would be lost. Drums are part of Africa's mystery. You cannot muffle them.'

Blanche shook her head and looked out of the window. She loved the wild open bush country. As warm air blew through the Land Rover drawing out the smell of petrol, her sense of panic slowly abated and her breathing became easier.

'Drums can reach areas where there is no television or newspapers. They carry messages to the wildest corners of this country. Places where people believe what the drums say. If they were muffled, then corrupt people in positions of authority could not use them,' she reasoned.

Fred nodded and ran his fingers through his hair. He understood only too well what Blanche feared.

'We have chosen to live here, my love, and must learn to live with African democracy.' He leaned towards her and took her hand. 'Remember they cannot completely destroy the beauty of the country or our love for it.'

Blanche squeezed his hand. They drove on to Inyati, their fingers tightly entwined.

Briar lifted the phone on half a dozen occasions to call her parents during the time the Andretti family spent at the Falls Hotel. Each time she replaced the receiver gently before the call was answered. She would not admit defeat before the safari even started. She would complete the three weeks and leave when the Andrettis returned to Italy.

Briar had now developed a deep dislike for Kirk Madden. She found him vain and arrogant. The heavily muscled man strutted round the hotel giving orders like a modern-day Napoleon.

She despised him for flirting with Tomasina when the Andretti men were absent. She hated the way he smiled at her conspiratorially as his hand brushed Maria Andretti's thigh or breast. He was playing with both mother and daughter and as his employee Briar felt sullied.

Grow up, she told herself in the privacy of her room. Kirk's behaviour has nothing to do with you. You've been hired to run the camp, not monitor his morals. She walked across to the window which looked out over the terrace. As usual tourists and waiters were woven into a kaleidoscope of movement and colour beneath the shady trees.

Her gaze moved to the spray rising high above the thundering Falls. Briar stared out at the mist, shimmering in the sun like a gigantic tangled cobweb, until her eyes watered. She was about to turn away and complete her packing – they were leaving for Kirk's camp later that afternoon – when she noticed two figures in close embrace at the top of the steps leading from the hotel gardens to a viewing site of the gorge.

There was something familiar about the couple. Briar put her binoculars to her eyes. She adjusted the setting and gasped. Kirk and Maria Andretti seemed to be in the room with her.

Maria's head was thrown back and her luxuriant hair swung in the breeze. Kirk's mouth covered hers and Maria's fingers dug deep into his bleached hair.

As Briar watched, unable to put down the binoculars, Kirk pulled Maria to him, both hands cupping her buttocks. She arched her pelvis forward and their bodies seemed to move to the pounding of the waters.

'No,' said Briar, turning away. When she looked again, Kirk and Maria were walking up to the terrace side by side. She could detect no trace of the intimacy she had observed, as they sat down opposite each other at one of the tables and ordered tea.

Clever, she thought. You're very smart, Mr Madden. At lunch you talk about the huge buffalo and elephant in the nearby Zambezi National Park. Then you wait until the men, Tara and Tomasina have gone there on a game drive, and you have the mother to yourself.

Briar flung open the wardrobe door and dragged out her shorts, slacks and shirts. She began stuffing them deep into her bag, careless of how they were creasing. Then her breathing became slower as she heard Blanche's soft voice saying, 'Never judge a man until you have walked at least a mile in his shoes.' She calmed down.

'Thanks, Mum,' she whispered to the empty room. 'I won't.'

Briar was able to smile at Kirk and Maria when they met in the entrance hall. She studied them carefully, but in front of the family they played their parts to perfection. Kirk was the efficient and polite hunter. The Andrettis were his clients.

Chapter Nine

KIRK'S CAMP surprised Briar. She had expected a simple bush camp with basic facilities. A great deal of money must have been spent on this place and she wondered once again who was funding Kirk.

She was standing in one of the round huts for clients. Built of brick, it was plastered with mud on the outside to look authentic, but the inside was painted white. The floor was of highly polished cement stained dark green. The round mat of woven grass in the centre of the room had an intricate border where the grass had been stained purple and green. She sat on one of the iron beds, which boasted an inner-spring mattress, inviting continental pillows in crisp white cotton covers and a neatly folded duvet at its foot, a necessity for the cold nights.

'Larney,' she said quietly and went to inspect the small bathroom which adjoined the main room. Her gaze roamed from the white enamel bath standing on four splayed legs to the toilet with a flush cistern. The basin was set in a slab of dark green cement. A mirror hung above the basin and there were cupboards on either side. She peered through the window, trying to see through the small mosquito mesh covering the opening.

Outside stood a 'donkey', the usual way of obtaining hot water in areas without electricity. The donkey consisted of a drum suspended in a brick structure with enough space beneath it to light a fire. A pipe ran in one end bringing in water. Briar supposed that in this sort of camp Kirk would have a generator to pump water up for the toilet cisterns and donkeys.

He probably has electric lights as well, thought Briar with a wry smile.

'Do you like it?'

Kirk's voice startled Briar and she spun round to see him leaning nonchalantly against the door frame, penning her in the bathroom.

'It's more like a hotel than a bush camp,' she said shortly.

'Why make clients rough it, when a little money gives them the comfort they crave?' he answered. 'By day they are all macho hunters, but when it gets dark they like a door that locks and a lavatory a few feet away from their beds.'

'I suppose the women enjoy the inner-spring mattresses as well,' said Briar and immediately regretted it.

'Oh yes, Briar,' he answered. His voice was soft and caressing as he walked towards her. Briar edged around the room trying to reach the door to the bedroom which was now unguarded.

As she did so she kept talking, hoping that he would not notice what she was doing. She felt as insecure as a schoolgirl about to have her first kiss.

Kirk seemed totally unaware of the direction she was taking. Yet, as she lunged for the open door, he shot across the room, snatched her arm and twisted her body into his.

'No!' she screamed but the sound was cut short by his mouth.

He pinned her arms to her side. She struggled to turn

her face away from his questing tongue, but could not break free.

His thick tongue filled and explored the inside of her mouth. His grip coiled around her as strong as a python slowly asphyxiating its victim. She had an image of Kirk as a snake with heat sensors in his upper lip seeking warm-blooded prey. His saliva was the saliva the snake smeared over its victim. She panicked as his arms squeezed her even tighter. Her usual common sense vanished. She bit down hard on his tongue and tasted his sour blood as it ran into her mouth.

Kirk merely laughed, his lips flecked with blood.

'That's not going to work, little Hanley,' he said, the pain in his tongue exciting him. 'I like women with fire. I knew you'd be good, the first time I saw you.'

Briar spat the blood out of her mouth and had the satisfaction of seeing the red spittle dribble down his bare chest. His words reminded her of the joy she had felt in Scott Gifford's arms. Their love had been so full of promise. Kirk was sullying something she still held precious.

'If only Scott was here he'd kill you,' she said in stifled gasps, still trying to breathe deeply.

'The Giffords.' His eyes lit up, they seemed to turn a dark, ominous green as he recalled his humiliation. He remembered hanging helpless as a cub in a lioness's mouth, as Scott Gifford threw him out of the dance hall.

That night, lying on the ground listening to the laughter from the hall, he had sworn revenge. He had achieved his aim: both Gifford twins were dead. Now fate had given him the chance to have his final revenge on Briar.

She had been the cause of his humiliation. She still showed her dislike of him, pulling away from any physical contact. Now he had her in his power. He longed to see her face as he told her how Scott was ambushed.

No, he cautioned himself. Save that story for later. This is not the time. I'll first take this hellcat, then tell her what happened to her precious Gifford lover.

Kirk's muscular physique belied his inferiority complex. At school he had been the runt in his class and was bullied by his peers. After school and during the war years he had exercised and worked on his body until his muscled torso took attention away from his lack of height. Constantly trying to prove himself, he managed to be both offensive and overbearing.

'So you think my camp is larney. Too fancy for you, is it? You disagree with sprung mattresses on the beds. In that case, Hanley, we won't let you try one of them.'

Briar tried to scream but one of his hands slapped down on her face and covered her nose.

He's mad, she thought as she fought to free herself. She felt the room spin as she struggled for breath.

For a small man Kirk held her to him surprisingly easily. He dragged her into the centre of the bathroom and kicked the door shut.

Briar felt the cold slab holding the basin cut into the small of her back as Kirk forced her against it. She tried to kick him.

'Don't,' he warned coldly. 'Or the Andrettis will sympathize with you because you slipped and broke your leg on the cement floor.'

Briar looked into his eyes only a few inches from hers. She saw the cold, implacable glare of the leopard, a solitary hunter of the night. There would be no mercy.

She would not give this man the satisfaction of hearing

her plead. His physical strength stunned and frightened her. She realized that she could not fight him.

'I swear that one day you'll pay for this, Kirk Madden,' she said. 'I call all the N'debele curses on you.'

'I look forward to that, Briar. I've felt your thorns,' he taunted, his tongue thick and unwieldy in his mouth. 'Now let's see the sweet roses of the Briar.'

In one swift, practised movement he unzipped her shorts and let them drop. The thin cotton of her panties tore as they were thrown on the floor. All the time he kept up the pressure pushing her against the basin. The cement edge pressed deeper into Briar's spine. She was certain that it would snap. She clenched her teeth as a new pain tore through her. Her eyes were shut tight. She would not call out, or allow him the pleasure of seeing her cry.

'A virgin,' Kirk hissed in disgust. 'So Gifford didn't even sample the goods before he was hung out to dry.' He stepped away from her and started to zip up his pants.

Kirk Madden did not see Briar's leg. It swung up hard and fast carrying all her hurt and hatred with it. He doubled over. He was unable to groan. Pain gnawed at him with the jaws of a hyena. He clutched himself as he tried to crawl to the toilet.

Briar seized the opportunity. Another well-placed kick doubled him over the porcelain bowl.

Briar knew that she would have to face the Andrettis soon and play her part as the camp supervisor. She splashed water over her face and combed her hair with her fingers. She tried to smooth out the creases in her shirt and made certain that her clothes showed as little sign of a struggle as possible. She stuffed her panties into her pocket.

Before she left the bathroom, she crossed to the toilet

and pulled the chain. Water stained brown by the rust inside the cistern gushed into the bowl and covered Kirk's face. He did not even lift his head. Another spasm of pain convulsed him and he continued retching.

She squared her shoulders and took a final look at herself in the mirror. The sound of Kirk vomiting was sweet music to Briar.

'Vomit like a pig because that is all you are, a pig.' At the door she turned back. 'Remember today, Madden. What evil you do will come back to you. You'll pay for this one day. My only prayer is that I'll be there to see you suffer.' She paused for a moment. 'If ever I or any member of my family meet you in the bush, watch your back.'

Briar walked through the bedroom and out into the boma.

The Andrettis were seated in camp chairs in the enclosure around a pile of logs which would be lit when it grew dark. The camp staff were obviously well trained. They had served tea for the women and beers for the men. The ranger appointed by the Department of National Parks to check that hunting regulations were strictly adhered to was in the kitchen having his tea.

'I had no idea a bush camp looked like this,' said Tara, munching a rusk as she studied the grass fence which enclosed the area.

'They don't, usually,' answered Briar, forcing herself to smile and not think about the scene in the bathroom. 'This camp has cost someone a great deal of money.'

Guido sat up a little straighter in his chair. He had been toying with the idea of buying a hunting concession himself.

'It's a beautiful camp,' Briar lied, hating anything that belonged to Kirk Madden.

'How much, Briar?' Guido asked. 'What would this cost?'

'That you'll have to ask Kirk.'

'Where is he?' asked Maria nonchalantly. 'We've not seen him since we arrived.'

'He's resting for a while. Something he ate at the Falls. Probably the *talapia* fish. Sometimes the fishermen leave it in the sun too long before they get it to the hotel.'

Maria pushed back her chair and placed her cup on the ground.

'I will see if I can help,' she said.

'Please don't get up. He was kneeling over the toilet bowl when last I saw him. He'll join us when he's ready.'

Maria relaxed and grinned.

'Men, when they have a stomach which is not good, are always near death.'

Well, this one does think he's dying, thought Briar, and it's a pity he isn't.

'I suggest the ladies shower now while it's still warm and light,' she said. 'It gets cold later and the mosquitoes may start biting.'

She could not wait to scrub her body and rid herself of all traces of Kirk Madden. She smiled in relief as the women stood up immediately and went off to their respective huts.

On the way to the hut he shared with his father, Marco noticed that there were openings in the bamboo screen around the outside shower which Briar, as a member of the camp staff, was using. He paused, not meaning to peep. Knowing that he was hidden from view – his family were all in the bathrooms in their huts – he stayed.

Briar's body was red. The bristles of the scrubbing brush left white streaks down her stomach and legs. Yet still she rubbed at her tender flesh. It seemed to Marco that she was trying to shed her skin, to rub away the old and emerge in a fresh one.

Briar was the sort of woman Marco would like to marry one day. She was well-mannered and quiet. Yet when she laughed she was young and beautiful and he wanted to laugh with her. He knew that he was expected to marry a girl from a good Italian family and breed children, to ensure that the firm remained in Andretti hands.

The few days he had spent in Briar's company made him restless. His neatly planned future seemed less exciting than it had before he left Milan.

'Staff,' shouted Briar suddenly, not yet knowing their names. 'Please send another bucket of hot water.'

Marco started and walked away quickly, feeling sick and guilty for spying on Briar. She did not deserve it.

Finally Briar stepped from the flat rock placed directly beneath the suspended drum of water and on to a smaller dry rock to one side of the enclosure. Here she pulled on a pair of slacks which she tucked into socks. She shrugged into a long-sleeved shirt and a padded gilet. Bending over to lace up her short canvas boots, she felt an ache deep within her.

'Mum, his shoes aren't worth putting on, let alone walking in for a mile. I hate him,' she whispered.

Briar looked up at the Zimbabwean sky which was now softening to accept the onset of dusk. Above her, perched on the branch which held the shower bucket, sat a robin. His bright dark eye peered at her as he cocked his head to one side.

Broad white eyebrow stripes and heavy brown spotting on his underparts would have identified him to Briar as a Heuglin, long before he broke into what she had always thought was the most beautiful song of any bird. As the robin repeated and varied the phrases of his song, the tears Briar had held back flowed at last. She did not try to stop them. Her shoulders shook and her hair, still wet, clung to her tear-stained cheeks.

Eventually the robin stopped singing and Briar dried her eyes.

'You should be giving us that as a morning wake-up song,' she said to the bird. 'You're not an evening bird. But thank you.'

At the sound of her voice the Heuglin fluffed out his feathers and flew away.

Briar leaned against one of the mopane poles. She realized that she could never tell her family of the rape. Her father would almost certainly tell his closest friend, Pat Gifford. Pat would feel responsible because it was his son who had hurt Kirk's pride at the dance. Erin was hot-headed enough to find Kirk and start a vendetta. Soon everyone would know about it. She would not be able to appear in public without being scrutinized by old ladies and young men, both wondering whether she had encouraged Kirk's advances.

If she kept it a secret she knew that Kirk would not be stupid enough to boast about raping her. The country brimmed with battle-hardened men who did not accept rape. Many of them had fought beside the Gifford boys. Some had been at school with her.

Kirk would be ostracized and would probably meet with an unfortunate hunting accident.

She stared up at the branch where the robin had sung, then raised her eyes to the soft grey heavens which seemed to stretch to infinity above her.

'I'm sorry,' she whispered, 'I was wrong to wish him harm. Revenge is yours, not mine.'

The words seemed to calm and cleanse her. With the birdsong still filling her ears, she left the shower.

Kirk excused himself from dinner pleading an upset stomach. Briar was relieved not to have to face him. The Andrettis accepted her suggestion that they should retire early as it had been a long day.

She thought that she would lie awake reliving the scene in the bathroom, but darkness was kind and closed her eyes. She awoke to the sound of the staff lighting a fresh fire and setting the table for breakfast.

Chapter Ten

KIRK'S SKIN pimpled into goose bumps as the warm water cooled on his bare skin. He was leaning over an enamel basin in front of his hut, shaving. As he flicked the shaving soap matted with blond hair into the bowl, the suds floated on the surface like scum on a stagnant drinking hole.

He had decided to remove the stubble he affected as a moustache. They had been in camp for a week and the moustache was still straggly.

Tomasina walked out of her hut pretending to brush her hair, but she was watching the muscles ripple across Kirk's back and shoulders as he moved.

She had enjoyed many liaisons in Milan. The fashion industry was filled with good-looking young men, living on champagne and cigarettes to meet deadlines for the shows. It was a fast-paced, frenetic life. Affairs were numerous and as short-lived as the applause which greeted each model on the catwalk. Tomasina liked the idea of returning to Milan to boast of bedding a 'white hunter'. It would give her a certain cachet with her friends.

Guido had made it clear to Kirk when they met at the Falls that his wife and daughters were to be treated with respect.

'I have heard how Africa heats the blood in a woman's

body,' he said, 'but in Sicily where I was born, men are killed for taking advantage of a man's family.'

Kirk had merely nodded, looked solemn and continued in his imagination to possess Tomasina.

As he turned away from the basin to pick up his towel, he caught sight of Tomasina watching him and smiled. She flushed, conscious that she had no make-up on and that her trousers were still unzipped. She turned her back on him, zipped up her cotton khaki slacks and went back into her hut.

Tara was sitting on the edge of her bed cursing her thick walking socks which bunched up each time she tried to force her feet into her short canvas boots. She looked up as her sister came into the room. Tomasina was flushed and flustered. She fiddled with her cosmetic case lying open on the table.

'Be careful, *cara*,' Tara warned, 'that one is not your usual Milanese. He is wild and dangerous, like the animals he hunts. He will hurt you.'

'Who?' queried Tomasina, pretending innocence.

'Kirk Madden. He has been making love to you with his eyes ever since we met.'

'Tara, my little sister, you imagine things which are not there,' said Tomasina. 'I have no interest in the hunter.'

Tara shook her head and pulled at the laces of her boots, wishing she could knot them around Kirk's neck. She understood Italian men. They were lovers, but she sensed that Madden had cruelty hidden in him.

'Never trust a man who is full of self-love,' she said.

Tomasina laughed and carefully outlined her full lips in bright red. Tara, with her elfin features and short stature, was completely unlike Tomasina. Not only did the girls differ in their physical appearance, but Tara was also disparaging about the shallowness of the fashion world. She knew of her sister's numerous affairs, but kept them secret from her father.

Tara had fallen in love once in her life. It had lasted a year, a magical year for her. They had set a date for their marriage and chosen an apartment. One night she received a telephone call from her lover's wife. The woman was in tears. She asked Tara to send her husband home, as their baby son had been rushed to hospital.

Tara never saw the man again. All his messages were left unanswered. She found a new apartment and left no forwarding address. She now kept all men at a distance. They offered the moon and stars, knowing that they could provide neither.

Kirk banged the copper disc which stood on the sideboard in the dining room. It was suspended between a pair of warthog tusks and gave out a hollow, mournful sound.

Tara shrugged into a padded anorak.

'Forget showing off your figure,' she said, watching Tomasina pull her wide studded belt in another notch. 'It will be freezing on that truck. Take your anorak and gloves and scarf,' she added as an afterthought.

The two sisters hurried to the dining room as their father hated to be kept waiting. He liked to be in the Land Rover before the sky lightened. It made him feel that he was having a full day's hunt.

Maria had tried to reason with him. 'If we're this cold how do you think the animals feel? They sleep outside and are stiff in the early morning. They need to feel the sun before they move.'

Guido was deaf to all entreaties. So each dawn saw the

family huddled miserably on the hunting vehicle peering into the still murky bush.

'Today will be an easy day,' said Kirk layering tomato, Worcester and HP sauce over his fried eggs. He could not understand why the Andretti family found this manner of eating eggs strange, when they munched Jalapeno chillies as if they were peanuts.

He had accepted a chilli on the first day in camp, thinking that if the women ate them, they must be mild. It had taken him all his will-power not to shout for water. His throat and nostrils reminded him for hours afterwards not to eat Jalapeno chillies again.

'We will check the leopard baits. Move those which have not been touched to another spot, and hopefully we will be able to choose our hide for tonight.'

Marco's eyes glistened. Guido had promised him the first leopard. What he had not been told was that Guido and Kirk would 'double tap' his shot, by shooting simultaneously in case Marco missed, or if his was a bad shot.

Kirk did not relish the idea of following a wounded leopard in the dark. Tracking any wounded animal was dangerous, but to search for an angry leopard in the long grass made even hardened hunters tense and nervous.

'This may be the first skin for your jacket, Maria,' smiled Kirk.

'Spotted furs, trapped or endangered species should not be used by furriers,' said Tara, putting down her knife and fork.

'Leopards are like cats, Tara,' said Kirk placatingly. 'Give them the right conditions, enough food and they breed like rabbits. Zambia, for example, is overpopulated with leopards. We have enough of them here to make thousands of coats and not even notice their loss.'

'Countries like this need the money, Tara, and shooting leopards is not cheap,' added Guido.

Tara dropped her argument. Her radical views on hunting had moderated since she started the safari. Issues which seemed clear-cut and simple, sitting with her friends in Milan, changed once she was in the African bush. Here she was faced with the harsh realities of existence in a third world country, where foreign exchange was of prime importance and the population explosion could not be controlled.

Politics had become a game of juggling people, animals and the preservation of their natural habitat. The two balls most often dropped were animals and habitat.

Kirk wiped his mouth, belched and pushed back his chair.

'Let's roll,' he said.

'Whew! What's that stench?' asked Maria, pinching her nose as the Land Rover lurched into a narrow wooded valley.

It was midday and the morning chill was long forgotten. Maria had tucked her hair up under her cloth hat and flicked up the collar of her shirt to protect her neck from the searing sun.

'This is our lucky bait, I hope,' answered Kirk. 'We've hung it in a tree which has been used by leopard. We've seen the claw marks on the bark and branches.'

'You said that about the last three trees,' said Tara.

They had bumped around in the vehicle all morning. Each prospective site had shown no sign of fresh leopard spoor. The leopards had ignored the sides of zebra and impala carefully concealed from the vultures beneath leafy branches, yet within fairly easy reach of a leopard up the tree.

'When do we stop for lunch?' asked Tomasina. She too had lost interest in looking for non-existent spoor.

'Not here,' said Maria, trying to think of her scented bathroom at home. She could not even recall the beautiful smell of a rich red rose.

Suddenly she remembered the mosquito repellent she carried in her pocket. She dabbed it on her wrists. The repellent stank, but Maria brought her hand to her nose, breathing it in as if it were Calèche perfume.

The valley they were in narrowed. The rocky sides rose up steeply, holding in both the heat and the heavy silence of midday. Suddenly the stories Kirk and Guido had been telling Marco about the habits of this solitary killer they were seeking seemed very real. The women felt small and vulnerable sitting in the open Land Rover.

Maria looked up at the overhanging branches of the Brachystegia woodland nervously. She expected to see a seven-foot feline stretched supine on one of the branches, its tawny colour and the clusters of dark rosettes on its skin copies of the shadows thrown by the leaves.

As the vehicle slowed to a walking pace Maria studied the largest trees, dreading yet hoping to see a long, black-tipped tail hanging down straight as a rifle barrel from one of the branches.

Kirk stopped the truck and switched off the ignition.

'Stay here and keep quiet,' he commanded. 'We're going to see if a leopard visited the bait last night.'

'Please let us come,' said Maria. 'I feel safe with you there.'

Kirk paused, then nodded.

'All right, everyone out, but walk quietly and no talking. Guido, you bring up the rear. No shooting,' he warned.

As they followed Kirk, trying not to snap dry mopane twigs and leaves, Maria cursed herself for having asked to leave the vehicle. Sweat drenched her shirt and she wanted to vomit. The smell of rotting meat and blood filled the air. She gasped, desperate for fresh air to breathe.

Suddenly Kirk stopped beneath the spreading branches of the large acacia.

Without warning a scream of absolute terror rang out. It bounced off the rocks and echoed eerily up the valley.

Tomasina jumped back as if stung by a scorpion. Kirk felt the familiar sick rush of adrenalin which always shadowed danger. He swung his rifle up at the tree but nothing moved.

'What is it, Tomasina?' he said. 'What have you seen?'

'Maggots,' answered Guido, fishing the wriggling grubs out of Tomasina's hair. Kirk turned on her, his yellow-green eyes flashing.

'That scream could cost us this leopard. There are fresh claw marks on the tree, the branches have been moved and part of the carcass has been eaten.'

'A leopard would eat meat which is full of maggots and dripping green slime?' queried Maria.

'I've watched a leopard on a bait sneezing maggots out of its nose as it fed,' said Kirk, calm now after the shock.

The women shuddered and sat quietly in the shade while Kirk supervised the camouflage of the hide. It was an old one built on a small rise downwind from the tree. It gave them a clear view of the tree and the bait.

The trackers hacked away a few small branches which might interfere with a clear shot. Then Kirk positioned

Marco and Guido in the hide and made a rest for Marco's rifle. Few hunters hold a rifle steady without flinching when they see their first leopard outlined against a darkening sky.

'Let's pray he's hungry and comes while it's still light,' said Kirk, finally satisfied that he and Guido would have clear shots over Marco's shoulders. 'We must get out of here and allow the place to quieten down.'

'Do you think the leopard will come tonight?' asked Tomasina, ashamed of her outburst.

'Yes, if he's brain-damaged or deaf,' answered Kirk.

'I am sorry, Kirk,' said Tomasina and put her hand softly on his arm. The movement threw open the top of her shirt and exposed part of her breast.

Kirk's attitude changed immediately. He put an arm protectively around her shoulders and squeezed her to him. It seemed a conciliatory gesture to Guido and Marco, but Tomasina felt the sexual charge in his body. It excited her and she decided that she would definitely have Kirk Madden before they returned to Milan.

'Here, you still have one or two grubs on you,' he said. 'Let me brush them off.'

He turned her to face him.

As he pretended to flick grubs from the front of her blouse, he quickly held and squeezed her nipple.

Tomasina winced with pain but it was pleasurable. Kirk stared straight into her eyes. What he saw made him want to throw her down in the shadow of the great old acacia and remain over her until she cried out for him to stop.

'Tonight,' he whispered. 'My hut. Midnight.'

Tomasina nodded, her back still turned to her family.

'Thank you, Kirk,' she said loudly. 'Those maggots are

loathsome. I hate crawling things which live on dead flesh. They remind me of graveyards and tombs.'

Maria crossed herself. 'Don't be morbid, Tomasina,' she said.

'We'll have lunch at a river with a beautiful waterfall, not far from here. I call it Kirk's Rest,' he said. 'Then we'll return to camp. The women can relax. The men will come back to the hide. I want everyone in place long before the shadows lengthen, in case our leopard comes early.'

'When will you men return to us?' asked Maria.

'That depends on the leopard,' answered Kirk, smiling at her. He still intended to have her and her daughter in his bed before the end of the safari. Maria's kisses were experienced and had excited him.

'If the Tom comes early we'll be back for dinner. If not we may have to wait for dawn. He may come for an early breakfast instead.'

Maria moved closer to him and held out her hand.

'I have a thorn in my thumb, please take it out,' she asked loudly.

Kirk bent over her hand which was free of any thorns.

'Make it early,' she whispered.

She had finally decided to have an affair with Kirk. He had suggested it at the Falls, but then she was still worried about the possible consequences. Things had a different perspective in the bush, away from any form of civilization. Here all was strange and exciting. She felt younger than her daughters.

Guido was totally engrossed in hunting and spoke of nothing but rifles, bullets and trophy-sized horns. At night, wearied by the day's tracking, he fell into a deep sleep. She was certain that he would suspect nothing.

Kirk's hut stood alone outside the fence enclosing the boma. It would be easy to sneak out of her hut to find his. If Guido woke to find her gone, she could always say that she had been unable to sleep and had gone to sit by the fire.

Kirk grinned and squeezed her hand. Two bedded in one night, he thought. That Tom better not wait for dawn.

'There you are,' he said, 'it wasn't in too deep.'

Maria smiled. She had wrestled with her conscience, had prayed nightly, but still her body betrayed her. She had developed a fixation on Kirk Madden. She had to have him. Their embraces at the Falls burned in her dreams. She relived every moment, retasted his mouth, felt his strength and arousal.

Her eyes, like trackers hot on animal spoor, followed his every movement. Maria knew that she was behaving like a teenage girl, giddy with her first love, unable to control her physical needs.

The three women spent the long drowsy afternoon lazing in camp. It seemed so quiet without the men.

As the sun slid behind the trees in its spectacular blaze of red and gold, the women gathered around the camp fire. Two of them were blind to the beauty of the trees standing out against the shining whorls and streaks which nature painted across the sky. They waited only for the concealing mantle of darkness.

Chapter Eleven

THE CESSNA bounced about on the heat thermals with all the aerobatic skill of a bateleur eagle. Unlike the eagle, Matamba's bulk was strapped tightly into the small front seat. Returning home after lunching with Fred and Blanche Hanley at Inyati, he was not feeling well. Each time the plane dropped his stomach rose. The flight seemed endless. He tried looking out of the window but the land beneath him seemed to swim and gave him vertigo.

The roast beef and treacle pudding which Blanche served for lunch was tasty and Matamba had partaken too heartily of fare more suited to the cool British climate than the heat of Zimbabwe. He now regretted accepting a third helping of pudding and custard.

He had not enjoyed the conversation after lunch with Fred Hanley. It added mental unease to his physical discomfort.

Over the years he had borrowed money from Fred, promising to repay it once his party came into power. Then the unexpected happened. When elections were held, an outsider won the race and Matamba was in no position to return the money.

He enjoyed the comfort it brought. After the elections he continued to borrow from Fred. Fred's father, a wealthy English landowner, had been a shrewd businessman who taught his son that if a man owes you something, you have him in your power.

When he realized how deeply in debt he was to Fred Hanley, Matamba was shocked. He was also aware that if news of this debt was leaked, it could destroy his political credibility and give the opposition a knobkerrie with which to beat him.

After lunch Fred sat on the verandah with Matamba and showed him the list of payments he had made over the years. Even interest free, it was a staggering amount. The figure sat as heavily in Matamba's stomach as the treacle pudding and custard. He knew that it would be impossible to repay the loans.

The alternative suggested by Fred terrified him. It meant out-manoeuvring Tigera. Many men had tried it, few survived. People who annoyed Tigera seemed to die in convenient accidents. Matamba had no wish to become a statistic.

Fred Hanley had suffered with Pat over the insane slaughter of the game on Ganyani. He understood men like Tsvakai Tigera. He knew that if Pat did not capitulate, he would lose Erin. An accident would happen and no finger would be pointed at Tigera. Erin resembled Scott so closely that secretly Fred looked upon him as a son-in-law. He loved the boy, as he loved and respected Pat.

Fred also knew that Kame and Ganyani were like the red blood in his friend's veins. Pat could not live without his game ranches. He would rather die than give up the land he loved. Fred had to persuade Matamba to speak to Tigera.

Once back in his own house Matamba's stomach settled a little. He eased himself into the leather chair at his desk and called for a Coke. His wife ran to obey.

Irritably he switched off the fan. The whirling blades whispered Fred's parting words. 'Contact me when you have news.'

Matamba swallowed the drink in one long gulp, then pulled a notebook from a locked drawer. He, too, had a long list, not of money debts but of the names of people who owed him favours. He was about to call in some of these. He did not enjoy crossing names from his list, but Fred was insistent.

Matamba's study grew dark as the evening shadows lengthened. His wife came in to switch on the desk lamp. Matamba was so engrossed in his thoughts that he merely nodded. He had tried to contact Tigera twice. Both times the secretary said Tigera was in a meeting and would return his call.

Matamba knew that she was lying. As she was secretly in his employ he knew that she would only lie to him if Tigera was in the room and she could not talk freely.

'Tell Mr Tigera that it is of vital importance that we talk as soon as possible,' he said. 'If you want a cheque at the end of the month tell him now,' he added softly.

Matamba replaced the phone. He leaned back in his chair and clasped his hands over his belly.

He could afford to relax a little. The terror of confronting Tigera empty-handed was over. One of his informants had just told him of a confidential deal between Tigera and a Far East consortium.

The deal involved granting rights for a hotel and casino in the Zambezi National Park, the magnificent rainforest area around the Falls. This had been created a World Heritage Site to protect the rich plant and animal life, as well as the unspoilt beauty of the Falls. Such a deal could have world-wide repercussions and cause the government great embarrassment. Tigera would lose his enviable position and all his credibility if it were known that he was involved.

According to Matamba's informant, the consortium planned to bring in bulldozers and earth-moving equipment by night and clear the area they needed before ecological pressure groups could react. Once the trees were removed they could not be replaced. It would then be logical to build the Casino, promising to be environmentally conscious, a promise easily made and broken before the last signature was on the document.

Matamba steepled his fingers as he mused over the plan. In a world which feeds on violence and bloodshed, the destruction of a small piece of forest in a Central African country would soon be forgotten. If the world's roar of anger could not halt the destruction of the great rainforests in Brazil, its voice would be only a faint whisper protesting about the Falls.

Tigera is clever, thought Matamba. But sometimes greed makes a man foolish. I think Tigera has at last given me a weak spot on which to apply pressure.

The sharp ring of the telephone cut across his thoughts. He leaned across and picked up the receiver. At the sound of Tigera's hard metallic voice, he shuddered and decided to use this new information only if all else failed.

'My friend,' Matamba said, 'it is good of you to phone when you are so busy.'

'I always have time for friends,' answered Tigera, emphasizing the word 'friends'.

Matamba spoke softly and urgently for a few minutes. Sweat beaded his forehead as he waited for Tigera to reply.

'Kame! What do you mean, I can't have Kame? Then our plan at Ganyani has failed,' snarled Tigera.

Matamba felt his stomach clench. Surely Tigera could not blame him for the Giffords' intransigence?

'They have not heeded the warning,' said Matamba. 'Pat Gifford made a statement at the polo meeting last Saturday. He told everyone that a spurious anti-poaching campaign had been carried out on his ranch. He said it was merely an excuse to slaughter his game and drive him off the land.'

'No!' roared Tigera.

'He swore that he and his son would remain on Kame and restock Ganyani with game.'

'Did he?' Tigera spat the words over the phone. Matamba held it away from his ear. Secretly he admired Pat Gifford for the stance he was taking from a position of such weakness.

'It seems that he's not afraid that he will lose his son,' said Matamba quietly.

'The son,' swore Tigera. 'He is as mad as his father. He says he would rather die than lose the ranches.' There was a long silence. 'Perhaps we'll grant his wish.'

'My friend,' said Matamba quickly. 'We must speak. I have a plan which can be of great benefit to both of us.'

So have I, my fat friend, thought Tigera as he clicked his fingers for a cigar. His secretary hastened to obey. She held the phone to his ear, as he clipped and lit the foul-smelling tobacco. She turned her head away from the phone as if proving to Tigera that she was not listening.

If clearing animals from Ganyani won't persuade them to move then I'll try other means, thought Tigera. Legless soldiers are always more demoralizing to people than a dead body. Perhaps kudu with their entrails dragging in the dust, antelope with legs slashed or staff with missing limbs will change the Giffords' minds.

Tigera well understood the importance of cattle and children to a man, but staff, servants and animals were there merely to be used. 'Excuse me a moment,' he said, 'I have urgent business to do.' He hurried from the room.

'Continue,' he said on his return a few minutes later, his thin lips lifted slightly at the corners.

His secretary gave an involuntary shiver. When Tigera smiled it was usually followed by some dreadful act.

Matamba breathed in deeply before he spoke. He had to convince Tigera. He had not mistaken the look in Fred Hanley's eyes when they spoke of his debt.

'My old friend,' he said. 'It will soon be known that we have bought Kame and Ganyani. Tongues will wag like dogs' tails. We do not need dung sticking to us when another British Legation arrives in Harare.'

He paused and took another deep breath.

'In money matters few are your equal. I could not attempt the things you do so well. But,' he paused, 'this is my idea.'

Tigera uncrossed his legs and straightened the creases in his pants. Matamba was still important to him, as he was held in high esteem by the N'debele. He could quieten them and stop their rumbles rising to a roar when the Shona annoyed them. Matamba was useful. Tigera was prepared to allow him to participate in some of his deals, though he made sure that he did not know of all his plans.

'Let us offer the Gifford boy the new hunting concession as his land. He is capable, an excellent hunter and the challenge will make him forget Kame and Ganyani.'

Tigera let the silence grow. Matamba hurried on before he could refuse.

'Let Pat Gifford set up and run the photographic safari area. He has a lifetime of experience in the bush. He will be near his son. It will stop him brooding over Kame. And most important of all, it will show that we did not take his land. A man does not take with one hand and give with the other.'

Tigera listened but gave no answer. Matamba realized that he had not swayed him.

'This way we do not have to pay Gifford for Kame and Ganyani. We merely give him new land in exchange for Ganyani. Land which is worthless to us until roads are cut through the bush, boreholes sunk, bush camps built and staff recruited and trained. Let them do the work. When it is finished – who knows what might happen?'

Tigera tapped the receiver with his gold pen. It was an ominous, irritating sound.

'The photographic concession could come up for renewal. We would have a well-run place to put out on tender, not a wilderness. It will also prove how liberal we are. Eventually the money for the concessions will be ours,' finished Matamba.

Tigera smiled and the gold filling of his front tooth glinted in light cast by the chandelier overhead.

The N'debele dog has proved himself, he thought. It is a good plan. When the time arrives to renew photographic safari concessions the billionaire benefactor with eagle eyes will be back in America, happy that he has helped conservation in Africa. Pat Gifford can then work for the new concession holder or leave. It will seem that we are doing our job honourably.

Perhaps, he thought, as he listened to Matamba wheeze over the phone, perhaps the N'debele will not be here to share the money. He lives too well and grows too fat. The heart, like a donkey, bows beneath weight for a time and then can go no further.

The thought of having all future monies to himself made Tigera grin happily.

'Your plan is a clever one, my friend,' he said. 'Once news of the new conservation area is made public, it will cause much excitement among the hunters and safari operators. Even the Giffords will be interested in the area and who will be chosen to run it.'

Matamba coughed in relief.

'Another idea,' he said huskily. 'Let Fred Hanley put the suggestion to Gifford. Pat trusts him and will probably take his advice. Let's talk to Hanley, then leave it to him to persuade the Giffords to move.'

'Good,' agreed Tigera. 'Sleep well tonight, my friend.'

Tigera stood up and stretched. The top of his bald dome would barely reach Matamba's shoulder. His narrow face and thin body betrayed the fact that he would never be as imposing as Matamba, but he was clever and cunning.

It was too late to cancel his orders. Let it be done, he thought. That Pat Gifford needs a lesson.

Night had come and with it the neon signs and gaudy lights which turned Harare into a seemingly noisy, glittering circus, set incongruously in the Zimbabwean bush.

The look of disgust on Pat's face still rankled. Tigera nodded. The plan for terror by mutilation would continue. Matamba need never know.

Chapter Twelve

PAT WRIGGLED his buttocks uncomfortably on the low round stool placed for him in the shade of the great teak tree. His long legs were jack-knifed with his knees pointing to the sky. He knew that within an hour his legs would cramp and he would have to change position. His inability to sit comfortably on this seat of honour would amuse the N'debele people gathered for the indaba.

He glanced at Erin and envied his youth and suppleness. Erin crouched flat-footed with his knees drawn up under his chin. His bottom skimmed the ground. Pat knew that, like the N'debele, Erin would remain squatting comfortably in this cramped position all afternoon.

Pat ran his hand over his bald dome. Sheeba laid her chin on his foot and her forehead wrinkled into tight frown lines as she gazed up at him. The people squatted a safe distance from the devil dog. Pat dreaded this meeting. He had put it off as long as possible. But after speaking to Fred Hanley, he realized that he would have to call it. The gathering settled down. Mothers put babies to fat breasts, old men sniffed snuff up their nostrils, children were quietened, chickens pecked on the outskirts of the crowd.

In simple words Pat explained that they were selling Kame and Ganyani to the government because poaching could no longer be controlled.

The crowd seethed and moaned like a dying animal. He waited until the consternation settled.

'You are my people,' he continued. 'I will always look after you.' He choked, then coughed gruffly, ashamed at his show of emotion.

'The government have given us new lands to work. Erin will hunt in lands near Chete safari area. He has already named the place New Ganyani.'

Pat paused as a prolonged cheer and delighted clapping broke out in the crowd.

'I too will have a new home. It will be near Chizarira. Tourists will come with cameras, not guns. We will need men to cut roads, build bush camps, and to run the camps, cook, wash and iron. Your wives and children will come with us. Soon you will have a village like this one. I will call my home Kame Two.' Here, Pat stopped speaking. He could not continue.

Jacob stood up and surveyed the people, most of whom had been born on Kame.

'We are N'debele,' he said. 'Our people go back to the N'guni warriors from the south. Mizilikazi was a name feared by all. He was a powerful and clever man, a man who knew that moving away from one's homeland was at times both necessary and wise.'

An old man with a cap of tight white curls took up the story in a reed-like voice. It was thin but carried clearly to all at the indaba.

'Mizilikazi was pushed north by the Voortrekkers in South Africa. He crossed the Limpopo River and set up his kingdom near the Matobo Hills.'

He paused and the crowd chanted for the story to continue. They loved stories.

'His impi took land and villages right to the Zambezi River. He was a man.'

Jacob cut in. He knew that once started, the old story-teller would continue for hours.

'Mizilikazi was a man. Let us too be men. Let us leave behind us what we must. Let us make for Mr Pat, Erin and ourselves a new Kame and a new Ganyani.'

This piece of rhetoric was greeted with an immediate roar of approval. The women ululated and formed small circles to shuffle their bare feet in the dust in a dance of acceptance. Babies bounced on their backs as they swayed. Flies flew up and circled waiting to return to the milk-rimmed mouths of the babies.

Pat stood up, eager for an excuse to stretch his legs. He crossed to Jacob and took his hands.

'You are my friend and my brother,' he said softly. 'Thank you.'

Erin left the dancing throng and joined the two men. Jonas followed him.

'Jacob, will you and Jonas stay with me?' Erin asked. 'It will be new land and I will need your eyes and ears.'

Jacob looked at Pat. His loyalty was divided. He knew that without a woman or sons Pat would be lonely. Pat nodded.

'Yes. But Rudo will of course stay to look after you, Mr Pat,' said Jacob. Erin laughed. Turning to Erin, Jacob's face was grave. 'I come on one condition.' Erin's smile vanished and concern took its place. 'I have to visit Kame and Mr Pat at least twice a month.'

'You mean you have to visit Rudo,' teased Pat.

'That too, Mr Pat. A woman's eyes grow like those of a

chameleon when her man is away. She looks around in circles. Who knows what she may see.'

Pat and Erin both roared with laughter. Jonas came to join them and hear the story.

'Jacob now has enough sons, he wants four daughters so he can have *lobola* when they marry,' said Jonas. 'A man always needs marriage money.'

'That would be good, but my sons will all be trackers for Erin and Erin's sons.'

Jacob grinned with impish delight as he saw Erin's ears redden in embarrassment. Erin had no experience with girls or women. The war had taken away his youth. Whispers of Aids, the thin sickness of Africa, curtailed his sexual appetite. He had been too scared to indulge in the occasional sexual foray enjoyed by his friends.

Pat turned away from the men to watch the indaba turn into a session of rejoicing.

'They are behaving like Israelites going to the promised land, not people being uprooted from their homes and made to start a new and uncertain life,' he said wonderingly.

'We are N'debele, not Tonga,' replied Jacob, referring to the most primitive tribe in Zimbabwe. 'It is not necessary for us, like the Tonga, to drag our ancestral trees from the ground and take them with us. We do not need the branches to assure us that our ancestors are near.'

Pat nodded. Superstitious beliefs were never buried deep in Africa. Education and missionary work merely sprinkled a layer of sand over them.

'We will truck out all livestock,' said Pat, suddenly businesslike. 'Do a count and let me know how many vehicles we'll need. By the end of winter we must be gone.'

Jacob and Jonas nodded. They knew what those words cost Pat.

'My heart is sad for Mr Pat,' said Jonas, as they watched Pat put his arm around Erin's shoulders and walk away.

'Life is hard. In Africa it is cruel. The strong survive. Mr Pat is strong. His cub Erin will be even stronger,' said Jacob philosophically.

Pat and Erin paused before moving out of the shade into the strong sunlight.

An area has gone and times have changed, thought Pat as he watched the villagers swirl dust over themselves as they danced. But the people have not. While there are people like this, there is always hope.

He quickened his pace. Soon the singing faded into the heavy midday silence which presses down like a steam iron on the African bush.

Chapter Thirteen

THE GROUP of men hidden deep in the tall thatching grass began to grow restless. The night was cold. The sandy footpath leading to the staff village on Kame lay as white in the moonlight as the innards of the antelope they had partially gutted.

These were Tigera's men, uneducated, the brutalized by-product of the Bush War. Pain excited them.

Rudo tucked the enamel dish of chops and rice more firmly under her arm. Pat insisted that she always took dinner home for her children when she worked late.

Rudo flicked her torch from side to side as she walked. She prayed that the beam would not pick up any red or yellow eyes in the bush. Usually Erin drove her back to the village, but this evening Blanche and Fred Hanley were having dinner and spending the night with the Giffords. She had slipped out of the kitchen, opting to walk the short distance rather than disturb the two families.

Tigera's men tensed as they saw the torch beam swinging across the path.

'It will be easy. Tonight she walks,' said the leader. 'We will not have to go into the village for her.'

Instead of waiting in ambush to surprise her as she

came level with them, they stepped out and blocked her way.

Rudo saw them. She dropped the dish and turned to run, but the way back to the house was barred by men who had cut around behind her.

This was what they enjoyed: an animal or human held at bay. The animals were easy. At night they stood still, transfixed in the bright beam of the *bulala* lamp, a high-powered light which was illegal for hunting.

Humans were more fun. They screamed, pleaded for mercy and promised anything for freedom.

Rudo did none of these things. She tightened her grasp on the heavy torch and shone it in their faces.

'*Bere*,' she hissed. 'You come like the hyenas at night. I smell the dung on you and it makes me sick. You run to do the bidding of others. For money you would kill your mothers. *Bere* have more honour than you.'

The man on whose face she focused the torch gave a strangled cry of rage. '*Bulala*! Kill her!' He jumped forward. Rudo swung the torch two-handed. She put all the strength she possessed into the blow. It caught him on his left temple and pulped his eye.

His roar of pain and anger stirred the men into action. Before Rudo could swing the torch again, her arms were pinioned to her side and she was thrown to the ground.

'*Bere*,' shouted the wounded man, 'hyenas are we?'

He pulled a knife from his pocket. The steel gleamed silver and beautiful as the moonlight danced on the blade. Blood poured down his face and ran into Rudo's eyes as he knelt over her.

The knife flashed.

'You will call no man *bere* again,' he said as he sliced at her lips and probed in her mouth for her tongue.

Rudo tried to scream but her mouth filled with blood and threatened to choke her. She heard her blouse tear. The man felt for and found her full round breasts.

'Neither will you be mother to children. No man will want to be with you. Children will run from you.'

Pain finally released Rudo from his voice. All was black; only the smell of her blood remained.

The sound of a vehicle was heard in the distance. The men looked up, startled. The leader jumped to his feet, wiping the blood from the blade on his trousers. The grass closed behind them.

Erin was whistling as he swung the Toyota round the bends. He was almost at the village and there was no sign of Rudo. She had obviously reached the village safely. He and Pat worried on the few occasions that she walked home. Hyenas often skulked around villages, scavenging rotten meat and faeces. At night they were bold. Erin did not want Rudo attacked by hyenas or lion. When he had gone to the kitchen and discovered that she had already left, he had decided to follow in the Toyota to make sure she was all right.

Suddenly he slammed on the brakes. There was a dead animal lying in the road. Immediately he thought of Ganyani.

'Don't let them have started here,' he whispered. He ran to the huddled shape. As he neared it, he recognized the bright yellow floral print skirt which Rudo had worn that evening. He turned her over, lifting her face from the dirt.

'No!' he screamed. 'Come back, you bastards. I'll kill you!'

He ran to the Toyota for his rifle which was always at hand. He switched the headlights full on, illuminating the grisly scene, and threw his rifle back on to the seat.

No, you fool, he thought, Rudo needs help. We'll find the swine who did this to her later.

Carefully he picked her up in his arms. He was strong but still staggered as he carried her back to the Toyota.

Tenderly he laid her on her side on the seat, making certain that her head would not loll and she could not choke on her own blood. He started the car and was about to reverse when something small and dark lying on the blood-soaked sand caught his attention.

He took his gun and ran to the spot. For a moment he stared in horror at the two dark strips.

Then he whipped out his handkerchief and wrapped Rudo's severed lips in the oil-stained cloth.

The Hanleys and Pat hid their shock and horror as Erin carried her into the house. They did their best to staunch the blood but, knowing she would have to undergo surgery, they were wary of giving her anything for the pain.

Fred telephoned a surgeon in Harare who owed him a favour. The specialist agreed to leave for Bulawayo immediately. Rudo would have to be taken to the emergency section of the General Hospital first but the surgeon promised he would have her transferred to the Mater Dei, the finest hospital in the country, and would operate on her there.

'The art of gentle persuasion,' said Pat bitterly. 'Unfortunately they've discovered that mutilation is more effective than death. Could they not have waited till you told them that we would accept their offer?'

'Mutilation changes a man's opinion very quickly,' answered Fred.

'I can't have this happen to my people,' said Pat quietly. 'We must leave Kame before the end of the month, we can't wait until the end of winter.' Tears filled his eyes as he looked down at Rudo. Fred turned away.

They put Rudo on a camp bed as a makeshift stretcher and Fred drove them to the airstrip.

Within minutes the plane was airborne and Rudo, with Erin and Pat by her side, was on her way to Bulawayo and hospital.

'We need Briar,' sobbed Blanche as she and Fred drove away from the airstrip. 'She did volunteer work in the hospital during the war. She can look after Rudo. The hospitals here are overcrowded and insufficiently staffed. Rudo will die if she doesn't have private nursing care.'

Blanche steadied herself against the dashboard as Fred swung his Toyota round and headed back to the airstrip.

'Fred! What are you doing?'

'Going to fetch Briar. I have enough gas to get to Madden's concession. I can refill there.'

Blanche caught his arm.

'How are you going to land in the dark?'

Anger sharpened Fred's mind.

'I'll call Madden up on the radio once I'm airborne. He can park his two hunting vehicles at either end of the strip with the headlights on. The staff can build small fires at intervals along the edges.'

Blanche looked unhappy. Fred took her hand.

'Just think how lucky we are that the curfew on night flying has been lifted. Pat is taking Rudo to hospital. I can fetch Briar. A short while ago we could not have done that.'

'I'm coming with you,' she said.

'Blanche Hanley, you are driving back to Kame village

right now. Jacob has to know what has happened to Rudo. He and Jonas must pick up the spoor of those swine for Pat and Erin to follow.'

She nodded. She knew that Fred was right, but she was afraid and wanted to be near him. As if sensing her fear, he leaned across and kissed her on the cheek.

'Assure Jacob that Rudo is alive and that we'll do everything to see that she is well looked after.'

As he climbed into his plane, he shouted, 'Tell Jacob to take the rifles they use when they go out with Erin. These men are to be treated as armed poachers. Jacob and Jonas can shoot to kill.'

Blanche's reply was lost in the roar of the engine as it caught and spun into life. She turned her face away from the flying grass and stones. As the plane lifted from the runway Fred saw the headlights wavering back over the bumpy road.

'Good girl,' he said and turned his concentration to the instrument panel.

Chapter Fourteen

KIRK MADDEN had the men seated quietly in the hide waiting for the leopard. He glared at Marco who was lifting his hand to swat at a mosquito. Her proboscis had pierced the soft skin at the base of his neck and she was sucking his blood.

Hunting for leopard had sounded exciting in Milan, when the family discussed it around the dinner table, but Marco had not envisaged sitting for hours in a cramped hide unable to move. He was developing a dislike for Kirk, whom he now considered to be his tormentor. What harm could there possibly be in scratching a mosquito bite? They were hidden by the leafy branches of the hide. No leopard could possibly see him rub his neck.

Marco glanced surreptitiously at his wristwatch. They had been sitting in this hide for three hours. He forced his mind away from his bladder and tried to concentrate on the black outline of a leopard which would balance on the branch as it tried to hook up the swinging bait.

The side of impala which had replaced the festering leg of buffalo had been secured just out of reach. The leopard would have to pose on the branch for a while as it tried to claw the meat close enough to swing it over. That would give the men time to aim and shoot.

The slits of light which filtered into the hide had faded.

The sun was setting. Marco could no longer see Kirk or his father clearly. He suddenly felt alone and vulnerable. The trackers had taken the Land Rover and parked it a long way from the hide. They would return only when they heard shots.

As the sun slid away, the bush became silent. Everything seemed to be holding its breath, waiting for the creatures of darkness to appear. The plaintive call of a fiery-necked nightjar broke the silence. The men listened as the descending notes came faster and closer together until it too was silent.

Without moving his head, Guido glanced at his son. Perspiration was beading Marco's forehead and neck.

We'll fire with him as Kirk suggested, he decided. We can always close up the extra holes in the pelt. Marco will not notice them or the noise as we fire. He will be happy that he shot a leopard.

A low cough followed by an indrawn breath came from the side of the hide. It was so close that it seemed to Marco that the animal was in the hide with them. He clenched his legs together.

Damn, thought Kirk. Tonight it has to take a different route to reach the tree.

The trackers had found pug marks in a heavily wooded area near the tree, where the leopard had forged a path through the undergrowth. They were certain that the animal would use the same route again. These big cats approached bait cautiously and usually from dense bush.

The leopard had forsaken its usual path and was walking silently and slowly past the hide. It must have sensed or smelt us, thought Kirk.

There was no need to gesture to Marco. He was holding his breath, straining to hear the next cough, waiting for the hide to collapse as the leopard discovered them.

Guido and Kirk waited. Marco longed to jump up screaming and watch the leopard melt into the bush. He wished that he had never asked to shoot a big cat. He had had no idea that the suspense would be as dreadful as this. He was certain that the leopard with its fearsome retractile claws knew that they were in the hide.

He could hear his heart pounding in his ears as loud as the drums which shook the earth at night. His hand trembled on the rifle. He was relieved that it was too dark in the hide for his father to see his fear.

Marco no longer felt the mosquitoes' sting or the black ants biting his calves as they crawled up the legs of his trousers. He strained his eyes, longing now to see a heavy shape crawl across the branch beneath which hung the bait. He needed to know the whereabouts of the leopard. He knew that he would not be able to remain silent and motionless much longer, knowing that the carnivore was circling the hide.

A hiss, faint as the first warning of the snake, alerted him. Something was moving up the tree. It was the leopard. The cat had decided the area was safe and was climbing up to the bait.

Marco felt his stomach churn and he wanted to be sick. He now had to shoot at an animal which was barely distinguishable against the darkening sky. Looking through his scope, he saw to his relief that the animal was not only larger but clearer.

Kirk had tied the rifle into position, hoping that it would help Marco not to flinch and let the barrel kick up. He hissed again. Marco tightened his finger around the trigger. He breathed in, held his breath and fired. He opened his eyes, hoping that his father had not noticed that he closed them when he pulled the trigger.

The three shots were so close together that they sounded like one great explosion. The leopard roared and fell from the branch, hitting the ground with a sickening thump. Marco shivered as the big cat twisted on the ground. It tore bushes apart and clawed at itself in its pain and anger. Gradually the chilling snarls of rage died away.

'I did it!' shouted Marco jubilantly and tried to stand up.

'Sit,' snapped Kirk. 'No one moves until the Land Rover arrives. We need the lights and trackers.'

'But it's dead. You heard it fall,' insisted Marco.

'Do you know how many idiots have died because they heard a leopard fall and went to claim the pelt?'

Guido put his hand on his son's arm. He understood the relief which comes after hours of huddling motionless and nervous in a hide, and the excitement which follows a kill.

'Kirk is right. Wait.'

Guido sat down until the lights of the hunting vehicle lit up the inside of the hide. He crouched over and unzipped his pants.

'Stand in the entrance. Don't walk away,' warned Kirk.

They would not use this hide again on the Andretti hunt, so the smell of Guido's urine would not matter.

'Stay here until we call,' ordered Kirk.

The trackers and Kirk took high-powered battery lamps and walked cautiously to the tree.

'But . . .'

Guido held up his hand. 'He is the hunter. Listen to him.'

Guido and Marco watched as the men reached the tree.

The lamps bobbed around like fireflies in the bush. Then they left the area beneath the tree and moved to the dense bush and tall grass.

'The leopard is not there,' said Guido as he chambered another round into his rifle.

'It must be, we heard it roar and fall,' argued Marco.

'But we did not see or hear it slink into the bush with the bullets deep in its body.'

Marco stared at his father.

'Bullet,' Guido quickly corrected himself.

'Here.' Kirk's voice rang out loud and clear in the heavy silence which always follows death. The lamps were now still and concentrated on something in the long thatching grass.

Marco gasped as he looked at the leopard lying on the dusty ground. It was a magnificent male.

'It's an excellent Tom,' said Kirk, holding out his hand to Marco. 'It will measure seven feet if not more from its head to the tip of its tail.'

'Maria will be delighted,' said Guido. 'This is the first skin for her jacket. The colour is very good. Look how the dark spots stand out on the tawny yellow fur.'

Marco knelt down and ran his hand along the cat's whiskers. Though death had claimed the fire from its eyes, they still glared up at him baleful and yellow. Marco wanted this cat. It was his first of the Big Five. His mother could have other pelts and other coats.

He was about to claim the animal when his father spoke. Guido already had lion, elephant, leopard, buffalo and even a rhino to his credit.

'I'll give you the two leopards on my licence, Marco. You may kill them. I have shot many in my time. That way the coat will be a gift from son to mother.'

Marco swallowed his disappointment. He could not gainsay the head of the Andretti family. 'Thank you, Father.'

Soon the trackers had layered the back of the Land Rover with armfuls of thatching grass. In death the leopard would be treated with deference. No one wanted the precious pelt damaged.

The blood had already been sponged from its fur and the holes plugged. Marco was told that his shot had probably hit bone and ricocheted back through the pelt causing two holes instead of one. Kirk and Guido knew that the two bullet holes were theirs. Marco had fired either over or under the cat.

Kirk forced himself to drive slowly. He did not want the cat jolted so that blood started seeping into its fur.

He kept glancing at his watch. The night promised the untasted delights of Maria and her daughter Tomasina.

The women heard the low growl of the Land Rover as it rumbled slowly into camp. They jumped up from their chairs around the fire and hurried to the grass-roofed shed where Kirk was parking.

Guido and Marco were the first to greet the women and tell them of the leopard.

Maria clapped her hands happily.

'My coat. Oh, my son, I am so proud of you. Thank you.'

She enfolded Marco in an embrace and then pulled away and wrinkled her nose.

'What is that smell?' she asked.

'Blood,' answered Guido, leading her around to the back of the Land Rover.

'And the smell of death,' added Kirk, as he shone the lamp on the leopard. The soft white fur on its chest and underparts blew softly in the chilly breeze. Maria ran her fingers down the long tail. She smiled as she stroked her face with the black tip. Tara looked away. There was something obscene about the act.

'It's magnificent,' exulted Maria. Tomasina nodded in agreement, though she had no wish to touch the dead carnivore.

'It was magnificent when it was alive,' said Tara. 'Now it's merely a mass of dead flesh. By tomorrow it'll be stinking.'

'Tomorrow it will be skinned. The vultures will clean up the mess and Mamma will have one skin towards her coat,' said Guido softly but firmly.

'Why aren't you satisfied with your minks and sables, Mamma?' asked Tara.

'Those are farmed like beef and leather, *cara*. Everyone has them. I want something different. I want a spotted skin. You heard Papa. Leopards are not endangered here.'

Guido came and stood behind Tara. 'Why don't you go back to the fire with Briar?' he said loudly. 'It's cold out here.' Then he added in a whisper, 'Don't spoil Mamma's pleasure in her first leopard pelt.'

Tara took Briar's arm and the two women walked back to the camp fire.

Briar poured Tara another beer and placed platters of chips made of sliced and fried green bananas beside her. She added a small bowl of fried mopane worms. Briar knew that the staff would eat them if the women did not.

Kirk watched them leave. He barked orders for the leopard to be carefully lifted and carried to the skinning shed. Maria's eyes shone and her lips were slightly parted.

She breathed in shallow pants as if making love. The dead leopard excited her. She walked over to Kirk.

'I must give you a hug of thanks,' she said. Guido and Marco smiled at her obvious enthusiasm. 'Tonight,' she whispered.

'I think I'll shower. I smell almost as bad as the *mbada*,' Kirk said.

He heard the huskiness in his voice. Maria had aroused him. He needed to get away from Guido and Marco. They must suspect nothing.

As he strutted away he was pleased with himself. The leopard hunt had been successful. The Andrettis were happy. He knew that Maria would show him just how happy she was, once Guido was asleep. He forgot the midnight tryst arranged with Tomasina.

Briar watched Kirk as he approached the camp fire. His hair was still wet from his shower and the sweet smell of aftershave lotion wafted behind him. He had more of a swagger than usual. She found it difficult to be near him and avoided him as much as possible. She spoke to him in monosyllables and only when necessary.

If she had thought of an excuse which would not arouse her parents' suspicions she would have contacted Fred and asked him to fly in to the camp to collect her. But her father was not a fool. He would wonder why she was not staying for the full three weeks. She had conjured up and discarded dozens of excuses. Finally she decided not to give Kirk the satisfaction of seeing her run away from him. She would leave with the Andrettis as planned.

Life in the camp had become easier when Briar formed a friendship with Tara. The two girls soon discovered that they had a lot in common. Tara listened eagerly to Briar's tales of growing up in the African bush. She was insatiable in her desire to know more about the animals and their habits. She soon learned both the Sindebele and botanical names for most of the trees and grasses.

Briar enjoyed her role as big sister cum teacher. It was pleasant to wile away the long hours talking to Tara. The Italian girl was happy to learn about the history of Rhodesia, as the country was called until 1980, when it became the independent republic of Zimbabwe.

Another bond the girls shared was their mutual dislike of Kirk Madden. Tara called him Romeo Madden, believing he was a frustrated gigolo.

She knew instinctively that something had taken place between Kirk and Briar. Briar would not discuss Kirk. Tara was content to wait. Now the girls sat together warming their hands over the flames. Neither looked up as Kirk strode past them. He had been called to the hut which housed his radio equipment. A few moments later he came storming out.

'Damn Hanley,' he fumed. 'The whole damn family are nothing but trouble. Why does he have to come tonight of all nights?'

'He looks like a rooster who has lost his hens,' whispered Tara to Briar as Kirk approached them.

'Talking to yourself is the first sign of madness,' she added loudly for Kirk's benefit.

Kirk quietened down. He had forgotten the two women sitting by the fire. He glanced at Briar.

'Your father is flying in to fetch you.' He was delighted to see blood drain from her face.

'What's happened? Why?' she whispered, scarcely able to speak. It must be Mother, she thought. Nothing else would make him fly down here at night.

Kirk did not answer. He was enjoying her fear. He

called to his staff and ordered one of the trucks to go to the landing strip, quickly choosing the men who were to make the beacon fires. He would follow with the Land Rover.

'Answer her,' shouted Tara. 'Why is her father coming tonight?'

Kirk saw Marco and Guido come out of their hut at the sound of Tara's raised voice.

'One of the staff has had an accident,' he said lightly. 'They seem to be flapping about it.'

'So why come here?' asked Tara, intent on finding out as much as she could for her friend.

'They seem to think that she can help nurse the person. They forget that she has a job here,' he sneered.

Briar's eyes flashed and Kirk stepped back. He did not want a repeat performance from her right foot. I need to be in working order tonight, he told himself. Perhaps I should calm the vixen down.

'I owe you nothing, Kirk Madden,' said Briar icily.

Marco and Guido joined Tara at the fire. They did not understand the undisguised animosity in Briar's voice.

'I will leave as soon as my father arrives. You will make up my wages. The full three weeks.'

'But—'

'You have no choice, Kirk Madden. My full wages or . . .' Briar left the threat hanging on the wire of tension which bound them.

Kirk turned away. 'I'll do it now,' he said.

'No, I've changed my mind, make it a full month's wages. Four weeks. I've earned it.'

Kirk was about to protest when Tara spoke up for her friend.

'She certainly has.'

Kirk swallowed hard. Had Briar told Tara about the rape? He had been certain that shame would seal her lips, but the two girls had become close. He could not afford an open confrontation with Briar in front of the Andrettis. They were important people and could send him other wealthy clients.

'A month's salary it is,' he said.

'We'll miss you, Briar,' said Marco. 'You have been wonderful to all of us.'

Tara had walked away from the group around the fire and now stood alone in the dark.

'I'm going with Briar. I'm not going back to Milan with the family.'

'What! What is this nonsense, Tara?' growled Guido. In his family the women listened to the men.

Tara heard his voice become hard. She quickly changed tactics. Hurrying back to the fire, she put her arm around his waist and snuggled her curly head on to his shoulder.

'Please, Papa. I would love to spend some more time here. It's such a wonderful place. There is so much more for me to learn. This bush is the perfect laboratory. Briar will look after me. I promise to phone you every week.'

Guido ruffled Tara's hair. He could not remain angry with his young daughter for long.

'Have you asked Briar if she wants you with her?' he asked.

'No,' said Tara. 'But her family need someone to nurse a patient. Remember I am a *sorella*, Papa. You made me do the course when I was uncertain what I wanted for my future.'

'That is one way of explaining why you did nursing. The real reason was that you considered yourself to be deeply in love with that Romeo of a student doctor.'

Tara giggled and hugged Guido harder.

'You were right, Papa. He was not for me. But the five long years of cleaning bedpans and giving injections will come in useful now.'

'Please let her come with me, Mr Andretti,' said Briar, speaking for the first time. 'I will need all the help possible. I am not a qualified nurse. Tara's training will be invaluable. My family will love her. I promise to keep her away from any doctors, good-looking or not,' she added.

Guido looked at Briar, her face soft and lovely in the firelight. He instinctively trusted her and when she smiled at him, he nodded.

'There are not many people I would allow to look after Tara,' he said, 'especially as she will be so far away from us and in a country which is so strange to her. But I know that Tara will be safe with you and your family, Briar.'

Guido put his hands on Briar's shoulders and kissed her lightly on each cheek.

'May Mother Mary be with you,' he said.

Marco looked at his father in amazement. He was not given to public displays of emotion with non-family members.

Soon there was a babble of noise as Maria and Tomasina joined the men and the family discussed Guido's decision. Tears mingled with laughter as the Andrettis bid farewell to Tara.

The young women ran to pack their bags and throw them into the back of the Land Rover. Briar stopped at the kitchen for a minute to explain to the staff why she and Tara were leaving. Then they jumped into the Land Rover and waited for Kirk.

He sauntered to the vehicle.

'Hurry,' shouted Briar. 'My father will need all the light possible.'

He slammed the Land Rover into gear as Guido and Marco ran towards the vehicle.

'We're coming too,' they said. Guido could not bear to see Tara leave.

'No, Papa. It is better to say goodbye here.' Her words were drowned by the roar of the Cessna as it flew over the camp and then on to circle the landing strip.

'*Ciao!*' she shouted as the Land Rover bumped down the road.

Tomasina was secretly relieved that Tara had left with Briar. Tara slept lightly and was too astute to fool. It would be easier to sneak into Kirk's hut without her in camp. She hoped that this unexpected interruption in the evening's plans would not interfere with her tryst with Kirk.

Maria watched Guido and Marco standing in the dark long after the Land Rover's headlights faded.

'Guido will sleep well tonight,' she said to Tomasina. 'I feel he is getting a little too old for these safaris.'

'Papa looks fine to me,' said Tomasina. 'Neither he nor Marco seem tired.'

Maria searched Tomasina's face and voice for any sign of sarcasm, but her brown eyes looked into Maria's tawny ones guilelessly.

During her teenage years the Andretti home had been filled with screams and tantrums as the adolescent Tomasina fought her mother for the right to Papa's affections and to choose her own clothes and boyfriends. Until Tomasina moved out into a flat of her own, each day brought a new battle. Maria saw in her what she herself had once been. Where men's eyes had once followed her, now they followed her daughter.

In turn, Tomasina saw that her mother was jealous of her popularity and beauty. She felt no pity for the woman who was desperate to make the most of her remaining years of good looks.

Her mother had everything that money could buy. Guido spoiled and still loved her. He might enjoy the occasional afternoon of passion in some young girl's arms but he did not love them, so it was not important.

'Maybe you are right.' Maria turned away from her daughter. 'Let us sit at the fire. You call Papa and Marco.'

The Andrettis were enjoying glasses of red wine and listening to the story of the leopard hunt when the roar of the Cessna once again drowned their voices. They stood up and waved as Fred dipped a wing in farewell, and headed for Bulawayo.

'In Africa the sky peeps out between the stars,' said Tara, her nose pressed up hard against the window of the plane. 'In Milan neon stars are seen in the city, but few in the sky. You are so lucky to live here, Briar.'

She turned round in her seat and smiled at her new friend. Briar had sat Tara in the front beside her father. It gave the girl a magnificent view of the glory of the heavens. The instrument panel lights outlined Tara's features. In the soft glow she was fresh-faced and pretty. Tara had none of the sultry beauty with which her mother and sister were blessed, though she did have the Andretti eyes with the rich, dark eyelashes.

But, whereas their eyes were an invitation to men,

Tara's were a challenge. She had the wonderful Italian ability to express both joy and grief openly and volubly. Tara left no one in any doubt about her feelings.

'You would make a good African, Tara,' answered Briar. 'Yours has been an instant and passionate love affair with my country.'

Tara turned back to look out of the window. Fred was silent. Sickened by the implications of Rudo's mutilation, he had taken no part in the girls' chatter.

'*Rien n'a changé mais tout est différent*,' he said softly.

'Excuse me?' said Tara.

'I was talking to myself. A bad habit for a man of my age.'

'But you were not talking English.'

'No. It was a saying my French grandmother used when things went wrong. It frequently returns to haunt me. It suits this country. The saying means that nothing has changed but everything is different. In Zimbabwe today everything has changed, but nothing is different.'

Tara frowned.

'Dad, that sounds Irish,' said Briar. 'You've changed Grandmother's expression completely.'

'I have,' he answered and lapsed into silence again.

The girls respected Fred's disinclination to talk. Tara lost herself in the beauty of the starry night and Briar worried about what they would find when they landed in Bulawayo.

'Dear God, let Rudo live,' she whispered, her lips barely moving. 'Don't take her from Pat and Erin as well. Please.'

Suddenly they saw the lights of Bulawayo, the second largest city in the country. They glowed in the darkness like reflections of the stars overhead.

Fred was speaking to the control tower at the airport

but Briar, seated in the back, was unable to hear the conversation. She looked at the stern set of her father's face and decided not to question him.

They touched down with a bump which bounced the aircraft back into the air. The second bump was softer and the wheels held the ground.

Dad must be worried, thought Briar. He usually treats his plane like a baby.

A tall, broad-shouldered young man came running out to the plane before the propellers had stopped turning. He ignored the indignant shouts from the uniformed man behind him.

He flung open Tara's door and held out his arms.

'Briar,' he said in relief. 'I'm so glad you're here. It's been hell.'

He stopped in mid-sentence and stared at Tara.

'Where's Briar?'

'Here, Erin. I'm in the back. This is Tara Andretti. She is a qualified nursing sister and has come to help me look after Rudo.'

Erin merely nodded. The events of the night had driven politeness from him. He wanted to return to Kame. He had to be there when Jacob and Jonas found the ones who had carved up Rudo. He had to see the same pain in their eyes which he had seen in Rudo's.

'I've borrowed a car. Come, I'll take you to the Mater Dei.'

'Then you probably won't need us,' said Briar. 'They'll look after Rudo well.'

'The hospital know that she is to have a private nurse. You,' he said to Briar. 'Now we'll tell them that Rudo will have a day and a night nurse. You and Miss Andretti. Someone up there is helping us,' Erin went on. 'When the specialist in Harare heard what had happened he contacted a plastic surgeon from South Africa. The man had just arrived in Zim on holiday with his family. He persuaded the man to operate on Rudo. We have a good chance that she will suffer only minimal scarring. Though the mental scars . . .'

'Those will fade with time. They always do,' said Briar softly.

Tara looked up quickly. There was a sadness in Briar's voice which she had not heard before.

You too have scars, Briar, she thought, but they have not yet healed and faded.

Tara helped unload their bags. She slung one over each shoulder and followed Erin. As they entered the airport building the bright lights burnished Erin's blond hair and pinpointed his clear blue eyes protected by lashes almost as thick and long as her own.

Erin had been striding through the building intent only on returning to the hospital to collect his father. Now, as he paused for a family to push a trolley of luggage past him, he glanced over his shoulder.

Tara almost fell over him. She had been following close behind, keeping a tight grip of the two heavy bags which bumped against her thighs as she walked.

'I'm sorry. Let me take those, Miss Andretti,' said Erin.

Tara handed the totes over gratefully and rubbed her numb fingers.

'Tara,' she said. 'I would like you to call me Tara.'

Erin decided that he would like to know this Tara. He smiled down at her. Suddenly the stern-faced man looked like a carefree boy again. Tara was pleased that she had persuaded her father to let her join Briar. She liked Erin Gifford and hoped that they would see more of him.

'Will you be staying in Bulawayo for a few days?' she asked.

'No. Dad and I will leave for Kame as soon as possible. We have something which needs to be done. We must move quickly.'

Tara felt a sense of loss and desolation quite disproportionate to the circumstances.

'Oh,' she said softly.

Erin looked at her quickly but she was looking at the floor.

'We will fly back to Bulawayo to see Rudo after the operation. Jacob, her husband, will want to be with his wife.'

Tara's spirits lifted. She would be seeing this good-looking man again. For once she controlled her instincts to put all her feelings into words.

'Where is Jacob now?' she asked instead.

'Where I should be. Tracking the bastards who did this to his wife,' answered Erin shortly. Her question stirred up the anger and hatred which her smile and presence had momentarily dispelled.

Briar took Tara's hand and squeezed it. The women sat silently in the back of the car as Erin sped through the quiet streets to the Mater Dei Hospital, set in nine acres of parkland.

In low voices Erin and Fred discussed the implications of this use of terror. The women caught only a few words. Briar was pleased that they were excluded from the conversation. She did not want Tara to lose her love for the beautiful country because a few amoral men abused their positions of power.

Briar still saw Zimbabwe through the eyes of a child. She found it hard to believe that after the horror and hatred of war, men would still perpetrate atrocities for their own gain. As she prayed for Rudo's recovery, so she prayed for the death of the men who had casually and callously maimed this woman. She also longed for retribution for the man or men who had planned the act.

Erin drew up in front of the hospital in a squeal of brakes. Pat was pacing restlessly outside the front door. He felt helpless and uncomfortable in hospitals. To him the smells and sounds were associated with death. He longed to be back in the familiar bush where he was in control.

'How is Rudo?' Erin and Fred spoke together.

'She has just been wheeled into the theatre,' Pat replied. 'The plastics guy gave me a long explanation on what he was going to have to do.' He swallowed hard and wiped his forehead. 'I thought I had a tough stomach after years of gutting animals, but by the time he had finished I had to run for the bathroom. The staff suggested I remain outside until you arrived.'

He managed a weak grin. Erin switched off the ignition and went to stand beside his father.

'Will they allow her private nursing?' asked Briar as she and Tara tumbled from the car with their luggage.

'The nuns are only too happy to have some help,' answered Pat. 'I spoke to a kind Italian nun who seemed to be in charge. The heavy rains in this area have turned Bulawayo back into the "place of slaughter", as Lobengula named it. Only this time it's mosquitoes, the anopheles, who are killing the population. The hospitals are full of people with malaria and meningitis. There have been quite a few deaths. They have gone back to using quinine and paludrine, the only drugs to which these mosquitoes are not resistant. Almost everyone we know in Bulawayo has had malaria this summer. There's a new wonder drug but it's causing hallucinations, hangovers and seizures in many people, so they are afraid of using it.' He shrugged and rubbed his arms as if he was cold.

Erin shivered. Dear God, does Africa always have to be so harsh and violent, he thought.

'If they need us, Tara and I will go right in,' said Briar. 'Oh, sorry, Pat, we haven't introduced you to our Italian *sorella*, Tara Andretti. Rudo will have the best possible care.'

Pat held out his hand. 'I'm pleased to meet you and, needless to say, relieved that you are able to join Briar.'

Tara's warm smile lit up her face.

'I love being on safari, but that Kirk Madden was becoming annoying. He hangs around women like your mopane flies.'

Her Italian accent put so much disdain on the 'mopane flies' that Pat laughed, and with the laughter some of the tension vanished.

'Dad,' said Briar, 'why don't we let Pat and Erin go off to Kame now? I know they want to join up with Jacob and Jonas. Jacob will be frantic for news of Rudo.'

Pat gave Briar a quick hug. 'Always the right suggestion at the right time,' he said. 'Thank you, Briar.' He turned to Tara. 'And I must thank you for cutting your safari short and coming to help us.'

'For me it is a pleasure,' answered Tara. She was rewarded with a smile and a squeeze on her shoulder from Erin.

'Mum is alone and worried on Inyati, Dad,' Briar continued. 'Please go back to the airport with Pat and Erin. Fly home and tell her that Tara and I will keep in touch. We'll give you a daily report on Rudo.'

The women waved until the car was out of sight, then they slung the heavy bags over their shoulders and walked into the hospital.

'*Fa caldo*,' exclaimed Tara as she staggered beneath the weight of her bags. 'I hope we don't have to climb up six flights of stairs to reach the top floor,' she said, eyeing the large L-shaped building. A sister came bustling to the door to meet them, wearing the brown dress and beige veil of the Franciscan nuns.

'I recognize this order,' whispered Tara as they waited. She nervously fingered the small gold cross which hung on a chain around her neck. 'It's an austere order founded by St Francis of Assisi.'

'They do magnificent work in this country,' said Briar.

'I have been expecting a nurse who is to help with a case we have in surgery at the moment,' the nun said briskly.

'That's me, Briar Hanley,' said Briar. 'And this is Tara Andretti, she's a qualified nursing sister. We thought that we could be of some use to you.'

'The Mater Dei is almost full. We are dealing with one of the worst outbreaks of malaria in Bulawayo that I can remember.'

The nun was still barring the entrance. She eyed their khaki slacks and walking boots sceptically. Only when Briar mentioned Pat Gifford did her expression soften.

'A fine man,' she said in a soft voice, 'with a fine son. They'll both make a good marriage one day.'

Briar was surprised, as she had never thought of Pat remarrying. Yet the sister was right. He was a fine man.

'In parts of Italy they say that the father is often better than the son,' whispered Tara.

Briar felt herself blush. Tara must have misinterpreted Pat's embrace, she thought.

'Pat always kisses me,' she explained. 'I was going to marry his eldest son, Scott, but he was killed in the Bush War.'

Now, Tara thought, she understood the reason for the pain she sometimes felt in Briar.

'You cannot see the surgeon dressed like that. I may be able to find uniforms for you,' said the nun over her shoulder as she led the way. 'They won't be new. We don't have the money to spend on luxuries like that here. You will look less like tourists and more like nurses once you are in uniform. We are short of lilac ones but I may be able to find RSN uniforms for you.'

'Thank you, sister,' answered Briar.

'RSN?' queried Tara.

'She means the Regulation State Nurse's white uniform,' whispered Briar.

'A nurse will bring the uniforms here,' said the nun, opening the door to a private ward. 'When you have changed you may want to spend some time in our chapel. That poor woman needs our prayers.'

She closed the door softly, then opened it again.

'The operation should take about five hours, so you have time for prayer.'

The two girls looked at each other and grinned.

'The Franciscans may be a strict order, but she's lovely,' said Tara.

'In this selfish world, I find that nuns are very special people,' answered Briar.

*

Briar and Tara both knelt and prayed in the chapel. In their crisp white uniforms they looked like novices.

'I always feel strong and peaceful after sitting quietly in a church, any church,' said Briar.

'I think it's the power of prayer which strengthens one,' answered Tara. She genuflected and stood up. As the girls tiptoed out they were surprised to see both patients and nuns sitting in the dimly lit chapel.

The hours passed quickly as Tara and Briar ran to do the bidding of the ward staff.

Eventually they were called to the private ward. Briar gasped as she looked at Rudo. She was heavily bandaged, her face swollen and her eyes closed.

Beside her bed stood a short, squat man. His hair was thinning on top but curled luxuriantly at his neck. He waited until the staff wheeled the trolley from the room, then turned to Briar and Tara.

'I understand that my patient is a family retainer and you have come to nurse her and relieve the pressure on the Mater Dei staff.'

The girls nodded. His voice was cool and his words clipped.

'The woman is fortunate that her lips were brought to hospital with her.'

Briar shivered. The mere thought of Rudo with raw strips of flesh where once she had smiling lips sickened her.

'Micro-surgery is a wonderful branch of plastic surgery. I was able to join the tiny severed blood vessels and veins to the main artery which runs from each corner of the mouth to the centre.' He paused and coughed delicately as if expecting applause from a medical congress.

'Arterial and venous anastomosis takes time,' he added.

The girls nodded and waited for him to continue.

'Her tongue was a jigsaw puzzle. They really cut it up. Fortunately it was not severed. The swelling will fill her mouth as it heals. Eventually she will talk again. Perhaps not as well as before, but she will talk.'

'Oh, thank God,' breathed Briar.

'Yes,' he said, eyeing the gold cross which Tara was stroking. 'Feeding will be a problem. We'll probably use a Ryles feeding tube for a few weeks.'

'Ryles?' whispered Briar to Tara, as the surgeon bent over Rudo and lifted her eyelids.

'A tube that threads through the nose and into the stomach,' explained Tara.

Briar felt nauseous and hoped she would not disgrace herself in front of the plastic surgeon.

'I understand that the ranch owner's son disturbed the butchers,' said the surgeon. He nodded at Rudo. 'She was lucky. We would not have been able to save her breast had they completed the job and severed it. But it's neatly back in place and there is every reason to believe that she will be able to suckle again.'

He ran his knuckles gently across Rudo's cheek and his lips moved wordlessly.

'The sister-in-charge will be in later to give you your nursing instructions,' he said. 'Remember, the most important thing you can give a patient is love and compassion. Touch her softly. Let her feel that you care.'

He swung out of the room, his coat flapping around his knees.

'Thank you, doctor,' Briar called after him. Her voice was swallowed by the sound of his footsteps as he hurried down the corridor. But it awakened some spark in Rudo's drugged mind. She opened her eyes and looked at Briar helplessly.

Briar hurried to her side.

'It's all right, Rudo. You are safe. Jacob will be here soon. We all love you.'

As she spoke she stroked Rudo's fingers rhythmically. Rudo's eyes closed. She again entered the oblivion afforded by drugs and the anaesthetic.

Briar brushed the tears roughly from her own eyes and stood up as the sister walked in. Her veil, soft and delicate as dust dancing in the wind, swung over and hid Rudo's bruised and bloated face.

Chapter Fifteen

KIRK MADDEN was in a bad mood. His men ran to smother the small fires lining the airstrip. Then they crowded into the truck driven by his head tracker.

'Idiots,' he yelled. 'Half of you come with me. Do you want that truck to break down on the way back to camp?'

He was relieved that Briar had finally left the camp, though he would miss gloating over her, knowing that mortification would silence her and safeguard him.

He glanced at his watch as he waited for his staff to climb into the truck. It was past eleven o'clock. He wondered when Maria would come to his hut. Midnight should normally have given Guido and Marco sufficient time to have a brandy after dinner then fall into a deep sleep. Tonight he ran the risk of Marco being too excited by the leopard kill and the departure of the girls to go to bed.

Kirk had listened to the Andrettis' stories at the Falls and around the camp fire. He had heard horrible tales of what happened to men who interfered with Italian wives and daughters. He lusted for Maria and Tomasina, but not enough to lose his life or, as Guido so succinctly described it, his manhood.

Kirk parked the truck and walked into the boma. To

his relief the camp fire was a mere glow and the chairs were empty.

He glanced at the huts. They were all in darkness. The camp was silent. He moved noiselessly into the kitchen where he knew his supper would be on the stove. The staff were accustomed to his eating habits and made certain that a plate of venison and potatoes was always ready for him.

Kirk perched on the edge of the table and ate voraciously. The stew was full of marrow bones, glutinous and good, the way he liked it. Kirk licked his fingers, belched and made his way to his hut.

Maria turned over slowly in her single bed. The springs squeaked and she froze. Guido mumbled and pulled the blankets up around his neck.

The hands on the clock beside the bed read five minutes past twelve. Maria flung off her blankets and swung her legs over the edge of the bed. This time the bedsprings seemed to co-operate. Guido lay undisturbed.

Maria selected a quilted satin gown and slipped it over her head. She shivered as she wore only a diaphanous black nightdress underneath. It was more in keeping with a boudoir than a bush camp, but she knew how enticing it was. She wanted Kirk excited when he saw her body gleaming through the soft chiffon.

Tonight she would be gambling with her future. She was going to make sure that it was worth the risk. The thought of Guido finding her lying entwined with Kirk made her blood race.

She walked quickly to the door. Suddenly there was a loud thud. To her guilty ears it sounded like a nuclear explosion. She had walked into Guido's gun case which he had placed to one side of the door. The pain in her foot was forgotten as she stared at Guido's bed.

144

'Maria?' he mumbled sleepily, fumbling at his mosquito net.

'Sleep, *caro*,' she answered. 'I have one of my migraines. I am going to sit at the fire for a while. The fresh air always clears it.'

'Mmm,' he sighed and turned over.

Maria stood at the door indecisively. She should go back to bed. There would be other nights to spend with Kirk. But somehow the sight of the great dead leopard and the smell of its blood and its death had excited her sexually. She wanted Kirk tonight.

She waited, motionless as an animal at bay, until Guido's breathing became low and regular, then tiptoed to the door and slipped out into the night.

She glanced around the dark boma nervously then hurried to the fire, eager for the slight protection afforded by the dying embers. She kicked one of the mopane logs deep into the coals. Grey ash covered the dust which had already settled on her satin mules.

Maria pulled a chair away from the log, which was being licked by small yellow tongues of fire. Satisfied that she had set the scene and feeling more secure with the firelight to guide her, she left the boma. She lifted the hem of her gown as she walked. It was beautiful and expensive and she did not want it impregnated with red dust.

Kirk heard the soft footsteps long before Maria reached the door of his hut. He stripped off his shorts and stood behind the door in the dark room waiting.

As her long fingernails scratched lightly at the door he swung it open and pulled her to him. He stifled her scream of surprise by clamping his mouth over hers.

He used his tongue as if copulating. Maria gasped. She dug her nails into his hard buttocks and pulled him to her.

'Not so fast,' said Kirk, breathing heavily. 'I want to enjoy you.'

He swung Maria up into his arms and dropped her on to his bed. She tried to pull him down with her, but he had moved away. She heard a match being struck and saw his wet lips and flushed face in the glow, as he held the flame to the candle-wick.

'Now let's see what we have,' he said as he pulled off the quilted gown and tugged at the ribbons which held the nightdress up on her shoulders.

As she lay stretched out on his bed with her legs wide and her full breasts rounded on her ribcage, Maria could have been a young woman of thirty. The candlelight was kind to the faint lines on her neck and face. Her position was both provocative and showed off her body to its best advantage.

'How should I take you?' he said softly. His eyes were as yellow as the leopard's which Marco had shot and they excited her.

'I think fast to start, then long and slow. No,' he mumbled as he ran his long tongue around her nipples and down to her belly button. He lifted his head and looked at her. Maria's large brown eyes were liquid with desire.

'No, we'll start long and slow,' he said as he buried his mouth in her warm flesh.

He pulled away, surprised at the sharp burn in his mouth, then grinned as he realized he was tasting the Jalapeno chillies which the Andrettis ate every day.

The sharp tang excited him and his tongue moved faster. Maria arched her body and gasped. She closed her eyes and gave herself up to his tongue. Kirk had just moved over her when she froze.

'Maria?' The word rang out clearly from the boma.

'Guido!' she gasped.

Kirk held her down hard. He wondered if they had time to complete the act, but Maria was struggling to get up, her eyes wide with the fear of discovery. She was frantic to leave Kirk's hut.

The frenetic mood of sexual excitement was broken. He released his hold and lay back on the bed, watching her struggle into her gown and mules.

She ran from his hut without looking back. He blew out the candle. Maria would not return that night.

'Guido,' he heard her call from the other side of the boma.

Crafty woman, he thought. She went around to the far side. He'll never know that she was near my place.

'Guido *caro*, why have you come out? You need your sleep. You have another long day of checking leopard baits tomorrow.'

'I woke and you were gone,' he answered. 'You were not at the fire.'

'No, the flicker of the flames made my headache worse, so I came to stand in the dark for a while. I feel much better now.'

Guido put his arm around his wife.

'You are wearing the gown I bought for our holiday in Rome,' he said softly.

Maria wondered whether she could reinvent her mythical headache. Tonight she wanted only the excitement offered by Kirk.

'Yes,' she replied dully, as he led her back to their hut and his bed.

*

The flames took hold of the log and suddenly the mopane exploded. It threw showers of sparks up at the stars, then, as if overcome with the splendour above them, they fell to earth, mere black smuts.

Tomasina was dozing when the golden display flickered through the window of her hut and painted strips of light across her closed lids.

She groped for her wristwatch in panic. I must have fallen asleep, she thought. It's probably five o'clock and the staff are stoking the fire.

With a sinking feeling, she realized that she might have missed her tryst with Kirk. She had heard his truck return, but decided to wait until one o'clock instead of midnight, as Guido and Marco stayed at the fire until eleven thirty. They would need at least an hour to fall asleep.

Her scrabbling fingers found her watch and she peered at the fluorescent numerals. One thirty. She still had time to meet Kirk.

Thank goodness Tara left with Briar, she thought to herself. She would have guessed where I was going before I opened the door. That one has the sixth sense of the animals she adores.

Tomasina breathed in the clean night air. She stood in the dark beside her hut and studied the boma. There was no movement near the fire.

A log must have fallen into the coals, she thought with relief. She tiptoed past her parents' hut then paused and looked behind her, trying to identify the noise. A warm flush covered her face and neck as she realized what was causing the squeaking she heard.

It embarrassed her that her parents, whose youngest child was twenty-one, still found sexual pleasure in each other. It did not seem correct for parents to indulge in practices considered by the young to be theirs alone. She hurried past, deliberately blocking out the noise of the bed springs.

Once outside the comparative safety of the grass fence encircling the boma, her breathing quickened. Every noise alarmed her. Every dark shadow was a lion or a hyena. She was shivering when she reached Kirk's hut.

Kirk tossed restlessly on his bed. Maria had aroused him and sleep was impossible. Suddenly he lifted his head from the pillow and sat up. There was someone at his door. Guido must be asleep, he thought, and she has returned. His breathing quickened and he padded to the door.

'Maria?' he whispered, his voice husky and deep. 'Is he asleep?'

The figure standing in the deep shadow of the hut was motionless.

'Maria?' queried Kirk. 'Don't play games. Come here.'

The woman turned and fled from him. He chased after her and caught up with her just as she was about to run into the boma.

His hand fumbled at the soft cotton of her gown.

'Touch me and I'll scream,' hissed Tomasina. The hatred in her eyes was that of a cornered carnivore.

Kirk suddenly remembered their tryst. He realized that if she called out she would bring Guido, Marco and Maria running from the boma. He dropped his hand immediately and stood away from her.

'Tomasina,' he whispered, 'you don't understand. Please let me explain.'

The sound of her hand connecting with the side of his head was like a pistol shot.

'Explain to my father,' she said.

Tomasina ran into her hut and knelt over the toilet bowl. The sour stench of vomit filled the room. Kirk paused in the doorway and watched her shoulders heave as she threw up. He turned and walked away. It would be no use talking to Tomasina until she had calmed down. He would have to convince her that calling her mother's name had been a harmless mistake.

I have until dawn to find an excuse, he told himself as he stripped and flopped across his bed. Damn hysterical women. She's behaving like a schoolgirl.

He rubbed his cheek ruefully. Three gifts from three women, he thought, staring up at the dark ceiling. Briar's mule-kick almost ruined my manhood. Tomasina has left me with an ear which will probably ring for days. My tongue and the inside of my lips are still burning from my session with Maria. Just as well it was interrupted. I wish they chewed gum or candy like Americans. Chillies are one helluva snack. He grinned suddenly as he thought of the stories he would tell his friends after this safari. None of them had had a Jalapeno mouth.

The only two people sleeping peacefully that night were Marco and Guido. Maria and Tomasina lay motionless on their beds. Their bodies were still but their minds raged restlessly.

Maria knew they had ten days left before the safari ended. She would still have a chance to be with Kirk. But the events of the evening had frightened her. She did not want to join the ranks of lonely ex-wives in Milan. She was no longer sure that one night with Kirk was worth losing her home and status. Yet he excited her. She knew that if the opportunity arose her body would betray her.

Tomasina too lay still. She was well aware of the family upheaval her news about Kirk and her mother would cause. It would involve relatives from the far-flung corners of Italy. Her father would be mocked by his associates. She cringed from the thought. She loved her father and still sought his approval. She knew that he had wanted his first-born to be a boy. For years she was conscious that she had been a disappointment to him.

'Bearers of bad tidings are always hated,' she whispered, as if the sound of her voice would solve her dilemma.

Suddenly she sat up in bed. Perhaps she should have given Kirk a chance to explain why he had called her Maria. Perhaps it had been a simple slip of the tongue.

Her mother would never consort with another man. She had just heard her mother with her father. They loved each other. Her mother was a faithful wife and a good mother.

Tomasina felt dirtied with shame. How could she have imagined that her mother would sleep with Kirk? She shuddered as she thought of the mayhem she would have caused had she told her father that her mother had broken her marriage vows.

Kirk's tryst was with me, she thought. I was late. He was half-asleep and said Maria, meaning Tomasina. The poor man wanted to know if Papa was asleep as he and Marco have been feeding Kirk horror stories about Italian vendettas. Tomasina closed her eyes. The mopane log was now a heap of red coals and her room was dark. Her dilemma was over. She slept with a small smile on her lips.

Kirk heard the Heuglin's robin greet the dawn and he groaned. It was time to get up and face the Andretti family.

Chapter Sixteen

PAT TAXIED the Cessna into its makeshift hangar in the shade of a huge teak tree. He and Erin forced the long bolt into place, locking the doors securely against hyenas, who enjoyed chewing the plane's wheels. The moon stood white and high in the sky. Pat and Erin swung into the Land Rover which was standing where they had left it when they rushed Rudo to hospital.

Erin glanced up at the moon. It was cold and featureless against the dull grey backdrop which precedes the delicate colours of dawn.

'It'll soon be light enough for Jacob and Jonas to move fast,' he said.

Pat merely nodded and pressed the accelerator pedal to the floor. The Land Rover roared down the dirt track, shattering the silence and hurling up dust and grass from beneath its broad tyres.

They stopped at the house long enough to unlock the gun safe and collect their rifles, ammunition and water bottles. As an afterthought Erin tucked the emergency first-aid box into his hunting vest. The tin was uncomfortable but cool against his skin.

He took the wheel and followed the path to where he had found Rudo. Pausing only to check that the tin trunks beneath the trackers' seat were firmly locked, he and Pat picked up the spoor.

It was easy to follow, as Jacob and Jonas had knotted grass, notched tree trunks and laid branches across the path to guide them. Father and son moved fast but Jacob and Jonas were setting a punishing pace.

'I don't believe it,' said Pat, pausing for a sip of water. 'Those two followed spoor at night and they are running on it.'

'They want these butchers badly,' said Erin. The men continued in silence.

'Son,' said Pat. 'Remember that though you found Rudo, the men who mutilated her belong to Jacob.'

Erin merely nodded. When he saw again the dark patches of blood-soaked soil where Rudo had lain speechless and writhing in agony, it rekindled his hatred for the men they were now following.

Dear God, forgive me, I know that vengeance is yours. But if Jacob and Jonas don't get them I will, he vowed silently.

Erin stopped short. In front of him was a mopane branch broken into a V and stuck upright into the soil.

'They have them,' he whispered. 'We must move very slowly.'

Suddenly an unearthly scream of terror rang out. Erin and Pat jumped involuntarily. The hair stood up on Pat's arms and he licked his dry lips. He glanced behind him. Erin motioned to his father and they sank into the bushes beside the path. The scream was followed by others, interspersed with pleas for mercy.

Pat wanted to plug his ears. He felt as if he was in hell, hearing the souls in torment. Choking gurgles followed the screams. He could visualize the men fighting for air as blood clogged their lungs and their entrails filled their mouths. He had to stop the torture. He stood up, but Erin dragged him back.

'Remember the men who did this are Jacob's,' he said, mimicking his father's words. 'Let justice be done, Dad. This is Africa. It's the only way Jacob will find peace.'

Pat sat down with his back against a tree and took a long drink. Then he splashed water over his face and neck. Even though he had been through the war years, such atrocities sickened and horrified him.

He closed his eyes. Time passed slowly. He fought sleep, while Erin sat watching the track they had followed. His eyes were wide and alert.

The first sounds which herald dawn broke the long silence. Grass rustled as small creatures ferreted for food. Birdsong grew tentatively stronger. Birds ruffled their feathers; soon they would be searching in the dew-laden grass for insects. Erin looked at Pat. His head had dropped forward and his breath was a low snuffle as he slept.

'It is done.'

The voice came from behind him. Erin swung his gun in the direction of the voice. Jacob parted the high grass and walked through, closely followed by Jonas. Both men were grave. Their faces seemed to be carved from the hard granite of the Matobo Hills.

'Rudo?' queried Jacob. 'Does she live?'

'Rudo is in the operating theatre. They have a specialist from South Africa to work on her. She could not be in better hands,' comforted Pat.

'Soon you'll see her yourself,' said Erin.

Jacob did not smile. He had done what he had to do, but torture was not a man's work. Before they died he had learned the name of the man who sent them. When the time was right he might tell Pat and Erin, but not now.

'The remains?'

'Today the great black birds will show the *bere* the way and tonight the hyena will feast,' said Jonas.

Erin sprang up as if bitten by black Matabele ants.

'Jacob, turn round,' he said sharply.

'It's nothing, a scratch,' said Jacob.

Pat went over to Jacob and unbuttoned his shirt.

'A scratch?' said Erin, looking at the gash which ran from below Jacob's ribs to his shoulder. He pulled the tin box out from his vest and quickly opened it. 'At least we can patch it up until we get to Bulawayo,' he said, squeezing a thick yellow coil of Betadine into the wound.

Pat helped him staunch the cut with gauze pads and bandage them tightly in place.

'We leave for Bulawayo in half an hour,' he said as they dropped Jacob and Jonas off at the village. 'Wash and change, but don't touch that dressing, Jacob,' he warned. 'Erin will collect you in twenty minutes.'

When they arrived at the Mater Dei, Jacob insisted on seeing Rudo before his wound was stitched and dressed. The three men walked gingerly into the ward. A petite figure dressed in an RSN uniform was intent on setting up a new drip. She turned to greet them.

'Good morning,' she said. 'We've been expecting you. I told Rudo you would be here early.'

Erin started. He had only seen Tara at night when he was distraught and angry and had paid her little attention. Now he studied her carefully. There were dark smudges under her eyes, which were the honey brown of new *masasa* leaves. Her heavy eyelashes drooped with weariness but her smile was bright. He felt comfortable with her, yet excited.

'Briar will be here in a few minutes to take over the morning shift. She'll be so pleased to see you.'

Tara turned to Jacob and held out her hand.

'You must be Rudo's husband?' she said.

Pat hastened to introduce Jacob.

'Briar and I will see that she is soon back with you and your children. Please don't worry. The worst is over. We are keeping her free of pain and the operation was successful.'

Jacob gave Tara a small smile of thanks. He stood at the foot of Rudo's bed. The heavily bandaged woman with tubes stuck into her veins and filling her nostrils was not his wife. This was not the mother of his children. He did not know the stranger.

'Speak to her,' said Pat. 'She can hear you but cannot answer. Comfort her, Jacob. She needs to know things that only you can tell her.'

Jacob shook himself as if breaking from a trance. He pulled up a hard chair and sat close to the head of the bed.

'Rudo,' he said, 'I see you, my wife. I wish to hug you but they will not allow it until you are well.' Jacob put his face close to hers.

'It is done,' he whispered. 'The dogs are dead. Never again will they hold a knife.'

Rudo opened her eyes slowly and looked at Jacob. Pat turned away from the pain and love in her gaze.

'Come,' he said to Erin. 'Leave Jacob alone with Rudo for a while.'

The two men were standing outside the door talking quietly when the swish of crisp cotton alerted them that they were not alone.

'It is a gentle day, Mr Gifford,' said the nun who had welcomed Briar and Tara into the hospital. 'I have come to fetch your man. The woman must have rest. Her husband has to see the surgeon who worked on his wife. I think the doctor wants to put a few fancy stitches into that nasty gash across his chest.'

She smiled at Pat and Erin as she walked into the private ward.

'Two fine young women you gave us. Not afraid of hard work. They'll make wonderful wives,' she said, as she ushered Jacob out of the ward.

They almost collided with Briar who was hurrying down the corridor holding a bedpan covered with a clean cloth.

'Jacob,' said Briar, 'I'm so pleased that Rudo has seen you. Now she will recover quickly.'

'Thank you,' said Jacob. 'Thank you for looking after my wife.'

The nun turned to Briar and gave her a few instructions in a soft voice before ushering Jacob away to the surgeon.

'Briar,' said Pat.

Briar turned to face him. Remembering Tara's teasing, she felt strangely shy of the man she had known almost all her life. He held out his arms to hug her, but she fiddled awkwardly with the bedpan, making it impossible for him to hold her. Unaware of her embarrassment, Pat kissed her on the cheek.

'Tell us,' he said. 'Is Rudo going to talk again?'

'According to the surgeon she should do. It will take

time. She'll probably never speak as well as she used to, but she will be able to make herself understood,' answered Briar, edging towards the door.

'Rudo is a fighter. She has the warrior blood of the Zulus in her. She'll make it,' said Erin.

As Briar turned the door handle to enter the ward Pat stopped her.

'Jacob wants to stay here until Rudo leaves hospital. Erin and I think it's a good idea. Erin has a hunt starting in two and a half weeks' time. Rudo should be able to leave Bulawayo by then.'

Briar nodded, wondering why Pat was telling her their plans. She had to relieve Tara. She also wanted to be away from Pat and collect herself. She felt that she was behaving like a teenager in his presence.

'Fred and Blanche have offered us their home here,' he continued. 'We thought that you and Tara would like to join us. It will be more comfortable than rooms in the nurses' section.'

'Jacob cooks almost as well as Rudo,' added Erin with a grin. 'Come on, Briar. I've always wanted a sister. Dad just couldn't find the right recipe,' he teased.

Pat punched his son on the shoulder.

'You of course would not be interested in a certain doe-eyed *sorella* with a delightful Italian accent,' he said.

Erin stared at his father dumbfounded.

'I saw your eyes sparkle when young Tara turned to speak to you,' laughed Pat, enjoying his son's discomfort. 'You have my blessing, son. She's lovely.'

'Dad!' roared Erin, red with embarrassment.

'Sshh,' said Tara, appearing in the doorway of Rudo's room. 'You'll wake her. She fell asleep after Jacob left and sleep heals the body.'

In low voices the men told Tara of their plan to spend a fortnight in the Hanleys' Bulawayo home.

'Give me two minutes to hand over my patient to Briar and I'll sleep anywhere,' she said.

Briar shrugged. Tara had made the decision for her.

Chapter Seventeen

THE TALL brown grass fell aside, as easily as hair to the teeth of a comb, as the N'debele woman, large with child, pushed her way through the shoulder-high clumps.

Her young daughter was tied tightly to her back with a brightly coloured length of cloth. The mother's lumbering walk had lulled the little one to sleep. Her head lolled as her mother wove her way across the grassy plain. Flies clustered on the child's face, sucking mucus below her nose and dribble from the corner of her mouth. She slept on undisturbed. Her brother, a thin five-year-old with a bloated belly and protruding navel, followed close behind his mother. He held his catapult tightly, ready to bring down any bird or rodent on the way.

The woman was uneasy. She knew that she should not have left the well-worn track which linked the two villages, but she felt the child thrusting down in her womb and knew that her time was near. She wanted to be in her mother's village for the birth. The route she had chosen cut the journey by half a day.

The night before she had shivered in fear and crawled close to her husband as the waning moon brought with it the hunting roar of lions. As the roars gradually died to a series of grunts, her husband whispered that the *shumba* were at least a day's walk away from the village. There was little to fear. She slept. The sun washed away the remnants of night terror and the lions were forgotten.

As she bent over the pot, cooking maize meal for her family, her belly contracted and she gasped. When her husband had eaten, she took the children and left the village, as unobtrusively as a lioness leaves the pride to give birth.

The day was cool and darkening clouds spoke of rain. The mother still felt uneasy and kept glancing behind her, yet she saw and heard nothing.

The grass rustled beside her. Instinctively she pulled her son in front. Her eyes searched for a tree but she could see only grass swaying in the wind. In the distance was a stand of mopane, but it was second growth scrub and of no use. She turned again to look behind her. To her relief she saw a teak tree, stark and black against the brooding sky. It had withstood a bush fire but still held its almost leafless branches up high.

To reach the tree she would have to retrace her steps. She hesitated a moment, looked longingly in the direction of her mother's village, then turned back.

The grasses closed behind the family leaving no trace of their passing. When they reached the tree she untied her daughter and placed her on the ground. She bent over letting her son use her back as a ladder. He scrambled up nimbly and she groaned as his weight compressed her swollen stomach. She then tied the girl into the cloth and slung the human bundle over her son's thin shoulders.

He continued to climb awkwardly up the tree. The toddler cried as her body bounced against the trunk and branches. The mother stayed at the bottom of the tree until she was certain that her children were as high as the boy could climb. She then made him wedge himself and his sister securely in a fork and tie the cloth around the tree trunk and then knot it around themselves.

Sweat painted patches on her blue print blouse and even the wind did nothing to cool her. An unreasoning terror possessed her. The whites of her eyes seemed to fill her face as they rolled up in fear. She searched the endless plain of grass. Nothing moved. All was silent and still. Yet instinct screamed at her to join her children.

She tried to roll up the long skirt wound around her belly, but her hands trembled so much that it kept falling back to her ankles. In desperation she took it off and lifted her arms to the lowest branch to pull herself off the ground.

Her arms never reached the branch. A tawny shape which she neither saw nor heard, only sensed, hurtled from the grass. It landed on her back. A foreleg muscled and hard as a steel rod pushed her head on to her chest. As she fell forward her spine broke and all was dark.

The gaunt lioness, her ribs standing out stark as old railway sleepers in her body, proceeded to rip open the woman's soft large belly. The cat gave a low roar of triumph and buried her face in the contents.

The boy screamed, a high shriek of insanity. His sister, infected by his screams of dread and horror, cried with him.

The lioness, ill and hunting alone, looked up at the tree. She growled at this new threat and lifted her head from the depths of the woman's belly. Blood and tissue dripped from her mouth and clung to her fur as she rushed to the tree. She was too weak to pull herself up more than a foot or two. Her claws raked the trunk deeply as she slid back. She tried again and then capitulated and returned to the half-eaten body at the foot of the tree.

Fearing that her prey might be taken from her, she tugged the woman's body deeper into the grass. The children were spared the sight of their mother being devoured, but they were not spared the contented slurps, grunts and gnawing of meat and bones.

With night came the rain. The boy cupped his hands, drank, and then made his sister drink. Darkness also brought bedlam. The lunatic laughter and ghoulish howling of the hyenas silenced the children. They knew that hyenas were the pets of *ngangas* and they did not want the witches to appear. They clung to each other numb with cold and terror. Eventually exhaustion granted the children sleep which was deep and still as death.

Chapter Eighteen

IT WAS cold in the first light of day. Erin's breath hung white as hoar-frost in front of his face. He rubbed his reddened fingers together and stamped his feet as he walked across the hard, sandy floor of the boma to the recently completed straw hut which served as a dining room.

He smiled as he saw bunches of bananas hanging from the pole on which the front of the thatched roof rested. The fruit was still dark green but a few showed a faint yellow flush. The ethylene gas given off by the ripe ones would soon turn the others deep yellow and ready to eat.

Erin looked around the camp he and his men had constructed and congratulated himself.

The grass huts for the hunters were each large enough to accommodate two iron camp beds. A clothes rail cut from mopane branches stood in the corner. A table of rough but neatly sawn branches was sturdily set on four thick poles planted into the ground.

The grass walls stood as high as a man's shoulder, affording privacy, light and air. There was no door, only an opening in the wall with a short zigzag path lined by a grass fence leading to it. The theory was that predators were wary of entering a confined space where they could not see far ahead. This notion calmed most of the wives and daughters. A camp fire burned brightly in the middle of the clean swept area.

The huts formed a circle within the boma. Erin's men had built a protective grass fence behind the huts.

'If *shumba* wants to come in he will,' Jacob had prophesied, as the sticks of grass in the bundles stuck into his shoulders and the perspiration trickled over his body and made him itch.

'I know, but it keeps our clients happy,' Erin had reasoned.

'Then why are the showers and toilets outside the fence?' Jonas had asked.

'*Shumba* knows that he must not take people when they sit on the square box or stand beneath the drum of water,' Jacob had teased.

'Katoro,' Erin shouted. Before the name had been fully uttered a small, powerfully built man appeared, carrying a red enamel coffee pot and a dark green mug. A raised cicatrice running from his ear to the corner of his mouth bore mute testimony to a fight with another skinner over a woman. Katoro when angry was a man to be avoided.

'Coffee is ready, Mr Erin,' he said. His face lit up at Erin's smile of appreciation. Katoro had recently been elevated from a skinner to the envied position of cook for the New Ganyani camp. Not only was the pay better but his prestige among the ladies in the village had risen enormously. Unlike most of Erin's staff Katoro was not married. He informed Erin that he was still choosing a suitable wife, and he had a selection of young girls living with him.

Erin's men had built a circle of huts for the camp staff a short distance from the main hunting camp. Wives and families from Kame and Ganyani had already moved in.

Chickens pecked around the huts and a few scraggy goats were penned in a kraal.

Pat and Erin had divided the staff between New Ganyani and Kame Two. During the week the Hanleys had spent with Pat and Erin, Briar had come up with a suggestion which Pat had seized upon eagerly.

'Instead of sending all these faxes cancelling your booked hunts, why don't you offer them something new, different and exciting?' she said.

Fred had been about to stop her, when Pat held up his hand. 'Such as?'

'Well,' said Briar. 'Offer them a Selous hunt.'

Pat looked nonplussed, as did Erin.

'You'll have time to put up a grass camp and find a few waterholes,' she continued quickly before the men could decry her suggestion. 'Let them sleep in grass huts, use long-drop toilets and the old drum with holes punched into the sides hoisted up on a rope as a shower.' Her eyes sparkled as she painted scenes of a bygone era.

'Selous Safari,' mused Pat, thinking of Frederick Courteney Selous, the young Englishman who had come out to Africa and become one of the most famous hunters in the country. 'It might just work, Briar.' He grinned, caught up in her enthusiasm.

'Offer Kame Two at the same time,' added Blanche. 'Many of your hunters would like a few days without wives or . . .'

'Or mistresses,' cut in Briar.

Blanche laughed. 'There is something romantic about the bush. It seems to have the same effect on people as an ocean voyage.'

'Wives – or whatever – would probably be glad of a day or two watching game from a Land Rover. Their blisters

166

could heal and a good hot bath works miracles,' said Fred. 'You have a wonderful old farmhouse down near Kariba and it's in your new concession. Use that.'

'It's a great idea, Dad,' enthused Erin. 'New Ganyani as the hunting camp and Kame Two for relaxation.'

'Suggest a combination of the two in your faxes. The hunt followed by a rest,' said Briar. 'I'm sure it'll work. Come on, let's get going on the faxes.'

The response stunned the Giffords. They were fully booked for the season.

Erin had settled into his new life easily and smoothly. His days were so busy, building the camp, arranging for water to be pumped up from the nearby stream, choosing areas for the long-drop toilets and finding flat rocks as a base for the open air showers, that he had little time to grieve for the old Ganyani and Kame ranches. Pat had given him an enormous task and he was determined to prove that he was capable of setting up and running his own camp.

He enjoyed making all the decisions. It was new and exciting. The old ranch had been built by Pat and was run according to his father's rules. New Ganyani was his and he felt the proprietorial air which a father has for his first-born son.

Katoro watched Erin sip the hot coffee. Then he trotted to his kitchen to fetch the maize-meal porridge. Carefully he lifted the pot from the old Dover stove. The stove was his prize possession. He still baked bread in a battered tin trunk set into a bed of coals, but the stove had been brought up to the new camp from Kame and he allowed no one to touch it. The walls and roof of his kitchen might be made of thatching grass but he felt that the stove made it the equal of any hotel kitchen in Bulawayo.

Katoro kept watch as Erin punched two holes into a tin of sweetened condensed milk and trickled the thick, sickly sweet liquid over the *sadza*. Anticipating Erin's next move, Katoro handed him the bowl of wild honey. Erin pushed the beeswax to one side and ladled honey over the condensed milk.

Katoro always stood and watched Erin eat. It amazed him that Erin could eat the stiff white porridge correctly at dinner, by dipping it into *kapenta* or meat stew, yet in the morning could not eat it with soured milk.

'It must be an English habit that the Big One taught him when he was but a child and knew no better,' he confided to Jonas.

Jonas agreed immediately. It was a wise man who was friends with the camp cook. It meant extra meat and sometimes tinned fruit.

Erin scraped up the last sticky trace of condensed milk with his finger and pushed his plate away.

Today they were going to complete the last of the three grass-walled huts they had built for hunters.

Erin held out his mug for a refill of coffee and watched the men coming into the boma laden with piles of freshly cut grass. Suddenly he put down his mug.

'Jacob, Jonas!' he shouted.

His staff echoed his call all the way to the village where his trackers were having their *sadza* and milk.

Within minutes they were with him.

'We will not build today. We'll leave that to the others, they know what to do. Get our water bottles. We are going to find the waterhole that my father saw when he flew over here last week.'

'It will be good to look for spoor again,' said Jacob.

Jonas nodded. He had secretly enjoyed the break from

the daily routine of the hunt, but would never admit to it.

Erin took his rifle from Jacob and shouted something in Sindebele which sent five men hurrying away to where they were clearing the grass to form an airstrip.

Pat wanted to spend the weekend with them and Erin was determined to have a strip of land cleared for the Cessna. He wanted to see the amazement on his father's face when he saw not only a completed airstrip but also a working bush camp.

'Any man who does not do a full day's work will not have *nyama* when we return tonight with a buck,' warned Erin.

The promise of meat for supper meant that the builders were all hard at work before the three men left camp.

Erin swatted at the tiny mopane flies hovering around his eyes and nose.

'Ignore them like the *shumba* ignores the tsetse flies,' advised Jacob.

'Perhaps if I could roar like him they would leave me,' answered Erin, missing the cloud in front of his face and swatting his neck instead. He winced as red finger marks were outlined on his skin.

The three men had walked until their shadows were directly beneath them, but had found no sign of the waterhole.

Ahead of them lay a deep grassy valley.

'A kill,' said Erin, pointing across the valley to where black shapes were hunched in a tree.

'Not a new one,' said Jonas, shading his eyes. 'There are no vultures in the sky, only the ones still in the tree.'

'Probably too fat to fly,' laughed Erin. 'Let's go and see what the kill was.'

Jacob was silent as they pushed their way through the grass. His eyes never stopped searching and like a bloodhound he sniffed the air as they walked.

Suddenly he veered away to the right and bent down in the grass. Erin and Jonas waited for a few minutes but when he did not reappear, Erin chambered a shot and moved cautiously to where Jacob had disappeared. They found him hunched over something in the grass.

'Jacob,' said Erin, 'what is it? What's wrong?'

Jacob stood up and kicked at the object with his foot. It unfolded. A scrap of blue cotton material encrusted with congealed blood and black with flies.

The men looked at each other and then back at the cloth.

'*Shumba*,' said Jacob, pointing out a barely visible pad print in the sand between the grasses.

He bent low over the spoor and conversed with Jonas. The men spread out, walking slowly. When they found further evidence of the lion they attracted one another's attention with the soft call of the Cape turtle dove which to Erin sounded like, 'Where is Ingwe? Where is Ingwe?'

Erin followed them silently. He was wary, knowing how easy it was to walk right up to a lion without seeing it. This one would be resting in the heat, content with a full belly.

Jonas and Jacob stopped and beckoned him to join them.

'It is an old female. She is alone and will not live long as she can no longer hunt,' said Jacob.

Erin did not question him. He still did not fully understand how his trackers could tell the history of an animal from a few footprints in thick grass, but he did not doubt their verdict.

Suddenly Jacob let out a whistle, shrill as a white crowned shrike. The men joined forces immediately on hearing the loud, nasal call. Jonas left the dried blood spattered on the grass stems and hurried across to Jacob and Erin.

Erin looked down at what Jacob had found, gagged and forced himself to stare up at a circling bateleur eagle, concentrating on the black trailing edge under its white wing. He tried to focus on whether it was broad enough for the bird to be a male. As the sour gall continued to rise, Erin studied the spectacular somersaulting flight which had earned the eagle the old French name for an acrobat.

'It was a woman,' said Jacob, staring at the gnawed bones lying scattered in a circle, where hyenas had fought over the remnants left by the lioness.

Erin was forced to look back at the pathetic remains. The grass had been trampled into an arena by the feasting hyenas. Scraps of material hung limp as flags at half-mast on the thatching grass stems.

'The lioness, we must find and shoot her. She has tasted human flesh and will kill again,' Erin said.

'There is no need,' said Jacob. 'The hyenas have done that for us.' He said something to Jonas who walked away quickly, his eyes on the ground.

'She tried to defend her kill but they were too many. Jonas will soon find her body. See here.'

Erin squatted beside Jacob and marvelled yet again at his tracker's eyesight. Jacob used his stick to turn over what had seemed to Erin to be a broken branch covered with sand lying deep in the grass.

It was the leg of a lion gnawed from the body at the shoulder joint.

As they were studying the grisly proof of the lioness's death Jonas reappeared.

'It is as you say. The body lies there.' He pointed a short distance away from where they crouched.

'She was not old, only too greedy. She tried to eat the soft underside of the *nungu*. Her throat and paws are pierced with the black and white quills of the porcupine. The sores ooze yellow pus. She was sick and would have died soon.'

A sound, weak as the mew of a newly born kitten, attracted the men. It seemed to come from the vultures. They studied the black shapes and made their way cautiously to the tree and the noise.

'Children!'

'What, Jacob?' asked Erin. 'What are you talking about?'

'Those vultures are children tied to the tree,' said Jacob.

Erin shuddered. He could still not distinguish the shapes. As they approached the teak tree he recognized the human forms. He hurried through the grass.

A hand shot out and pulled him back. He spun round, angry and ready to remonstrate with Jacob.

'There may be another lion here. See how claws have marked the tree. A lion knew the children were there.'

Erin nodded soberly. He had no wish to be caught between some other lion and what it considered was its prey.

'It may be hungry,' continued Jacob.

Erin was staring at the wide expanse of grass, watching for any movement of the seed-heads in the windless day, when something soft wrapped around his ankle.

He stifled a scream. Looking down at his foot, he whistled for Jacob. He had walked into a coiled length of patterned cloth. He stood still, as Jacob and Jonas scouted the area, pointing out signs to each other with long sticks broken from an old mopane tree.

'She could not climb the tree after her children,' said Jacob.

'So she took off her wrap. Perhaps she was too fat,' continued Jonas.

'And that was when the lioness got her,' said Erin softly.

'It started eating her here.' Jacob pointed. 'See how the ground drank the blood. *Shumba* was disturbed and dragged her body away.'

'Slowly,' added Jonas. '*Shumba* was weak and the woman was heavy. It ate her there in the long grass.' He indicated a few feet away with his stick.

'The *bere* smelt the meat and blood and came to eat. They fought and pulled away pieces of the woman's body to where I found the first scrap of blue cloth,' finished Jacob.

The two trackers stood at the base of the tree and called to the children but the little ones were silent. It seemed as if death had stiffened the two bodies into one.

Jonas handed his rifle to Jacob and swung himself easily into the tree.

'They are dead,' he called down.

'Climb higher,' instructed Erin. 'See if you can touch them. Get above that fork.'

Jonas worked his way along the branch until it seemed that it would break beneath his weight. Then with the extraordinary agility usually exhibited only by primates he flung himself into the air. He scrabbled frantically for the branch above him, feeling his nails tear as his fingers found purchase on the bark.

173

Erin closed his eyes, expecting to hear a heavy thud as his tracker fell to earth.

'Bring them down,' shouted Jacob.

Jonas untied the cloth from the tree trunk and retied it tightly around the children. Then he slung the bundle across his back and climbed carefully down the fire-blackened teak.

Jacob lifted the bundle from Jonas's back as soon as he was on the ground. The three men bent low over the two bodies. The little boy had his arms wound tightly around his sister. Her face was hidden against his torn vest.

Erin felt for a pulse beneath the boy's small jaw. He started.

'I think I felt a beat,' he said. 'Soak this in water and give it to me,' he commanded, ripping off the cotton bandanna he wore tied around his forehead.

He held out one hand for the wet cloth and the other he placed back on what he thought was a pulse. Yes, he breathed to himself. Yes, it was there, as faint as the heartbeat of a fledgling, but the boy was alive.

He wadded his headband and held it to the child's mouth, slowly squeezing a few drops on to his lips. When he saw a slight tremor in the mouth, he gave the cloth to Jacob.

He turned his attention to the girl.

'Your water bottle,' he said to Jonas.

Jonas handed him the metal bottle encased in camou-flage netting and watched as he trickled water over the child's face and body.

He could find no pulse but persisted in stroking her limbs with long movements towards her heart.

'Wet your finger and put it in her mouth.'

Jonas did. He turned so that the small shadow thrown by his body would fall over her face.

The two men worked over the child, oblivious to everything except beating death. They heard Jacob talking to the boy but did not turn around.

A small, cracked voice whispered something they could not hear.

'Yes, there was a lion,' answered Jacob. 'But your mother is not dead, only her body is not here. Her spirit is with the ancestors and she will live there for ever. You must be proud of your mother, for she was as brave as a man.'

This was followed by a long silence, then Jacob said, 'We have found the lion. It is dead. This I promise you.'

Erin glanced over his shoulder. The boy was now clinging to Jacob's neck, his skinny legs with scabbed and scarred knees wound tightly around his waist.

'If Jacob says the lion is dead, you must believe him, because Jacob is the best tracker in the country. All the *shumba* fear him.'

Even though Erin spoke in Sindebele the boy turned his face away and seemed to burrow into Jacob's body.

'It will take time,' said Jacob in English. 'He is of an age to remember. The girl child is lucky. She will remember nothing.'

If she lives, thought Erin, turning back to where Jonas was still sponging and stroking the small body. Erin had just removed his finger from the pulse when the girl made a sucking sound and her mouth pursed as if tasting a sour lemon.

He instinctively recoiled in shock and Jonas laughed.

'These children are strong. They were found in a tree like monkeys. We must name them.'

'Oh no,' said Erin. 'If we name them we must keep and look after them.'

Both trackers nodded. If you saved a person's life, they belonged to you and were your responsibility.

'Jacob, Jonas,' pleaded Erin. 'These children have a father, a family. They must go back to their village.'

'It could take a long time to find the village,' said Jacob.

'Perhaps the father is dead,' added Jonas.

They spun round, like a single spinning top, as the baby girl squalled. She lay on the ground gazing up at the men beseechingly. Her huge black eyes seemed too large for her face, now tinged grey and drawn.

'This one is Buna,' said Jonas.

Erin nodded. 'Yes, she does have both the eyes and voice of a Galago. As she is small we will call her a bush-baby. Buna is her name.'

Jonas smiled and nodded at Jacob.

'This one,' said Jacob, still in the grip of the boy's arms and legs, 'will be Shoko. He clings to me like a vervet monkey and as you see his arms and legs are as long as those of a monkey.'

Erin studied his trackers. He had the feeling that he had been led into this situation very skilfully.

'Shoko and Buna can stay in camp with us.' At their delighted grins he held up a hand. 'Until we find their family.'

The small party wound their way through the tall grass, each tracker carrying a child. The children now sucked eagerly on the wet cloths.

Jonas and Jacob chatted quietly as they walked. Jonas's wife was still in milk from the last baby and could suckle Buna until she was strong enough to eat. Shoko would be able to eat watery *sadza* the next day.

Jacob said something to Jonas. He nodded and Jacob turned to Erin.

'Let Jonas carry Buna and Shoko back to camp. It is not far. We will shoot meat for the camp. Jonas can leave the children with the women and bring the truck to fetch us and the meat.'

The trackers were happy. The camp would now be successful as they had found mascots. Mr Pat had Sheeba and everyone knew that the 'red devil-dog' brought him luck.

Chapter Nineteen

TARA AND Briar stood side by side at the window overlooking the parkland in which the Mater Dei Hospital was set. The grass was still surprisingly green, as the chill mornings and evenings warned of the approach of winter.

Briar had just arrived to relieve Tara after her night shift. Though it was no longer necessary to have two nurses on duty, the girls enjoyed working in the hospital. They were both good-natured and hard-working, qualities admired and appreciated by the staff and nuns.

There was always someone in the Hanleys' home when the girls came off duty. Tara and Briar were surprised at how well Pat and Erin cooked and ran the house.

'It's easier than running a bush camp,' answered Erin, when Tara complimented him on a breakfast he had prepared for her.

Pat and Erin took it in turns to fly to New Ganyani and Kame Two. The staff were working well and both camps had fallen into a good routine. Jacob had returned to new Ganyani the week before, much to the hysterical joy of Shoko.

Rudo was pronounced out of danger. Though she was progressing well, her doctor had decided to keep her in the Mater Dei for an extra week as she was still not speaking.

He was not sure whether it was due to shock or some problem with her slashed tongue.

Briar sat beside her bed for hours, telling her about Kame and Jacob. Rudo's eyes followed Briar's lips but her own never moved.

Tara stretched and yawned.

'Well, I'd better leave now. Erin is at New Ganyani so I'll be making my own breakfast today.'

'No, Pat said he'd surprise you and be cook for the day,' said Briar, unconsciously ruining Erin's surprise.

'I thought he was still at Kame?' said Tara.

Briar flushed.

'He flew back last night. He said that he didn't want me to be lonely in that big house.'

'Aha!' said Tara, her eyes sparkling.

'Tara, Pat could be my father,' stammered Briar.

'I suppose he could just have made it,' admitted Tara, doing some quick calculations. 'My father is much older than my mother and they love each other. Well, in the Italian way,' she concluded. 'Pat is not so much older than you. In any case he only looks about thirty-five. I think he's sexy.'

Briar grinned impishly.

'I thought you found Erin sexy?' she said.

Tara did not look at all discomfited.

'Oh I do. He's—'

There was a noise from the bed. Tara and Briar spun round. Rudo was trying to speak.

'Briar?'

'Rudo,' said Briar jubilantly. 'You can talk again.'

'Briar,' said Rudo indistinctly. 'Marry Mr Pat. Man needs a woman.'

Briar was so thrilled to hear Rudo speak that the import

of her words did not register at first. She moved quickly to the bed and hugged the woman who had been to hell and back.

'I agree with Rudo,' said Tara.

'What?'

'You should marry Pat and live on Kame.'

'Live with Mr Pat and me,' whispered Rudo, still having difficulty in shaping the words.

'That's ridiculous,' said Briar shortly. 'But I am going to phone and let him know that you are talking. Now you will be able to come home, Rudo.'

She ran out of the ward and almost knocked over one of the nuns.

'Sorry, sister,' she said and ran on. 'Rudo's talking,' she called back over her shoulder.

The sister smiled and walked into the ward. Tara jumped up from the edge of the bed where she had been sitting holding Rudo's hand.

'Your doctor will be in to see you shortly, Rudo. He will probably let you spend tonight at home.'

She was rewarded with a lopsided smile and a mumbled 'thank you'.

'Amazing,' said Pat when the doctor phoned to say he was releasing Rudo from hospital. 'Yesterday she lay there dumb and listless. Now you tell me that she is sitting on a bench under one of the trees. Thank you. We really owe you more than we can ever repay.'

'What is amazing is how those young women you sent us have worked, Pat. Briar has spent hours sharing her strength with Rudo. It was her love that put words into Rudo's mouth.'

'Yes, Briar is like that,' said Pat, as he gently replaced the receiver.

On his way to collect Rudo, Pat decided that he would persuade Briar and Tara to come to Kame Two. Rudo could recuperate. Briar and Tara could keep an eye on her and have a well-earned rest from nursing.

Chapter Twenty

THE ATMOSPHERE had soured in the Madden camp since the departure of Tara and Briar. The safari was nearing its end and they had still to find another leopard.

Kirk Madden and his trackers spent day after long day checking and rehanging baits. Yet for all his skill at choosing new locations, they found no fresh signs of leopard.

The women were tired of jolting over rough tracks all day, only to sit and watch the men cut down stinking carcasses and rehang fresh ones. Mother and daughter had remained in camp, reading and bickering with each other. They were bored with the slow pace of camp life.

'Come with us today,' pleaded Guido after breakfast. He put his arms around the shoulders of his wife and daughter. 'You bring us luck. I know we will be lucky today if you are with us.' He kissed Maria on the cheek. 'Please, *cara*.'

Guido looked at Kirk for help.

'Kirk,' he called, 'ask my women to join us today. Perhaps they will do for you what they won't for me.'

I'm sure they will, thought Kirk lasciviously.

'Maria, Tomasina, please join us. We need luck today. I have a feeling that with you in the hunting vehicle we'll find that last leopard we need.'

The women hung back a while longer, making Marco join in the exhortations. Then they agreed and climbed into the Land Rover accompanied by cheers from the men.

Kirk watched as the shorts stretched tight across Tomasina's buttocks. He was still determined to have her before the end of the safari. Having decided that Maria was afraid of Guido and expecting no future night calls from her, he had been playing Tomasina skilfully. He ignored her during the day, then embraced her furtively when out of sight of the family. She responded readily. She, too, was eager to have Kirk. She still wanted to add a white hunter to her list of trophies.

The first bait they checked had been visited by a leopard the night before. Fresh claw marks were visible in the old meat and it had eaten a little.

'It will return tonight to eat again,' said Kirk. 'We'll wait here while the trackers build a hide.'

'*Cara*, you brought us luck. Tonight you will have your leopard,' exalted Guido.

'And soon your jacket, Mamma,' added Marco.

The National Parks ranger was walking round the base of the tree looking unhappy.

Kirk hated having what he called a 'watchdog' with him, but he treated the man politely. He realized that if the ranger filed bad reports he could lose the concession.

'What's wrong?' he called. 'Are you not happy that we've found our leopard?'

The ranger said a few words to the trackers, then walked to where Kirk stood in the meagre shade of a mopane tree.

'Your trackers agree with me. The leopard is probably a female with young.'

Kirk felt ill. He needed this leopard. If he was to receive

clients from Guido Andretti's recommendation then the safari had to end on a high note. He was determined that the high note would be a rifle retort and a dead leopard.

'But we cannot be sure until we see it,' argued Kirk.

The ranger merely nodded and turned away. Idiot, thought Kirk, there are so many cats here, what does one female more or less mean?

'What is the matter?' asked Maria. She had watched the exchange, but understood only the warning and anger of the body language.

'My watchdog thinks that it's a female with cubs,' said Kirk bitterly.

'But you will still shoot, will you not?' asked Maria anxiously. She turned to her husband and broke into Italian.

'Guido,' she said, 'Guido. You promised that I could have my jacket. Now because some ranger thinks the leopard is female I won't have it. Oh Guido, oh *caro* Marco, shoot my leopard.'

Maria burst into tears. She peeped at Guido between her fingers. Tears never failed with him. He could not bear to see her unhappy.

Guido crossed to where she was now squatting near the bait.

'Kirk,' he bellowed.

Kirk stood up and followed Guido to a nearby anthill.

'Kirk, my wife very much wants this leopard.'

'I cannot afford to shoot a female with cubs especially after a warning from the ranger. I could lose my licence,' Kirk replied.

'I have many very important friends in Milan. Many who would like to make an African safari. They would hunt with the man I recommend. I can count at least five who would take an elephant hunt.'

Kirk licked his lips. The fees from five big hunts plus handsome tips were worth one female leopard. He could probably fill the ranger's mouth with money to quieten him.

'I would be very grateful,' continued Guido. 'Let us say grateful enough for a bank account in Milan to hold twenty thousand dollars in the name of Kirk Madden.'

Greed ran its fingers up Kirk's spine but he kept his face impassive.

'You see,' said Guido, 'man to man, I had a little indiscretion in Milan. Maria found out about her. I need skins shot by her son to make up for it.'

Kirk nodded. He had made up his mind. He called loudly to his trackers in Shona.

'The ranger thinks this *mbada* is a female with young. We will look at another bait. Let's go.'

'Do you wish us to break down the hide now it is useless?' asked one of his trackers.

'No,' Kirk answered nonchalantly, 'leave it. I want to check the bait at the river. We will have lunch there.'

Kirk was silent on the drive to the river. He was determined to return for the leopard but he would have to think of a way of losing his watchdog.

They jolted over the rocky track which led down to shallow pools made dark by the overhanging branches of teak trees. The rough road gave him an idea. He laughed and hit the steering wheel. Marvellous, he thought, you're bloody marvellous. He would fake a breakdown with the Land Rover. The ranger could escort the women back to camp – it was within easy walking distance.

185

He, Guido and his one tracker would stay to repair the vehicle. He would give the other tracker orders to keep the ranger in camp, perhaps by finding a willing woman to amuse him.

They would return to the hide taking a *bulala* lamp with them. Whatever time the cat came they would get it. The returning vehicle would not be heard in the staff camp. The ranger could be told that they had all returned early and were in camp for the night.

His trackers would be well paid to keep quiet about the night's kill. Fortunately neither of the trackers liked the ranger, who tended to give them instructions. He would order a very early start the next day. The ranger would not have time to check the skinning shed. The leopard would be skinned and the extra skin packed and hidden before they returned that night.

Kirk grinned at Guido sitting beside him. 'Done,' he said.

Guido smiled at Maria, who was sitting up high on the trackers' seat.

'It is yours,' he said in Italian. Maria mouthed him a kiss. Guido knew his life would be peaceful for a while. Morals and money have never made good bed-partners, he thought, looking at Kirk.

The river was cool and dark, a welcome respite from the bright light and the dust. The women jumped down from the Land Rover and ran to splash in the water.

'Keep in sight of the truck,' shouted Kirk. 'Animals come down to drink and I don't want you stumbling over an old mud buffalo.'

Tomasina splashed water over her face and neck. It trickled inside her shirt, plastering the thin cotton to her skin.

'Be back in a few minutes,' she called as she walked behind a conical anthill whose rich red soil moulded by termites now afforded anchorage to trees and shrubs.

Kirk watched her go then lifted his rifle and swung out of the Land Rover.

'I'll just check that the area is safe,' he said to Guido. 'Would you see that Maria and Marco have lunch. Be back in ten to fifteen minutes.'

Tomasina unzipped her shorts and stepped out of them, enjoying the coolness of the air on her sweaty skin. She squatted on an open patch of sand, wary of snakes or spiders.

Kirk came noiselessly around the anthill. He watched Tomasina unobserved. His breathing quickened. He knew he had to have this woman. As she fumbled in her pocket for a tissue, he stepped forward. Tomasina gasped and scrabbled for her shorts. Kirk put his foot on them and studied her lower body. Tomasina felt herself flush then she drew herself up and placed her hands on her hips.

'You are truly lovely,' he whispered as he came towards her.

'No, not here,' she protested as his fingers became urgent.

But the thought of the Andrettis lunching a few yards away, unaware of what he was about to do to their daughter, excited him even more.

'Yes. Here. Now,' he said, pushing her up against the hard clay.

Tomasina stifled her initial cry of pain as his weight bore down on her. Then she gave herself up to his brutal love-making.

'Tomasina?' Maria's voice drifted across the shallow river.

'Answer your mother,' commanded Kirk, still holding her against the anthill.

'Can't,' breathed Tomasina.

'Answer,' said Kirk and she bit her lip as a lump of rock-hard clay dug into her buttock.

'I'm all right, Mamma,' she called breathlessly.

'I told you not to worry,' said Guido. 'Kirk is having a look around to make sure that there are no animals. Tomasina is quite safe.'

Maria sank back on the tarpaulin. She pillowed her head on Guido's leg and closed her eyes.

Kirk grunted, then pulled away from Tomasina. He zipped up his shorts and turned to go.

'Kirk,' whispered Tomasina, holding out her arms.

Kirk ignored her. Hunting women was like hunting game. It was the chase that was exciting, not the aftermath of love-making, not the gloating over the dead animal.

He had pursued and enjoyed Tomasina. Unless he had the desire to take her a second time, she was unimportant in his life.

Tomasina watched him strut away. '*Porco*,' she hissed.

She pulled up her shorts, now stained and crumpled where his feet had ground them into the earth. Dusting off as much of the sand as she could, she dragged them on. She let her shirt hang loose over the shorts.

If I stop and pretend to wash my legs and arms in the pool on the way back, I can probably slip and soak the shorts and shirt. That way Maria will notice nothing, she thought.

Maria sprang upright at the sound of the splash.

'What's that?' she said.

'Only Tomasina,' answered Marco, stuffing another sandwich into his mouth. 'She's slipped into the pool and is now splashing around with her clothes on.'

'Crocodiles?' asked Maria, looking at the dark pool.

'It looks deep, because it's dark in the shadows. In fact it's quite shallow,' said Kirk, appearing from behind the Land Rover. 'She's safe there.'

He sank down beside them and watched Tomasina clean herself whilst pretending to splash in the water.

Women, he thought. They should be the ones to run governments and rule countries. They are far more devious and clever than men.

'I'm going to check the Land Rover. It has been giving some trouble,' he called to his men in Shona. He knew that the internal combustion engine was not in the ranger's area of expertise.

'I'll be a few minutes,' he said to Guido. 'I didn't like the sound of the transmission as we came down the hill.'

Maria looked alarmed.

'Don't worry, Maria,' he said loudly. 'Look at your daughter, totally happy and relaxed.'

Tomasina was stretched out on a rock in the dappled sunshine, letting her clothes dry on her body. She knew that the remark was meant for her, but she chose to ignore it, just as she decided to ignore Kirk for the rest of the safari.

Chapter Twenty-one

IT WAS the last day of the Andrettis' safari. Kirk's plan had worked perfectly. They had shot a female leopard. She was large and her coat beautifully marked. Once skinned, she could pass for a small male and no one would ever know that he had broken the law. Maria was ecstatic and Kirk knew that he would receive a handsome bonus from Guido, plus a run of future clients.

It was still dark when the gong was struck calling them to breakfast. Kirk explained that they should not miss one minute of the last day.

'This is the first time I have eaten breakfast by moonlight,' laughed Maria, as she held out her cup to be refilled with coffee.

'If we hurry we may see some of the night creatures on the road,' said Kirk. He was eager to get the game ranger into the Land Rover and away from the skinning shed. He would make sure that they returned only at nightfall, by which time the skin would be hidden.

If the ranger discovered the skin he would tell him that they had found the leopard on their way home after he had fixed the Land Rover. He would explain that it must have been going to the bait tree. Guido shot it. They returned too late for the ranger to see it. In order to keep the skin in top condition, it was taken straight to the skinning shed.

Kirk shouted for his trackers and the ranger. His trackers arrived at a run.

'Where is the ranger?' he asked. 'I want to leave now. Not when it suits him.' Both trackers suddenly developed selective hearing. They looked up at him blankly and busied themselves with packing the Land Rover.

Suddenly a door opened and a path of golden light led to Kirk's radio room. A tall dark figure stood starkly outlined in the doorway.

'What are you doing there?' shouted Kirk in Shona. 'No one goes into my radio room. It is private. Come here and explain yourself.'

'In English so that your clients can understand or in Shona so that only you and I know that you will no longer hunt in Zimbabwe?' asked the ranger coldly.

Kirk felt clammy.

'I don't understand what you mean,' he said, his tone now reasonable and conciliatory.

'I believe you do, Mr Madden. I have overlooked many things whilst I have been in this camp, but shooting a female leopard with cubs after being cautioned, using a *bulala* lamp to take her at night and bribing your skinners to say it was a male are all good reasons for you to lose your hunter's licence.'

The ranger seemed to tower over Kirk as he spoke. Kirk knew he had to plead with the man, but was conscious of the Andrettis watching the scene being enacted in the lighted doorway.

'Could we talk in the radio hut?' he asked politely.

'No, Mr Madden. You have just ordered me out of it and, besides, it is too late. I have put through a call to Mr

Tigera in Harare. He will receive the message when he arrives at his office.'

'Tigera?' said Kirk. 'What has he got to do with this?'

'Everything, Mr Madden. It is common knowledge that he obtained the concession for you.'

'That's not true. I . . . I . . .' blustered Kirk.

'I understand, Mr Madden. What is it that you colonials say, "One hand cleans the other"?' The ranger laughed, a small, mirthless sound. 'Let us go. Your clients are waiting.'

If he lost his licence, Kirk knew he would lose his livelihood. He would be forced to become a tour guide in some remote African country where they were not too particular about a man's credentials. His life of ease and prestige would end.

'Self-satisfied swine,' he muttered as he stamped back to the Andrettis.

'Is there trouble?' asked Guido.

'No,' snapped Kirk, then realizing that he had not yet received his bonus from Guido, he added more politely, 'the local officials they foist on us drive me mad with their incompetence.'

He sneered up at the ranger who was standing beside the Land Rover.

'This one was in my radio room, fiddling with my equipment. They understand nothing and break everything they touch.'

Kirk could feel the anger in the ranger, but he was beyond caring.

'One can expect little from a country which is run by the inept and where corruption is the currency. These National Parks game scouts are supposed to see that hunting is strictly controlled. They are mere lackeys, paid informers.'

The ranger opened his mouth to protest. He was proud to be employed by the National Parks, which enjoyed an excellent, well-deserved reputation. He waited in silence for Kirk's verbal explosion to end.

Mr Tigera will be interested to know that he is considered inept and corrupt by the man he feeds, thought the scout.

'Sshh,' said Maria, placing her fingers over Kirk's mouth. 'Let us not spoil our last day.'

'Maria is right,' said Guido. 'You can sort out the problems with your scout when we have gone.'

Kirk smiled. He became a different man. Once again he was their charming solicitous hunter.

Chapter Twenty-two

TIGERA WHISTLED as he walked into the office. His secretaries immediately stood up to greet him. The one in Matamba's pay studied him carefully. Some deal must have been successfully concluded or he was about to engage in something underhand. She would listen attentively today.

Tigera switched on his answering machine. As he listened to the messages, he lifted his hand when he wanted one of them noted. The secretaries held their pads and pencils ready.

A deep voice spoke in Shona. Tigera sat very still as he listened, then punched the repeat button. He gesticulated for one of the secretaries to approach his desk.

'Take a letter,' he said.

'"Dear Mr . . ."' he began. The secretary waited with her pen poised. Tigera glared at her. 'I will fill in the name.'

'Sir,' she said.

'"I have found a suitable candidate for the vacant post on the Somali border. I quite understand your position with the parties of raiding *shufta* in the area and the difficulty in manning the outposts. These bandits are a problem but, I assure you, my man is expendable. No questions will be asked."'

Another one of his stinking favours, thought Matamba's eyes and ears. I wonder who the unfortunate candidate is.

'"I remain your good friend, Tsvakai Tigera." Bring it to me for my signature when you have typed it. I will fax it personally,' he said.

'Yes, sir.'

Tigera sat back and sucked thoughtfully on one of his cigars. The probability of Kirk Madden being killed on the Kenya border with Somalia was high. The idea delighted him. With Madden dead, no one could connect him with many of the Bush War atrocities, including the ambush on the Gifford boys.

Tigera now had a new hunting concession to auction. It would be worth at least six million Zim dollars. The concession fee of fifteen per cent of the total quota issued to that area would be high, as it was rich in game.

The wealthy would be fighting for the concession. He might even be able to wangle it so that the payment for every animal on the quota was made in US dollars instead of Zim dollars. Hunters liked to sell the animals to their clients in US dollars and pay the government in Zim dollars. They would be furious if they couldn't do so, as their profits would be drastically reduced. However, Tigera was certain that as hunting areas in Africa diminished and competition intensified, the hunters would eventually be forced to pay in US dollars.

The future did not concern men of Tigera's calibre. He lived in the present and he placed himself at the head of every queue.

Kirk Madden was an embarrassment. He was pleased to get rid of him.

'Perhaps I'll reward the ranger,' he muttered, then shook

his head as he thought of the possible implications of offering money to one of the National Parks employees.

Every man has a price, he thought, but I have yet to find one of the rangers for sale. I know, some words of praise to the head of the Department of National Parks should do the trick. I can explain that he radioed me instead of the department as I personally asked him to check on Madden. They should accept that. It sounds reasonable.

'Get me the Department of National Parks and Wildlife Management on the phone,' he shouted and both secretaries sprang up.

Chapter Twenty-three

A SWIRL of brown dust greeted Erin. Sheeba rushed at him from the plane which had just landed at New Ganyani. She spun in circles, her feet hardly touching the ground and her yellow eyes filled with joy at seeing him again.

Pat followed his dog to call her to heel but Erin had already scooped her up in his arms and she was covering his face with wet licks.

'Watch it, Erin,' warned Pat. 'She'll expect me to carry her around soon and that's not going to happen.'

At the sound of Pat's voice, Sheeba gave Erin's ear a final lick and wriggled free to take up her position at Pat's side. He fondled her ears and she grinned up at him.

'All right, girl, I forgive your behaviour. I know you've missed Erin. But remember you are a hunting dog, not a puppy.'

Erin walked across to Pat and the two men clapped each other round the shoulders. Pat had missed the companionship of his son. Time passed slowly for him now as he had less work to do than Erin. The farmhouse with its eight bedrooms merely needed painting, the vegetable garden replanting and odd furniture mending.

Rudo was recovering well and had already taken over the cleaning of the house with a squad of workers who had come to Kame Two by lorry from the old Kame. The workers had settled into the existing village easily and quickly.

Pat had spent most of the time flying over the new territory pinpointing interesting rock formations, pools and streams on his large scale aerial map. When he returned, he, a National Parks ranger and two men he had chosen would plan walks for clients.

He proposed to use part of the rugged and magnificent Chizarira Park for the young and hardy, who wanted to look for the rare Taita falcon in the steep gorges and follow black rhino. The park was remote and difficult to enter without a four-wheel-drive vehicle, a part of Zimbabwe which was still relatively unexplored. Pat loved the place. He planned rough overnight camps, where visitors would sleep around the camp fire and wash in a bucket of water heated over the coals. He looked forward to discussing his plans with Erin.

'You have been working, son,' he said, giving the airstrip his nod of approval. Erin glowed. Praise from Pat had to be earned. Erin could hardly wait to show his father the New Ganyani Camp.

'Come, Dad, let's go,' he called as Pat walked back to the plane.

'Just a minute. I've brought a present for Jacob.'

The small plane bounced as Pat reached to help someone out of their seat.

'Rudo!' shouted Erin as he recognized the woman struggling to get out of the Cessna. 'Oh, it's good to see you. Jacob,' he called, 'come and help us unpack the plane.'

'You stay here, Shoko,' said Jacob as he climbed down from the trackers' seat on the back of the Toyota. His feet had no sooner touched the ground than the small boy was beside him. Shoko had accepted Jacob as both father and mother. He was as hard to shake off as a tick deep in a buffalo's ear.

Jacob's face broke into a wide, wonderful, white grin when he saw what the present was.

'Thank you, Mr Pat,' he said. 'I was getting thin and weak. Jonas's wife cannot cook like Rudo.'

Rudo puffed out her chest with pride. The slight difference in the size of her breasts after the operation was not noticeable.

'Who is that?' she asked as Shoko peered around Jacob's legs.

Jacob was delighted to hear that her voice was normal. He had been afraid that she would talk indistinctly for ever. The only outward signs of her ordeal were raised pink lines around her lips.

Briar and Tara teased her, saying she would set a new fashion in the village. All the women would buy pencils to outline their lips, as she looked so pretty.

'It is your new son,' said Jonas, before Jacob could answer.

'I will tell you the story,' said Jacob, glaring at Jonas.

'Come here, little man,' said Rudo softly, seeing fear in the child's eyes.

Cautiously the boy released his hold on Jacob's leg and approached the woman who seemed as large and comfortable as his mother had been.

'Shoko is his name and he has a sister called Buna,' said Jacob.

Rudo took Shoko's hand and as the small fingers gripped hers she smiled.

'I leave you for a few weeks and when I return I find that I have two new children, Jacob. Erin is not making you work hard enough.'

Pat and Erin laughed at the look of dismay on Jacob's face. He had never worked harder. His position as a tracker was a privileged one. Here at New Ganyani he had cut thatching grass, built huts, hacked down mopane trees for poles and even helped dig the deep holes for the long-drop toilets.

Erin took pity on his tracker.

'I don't know what I would have done without Jacob,' he said to Rudo. 'He has done the work of five men every day.' He paused. 'Today, Jacob, you may have the day off. Tomorrow we'll show my father the pans we have found and see what spoor there is to follow.'

Erin studied Pat surreptitiously as they climbed into the front of the Toyota. He was looking relaxed and happy.

Perhaps leaving Kame with all its sad memories has been good for him, Erin mused as he eased the gear lever into position. He looks years younger. In fact he looks almost as if he's in love.

The thought of Pat loving anyone but his mother alarmed him.

'Dad,' he said as the Toyota jolted over the recently cut road. 'Have you found someone to stay with you at Kame Two?'

'Stay with me?' answered Pat. For a moment his son's question perplexed him. 'Oh, you mean a lady-love,' he teased.

Erin blushed. It did not seem right to discuss sexual matters with his father.

'No, my boy. I'm happy as I am. I have everything I

want. When one has had the very best in life, why then settle for what could only be second-best? I have no wish to replace your mother.'

He put his hand on Erin's shoulder and squeezed it. Pat knew that Erin still missed his mother, but had not realized that his son was afraid that he would remarry.

Pat held on to the handle over the cubby-hole as the Toyota bucketed across a stretch of flat grey granite which lay in wide layers on the road.

'We dug up a lot of this as floors for the showers,' said Erin, eager to change the subject.

The road wound down into a hollow.

'You've made the camp down here?' queried Pat. 'It'll be a few degrees colder in the early mornings and evenings than if you had put it up where the granite slabs are.'

'I know, Dad, but we have a marvellous spring of fresh water right on our doorstep at New Ganyani. Wait and see.'

As they drove into the camp, the staff, smart in freshly washed khaki uniforms, lined the road. The villagers stood behind them singing and shuffling their feet in a dance of welcome for Pat.

Pat felt his eyes prick. He loved those people. He coughed to clear his voice, and greeted them.

They drove straight to the village where Rudo, Jacob, Shoko and Jonas climbed down. Pat inspected the huts, the straw hen coops built up high on mopane poles to keep the chickens safe at night, and the goat kraal fenced in with thick thorn bushes. He nodded his approval and the villagers beamed.

'The Old One is satisfied. He is happy,' they said. They proudly showed him the pipeline leading from the river to the village. An old stopcock controlled the flow.

'I thought this was a Selous-style camp,' said Pat, looking askance at the modern pipe.

'The hunting camp is traditional, Dad, but I gave them this as a gift for working so hard. They are very proud of their running water.'

The two men left the village to a song of thanks and praise. The beauty of the Africans' singing and their ability to harmonize always delighted Pat.

'Tonight the drums will sing,' said Erin. 'Tomorrow I'll have no workforce. They will all be stricken with a sudden, grave illness.'

'Usually called a hangover,' smiled Pat. 'Now let's see your baby, New Ganyani.'

Erin sat quietly on one of the carved wooden stools while Pat inspected the camp. The staff stood to attention in silence, waiting for the Old One to speak.

Pat took so long that Erin felt his stomach contract. He had obviously done something wrong.

Eventually Pat emerged from the kitchen chewing a stick of biltong which was not quite dry. He preferred eating the venison when it was still 'wet' inside. He walked across the boma to his son and held out his hand.

'Congratulations, Erin. I could not have built a better camp. I can think of nothing to improve it. You are one of Africa's children.'

Eric stood up and hugged his father.

'Katoro,' he shouted. His call had been anticipated. Katoro arrived with a tray of tea and sandwiches.

Pat took one of the sandwiches and smiled when he saw the thick smear of scrambled egg and mustard.

'Well done, Katoro,' he said. 'Thank you.'

The time had arrived to tell Erin his news. He had

forced himself to keep silent, but now he had to share it with his son.

'In a strange way I think those devils Tigera and Matamba did us a favour,' he began, 'though it broke my heart at the time. No, not a favour as I don't believe they could ever do anything good.'

Erin added a fourth teaspoon of sugar to his tea. He said nothing, but waited for his father to continue. Tigera and Matamba were dirty words in his vocabulary. He wanted to hear nothing good about them.

'The subject of land compensation came up a few weeks ago. Fred persuaded me to let him handle it, as he knows so many men in the government and is on good terms with Matamba.'

Pat paused and let the tension build up. Sheeba padded into the boma. She tucked her tail up high under her belly and tried to hide the enormous bone hanging out of her mouth. She had shamelessly made a fuss of Katoro in the kitchen and had been rewarded with a bone from the leg of an impala.

Pat made Erin wait, while he found out if Sheeba had raided the kitchen or gained the bone honestly. He then patted Sheeba and called her to lie at his feet. She dropped the bone on to the sand and holding it down with one large paw, began to gnaw at the meat Katoro had left on it for her.

Erin shifted on his stool. He was about to break the one unwritten childhood rule in their home – 'Don't interrupt when Dad is speaking' – when Pat continued.

'Fred returned a few days ago. He assures me that he didn't twist any arms. But he must have broken a few. He calls it returning old favours.'

Erin nodded as he drained his cup.

'Instead of monetary compensation, which would never be what the land is worth, we are being given the same amount of land as we've lost.'

Erin stared at his father. He ran his fingers through his blond hair, only to have it fall back over his forehead.

'Don't you understand, Erin? New Ganyani will be ours. We will own it. You can hunt without a game ranger as a watchdog. It will not be put out to tender. It is our land. But . . .' Pat held up his hand to stop the explosion of joy and relief he knew would follow the announcement. 'We are only allowed an area which is the exact size of the one we lost.'

'Only!' shouted Erin. His voice echoing across the camp. 'But they don't do this! They never do this! I can't believe it,' he exclaimed.

Neither could Katoro or the kitchen staff, as they peeped around the boma fence and saw the Old One and Erin dancing and slapping each other on the back. Sheeba was torn between consuming her bone and the need to guard the two men who were behaving so strangely. Her forehead folded into deep furrows as she watched them. Finally satisfied that they were in no danger, she returned to her bone.

'Fred is a miracle man,' said Erin. 'Oh, how I love him.'

'Fred's miracles mean knowing the right people in the right places.'

'And the right secrets about them,' broke in Erin. 'Dad, I don't care what threats or blandishments he used. They worked. We have New Ganyani. We have a future. I'm no longer building a camp which could be taken away at any time.'

Pat looked at his son and rejoiced in his happiness. New

and often harsh countries were for the young. He still hankered after his old home at Kame and the memories that went with it, but he would never let Erin know.

Suddenly Erin grew quiet. 'But you, Dad, what about you and Kame Two?'

'That's a little different to New Ganyani,' answered Pat, thinking of the choice he had been given. Outright ownership of either the new hunting area, or the photographic safari area, but not both. He had decided to ask for the hunting area, New Ganyani, for Erin. His son was young and would have a family.

Pat had memories to pillow his dreams at night. A wife, sons, ranches. He had been a fortunate man. Now it was Erin's turn.

'I've decided to take life a little easier,' he lied. 'Fred stirred up some muddy waters. Those in power paid me enough for Kame to enable me to buy the photographic safari concession to Kame Two for a period of ten years, renewable at the end of the term. Kame Two will not be put up for tender for the next twenty years.'

'Dad, that's marvellous.'

'We must hope that the agreement is more solid than the Lancaster House Agreement or I'll lose Kame Two before ten years have passed.'

'If Fred wrung concessions from them, then they must have some secrets they cannot afford to have aired,' said Erin. 'I have a good feeling about Kame Two, Dad.'

Pat walked across to the dining hut, stretched up and twisted a banana from the bunch. He peeled it carefully and savoured the slight lemon flavour which comes only with bananas ripened on a bunch.

'I agree, son.'

Sheeba placed both paws across her bone as the staff

moved into the boma to prepare the camp beds for the night. One man walked too close to where she was lying. The double ridge of red hairs on her back stood up straight as a punk's haircut. She growled and lifted her lips to show her canines. The man dropped the fresh towels in the dirt and fled.

'Sheeba,' admonished both men.

The ridgeback merely grinned at them, wagged her tail and returned to her bone.

Pat and Erin sat over the camp fire cradling mugs of whisky and spring water. In the distance they could hear the drums beating. Outside the grass fence of the boma, Katoro's slender fingers plucked and flicked at the flat steel keys of his *mbira*. The hollow gourd gave resonance to his delicate music. The two men listened in silence.

'It sounds as if the *mbira* is a woman singing to the male beat of the drums,' said Erin.

'It is the chamber music of Africa,' answered Pat soberly. 'I had no idea that Katoro could make it sing like this. Usually the "African piano" sounds metallic and discordant. He seems to find the depth in his little *mbira* that Anne-Sophie Mutter draws from her violin.'

Katoro had prepared a traditional meal of *sadza* and stew, using the tail of the buffalo which Erin had shot for staff rations a few days before. Warming on the stove was a bowl of deep-fried mopane worms. The harvesting season for this delicacy had almost ended. Pat and Erin both enjoyed the worms with hot *sadza*.

Sheeba lay near the fire, her ears pricked to the sounds of the night, but she never took her eyes from the men's faces.

Erin breathed in deeply. He had wanted to broach this subject ever since his father had assured him that he had no wish to remarry. But he was still a little nervous of giving Pat advice.

'Dad?' he said.

Pat looked up from his plate and frowned. As a child, whenever Erin wanted something he pulled at his fingers. He was doing that now.

'Yes? Out with it, son. What is it that you want?'

Erin looked up at the sky. A sliver of a new moon was sliding across the heavens. It was pale in comparison to the sparkling canopy of stars. He breathed a silent wish as he gazed up at the new moon.

Let Dad accept my suggestion.

'Well?' said Pat.

'Sorry, Dad, I was just wishing on the new moon. I always do it. Mum said it was lucky.'

Pat smiled. 'I do too.'

'Dad, you'll need someone to pamper the guests at Kame Two.' Erin hurried on before Pat could say that Rudo was perfectly capable of doing that. 'Someone to go out with your photo buffs. Someone knowledgeable about photography, birds and animals. Someone attractive to make the men want to come to Kame Two, as well as the women.'

'And you know this paragon?'

'Yes. Briar Hanley.' Erin stopped for a moment to judge Pat's reaction. 'She wants to work and meet people. She is the right age, she's good-looking and she signed no contract with Madden. Briar would never go back to work in Kirk's camp. It would be like living in close proximity to a hyena. She's been with you and Tara at Kame Two. I know she loves the place and you get on well with her.'

Pat nodded slowly. He liked the idea. He had always been fond of Briar. When she was a young girl being courted by Scott, he had looked forward to having her as a member of their household. Now she had grown into a beautiful and capable woman. He had seen a lot of her whilst she nursed Rudo. He would certainly miss her if she left Kame Two and worked for a tour company.

'Ask her quickly before she commits herself to something else,' urged Erin. 'I hear that another new company is starting a white-water rafting venture and looking for someone like her.'

Pat kicked one of the mopane logs, pushing it further into the flames. It cracked and spat. The resin, which contains turpentine, exploded into a fountain of gold and yellow sparks. Pat watched the display until his eyes ached and the fire died to a glow of red coals.

'Good idea, son,' he said.

Erin looked up at the heavens. It seemed to him as if the stars were smiling.

Thanks, he said silently.

The two men walked side by side to their grass huts with Sheeba leading the way.

Erin was desperate to show his father how good the hunting was on New Ganyani. They had picked up buffalo spoor early that morning at the hot springs. The buffalo had been wounded, as they found a few blood spots.

Pat, Erin and the two trackers now stopped short of the sprawling clump of jesse bush. The intertwining grey branches were tangled as hag's hair and equally uninviting. Jacob stepped down and scooped up a handful of dust. He trickled it through his fingers. Pat, Erin and Jonas then repeated the ceremony.

The slight breeze was holding steady, but they all knew

that once they were in the cathedral-like confines of the combretum the wind would eddy and swing, teasing their eyesight and testing their nerves as they sought an elusive blood spot on the edge of a twig or painting a fallen leaf.

Jacob studied the buffalo spoor once again before taking up his position at the head of the line. Pat and Erin checked their rifles. Each chambered a shot. The spare ammunition was tucked into canvas belts around their waists. Jonas took his place at the rear. It would be his duty to see that they were not ambushed.

The spoor told the trackers that the animal was in pain. It was not moving easily. If it sensed that they were following it, the buffalo might walk in a circle and wait for them. The hunted would become the cunning hunter.

Pat had no wish to see Erin, or his trackers, gored and tossed by the massive four-foot-long curved horns of a buffalo weighing one and a half thousand pounds. He knew that while they might sound, smell and look like cattle, African buffaloes had killed more hunters than any other animal.

He was holding his breath as he placed each foot carefully in the prints made by Jacob. In this way, he hoped, the animal would hear only one twig crack or one of the winged fruits crunch, instead of two separate sounds.

They were now deep in the jesse bush. Jacob held up his hand. The men froze as if playing the childhood game of statues. Jacob let more sand filter through his fingers. It swirled in a soft cloud, giving the men no direction. Jacob did not move. Only his head turned slowly from side to side. His eyes were wide as they tried to penetrate the gloom.

Erin shifted his weight from one foot to the other. Jacob flattened his hand, the sign to stop all movement. His hand moved so slowly that Erin wondered whether he had signalled at all.

Eternity seemed to stand still with them. Erin could smell the rank odour of their perspiration. He dared not wipe the stinging droplets from his eyes.

Pat longed to straighten his back and rub his neck. They ached after hours of bending low to avoid the lattice of overhead branches. The absolute quiet was ominous. Danger and death seemed very near. Jacob was his geiger counter. He fixed his eyes on Jacob's hands.

Jacob's forefinger rose from his side and pointed to the right. Pat squeezed his eyes tight to clear them, then stared to the right. Nothing moved. He was just about to look away when a movement, quick as the dart of a dragonfly, caught his attention. There were still some leaves on the jesse bush and he was unable to see what had alerted Jacob. Some of the leaves seemed to be flecked with the buffalo's blood, but they were only stained the dark red of autumn.

Pat studied the spot. No other flicker or bulky outline gave away the presence of an animal. He saw his son raise a finger, showing that he had seen the buffalo. The animal had betrayed its presence with a twitch of an ear. Still Pat could not distinguish the massive creature. It had become part of the jesse.

He knew it was watching them, waiting to explode into a killing rage to relieve itself of the pain it did not understand and could not bear.

As Pat searched the jesse, the almost impenetrable branches splintered and the buffalo, its head held high, burst out grunting and coughing with rage. Pat and Erin raised their rifles as if in a practised pattern. Pat's four-sixteen Rigby rang out a few seconds before Jacob heard the shot from Erin's four-five-eight Lott.

Both bullets struck deep into the animal's shoulder. Yet it thundered on, breaking through the jesse as if cracking matchsticks.

The rifles repeated their death calls, but the buffalo showed no visible signs of weakening.

Erin's last shot rang out. Pat knew he would have to reload. They had both chambered a shot, and had three in the magazine when they entered the jesse. He raised his Rigby and aimed low in the shoulder, hoping to smash bone and penetrate the buffalo's heart and lungs.

The animal turned and headed straight for Pat. He had no time to reload. Erin would have to try to break the enraged animal's shoulder to bring it down and that meant shooting close to his father.

Pat could smell the rank cattle and dung odour as the bull bore down on him. Now it seemed to gallop in slow motion. He had time to assess the spread horns where they splayed across the animal's forehead and formed a solid battering ram. Its boss was black, rounded and formidable.

Erin's hands were steady as he took aim. The animal had dropped its head and its ears almost brushed the ground. It was ready to use its horns to impale and toss its adversary.

Pat saw Jacob standing beside Erin, ready with fresh ammunition. It's too late, he thought. The charge is over. The bull is coming in for the kill.

Suddenly his feet were knocked from under him and his head hit the ground. He felt his teeth jar. Pain shot up his neck and into his skull, blinding him. There was an enormous weight on his legs. He was paralysed.

'Dad!' screamed Erin. 'Dad, can you hear me?'

Pat struggled to open his eyes. His son needed him. He had to get up. He struggled to stand and panic took over. He could not move. As if in a dream, he heard Jonas say, 'Help us get the *nyati* off his legs before the weight breaks his bones.'

Pat smiled. His wife was kissing him softly on the mouth, her lips sweet and cool. He sighed in happiness and opened his eyes.

Erin was bending over him, dribbling water into his mouth and dabbing his face with a wet cloth.

'Thank goodness you're all right, Dad. We were so worried about you. Jacob has gone to fetch the truck so you don't have to walk.'

Pat was about to protest, but as he sat up the jesse tilted sickeningly around him. He leaned against Erin gratefully.

'Thank you, son.'

'It died as it hit your feet, Dad,' said Erin. He suddenly felt nauseous and held the water bottle to his lips for a long time.

'It's not that difficult to kill a buffalo,' said Pat, watching Erin drink. 'The hard part is persuading the animal that it's dead. I've seen them continue a charge when their heart and lungs have been pulped. They shouldn't have been able to blink.'

He pulled himself away from Erin's embrace and felt his head gingerly.

'Jacob,' he called. 'Come and help me up.'

Jacob and Erin knew it would be no use remonstrating with him so they each took an arm and helped him to stand. He held on to them for a few moments and then hobbled towards the buffalo. 'Where was this poor thing wounded?'

'We haven't looked, Dad. Our only concern was to get you out from under it.'

Pat walked around the buffalo. The hum of bluebottles was loud. Ticks and parasites scurried from the body cooling in death.

The jesse held the stench of blood and cordite in its grey branches. The brush had become a temple to the sacrifice of the bull.

'Here,' called Pat, holding up the buffalo's tail. 'Look at this.'

'*Shumba*,' said Jacob, tracing the deep, racking claw marks down the animal's rump.

'Yes, she must have jumped on to its rump and either lost her hold or been shaken off.'

'But not before she opened the skin,' said Erin, wrinkling his nose at the smell of putrefaction which came from the gaping wounds.

'Done some time ago,' said Pat. 'Maggots are in already.' He dug at one of the long wounds with a twig broken from the jesse. White, limbless grubs fell on to his boots. 'It must have suffered the torments of Hades with every fly and blood-sucking insect homing in on it.'

'Those cats have claws like razors,' said Erin, 'yet these old buffalo-skin boots of mine have lasted for years. Nothing ever seems to scratch them.'

'Your boots couldn't resist the power that cats have in their forelegs when they strike,' answered Pat with a smile.

'Here's Jacob.'

They looked up. Jacob was reversing the Toyota as close to the jesse as he could. The buffalo would be winched on the back of the hunting vehicle and taken to New Ganyani. It would provide meat for the staff for weeks.

'Erin,' said Jacob quietly, 'I have found tracks. The ones we have looked for since the last full moon.'

Before the buffalo hunt the news would have filled Erin with excitement, but now he felt only weariness.

They had found animals caught in poachers' traps and wires the length of the river bank, but until today there had been no sign of the poachers.

'How old?' asked Erin.

'The prints are only a few hours old. They are walking to Nzou Trees.'

Erin knew the sandy spit well. The river gouged an S-bed across the land and enormous acacia trees had dipped their deep roots into the wet soil. When the long pods ripened, the place rumbled to the contented feasting of elephant herds.

'We'll have to ask Dad to drive the Toyota back to New Ganyani with Jonas,' said Erin.

Jacob shook his head. 'We need Jonas with us. Two cannot surprise and capture poachers. The tracks show four, maybe five men.'

Erin was about to protest when Pat joined them.

'If that's what you two consider to be whispering, the poachers at Nzou Trees will hear you.'

Jacob and Jonas exchanged knowing glances. The Old One still had the ears of a young man.

'I will take the buffalo back to camp then meet you at Nzou Trees.'

'You don't know where they are, Dad,' said Erin.

Jonas shuffled his feet uncomfortably and Jacob busied himself with securing the buffalo on the back of the truck.

Pat realized that for the first time he was not in control of the situation. New Ganyani belonged to his son and Erin would make the decisions. He felt as if he had lost something precious. His son would no longer rely on him. His baby boy was a man.

As if sensing his father's dismay, Erin said loudly, 'What do you think we should do, Dad? I feel we have to follow this spoor. It's the first time we've found anything less than a week old.'

Pat wanted to hug Erin.

'Having that old buff lie down on me was a bit tiring. I think you should get on to the spoor immediately. I'll see if Katoro can pour a decent whisky. A little Scottish water and a hot shower should have me ready to drive your poachers to the police post tomorrow.'

As they were about to leave, he called Jacob. 'Here,' he said, 'you may need this. Look after my son. Today he is a man. But parents always see their young as children.'

Jacob took Pat's Rigby reverently. Erin was stunned. His father never let anyone touch his rifles.

'Drop that and you are a dead man,' teased Erin.

Erin's mother had dubbed Pat's gun room 'the chapel'. She said that he spent as much time in there loading bullets and cleaning his rifles as a novice spent on his knees praying in a monastery.

Erin and the trackers stood by the matted jesse until the beige Toyota had bumped and lurched into the distance, then they turned and headed west. Soon they broke into the natural swing of walking in the bush. The only stops they made were to check the human footprints they were following. Two of the poachers wore shoes with rubber soles. The ridges were clearly defined in the sand. The other two were barefoot, but one limped and seemed to have his foot bandaged.

'With a little luck he caught his foot in one of his own traps,' said Erin bitterly.

After a while, Jacob stopped and pointed ahead. Standing at one of the shallow pans was a solitary elephant. The human footprints seemed to lead straight to the pan.

'The weak one needed to drink,' said Jacob.

'We cannot wait for the *nzou* to drink and dust himself,' said Erin. 'We must move fast if we are to catch up with the men.'

They all studied the massive elephant. None of them wanted a confrontation, but to skirt around it meant losing the spoor and taking hours to cut back on to it.

The elephant swayed from side to side as if enclosed in a cage. Its skin hung in loose folds.

Erin ran his binoculars over its head and trunk. He gasped and handed the binoculars to Jacob, who merely nodded and passed them to Jonas.

'It has not eaten or had water for many days,' Jacob said, pointing to the raw band of pink flesh from which dangled the tip of the beast's trunk. 'He put his trunk in a noose meant for another, not an elephant.'

Erin's finger itched to pull the trigger and put the great animal out of its agony. He could not bear to stand by and watch it try to suck up water with the almost severed tip of its proboscis.

The elephant seemed to sense their presence and tried to lift its trunk to suck in the air and smell their odour, but it gave up and let the tip hang helplessly.

'It's taken twenty million years for the elephant to develop that multi-purpose trunk. Without it he's dead. He uses it to breathe, smell, feel, gather food, drink and keep his body free from parasites,' raged Erin. 'Now some idiot sets a line of snares and almost cuts it off.'

Jacob touched Erin on the arm.

'I know how you feel. We too respect the great grey

men of the bush. But if you shoot him you'll lose your hunter's licence. That means we all lose New Ganyani.'

'Let us talk,' said Jonas.

The three men squatted in the shade of an acacia tree.

'It has to be shot,' said Erin.

'I agree,' said Jonas. 'But we ought to report it to the Department of National Parks. They send a ranger to make sure that the animal cannot be saved. Papers then have to be signed and permission given to shoot it.'

'By that time the grey man will be miles away or dead,' answered Jacob.

Jacob and Jonas exchanged a long look and then nodded. They had silently agreed on a course of action.

'I am not a hunter, merely a tracker,' said Jacob, drawing a circle in the dust with a stick. 'I do not hold a hunter's licence. I also have the Rigby.'

'It was fate that made the Old Man give it to you,' pronounced Jonas. 'The spirits knew that you would have need of it today.'

Erin shook his head, but was silent.

'Your father ordered me to look after you when he put the rifle in my hands,' said Jacob. 'It is only right that I shoot the elephant.'

'They will think poachers killed it,' said Jonas persuasively. 'You will not lose your licence and your conscience will be clear. You will have saved the old bull from a long slow death.'

The men looked across the pan of green water to where the elephant swayed. It tried again to slurp water with the delicate tip of its mangled trunk. Its grey skin hung in deep folds below its tail as if it was an old man unable to keep his trousers up.

Erin felt his eyes burn. He could shoot animals. He could watch overseas hunters shoot animals, but he could not watch an animal suffer.

'Jacob, shoot it. Put it out of its misery. Do it quickly. It's presenting a perfect broadside.'

Erin had often seen Jacob shoot. He was an excellent shot, yet he still coached him.

'Remember, aim for the bottom of the ear slit and then move your sights about two inches over.'

Erin wanted a brain shot. A quick death. He knew that even though an elephant has a large head in relation to the rest of its massive body, the brain is only four times the size of a human brain. The bone tissue between the inner and outer tables of the skull is filled with cavities and air cells and it is easy to miss the brain and have the bullet lodge in the cancellous area.

Jacob raised the Rigby and took his time perfecting his aim. Erin wanted to shout at him, terrified that the elephant would turn away and present them with a more difficult shot. But the old bull was weak and in too much pain to move around. He had found water and was desperate to feel the cool liquid trickle down his throat.

Even though Erin had been expecting the shot, he jumped as it cracked in his ears. As he watched, the elephant stood still for a second, absorbing the shock, then crashed over like a tower block imploding. It lifted its mutilated trunk to the heavens as if searching for a reason for the pain. Then all was quiet.

The men waited for the dust to settle before cautiously approaching the elephant. Many were the tales told around camp fires of dead animals suddenly exploding into life at the approach of the hunter.

'The old grey man has gone to join the others in a place where rivers are full and the grass is green,' said Jacob.

Erin pulled up a handful of Rhodes grass and placed the red-tufted spikelets into the elephant's mouth.

'For your journey,' he said as they turned away. It was a custom Pat had taught him when he shot his first antelope: 'Always respect the animal whose life you have taken.'

Erin turned to Jacob. 'Thank you,' he said soberly.

Jacob merely nodded. They formed a single file.

'They are less than two hours ahead,' said Jacob, kneeling to examine the broken stem of a flame lily which trailed down from an ochre clay anthill.

Erin bent down and snapped off the flower. Its wavy petals formed a cup of glowing red merging into gold at the stem. He tucked it into his ammunition belt and hurried to catch up with Jacob.

'There are the Nzou Trees,' said the tracker.

The circle of huge acacias rose up tall and flat-crowned ahead of them. The men had walked fast. Now they paused for a mouthful of water.

'They are not aware that we are here,' said Jacob, once again examining the footprints. 'Blood is coming through the bandage of the one with the bad foot. He has slowed them down.'

'They will check their trap lines at the river,' said Jonas. 'That will take some time, as they must untangle and kill the animals which have not yet died of thirst or been strangled to death.'

Erin felt a cold, killing rage cloud his reason.

'Kill them,' he said. 'They must die just like the animals which have been tortured in the snares.'

'Erin,' reasoned Jacob. 'It will be better for you to stay here on this hill. Then you can whistle to let us know if they see us and attempt to run. Jonas and I will walk the horns of the *nyati* and take them on either side.'

Erin was about to protest when Jacob smiled.

'We are black and could be rich poachers. Poachers with guns and uniforms. There are many today who pose as rangers, but fill their pockets by selling ivory and rhino horn. This way we will have them. You are a good hunter, but for this work you are the wrong colour.'

Erin grinned. 'You win. I'll stay here, but only until you have them.'

Silently as wind whispering in the grass, the trackers vanished. Erin scanned the river bank with his binoculars. Nothing moved. The poachers seemed to have disappeared as completely as his trackers.

He heard a faint rustle and scratching on a rock behind him. Slowly he turned his head, expecting to look into the muzzle of an AK-47. Instead a pair of beady eyes regarded him steadily. After a few moments the monitor lizard decided that it had outstared him and could leave. Erin watched the predatory lizard drag its scaly body over the rock and slide into a deep crevice. It resembled a reptile conjured up by producers of science fiction movies. He shuddered and returned his attention to the stand of acacia trees and the river.

Suddenly the wild, haunting call of a fish eagle rang out. It meant, 'Come, all is clear. It is safe.'

Erin hurried to the river. As he neared the bank he saw a group of men who had been hidden from him by the thick scrub.

Four men huddled on the ground, their hands clasped over their heads. Jacob and Jonas stood over them triumphantly. It had been a perfect hunt. The men had not realized that the trackers were near until the Rigby was pointed at them. Unarmed and terrified, they now sat shivering. The whites of their eyes rolled up and they dared not raise their heads to look at Jacob and Jonas who were heaping scorn and abuse on them.

Erin jogged towards the group. He was still sickened by the mutilation of the elephant. He wanted these men to suffer.

'Tell them to get up,' he commanded. 'They can show us where their trap lines are laid, then they can undo them, roll up the wire and carry it all back to New Ganyani.'

Jacob and Jonas smiled. This was the sort of justice they understood.

The poachers, tied together and carrying rolls of wire around their necks, would stumble and fall as they struggled to keep up with the trackers, unable to use their hands to help them. Their shoulders would soon ache unbearably as the knots Jacob tied tightened and pulled their arms together behind their backs.

They stood jerkily, like puppets on broken strings, at Jacob's command.

The one with the bandaged foot looked up into Erin's face. Urine stained his torn shorts and trickled down his leg, soaking into the bloodied bandage. Erin looked away. He was suddenly ashamed to be the cause of another man's abasement. His anger was turning to pity. He looked at the poachers, who stood with their heads bowed, and their hands trembling.

Their limbs were as thin and brittle as kindling twigs. The rags they wore covered only parts of their dusty shrunken bodies.

'These men are not the vultures who get fat on selling

meat,' Erin said to Jacob. 'Look at their clothes. Look at their shoes.' The canvas shoes were as torn and old as their clothes.

'The police will discover whether the snares were set for meat for their families or for the men from the city,' answered Jacob in Shona so that the poachers would understand.

'I hate poaching, but I can understand starving men without rifles catching animals to eat and to keep their children alive. There may be money and cars in the cities, but here they need food and medical care.'

Jacob and Jonas shook their heads. They did not understand this softness in Erin.

'Poachers know that the animals are like cattle, they must be protected. If they take the risk of setting snares they must also take the risk of being caught,' said Jonas.

'But we all know that the lazy one at the police post is bored. He has no work to do and no one comes to check on him. He is drunk from when the sun rises until it sets,' argued Erin in English. 'He will beat these men until they cannot stand. He will then throw them into that tin hut, where they will bake by day and freeze in the night. If he remembers, he will radio through to the police in Harare. They will spend another day or two stamping papers. Finally these men will be taken to Harare and sentenced.'

The poachers stood still. They did not understand the language but sensed that their fate was being decided.

'You cannot have pity for both people and animals,' said Jacob.

'Today I pity everything in Africa,' answered Erin softly.

Jonas wandered away towards the river. Erin knew that his tracker was right. When they had found a kudu cow caught in a wire noose and she had looked up at them with huge liquid eyes filled with agony and incomprehension, he had wanted to kill any and every poacher he could find. Now, with four terrified, skeletal men in his power, he felt only compassion.

Jonas whistled. Jacob went to join him at the sand spit leading down to the water.

'Jacob says will you go and see what is in the snare,' said Jonas, returning to Erin. 'I'll look after these hyenas.'

Erin nodded and went over to where Jacob squatted on the sand. His mouth set in a straight hard line as he looked down at the wire drawn into a tight bracelet around the gnawed-off foot of a leopard. The solitary cat had chewed through its leg rather than be held captive in the handcuffs of a snare.

'Get the men to collect the wires and traps. Call me when you're ready,' he said.

He sat on the sand, resting his chin on his knees. He stared across the water and dry sobs shook him.

Oh God, he prayed silently. Let the tsetse and the mosquito turn Africa back into a place where only the most primitive tribes and the hardest can survive. Let the animals once again roam this great continent, moving only to the song of the seasons.

Even as his thoughts formed, he realized that man, whether dangerous or kind, is the only creature all animals fear.

For a moment he felt a deep hatred for the Africa he loved.

You are a harsh land full of contradictions, his mind raged. We have made sanctuaries to protect the animals and now have to kill what we love, to stop them destroying their own refuges.

Jacob whistled to let Erin know that they were ready.

He walked to the river's edge and splashed water over his head. It felt cool as it trickled over his face and seemed to cleanse the turmoil in his mind.

'Untie their hands,' he said as he approached the four men. 'Leave the rope linking them together, but let them use their hands to carry the wire.'

Jacob and Jonas obeyed, but the rigidity in their shoulders and necks showed their displeasure.

'Tell the men to take us to their village. We will search it for horns and skins and perhaps we'll find the "fat one" who pays these men to run snare lines,' said Erin.

'Today the traps are empty. They have reaped only a leopard's paw,' said Jacob. 'But who knows what they usually find?'

'They have not shown us all the traps,' suggested Jonas. 'There are more hidden deep in the bush. They have shown us only enough to satisfy you.'

Erin knew that Jonas was right, but he merely said, 'Let's move, I want to see the village before dark.'

They had walked for a little less than an hour when the shrill calls of children alerted them that they were approaching the village.

Jacob and Jonas moved up beside the men and warned them that they would be shot if they raised the alarm and gave the villagers time to hide the horns and skins.

The poachers were too afraid to lift their heads. The children noticed the men shuffling into the small village, as if part of a slave gang. They ran screaming to their mothers, who disappeared into the huts.

Erin fired a shot into the air.

'Call for the headman,' he said to Jacob.

Within minutes, a figure whose belly belied the poverty

suggested by his hastily donned rags emerged from one of the huts.

'He eats well, this one,' said Jacob in a whisper. 'Let us search his hut first.'

Erin ordered Jacob and Jonas to conduct the search. The headman blustered, threatened and then became belligerent. But when Jonas appeared in the doorway holding a fine set of roan antelope horns in his hands, the headman sank on to the small carved stool outside his hut and held his head in his hands.

The roan antelope is an endangered and protected species. He knew that he would spend a year or so in jail. He also knew that the man to whom he supplied the horns and hides would disown him. He was alone and could expect no help.

His creased face when he looked up at Erin seemed about to crack, like mud baking in the sun. Tears trickled down his cheeks as he looked around his little village. His wife came and threw herself at Erin's feet, while the remaining women ululated and children wailed.

Erin turned away. He knew that most of it was stage-managed to sway him, but his heart ached for the people and their poverty.

This must be done, he told himself, otherwise within the next sixty years over fifty per cent of the animals in Africa will become extinct. They have to learn to protect the game.

He looked up at the sky, to avoid seeing the huge, terrified eyes of the ragged urchins and pleading mothers and wives.

'How can conservation take root when poverty and over-population increase daily?' he muttered to Jacob.

'Children and cattle are a man's wealth,' the tracker answered. 'Without them a man is nothing.'

'Without animals and the wild plains they live in, Africa is nothing,' said Erin softly.

Jacob and Erin watched as Jonas emerged from a hut, dusting thatching grass from his hair. He held a second pair of horns.

'You will not see the light of the sun again,' said Jonas to the headman of the small village. 'You will remain in jail until you die.'

'Do not look back,' advised Jacob as they left the village. He was afraid that Erin would weaken and release the men. 'The pots on the fires all have meat cooking. They have taken many animals. Now they cry because they must pay for it.'

Erin sniffed the air. The rank smell was of meat which had lain in the sun too long.

'You are right, Jacob,' he said. 'But they have not eaten today. The headman may have, but the others have no flesh on their bones. Give these poachers a meal and let them sleep in camp tonight. They may as well have a full belly when they face the police tomorrow.'

'The police in Harare are not like the lazy one in uniform, *bere*,' hissed Jonas to the poachers as he tugged at the knots holding their wrists together. 'You will tell them who pays you to trap our animals. You will show them all your lines and snares.'

'They will kill you if you lie,' added Jacob.

'And we will kill you if we see you in our hunting area again,' said Jonas. 'This is our land now. This is New Ganyani. You know you cannot have villages in our concession area. So if the police don't kill you in Harare, then move away from here when you return.'

The poachers winced and rubbed their wrists as circulation returned bringing pain with it. Jacob loaded the heavy horns on to the headman.

'You receive the money. You carry them,' he said. 'If you don't move away from this area we'll find you and the *bere* can crunch your bones.'

The men looked around fearfully as if expecting to see the spotted hyena, pet of witches, behind the trackers.

Chapter Twenty-four

PAT GIFFORD stood on the verandah of the old farmhouse on Kame Two. The floor was made of wood and was not as cool to his bare feet as the cement verandah at Kame had been.

As he gazed to the east, he no longer saw the white spray over the Falls. Instead the dull thunder was replaced with birdsong and the soft chatter of camp staff as they warmed themselves over their cooking fires.

Winter had stripped the mopane trees. The leaves, brown, tan and dull gold, lay thick on the ground. Pat had thrown a gilet over his long-sleeved cotton shirt, the only concession he made to the season. He still wore khaki shorts and his legs were bare.

New Ganyani and Kame Two had exceeded all expectations. Both camps were fully booked for the whole of the winter and well into the following summer.

Erin had flown to Johannesburg and bought a second-hand Cessna. The reason he gave was that clients felt safer if there was a plane at the camp to fly them out, in case of an emergency. Pat knew the real reason for the purchase was so that Erin could visit Kame Two and a certain Italian nursing sister more often. He had seen Erin and Tara's friendship deepen, during the time she and Briar were on Kame Two nursing Rudo back to health, and it delighted him. He loved the joy with which Tara embraced life. She scrambled up and down the steep ravines in Chizarira looking for the Taita falcons, heedless of mopane flies, ants or snakes. She studied bird books showing the robust little falcon with its white throat and black moustachial stripes until she was certain that she would not confuse it with the African hobby, another small falcon. She did not want to appear uninformed in front of the clients. She had a love for the bush usually shown only by those born in the country.

Rudo had taken on the task of teaching her to speak Sindebele and Tara surprised her tutor with her quick grasp of the language. Her friendship with Briar had deepened and the two women were almost inseparable. The farmhouse was now filled with song and laughter.

Pat did not dare think ahead to a time when Tara would leave and Briar might become bored with the job and return to Fred and Blanche at Inyati.

He depended on Briar totally and could not imagine Kame Two without her. Occasionally in the still, dark hours of the night he tantalized himself with the fantasy of Briar loving him as she had loved Scott. But when he totted up the difference in their ages he discarded the idea and punched his pillow, seeking the evasive oblivion of sleep.

Suddenly Briar's laughter rang out loud and clear. Pat spun round and leaned on the verandah railing. The wood was damp under his arms, but he did not feel it. His attention was focused on Briar and Tatton Boyce.

Tatton had booked into Kame Two for a month. He was doing an article for the *National Geographic Magazine* on the Taita falcon. Small and very rare, the bird had the speed of a peregrine and was found only in high gorges along the Zambezi River and in the mountains of Zimbabwe.

Pat watched with dismay as Briar took an obvious delight in Tatton's company. The man was dark with the rugged good looks of an outdoorsman. He spoke well and humorously of various assignments around the world. He was open in his admiration of Briar. They spent more and more time together.

'They make a good couple, don't they?' Tara walked up quietly behind Pat. She had given up hoping that Pat would fall in love with Briar. He seemed content to have her as a member of the staff.

Pat merely grunted. Tatton had put his arm loosely around Briar's shoulders. Pat longed for her to shrug it off, but she seemed happy to stroll down to the river with him as if they were lovers.

Lovers! Oh no, thought Pat. Briar cannot fall in love with Tatton. If she does she will leave me and Kame Two. They will roam the world together. I'll never see her or hear her laugh again. Like the numbness which follows a bullet strike, Pat realized that he needed Briar in his life. Idiot, he said to himself. You deserve to lose her to Tatton. Lose her? You could never have her. You are too old, Pat Gifford. Remember it was your son she loved.

'Sorry, Tara, I was day-dreaming.'

'Pat,' said Tara quietly, 'could I talk to you?'

'Sure.'

'In private.'

She probably wants to return to Milan, thought Pat as he led the way through the house to his office. The Andrettis had phoned again the day before. Tara had looked pale and distraught after the call and would not discuss it with anyone.

'Please sit down, Tara,' said Pat, pulling up an old button-back chair for her.

They sat in silence. Only the regular ticking of the grandfather clock standing in one corner of the large room broke the stillness.

'Pat, my parents want me to return to Milan immediately,' she said in a small voice, looking down at her lap.

Pat waited, but Tara lapsed into silence again.

'I can understand them wanting to have you at home,' he answered, playing with the paper-knife on his desk. 'We'll miss you here. You have been a wonderful friend to Briar.' He paused. 'And to Erin,' he added.

At the mention of Erin's name Tara shifted uneasily in her chair. Then she lifted her chin, squared her shoulders and stared at Pat.

'I told them that I am going to spend the rest of the year at New Ganyani with Erin.' She hurried on before he could compose a reply. 'Erin has asked me to help him run New Ganyani – just as Briar is doing here at Kame Two.' She paused and her huge brown eyes filled with tears. 'Pat, won't you phone them? Tell Papa and Mama that I'll be safe. Tell them what a special man Erin is. Tell them that it's just a job.'

She pulled her fingers. The gesture, so like Erin's when he wanted something, decided Pat.

'Papa is so angry. He says I am an Andretti and have a duty to be at home. I hate Milan. I want to stay here. Please, Pat, help me.'

Pat had already lifted the phone.

'Let's see if the lines are in order today and I'll do it now,' he said.

Tara flew around the table which served as a desk and flung her arms across his neck.

'Oh thank you, Pat. I love you.'

The door burst open. Briar, Tatton and Rudo filled the doorway.

'Sorry,' said Briar, overhearing the last part of the conversation. 'I didn't know you were busy.' She felt sick and hurt. Tara had given her no hint of her feelings for Pat. Briar had thought that she and Pat had a special friendship. Now it had fallen apart. He and Tara were in love.

'Come,' she said, hooking her arm through Tatton's. 'I can smell bacon frying and I'm starving.'

'Breakfast is on the table,' said Rudo with a disapproving look at Tara.

Mr Pat is for Briar, she thought. Tara knows that. Why is she taking him away? She sighed as she closed the door quietly.

'Men are creatures not to be understood,' she muttered. 'He has a good woman, Briar, but like a monkey who stretches out for the melon which is brightly coloured, he reaches for one who is younger.'

Briar and Tatton looked up from their plates as Rudo swept through the dining room and into her kitchen.

'Oh dear,' whispered Briar. 'We'll have to tread carefully today.' She giggled as Tatton stood up and tiptoed to the sideboard to heap scrambled eggs and bacon on his plate.

She found Tatton Boyce both attractive and fun to be with. He was her senior by only nine years. In a strange way she was reliving her youth through him. She felt young and carefree in his company.

Tatton was a loner and happy in his chosen profession. He needed to roam the world. He had formed the occasional attachment, but did not want to settle down and have children.

Briar Hanley was breaking down his resolve. He found to his dismay that he enjoyed the days when she was present more than when he was alone with the scouts or with Pat and Tara. He wanted to hear her voice in the mornings and had discovered that, if he rose early, he could join her on her morning walk to the river. She was becoming much too important and he could not control his desire to be near her.

Pat had found the Taita falcon for him and he knew that he had some excellent shots of the bird. Yet he extended his stay, explaining that the magazine had asked for extra shots as they planned to make the little falcon a major feature in the next issue.

Pat paused with his hand on the knob of the dining-room door. Briar's laughter pealed out, accompanied by Tatton's deeper guffaws. She looked up as Pat and Tara entered the room then turned her attention back to wiping a marmalade moustache from Tatton's face.

'I keep telling Tatton,' she said to Pat and Tara, 'that if he insists on putting two inches of marmalade on his toast, then he must learn to open his mouth wider when he bites into it.'

Tara merely smiled. The telephone line had been down and Pat was unable to contact the Andrettis. He was her only hope. She was certain that her mother and father would allow her to remain if he spoke to them personally. Secretly she had decided that she would go to New Ganyani with or without her parents' approval. But Tara

233

was sensible enough to realize that she would not enjoy her time with Erin if she knew that her father, whom she adored, was angry.

Briar took Tara's silence at breakfast as a sign that she was embarrassed at having been found with her arms around Pat.

Pat too was quiet, disliking the growing intimacy between Briar and Tatton. He was also worried about the implications he could face with the authorities should the Andrettis give Tara permission to stay and work at New Ganyani. They could hardly pretend she was a visitor when the local people saw her working in the camp and with the hunters. Soon the awkward matter of a work permit would arise. She would have to apply for a permit in a country where almost forty per cent of the population were unemployed.

Suddenly Pat was aware that Briar had been speaking and he had not heard one word.

'I'm sorry, Briar, my thoughts were elsewhere,' he apologized with a smile. 'You were saying?'

'That I thought it would be a pleasant break for Tatton if I took him down to the Fig Tree Camp tonight,' replied Briar. 'He's climbed up and down mountains for three weeks. I'm sure he'd enjoy a night in our tented camp at the river.'

Pat Gifford sought desperately for a reason to stop Briar from going with Tatton, but his mind was an obstinate blank.

'What a good idea,' said Tara innocently. 'It would be a break for you too, Briar. You've been working so hard. I can easily stand in for you.'

No, no, Pat wanted to shout but he merely nodded.

'Set it up, Briar,' he said. 'The lines are down again and

I need to put a call through to Milan. Tara and I will fly across to the office at Chizarira and see if we have better luck there.'

Tara grinned happily.

'Oh thank you, Pat,' she said. 'It'll mean so much to me if we can talk to Mamma and Papa today.'

Briar felt her smile freeze on her face. It was true. They were going to be married. There could be no other reason to phone the Andrettis so soon after their call to Tara.

She pushed back her chair. She had to leave the room. Tears were pushing at her eyelids and she would not let them shame her.

'Excuse me,' she croaked, 'I must make arrangements for tonight.' She turned back at the door. 'I hope the phone is working up there. See you later, Tatton.'

The meal was finished in silence, with everyone engrossed in their own thoughts. They left the room as Rudo came in to clear the plates away.

Briar and Tatton reached the tented camp in the late afternoon. Tatton had asked her to stop on the way as he wanted shots of the enormous termitaria, the fortress homes of termites.

Briar knew of one with twin spires, which would shelter more termites than a large city would house people. Tatton was fascinated by the puny creatures who, given their size, built homes to equal pyramids or skyscrapers.

The photographer spent some time wriggling the pointed end of his tripod into the base of the 'anthill'.

'This stuff is like cement,' he groused as he checked his light meter.

'It's actually excrement which has passed through several

termites,' said Briar, then laughed as the expression of disbelief on his face. 'They pass food to each other either by mouth or via their tail ends. By the time the excrement has been through a few termites, only a dark brown paste remains. That is their building cement. You can see how effective it is.'

'It certainly takes care of any sewerage problems,' answered Tatton, standing away from the camera to check the shot he had composed.

'They also eat all the corpses and old skins,' said Briar. 'So the insides of termitaria are kept perfectly clean.'

Tatton shaded his eyes and shook his head.

'Mum and I used to collect the small black termite mounds and throw them into the fowl pens. The result was a frenzy of feasting.' Briar smiled at Tatton. 'Our chickens loved them. I must admit that when I was at boarding school we used to wait for the termites to fly after a good rain. We would catch them as they milled around on top of the mound. They were probably confused and blinded by the light. We'd rip off their heads and tails and eat them. They tasted a little like condensed milk.'

'Ugh,' said Tatton.

'One day I'll catch some for you,' threatened Briar.

'You are impossible, Briar Hanley,' he said, 'but I would like you to be at my side always.'

Briar did not answer. She merely stared at him.

Tatton placed his hands on her shoulders.

'I should not have said that, Briar, but I mean it,' he said. 'I cannot offer you marriage because I am too restless. The great wilderness calls me constantly. I know that I am not good husband material, but I sense that you and I are kindred spirits.'

Still Briar said nothing.

'I can offer you an exciting life. I can offer you love and laughter. We can roam the world hand in hand. There is nothing for you here, Briar. Come with me '

'You have another week at Kame Two, Tatton. It sounds a wonderful idea, but I must think about it.'

Briar lifted her face as Tatton enfolded her in his arms. She liked him but something was wrong. There was no feeling. It was merely a pleasant kiss and hug.

You are still romanticizing what you felt with Scott, she told herself. Over the years you have made yourself believe that angels sang every time you kissed. You know nothing about adult love. This is all there is.

'Briar, you are so lovely,' said Tatton huskily.

See, she thought silently, Tatton found it exciting. She swallowed nervously as Kirk's sneering face slid into her mind. Perhaps I'll never again feel anything for anyone, she thought. Kirk has probably killed my natural feelings for ever.

A cold fist clenched her stomach muscles and she wanted to cry.

'I want to love you,' she whispered.

'You will, Briar. You will,' promised Tatton.

She tucked away all thoughts of a possible future with Tatton as she drove into the camp.

'It's too good to be true,' said Tatton, looking at the neat green tents pitched in the shade of a dramatic wild fig tree. Butterflies fluttered over the round fig fruits.

'I suppose it does look a little theatrical,' Briar admitted. 'But where else could one find so perfect a setting?'

The camp was quiet. Briar knew that only a family from Geneva was booked in for the night which meant she and Tatton could have separate tents. They would not have to share the partitioned staff tent.

She called to the man who ran the camp to help unload the Land Rover, then cursed under her breath as she realized that she had left her rifle at the farmhouse. Mentally she worked out how long it would take her to fetch the three-seven-five, but discarded the idea when she saw the game scout with a rifle slung over his shoulder shepherding the Swiss family back to camp.

Briar ordered hot water to be put into the shower drum for Tatton and went out to meet the clients. They were in good humour as they had seen crocodiles and a hippopotamus with a baby.

The scout called Briar aside as the family sat themselves at the tea table.

'Do you have your rifle?' he asked.

'No. I left it up at Kame Two. Why? You have yours.'

'I do,' answered the scout. 'But the grandfather tried to climb on to that branch which overhangs the hippo pool for a better photograph of the baby. The mother had hidden it in the grass at the edge of the water.'

Briar clucked in disapproval.

'I grasped for his arm to drag him back and dropped my rifle.'

'Yes?'

'The bolt seems to have jammed. I can't use it.'

Briar uttered an unladylike oath.

'Rifles are made for rough handling,' she said. 'I wonder why this one should have jammed. I'm sure Pat will be able to fix it.'

The scout nodded but still looked worried.

'Of all times to have forgotten mine,' she said.

'It's been very quiet here,' said the scout. 'We've had no trouble at all.'

'Don't speak too soon,' said Briar, crossing her fingers.

'Don't worry. It's the last night at the river camp for the Swiss. I'm sure we'll manage.'

'They didn't annoy the hippo, did they?' she asked, as they walked back to the party at the tea table.

Her father held very strong views on hippopotami, believing that they were the most dangerous animals in the African bush. He cited dozens of cases where little herd-boys looking for stray cattle had wandered into the reed beds and been cut in half by the flattened shear-like edges of the tusks of angry hippo. Hippo were always dangerous when cut off from the river.

Briar remembered, as a small child, hearing of neighbours whose boat had been attacked by an irate hippo cow. She had been walking on one of the hippo trails under water with her offspring. As the people fell screaming into the river she had killed all of them.

'The hippo was agitated,' said the scout, 'but I don't think she will leave the area. The calf is still very young.'

Briar nodded and fixed a smile across her lips as she approached the family. They had finished the last of the fruit cake and emptied the teapot. She advised them to anoint themselves with mosquito repellent after they had showered as the camp was near the river. Though the evenings were cold up at Kame Two, it was warmer down in the valley. She did not want any latent cases of malaria developing once they returned to Geneva.

The African sun was setting in a great red ball of fiery splendour. The orb seemed to fill the sky and turn the river to blood.

Briar joined Tatton, who was engrossed in his light meter readings as the sky changed from sparkling gold to bronze.

She stood beside him quietly, knowing that he did not

have long to capture the beauty. Already the trees were etched starkly black against a crimson backdrop. She stared at the sinking sun until her eyes ached, longing to imprint the colours on her brain for ever. Soon the sun would drop below the horizon with the rapidity of the shutter closing on his camera. In the distance sonorous roars joined by deep laughter told of the hippopotami leaving the water to graze along the river banks through the night.

The faint smell of woodsmoke curling and twisting among the branches of the gigantic wild fig prodded Briar from her reverie. She left Tatton and made her way to the kitchen, which was screened from the camp by a green tarpaulin sheet.

The Swiss family were to eat curried *kapenta* fish followed by crocodile tail stewed in tomatoes and onion. Whole pumpkins and sweet potatoes were roasting in the coals. The flesh would be scooped out and sprinkled with garlic oil. There would be bread baked in an old tin trunk. For dessert the cook had resorted to bread and butter pudding smothered with custard.

Briar had misgivings about the crocodile tails. Only a few hours previously the family had watched what Briar considered to be loathsome creatures. Like her, the cook hated crocodiles. He enjoyed feeding the tails, which tasted like a cross between lobster and chicken, to the guests at Fig Tree Camp.

When Briar emerged from her tent Tatton was at the fire with the Swiss family, telling them horror stories about lions and leopards.

'Stop it, Tatton,' said Briar as she joined them. 'No one will sleep tonight if you continue with this nonsense.'

'No. No,' said the grandfather, a sprightly seventy-year-old. 'What he says is true. I have heard how lions come into camps and take people from their beds.'

Briar looked at Tatton in exasperation. Night had set in. All was dark beyond the glow of the fire. She knew how nervous clients became at night when strange calls were magnified and they lay in bed straining their ears for the sound of soft footfalls.

Her job was to help the visitors enjoy the experience of sleeping outdoors in a tent. She did not want them to return to Switzerland terrified, warning their friends to keep away from the dangers of the bush and Zimbabwe.

'Humans are not normal prey for lions,' she said. 'They don't usually seek out places where there are people. The only attacks have been by lions who are weak, ill and can't hunt.'

'Or those who develop a taste for human flesh such as the ones up in Kenya when they built the railway. Remember?' said Tatton jokingly. He enjoyed teasing people.

'The man-eating lions of Tsavo were the exception not the rule,' Briar admonished.

'Tsavo?' queried the grandfather, always eager for a story about the bush.

'Tsavo was a camp on the Uganda railway line,' Tatton explained. 'It was a place feared from the time of the early slave traders. In fact it was probably the slavers' habit of throwing corpses of slaves who died en route into the bushes, which gave the lions the taste for human flesh.'

The Swiss family shivered and pulled their chairs closer to the fire.

'If I'm not mistaken Lord Salisbury, the British Prime Minister, referred to the Tsavo lions in the House of Lords, bemoaning the fact that work on the line was held up for almost a month, because man-eating lions had developed a taste for the workers,' added Tatton.

'You're safe here,' said Briar. Then, remembering that they had no guns in camp, she hoped that her words would not tempt fate to prove her wrong. 'The Tsavo lions incident happened in the early nineteen-hundreds and Fig Tree Camp is a long way away from Kenya.'

'What do we do if lions come here?' asked the mother. 'I do not wish to leave my bed and walk in the dark to the toilet tent.'

Briar patted the woman's hand, which was firmly clenched to the arm of the chair.

'You will find an enamel chamber-pot with a lid beneath each bed. Use that. Put it back and tomorrow the camp staff will see that the pots are emptied.'

The mother grimaced at the thought.

'And now,' Briar suggested, 'how about a good *marula* liqueur before we go to our tents.'

'*Marula*? What is that?' asked the grandfather.

'Curious old dodger,' whispered Tatton as he followed Briar to collect the tray of liqueurs set out by the cook.

'Curious, but he could send other clients,' said Briar, 'so ease up on the horror stories.'

'Your wish,' he replied.

'*Marula*,' Briar explained as she handed round glasses full of the creamy liquid, 'is a famous tree believed to have magic properties. The fruit is enjoyed by all animals. It's like a plum with juicy white flesh. It can be made into jelly and brewed for beer. They say elephant get drunk when the fruit ferments in their bellies.'

'They do. I've seen them staggering round after a *marula* feast,' said Tatton. 'I've also photographed them wreaking havoc on the vegetation the following day because of their hangovers!'

The Swiss family laughed, sipped the liqueurs and had their glasses refilled.

'That should put them to sleep,' said Tatton as he and Briar watched them disperse to their allotted tents.

'I hope so,' said Briar.

'Why so serious?'

'We have no rifles in camp tonight. I forgot mine. The scout dropped his and it's jammed.'

Tatton came up behind Briar and put his arms around her.

'When we are in Antarctica or Nepal, none of this will matter. Life is going to be fun, Briar. You are coming with me, aren't you?'

Briar rested her head on his shoulder. She looked up at the moon forcing its way through the thick black branches of the wild fig. Why not? she thought. He's offering me a carefree life. I probably need a change. I need to leave Zimbabwe for a while.

'Miss Hanley?'

A quavering voice saved her from answering. Briar gave Tatton a quick hug.

'See you later,' she said and hurried to one of the tents.

Tatton watched her go ruefully. She's worth waiting for, he said to himself, as he saw her disappear into one of the clients' tents.

Tatton was beginning to feel that Briar could be the one woman to end his nomadic life. For the first time, the thought of shouldering responsibility did not appal him. He did not want to change his lifestyle immediately, but after he and Briar had roamed the world, settling down could be a possibility.

He knew that Briar liked his company. He was certain that she would enjoy his embraces. She did not pull away when he hugged or kissed her, which he took to be a good sign.

Yes! He punched the air in a victory gesture. By the end of the week her answer would be yes.

He scuffed up the sand. It danced in small clouds of dust at his heels as he walked to where his tent was pitched. At the entrance he spun on his heel and crept across the camp to Briar's tent. It was dark inside. He felt his way to one of the beds and lay down to wait.

Half an hour later, after trimming the wicks of the candles and lacing up the openings of the tents, Briar made her way wearily to her own tent.

She was too tired to shower and change. She kicked off her boots, dropped her clothes on the floor and flopped on to the bed. The faint wail of jackals hunting in the silver moonlight lulled her and she sighed.

'Briar?' Tatton's voice was no louder than her sigh. She felt his weight tilt the bed as he sat beside her. His fingers, sensitive as those of a blind man, traced the outline of her face then followed the curve of her ears. They stroked her throat and moved on.

Briar lifted a hand to stop him, but he was so tender and his touch so gentle that she closed her eyes and her hand fell back to lie loosely on the bed. Even when his lips became urgent and demanding she could not rouse herself to protest.

Eyelets of moonlight edged themselves between the lacing on the tent.

She opened her eyes and watched the slivers of light flit like fireflies in the dark. The smell of sun-baked canvas and dust was warm and familiar. The bed groaned as Tatton moved over her. Briar opened her mouth. 'Con—?' she whispered.

'—doms?' said Tatton, finishing the word for her. 'Don't worry, you're safe, my love.'

She sighed and wound her arms around his neck, giving herself up to his love-making.

The shattering clang of a gong deafened her, but loving and the *marula* liqueur held her captive. She tried to sit up and think clearly.

'Lions!' Between the ear-splitting crashes of the gong, she heard the screams.

Instinctively she reached for the rifle beside her bed. She froze. Her fears had materialized. There were lions in camp and she could not protect the clients, neither could she make herself heard above the clamour to warn them to remain in their tents.

'Why do they not come?' quavered the grandfather as he hit the enamel chamber-pot with the lid. Splinters of blue enamel flew across the tarpaulin floor. 'They must hear this noise. Shout again. Tell them the man-eating lions came for us.'

His wife obeyed. Briar covered her ears with her hands. There was nothing she could do. It would be foolhardy to venture into the darkness where only the faintly putrid odour and feeling of fear would tell of the lion. If it has any sense it will leave camp, thought Briar. The noise is enough to scare away every lion in the area.

As if in response to her thoughts, she heard a series of short coughing grunts behind her tent. The banging intensified, as did the screaming.

'You are safe,' shouted Briar. 'Go back to sleep. It has gone.'

Her voice was lost in the din.

'Pity it isn't hungry enough to take them and put a stop to this infernal noise,' Tatton whispered in her ear.

'Perhaps the old man's arm will get tired and he'll be quiet,' she said hopefully. She tore tissues into small pieces and stuffed them into her and Tatton's ears. She could still hear the grandfather tirelessly beating the chamber-pot.

She put her head under the pillow, and waited for dawn and the noise to cease.

Shortly after sunrise the cook struck the iron bar which hung from the branch of a tree near the kitchen. 'Breakfast,' he called.

The Swiss family peered fearfully from right to left before emerging from their tents.

Briar was waiting to greet them. She had left her tent early, not wanting the staff to know that Tatton had slept with her.

'What an exciting night,' she said. 'You are so lucky to have been in camp when a lion visited us. I can't remember it ever happening before.'

'And hitting the chamber-pot to frighten it away was a stroke of genius,' muttered Tatton.

Sleeplessness had smudged blue streaks beneath his eyes and on the Swiss clients it had deepened the blue to purple.

'How do you manage to look so good?' Tatton whispered to Briar.

'Tissues in my ears, a pillow over my head and a cold shower,' she whispered back.

After their third cup of coffee the Swiss family had made themselves heroes of the night's adventure. They squabbled excitedly over whose idea it had been to use the chamber-pot and lid as cymbals.

The scout arrived after breakfast. He wisely made no comment on the night's proceedings. It had been a bright night with a full moon, not one of the dark overcast nights when lions usually hunt and are dangerous. He had heard the lion long before it reached Fig Tree Camp and judged from its grunts that it was merely taking a short cut through the camp. If it was hunting he would have heard nothing, unless it gave a full-throated roar. That terrifying sound would chill even a hardened hunter.

Excitement reached fever pitch when Briar and the scout showed them the lion's pug marks. They traced its route through the camp. The family showed only slight disappointment when they saw that the lion had passed close to Briar's tent, not theirs.

'Sorry, Tatton,' said Briar as they climbed into the Land Rover to return to Kame Two. 'I promised you a break from hard walking and climbing in the Chizarira area. You now look as if you spent last night at a disco.'

'I did. Noise level was the same,' he teased. His voice became soft and serious. 'Briar, last night was very special. I love you. Do you feel the same?'

Briar concentrated on the rough track. She did not have an answer to Tatton's question. Something seemed to stop her from accepting the life and love he was offering her. She liked him. Last night she had even thought she loved him. Yet she knew that she was not ready to leave Zimbabwe.

'Guido,' screamed Maria Andretti, her high heels clacking as she ran across the marble hall of their home in Milan. 'Guido!' She pushed open the door to his study. 'Quickly, lift the phone. It is Tara.'

He pushed aside a sheaf of papers and waved his secretary from the room. Guido now spent two days each week working from home. Since their return from

Zimbabwe he had decided to let Marco shoulder more responsibility at the Andretti headquarters.

At times like this he pondered the wisdom of his decision. The house was never quiet. There was always some domestic or personal crisis in Maria's life.

His study was used as Solomon's judgement chamber. Everything was brought to him to solve. Now he had to contend with Tara. He knew it would not be easy. She had his genes and pursued what she wanted with a single-minded purpose.

'Tara *cara*,' he said soothingly.

'Good morning, Mr Andretti,' answered a deep, masculine voice. 'We have not had the pleasure of meeting. I am Pat Gifford, a friend of the Hanleys. Briar and Tara have been on Kame Two helping Rudo, and also helping me set up my new photographic safari concession.'

Tara squeezed as close to Pat as she could. She crossed her fingers tightly as she strained to hear her father's voice.

'Good morning, Mr Gifford,' Guido answered coolly. 'Is it possible to talk to my daughter?'

Pat looked down at Tara, who shook her head. She looked up at Pat imploringly. He covered the mouthpiece with his hand.

'You must speak to your father,' he whispered urgently.

'We will only fight and he'll make me go home. Please, Pat. You promised you'd explain everything to him.'

Pat sighed and uncovered the mouthpiece. Tara smiled.

'Certainly, Mr Andretti. She will be here shortly. While we wait for her, could I have a few minutes of your time?'

Pat continued, sensing that Guido was about to make an excuse.

'Tara is a fine young woman, Mr Andretti. You can be proud of her. I had three sons of whom I was extremely proud. Two were killed in the Bush War. I now have one left. His name is Erin and he runs a hunting area called New Ganyani. He is an excellent safari operator, a superb shot, extremely capable and above all a gentleman. He needs someone like Tara to help run the camp. Your daughter is longing to accept the position.'

Still there was a silence from Guido.

'I fly up to New Ganyani at least twice a week. Erin has his own Cessna so if necessary Tara could get to us within an hour. I assure you that she will be as safe with Erin as she is with me.'

Tara gave Pat the thumbs-up.

That's obviously the line she wants me to adopt, he thought.

'I am listening but I am not convinced, Mr Gifford,' answered Guido. 'Tara is very dear to me. Our agreement was that once your Rudo was well, she would return.'

The man is inflexible, thought Pat. I wouldn't like to do business with him.

'I understand your feelings perfectly,' said Pat calmly. 'I too have a precious child. Please believe me, Mr Andretti, I would not ask you to agree to anything which could harm Tara. She loves the country and is having a marvellous time. I believe that life is better for her here than in a city full of temptations.'

Guido watched Maria pacing up and down his study. At each turn she stooped and straightened the silk Qu'um lying in front of his desk. He let his eyes play over the birds and beasts skilfully knotted into the design of the carpet.

The smells and sounds of the bush returned to haunt and tantalize him. He was afraid that if Tara remained in Zimbabwe too long, Africa like a jealous lover would not release her. He could make her return to be with him in

Milan, but her heart would always beat to the rhythm of the drums of Africa.

He was conscious of Pat waiting for his reply. Yes, he mused, perhaps Pat Gifford is right. I cannot foresee Tara's future. Maria was stamping her foot impatiently. Let her stay, Guido decided. I do not want her to be just another lovely woman in Milan. Tara is special. Let the bush keep my child a little longer.

'Mr Gifford, can you assure me that you will care for Tara as if she was yours? If you have any fears for her safety or well-being, put her on the first plane back to Milan.'

Guido's voice broke as he realized the enormity of what he was saying. He would have to face Maria and the family. He could imagine the recriminations which would follow. Already Maria's eyes were flashing and her nails dug deeply into her palms.

'You have my assurance, Mr Andretti,' said Pat. 'I already look upon Tara as a member of my family.'

'Pat, I love you,' Tara whispered, as she took the receiver from him.

He turned away and walked out on to the verandah as a torrent of Italian filled the room. Picking up his binoculars, he trained them on the dirt road which led to Fig Tree Camp.

He both longed and feared to see Briar. He had missed her, but he was scared that when she returned he would see love for Tatton in her face.

Wisps of dust, delicate as tendrils of smoke from a dying fire, danced over the road. Pat felt a strange excitement. It was the Land Rover. Briar and Tatton were returning. He held the binoculars to his eyes.

Tatton's hand resting on Briar's bare leg was magnified in the lens. Pat knew he should put the binoculars away but he was unable to move. He studied Briar's face. She and Tatton were laughing, but their eyes were hidden behind dark glasses. Briar's soul was curtained from his gaze.

Pat dropped the binoculars on to the table, so he did not see Briar remove Tatton's hand. As the Land Rover pulled up at the steps Tara whirled on to the verandah. She stood on tiptoe and kissed Pat.

'Thank you, Pat. You've made me so happy. I'll never forget this.'

Briar was about to remove her glasses, but at Tara's words and display of emotion she left them on. They would shield the shock in her eyes and give her the time she needed to absorb the sudden nausea which Tara's words caused.

'Pat finally reached my family. He was wonderful, Briar. He has convinced Papa. I have never been so happy.'

Briar merely nodded and pretended to fumble with the ignition key. She then managed a weak smile.

Pat studied her.

She's probably uncertain as to how I'll accept the news that she is in love with Tatton and will leave with him, he thought.

Tatton climbed out of the Land Rover and stretched.

'Fig Tree is a beautiful camp,' he said. 'We had a marvellous time. I think we fell asleep at three a.m. or was it four, Briar?'

Pat had an overwhelming urge to punch him. Instead he excused himself, saying he was going to find Rudo, tea and cake.

When he returned to the verandah, he found the party who had spent two days on one of his houseboats on Kariba seated at the table with Briar, Tara and Tatton.

They were delighted with the shots they had taken of

the elephants swimming across to the island, their trunks breaking the water like black periscopes. It had been a successful adventure and they were eager to tell their stories. The verandah was a hubbub of noise and laughter. Pat was able to turn his attention away from Briar and Tatton and listen to his clients.

'You are not sleeping, Mr Pat,' said Rudo quietly. She replaced plates of cake and put down a fresh pot of tea. 'You work too hard.'

Pat merely smiled at her and patted her hand. She waddled back to the kitchen shaking her head.

Why do men remain like children? she thought. They never see the sensible thing to do and they do not listen to women.

Rudo's words remained with Pat as he pretended to join in the conversation and laughter. At last the clients filed away, still boasting of the prizewinning shots they had obtained.

Pat looked across the table to where Briar and Tatton sat side by side.

'Briar,' he said, 'Tara and I are flying to New Ganyani tomorrow. We leave at dawn. Will you book out this party? The new clients should be here by noon. They are flying up from the Falls.'

Briar looked surprised. Pat usually collected his clients in the Cessna.

'One of them owns the airline which does the Flight of Angels over the Falls,' he explained. 'He is using his planes to bring his party to Kame Two. They'll only be here for two days. They are a high-powered business group who are determined to see everything in a week.'

'Certainly,' she said to Pat. 'Don't worry, I'll manage.' Then as if the devil had taken command of her tongue she heard herself say, 'Tatton has asked me to leave with him at the end of the week. He has assignments in Antarctica. I'd love to see that part of the world. Tara is quite capable of running the domestic side of Kame Two. In fact she already knows as much as I do about the business.'

'But—' Tara interjected. She was horrified at the thought of not joining Erin at New Ganyani. Pat squeezed her hand to quieten her.

'That's wonderful, Briar,' he said. 'I'm sure you'll be very happy.'

His words were nails in the coffin of her emotions. They proved that Pat had no feelings for her. He was obviously pleased that she was leaving with Tatton.

Tatton leaned across and kissed her. 'Thank you, Briar,' he said softly.

Briar wanted to run away. She wanted to be back at the waterhole where she had gone so many times with Scott. She could not bear to look at Tatton or Pat.

How could I have said that, she thought bleakly.

Pat felt his world close in. Life would be meaningless without the woman sitting opposite him. Kame Two would be like a rose without perfume. Beautiful, but the essential part would be gone.

He forced his lips to open in a wide smile.

'I'd like to take you on the *Gola* for a weekend before you leave. It'll be a break for all of us. Rudo has just told me that I need a rest,' he laughed. 'Perhaps she's right.'

'What is the *Gola* and where is it?' asked Tatton, with keen interest.

'*Gola* is Pat's personal houseboat,' answered Tara. 'He has two others for guests.' Pat had already taken her and Briar to the group of islets near Binga on Lake Kariba where he kept his houseboat.

Compared to the ones run by the holiday resorts on the lake, *Gola* was old-fashioned, but Pat used it only for friends and family. It was moored off the Sjarira Forest area and the islets gave him the privacy and peace he loved.

'*Gola* must be the Sindebele name for an animal,' said Tatton.

'For the wild grey cat,' answered Pat. 'Cats don't like water and when the waves chop on Kariba neither does *Gola*.'

The mention of the houseboat made Briar even more miserable. She would miss everything in this hard but beautiful country. As if to echo her distress, the drums set up a monotonous beat in the distance. She shivered.

'Now what?' said Pat. Drumbeats still recalled the slaughter at Ganyani. He knew that now he would always associate the throbbing resonance with death.

'A chief in one of the *kapenta* fishing villages has died,' said Rudo, wheeling out the wooden trolley to clear the cups and saucers.

Inwardly Pat breathed a sigh of relief. 'Thank you, Rudo,' he said.

She nodded. Rudo understood that it was the secret messages hidden in the songs of the drums which worried those unable to read them. Never again would she keep the drumbeats a secret from Mr Pat. She owed him her life.

'Rudo,' he said, 'Tara and I are flying up to New Ganyani tomorrow. Would you like to come and surprise Jacob?'

'May I take Buna, Mr Pat?'

'Of course. If Erin can spare them, we'll bring Jacob and Shoko back with us for a week. Jacob can terrify my clients by leading them up to count the hairs in the tails of the elephants.'

Briar looked up at Pat. 'Will you have room in the plane?' she asked.

'Oh yes,' Tara babbled. 'I'm staying at New Ganyani.' She laughed at the look of amazement on Briar's face.

'That's why Pat phoned Papa. Papa would not give me permission, but Pat was wonderful. He made Papa agree.'

Briar jumped up and hugged Tara. 'Did he tell your papa how good-looking Erin is?' she whispered.

'No,' Tara flushed, then retaliated. She pretended to enfold Briar in a bear hug.

'Is Tatton as sexy as he looks?' she said.

At the mention of Tatton's name Briar felt nauseous. She had foolishly misread the situation between Pat and Tara, but things had progressed too far with Tatton and she was now committed to leaving Zimbabwe with him.

'Rudo,' bellowed Pat. Rudo hurried out on to the verandah. 'We leave for *Gola* in three days.'

'Good, Mr Pat, that is very good,' she said.

Rudo smiled happily as she returned to the kitchen, wiping her hands on her apron. At last he thinks and behaves like a man, not a child. Now he must make Briar stay with him, she thought. That Tatton is not for her. He is like our *shongololo*. He, like the millipede, walks slowly but with great determination. He will always be moving and he will tire Briar. She is not made to wander like a spirit which has lost its way. This is her home. I will pray to the God of the nuns at the Mater Dei. He is a powerful God. He can keep Briar with us.

To the amazement of the kitchen staff, Rudo knelt down on the cement floor, threw her apron over her head to resemble a veil and prayed to the White God.

Chapter Twenty-five

TARA LOVED the simplicity of the grass huts and freshly swept earthen floors in New Ganyani.

She fitted into the lazy rhythm of camp life as easily and quickly as trackers running on spoor. For the first few weeks she made no suggestions, though her bright amber eyes noticed things which could be changed.

Erin left at dawn each day with his clients and returned at dusk. While he was away Tara was content to make friends with the staff and learn what part each played in the running of the camp.

On the last night of the hunt Erin and the hunters returned late. The men were elated as they had found and taken a trophy kudu. It now lay in the back of the Land Rover. Its massive and beautifully spiralled horns were twisted awkwardly over its back. It seemed to Tara that the eyes, dark and long lashed as her own, stared at her beseechingly.

She ran her fingers gently over the two spots on its cheeks. They seemed to have been dabbed on hastily with a powder-puff and gleamed white in the torchlight. She trailed her finger across the broad, white chevron between its eyes. The white hairs fringing the inside of the large ears tickled her fingers.

Poor creature, she said silently. You should be guarding

your cows and calves tonight, not lying here with your swollen tongue flopping from your mouth and blood cradling your head.

Yet, when she turned to face the men her face was bright and her voice cheerful.

'A magnificent pair of horns,' she said. 'Congratulations. What do they measure?'

'We did a rough measurement along the outside curve and they must be all of sixty-eight inches,' said Erin. He was relaxed and happy. He had given his client a superb greater kudu.

'I'd say closer to seventy,' teased Tara.

'If that was true we'd be only half an inch short of the record taken in South Africa,' said Erin. 'No. We'll have to be happy with what we have.'

'Happy? Let's drink to happiness,' said the hunter.

'There's hot water in the basins on the tables in front of your huts,' Tara said. 'You'll feel better once the dust is off your hands and faces. It'll make the popcorn taste better.'

'Popcorn!' yelled the Texan who had taken the kudu. 'You've made my day, gal. I've been on a diet of worms and fried banana chips for days. The whisky washes it down. But popcorn . . . Now we're cooking with gas.'

Erin was stunned. Where had Tara found popcorn? Coke and chewing gum were readily available but popcorn trailed way behind.

Tara managed to leave the men at midnight. She lay in bed with the blankets pulled up high around her ears. She could still hear them laughing and talking around the fire. She knew that no matter how hard she tried she would never thrill to the death of an animal, but she was beginning to understand the fascination of hunting.

The sun was high and the camp strangely quiet when she awoke the following morning. The Land Rover and the men had left. There was an envelope at her place in the dining hut. She was about to open it when Katoro arrived with a plate of *sadza* and soured milk. Tara enjoyed the traditional breakfast.

'Mr Erin told us to let you sleep today. He has taken the men to Harare,' said Katoro. 'That corn we popped in the pan last night was good,' he continued. 'We all have very big tips and in dollars!'

Tara smiled and tore open the envelope.

Dear Tara,

We cannot buy you flowers or chocolates. Any girl who finds popcorn in the bush deserves both.

Please accept this and buy chocolates when you are in Harare.

Thank you for making our hunt so special. We'll be back.

Yours, The Texans

Tara thumbed through the notes and shook her head. She would give it to Erin. I can't possible accept this, she thought. Then, as her fingers danced through the bills, a small smile stole across her face. Perhaps I can. Yes. I certainly can.

'Katoro,' she shouted. 'Where are the camp builders? I need them.'

Soon the silence was shattered as men ran to do her bidding. They were bowed down under bundles of thatching grass and mopane poles. They fetched balls of bark plaited into twine which they laid in water to make them pliable. Tara squatted on the sand and with a twig drew what she wanted. She paced out the length and breadth with the men.

'Tell them it must be finished before Mr Erin returns,' she commanded Katoro.

Tara was not sure what he said but the men hurried to obey orders. Soon the framework was standing. Then the thatchers moved in, to tie the grass bundles into place. Next year, the old insect- and spider-infested grass would be replaced with fresh grass.

Tara had set up her building beneath a grotesquely contorted baobab tree which Erin had told her was the only one in the area. She knew that it was a fertility tree, used by medicine men in Africa. It was the perfect site for her 'bush clinic'. She could not wait for Erin to return.

The Texan money would buy the first supplies for what she envisaged as a simple day clinic. The men had built an open-sided thatched-roof shelter beside the large grass hut. They were now binding poles together to make rough benches.

Tara intended giving classes to the camp staff, especially the women, on hygiene, contraception and child care. Katoro would be her interpreter. Though she could now give basic orders in Sindebele, she knew that her command of the language was not good enough for the information she wanted to impart.

The sound of the Cessna made the men scatter to the staff village. Katoro had warned them not to be around when Mr Erin arrived. Miss Tara wanted to greet him at the new building alone.

'It is because she is afraid that Mr Erin will be angry. Building camps is not woman's work,' said one.

'But she plans like a man,' said another. 'The building is good. But why does she want to stay on her own and why between the camp and our village?'

'It's the tree!' ventured a third. 'She wants to sleep near the tree which grows with its roots in the air.'

'Perhaps she wants to work magic and have Mr Erin as her man.'

Tara gulped as the Land Rover approached. She was apprehensive. This was Erin's camp. She had given his staff orders and constructed a building without his permission.

The Land Rover stopped in an cloud of dust as Erin saw Tara standing with her hands on her hips in the middle of the road. He did not notice the building. He had eyes only for the petite woman whose presence had made the last hunt so successful.

He was looking forward to a few days rest before the next group arrived. He planned to show Tara New Ganyani and take her on a buffalo hunt. A hunt without clients would enable him to assess how she acted under pressure in the bush. He could not afford to have someone working for him who behaved irresponsibly, ruining the hunt and perhaps endangering lives.

'Welcome home,' said Tara as she waited for Erin to comment on her clinic.

'Thank you, Tara. It's good to be back. The hunt was very successful. I must thank you for charming them. I've never known hunters so eager to return to camp every evening.'

'That was the whisky calling,' she said laughing.

'Yes. Italian whisky,' he teased. 'Jump in, let's see what Katoro has for dinner. I'm starving.'

'How do you like the New Ganyani clinic?' she said, pointing to the grass hut standing at the foot of the baobab.

Erin was silent. He climbed down from the Land Rover and walked to the hut. He circled it slowly, checking the workmanship. He kicked at a few of the mopane poles but they were buried deep in the hard ground and did not move. Tara trailed behind him, trying to judge his reaction from the set of his shoulders.

'Explain,' he said, sitting on one of the rough benches.

Tara started hesitantly, but as she spoke she saw herself helping the women and children. Her voice became animated and her hands flew in the air like a somersaulting bateleur eagle. Erin's reserve broke down and he roared with laughter when she described the part Katoro would play in her plans.

'You are marvellous, Tara Andretti,' he said. 'It's a wonderful idea. I cannot believe you managed to build it all in one day.'

'Your staff did all the work,' Tara answered, delighted by his reaction.

'You have obviously worked the same magic on the staff that you did with the Texans. Well done.'

Tara glowed in his praise.

'It is well,' whispered the villagers peeping from their huts. 'Mr Erin laughs.'

Soon a stream of villagers squatted round Erin, waiting for an explanation. Silence greeted his speech, then the women started clapping and singing.

'They are thanking you,' said Erin. And he omitted to add, advising him to take Tara as his first wife, to bear him many sons.

'They have also given you a praise name. It is Nsimba, their name for the genet. They say that like the "half-cat" you are intelligent and clever. You also have the same large amber eyes.'

'Nsimba,' said Tara, rolling the name around her tongue. 'I like it. Please thank them for me. Say I am proud to be Nsimba.'

'Tomorrow is a day of rest for everyone,' said Erin. He coughed, as their stamping feet pounded the red soil into dust. He looked for Jonas in the throng.

'Jonas,' he called. 'The day after tomorrow we take Nsimba to track her first buffalo.'

Jonas nodded and led the staff back into the village.

Jacob was still at Kame Two with Rudo. Jonas was uneasy about hunting the wily *nyati* without Jacob at his side, for he relied heavily on Jacob's expertise. As a team they were superb, but Jonas knew that he came second to Jacob in both tracking and sighting game.

Chapter Twenty-six

THE *Gola* swung gently on her moorings. Nyaminyami the River God was in a benevolent mood and the sparkling waters of Lake Kariba were placid. Yachts and sailing vessels skimmed the burnished surface with the grace and speed of white-winged gulls. Animals grazed peacefully beneath the large mahogany and acacia trees growing on the new shoreline.

Pat had chosen to moor his houseboat a little way into an inlet. Here it was protected from the unpredictable and violent storms which within minutes could whip the waters of the lake into fourteen-foot waves.

A pair of pied kingfishers sat on the mooring line, swaying like children on a see-saw. They seemed to take turns to hover over the water then dive into the clear depths and return with silver fish held firmly in their strong, pointed bills.

The young N'debele man chosen by Pat to look after the *Gola* squatted on the rear deck peeling a dish of potatoes. He had caught six bream that morning and was humming as he worked.

'There she is,' shouted Briar excitedly as she caught sight of the double-decked boat through the window of the Cessna.

Tatton was absorbed with his cameras and merely grunted.

'I don't think the window is clean enough for good photographs,' said Briar. 'Look at the boat instead of seeing everything through a lens.'

'Sometimes one can obtain unusual effects this way,' replied Tatton.

'Isn't she lovely?' said Briar, turning to Pat and leaving Tatton to fiddle with his lenses.

'Beautiful,' Pat answered, as he circled the boat before heading for the landing strip. 'And it seems as if I'll be eating smoked bream and potato salad again. I should never have told Gola that I enjoyed it.'

'Gola? I thought that was the houseboat's name,' said Tatton, looking up from his camera for a moment.

'It is,' said Briar, 'but the young man wanted to be called Gola G. as he fishes, cooks, cleans and looks after her. We should never have agreed as it is confusing.'

Tatton merely shook his head. Briar and Pat laughed.

'I didn't realize how much I've missed the *Gola*,' said Briar. 'I think I'd like to live here for ever and never see anyone.'

Tatton's expression set and Pat said hurriedly, 'What, and do Gola G. out of a job?'

Briar was quiet but she looked greedily at the beauty of Kariba.

Pat bumped the Cessna down on the short runway.

'There's certainly a difference in temperature down here compared to Kame Two,' said Tatton, wiping his neck with his peaked cap.

'You don't want to be here in summer if you find this hot,' said Pat. 'Temperatures can reach 122°F.'

'Antarctica, here we come,' answered Tatton.

Pat flinched at the use of 'we'. He was determined to enjoy every moment of Briar's company. He refused to let himself think of her imminent departure.

'Look,' she shouted, pointing to where an elephant bull stood in the deep shade of an acacia tree. He was resting and had draped his heavy trunk over one of the branches. He coiled it in a thick grey pad over the branch and it hung to the ground like a mamba.

'I must photograph that,' said Tatton. 'Please stop.'

Pat hit the brakes and the jeep jerked to a halt. The elephant flapped his huge ears slowly and ignored them.

'I need to get closer.'

Pat picked up his gun and led them towards the animal.

'They have poor eyesight, but be ready to move back if I say so. Do not run.'

The three moved closer to the great beast. Briar gasped. She had never been this close to an elephant before. It seemed to tower above them like a skyscraper. Suddenly she wanted to be back in the jeep and on the road to the *Gola*.

As if sensing her fear, the elephant uncurled its trunk and turned to face them.

Slowly it placed one ponderous foot in front of the other and walked towards them. Briar watched in sick fascination as puffs of dust swirled up in front of its massive feet.

The elephant paused and peered at them, then stood swaying indecisively.

'He thinks we are antelope,' whispered Pat.

As if to refute this suggestion the elephant advanced.

'Back,' said Pat. 'Walk backwards slowly.'

Briar felt ill. The elephant seemed to blot out the sky. She forced herself to walk backwards watching Pat and the elephant. 'Almost safe,' Pat said to himself. 'Another few yards and he'll lose interest.'

Suddenly the elephant squealed and threw its trunk in the air. He had seen Tatton turn and run.

In a swift practised movement Pat lifted his rifle. The retort stunned Briar. Her ears rang. She stood absolutely still waiting for the elephant to drop. Instead it wheeled in a cloud of dust and hideous trumpeting. It was soon lost in the trees.

'I said walk backwards slowly,' snapped Pat, turning to Tatton.

'That elephant would have killed us all,' said Tatton, still pale with shock. 'It was not stopping.'

'That elephant had satisfied its curiosity and was about to return to its tree,' said Pat coldly. 'We were just lucky that the shot I put over its head was close enough to turn it.'

'Poor thing will have a headache for days,' said Briar, eager to defuse the situation between the two men. Let's get to *Gola*.'

She sensed that she was the reason for the sudden animosity, not the incident with the elephant.

They walked to the jeep in silence. Tatton was smarting because Pat had shown him up to be a coward. Briar put her hand on his shoulder. She didn't want anything to upset the few days on the houseboat.

'Can we take *Gola* out to your mugger sandbank?' she asked Pat. 'I'd like Tatton to see our old crocodile. I bet he's never seen one as big.'

'I'll win that bet,' said Tatton, eager to talk of anything but the elephant. 'I saw one on an island off the Great Barrier Reef which was at least twenty-two feet long.'

'That's not fair,' retorted Briar. 'Yours was a salt-water

crocodile. They are always bigger than our Nile crocs.' She thought for a moment. 'I bet ours is fatter. Ours is almost as wide around the belly as it is long.'

Pat's anger abated. 'That's a bit of an exaggeration, Briar. Even with a kudu inside him he could hardly match that description.'

'I hope he's still there,' she said. 'He's been on the same bank every time we've come down to *Gola*,' she explained to Tatton.

'If he's not, then his belly skin is probably a bag slung over someone's shoulder or a belt buckled around someone's waist,' said Pat.

'I hate crocodiles.' Briar shuddered. 'They are so sneaky and look so evil.'

The pied kingfishers flew up with harsh, high-pitched cries of alarm as Pat parked beneath a tamarind tree and Gola G. hurried to meet them.

The birds hovered over the water waiting to settle down on the mooring lines, but Pat decided to move the *Gola* out to the cove opposite the sandbank while it was still light. A current from one of the rivers which flowed down into Kariba ran into the cove. It kept the water moving and clear of the bright Kariba weed. Pat did not like the remaining patches of weed, even though they now covered less than two per cent of the lake. They were a perfect cover for hippopotami and crocodiles and he never felt safe if he plunged into the water for a quick dip near them.

Like Briar, he disliked crocodiles. They were powerful and fast in water, yet when necessary could slide into the shallows and settle silently into the mud, leaving only a faint diamond pattern from the keeled plates on their backs to tell of their presence.

'He's there,' called Briar triumphantly. She had scrambled

up the ladder to the observation deck as soon as they were on *Gola*.

'Go and see her crocodile,' said Pat.

Tatton left Pat's side, still ashamed of the part he had played in the elephant incident. He now stayed close to Pat, helping where he could, attempting to atone for disobeying the command not to run.

Pat let out a long sigh as Tatton disappeared up the ladder. Gola G. looked up from where he was securing the new mooring for the houseboat. He dropped his eyes, his face inscrutable as Pat moved across to check the lines.

There is bad feeling between the men, he thought. Like two bull hippos they wish to slash each other for the woman.

'See,' said Briar. 'Yours could not possibly have been as fat as this mugger.'

Tatton studied the crocodile, a fine member of the Archosauria, the ruling reptiles, as it lay basking in the sun. Its heavy cylindrical body was splayed on the sand as if for skinning. The large, triangular head was pointed towards *Gola*. Its fearsome jaws were closed. The teeth formed a single interdigitating row except the fourth tooth of the lower jaw which curved up like a hook and clamped down over the top jaw.

'He's certainly big,' agreed Tatton, with an involuntary shudder. 'I'd say he's all of twelve foot in length. I'd hate to be in the water with that one. He'd have you drowned in minutes.'

'Ugh,' said Briar. She turned as Pat padded barefoot up the steps.

'Tatton agrees that our mugger is huge,' she said.

'Have you ever seen him take an animal from the

sandbank?' asked Tatton, thinking of the shots he could get.

'Only once,' answered Pat. 'I'm not sure that it was him, though it must have been a big croc. We were sitting up here, having sundowners, when my wife pointed out a group of impala coming down to drink.'

His voice was soft and his expression sad as he recalled a time when his wife and sons were all with him.

'The impala were red in the light of the setting sun and the dust they kicked up was pink around their feet. The ram dipped his mouth into the water and flipped his head back quickly. He looked around to make sure that his females and young were with him, then he seemed to peer into the water as if he was trying to see the gravel on the bottom of the shallows.

'Eventually he lowered his head to drink. As his mouth touched the water again, there was a huge swirl and he vanished. Within moments it was all over. Only ever-widening circles on the water told of the antelope's death.'

'Did you not see the croc?' asked Tatton.

'All we saw was the dust as the impala stampeded back on to the mainland, and a dark shape outlined in the water. He probably dragged the buck out into deep water to drown it and swallowed chunks from it when it was no longer struggling.'

'I can imagine no worse way to die,' said Briar, 'than knowing that a croc has got you. Until you drown you see this loathsome thing staring at you with those eyes stuck on top of its head.'

'It must be a quick death,' countered Tatton.

'Not if you're the one being held under water,' said Briar.

Gola G. appeared balancing trays of smoked bream and potato salad. Painstakingly he arranged the cutlery and crockery on the wooden table.

'The canoe is ready,' he said to Briar.

Pat looked surprised.

'I thought we could take Tatton along the shoreline after lunch and see if any game is drinking,' Briar explained.

Tatton looked across at the sandbank. The mugger had opened its mouth and its pointed teeth gleamed in the sunlight as a courser hopped around busily picking out and swallowing pieces of rotting meat wedged between them.

'How big is the canoe?' asked Tatton.

'Big enough,' answered Briar, 'and it's aluminium. A hippo took a piece out of the old wooden one.'

Pat laughed at Tatton's expression.

'She's only teasing, Tatton,' he said. 'It's a wonderful experience to drift along the shore and watch the animals. I often think that Zimbabwe is what the Bible described as the Garden of Eden. There is no other country in the world where you can experience this.'

Briar wondered once again how she could have thought of leaving Africa. She had been so stupid. She could not imagine what her parents' reaction to the news would be. She felt alone and trapped, unable even to talk to Tara.

Resolutely she pushed her departure from her mind and concentrated on flaking the bream on her plate.

The days drifted by as swiftly as the quiver of dragonfly wings.

They fell into an easy routine on the houseboat. Every

morning Pat would go to the rear deck, strip and soap himself and drop over the side of the boat. The current would carry him parallel to the *Gola*. Before it veered away and took him out into the lake, he would reach up and grab the pole outside the front cabin and swing himself on to the deck. There Gola G. placed a pair of shorts which Pat dragged on, letting his body dry in the early morning sun. He called this routine his *Gola* shower.

Tatton preferred to use the shower on deck, saying he did not trust deep water. Briar swam only where she was certain there were no hippo or crocodiles.

Their last night on *Gola* had arrived. They sat up on deck in silence, each absorbed with their own thoughts. The African sky glittered as if a giant crystal ball had been shattered and pieces flung across the heavens.

The lights bobbing in the bows of the *kapenta* fishing boats reflected brightly in the dark waters of Kariba. The lake and sky became one.

'The whole world seems studded with stars tonight,' said Briar softly. 'It's so lovely.'

Tears trickled slowly down her cheeks and she was glad that it was dark and the men could not see her cry.

The pied kingfishers had discovered the *Gola*'s new moorings and they once again swung happily on the mooring lines.

Pat climbed up to the observation deck at dawn to find Briar huddled in a blue anorak, cradling a cup of coffee in her cold hands. She was staring across at the empty sandbank. Pat watched her in silence for a few minutes.

She had not yet plaited her hair and it floated pale as dandelion fluff on the light breeze.

He wanted to put his arms around her and beg her to reconsider her decision to leave with Tatton, but he was determined that he would cause her no pain. He had seen how she suffered over the loss of Scott and he was not going to persuade her to give up Tatton.

He did not believe that Tatton would be able to make Briar happy. She was an African and would pine for the smells and sounds of Africa. He only hoped that once she had been around the world she would return to Zimbabwe.

His main concern was that she might marry Tatton and be lost to him for ever. In the long sleepless nights on *Gola* he told himself that his longing for Briar was merely a middle-aged man's desire to regain his youth. But he knew that it was not. Briar had become very important to him. Suddenly, as if sensing his presence, she turned round.

'Pat,' she said, her voice high and welcoming. 'Come and join me in a cup of coffee. It warms the belly.' Her breath hung like river mist in the cold air and her nose was pink.

She poured him a mug of coffee from the flask and added two spoons of brown sugar. Briar stirred the sweet mixture and held it out to him. As Pat took the mug his fingers folded over her cold ones.

'Thank you, Briar.' He pulled his hands away from hers as if they were on fire. 'I'm going to miss you.'

'Don't let's talk about it, please, Pat,' she answered, her voice breaking. Her eyes were hot with tears. She swallowed determinedly. 'Look, the mugger has gone. He must know we're leaving today. He has lost interest in us.'

'He's probably hungry and has moved to a more

profitable area,' answered Pat. 'There haven't been many buck down to drink lately.'

They leaned back in the deckchairs in companionable silence and watched the lake awaken to the sun.

Eventually Pat stood up and stretched.

'Time for my *Gola* shower,' she said.

'I'll come down with you,' said Briar, picking up the empty mugs. 'I promised to show Gola G. how to make French toast.'

She walked to the front deck to allow Pat his privacy. A breeze had sprung up and wavelets slapped the bottom deck of the *Gola* as the houseboat rocked to the new movement in the water.

She put the mugs on the wide rail and bent to pick up Pat's shorts, which Gola G. had placed on the decking for him. They were getting wet as water splashed on to the boards, now only a few inches above the level of the lake.

She flipped the shorts over the rail, close to the pole he caught to swing himself on deck at the end of his swim. There was a loud clang as the mugs careened against each other and toppled overboard.

Briar gasped. The mugs were Pat's favourites. She knelt on the deck and bent over the side. The white porcelain mugs painted with flame lilies seemed to taunt her as they spiralled down in the clear water. She stretched her arm down and her fingers brushed the handle of one mug.

'Damn,' she muttered.

Her sleeve was already wet. Determined to retrieve the mugs before they were lost in the deep water, she hung over the side and, taking a breath, plunged her head and shoulders beneath the water. She scrabbled frantically for the mugs. Her fingers closed around one. She knew she had to lift her head to breathe, but the other was so close.

Suddenly she sensed something watching her. She froze. Her lungs were burning. She was becoming light-headed. Yes. Deep in the shadows at the back of the boat lay a dark shape.

Briar recognized, with all the horror of a nightmare, the two hard lumps on the head and the snout just breaking the surface. She opened her mouth to scream. She had to warn Pat not to jump into the current.

Cold water poured down her throat and her legs flailed wildly on the deck.

Gola G. was waiting patiently in the kitchen for Briar to come and show him how to fry this new toast. He looked at his watch. Pat would soon call for breakfast. He should have finished his swim.

Gola G. could not understand Pat's habit of splashing in the current then swinging back on to the boat. He lived in fear that one day Pat would miss the last pole and be swept into the deep waters of the lake. He whipped up the eggs with a fork, counted the slices of bread, then with another glance at the clock he went to find Briar. Breakfast could not be late.

'Miss Briar!' he shouted as he saw her lying on the deck with her head hanging over the side. 'Miss Briar.' His muscled arms caught her around her waist and he lifted her up. She hung limp as a netted fish in his arms.

Pat heard Gola G. shout. Panic was loud and clear in his voice. Pat's hands were slippery with soap and he found no purchase on the pole as he tried to swing himself back on to the deck. He had to reach Briar. Terrified, Gola G. stared at her. Her eyes rolled back in her head and her face was as pale as a filleted bream.

'Mr Pat,' he shrieked as he dropped Briar on to the deck. 'Mr Pat, come quick.'

Gola G. raced to the back deck to see Pat's hands slipping down the pole. He grabbed his wrists and braced himself against the cabin door for purchase. Pat was a heavy man and he could feel his hands slipping.

'You must come. You don't swim today, Mr Pat,' he gasped. 'I think Miss Briar is dead.'

The words galvanized Pat as nothing else could. With strength born of desperation, he heaved one foot up on the deck and Gola G. was able to haul him aboard.

Pat ran to the front of the boat followed by Gola G. waving his towel.

Tatton emerged from his shower to see Pat racing naked past his cabin followed closely by Gola G. He pulled on a pair of shorts and followed them.

Briar was still lying on the wooden planks but her eyes were now focused. A pool of water and vomit lay beside her. Gola G. ran to fetch a bucket of water and clean the mess, while Tatton and Pat knelt over Briar.

She ignored Tatton and held out her arms to Pat. He lifted her to him. She buried her face in the soapsuds on his shoulders.

'Oh Pat, I nearly lost you,' she sobbed.

Pat glanced at Tatton, who stared back expressionlessly.

'There, there,' he soothed, stroking her wet hair. She was obviously hysterical. Perhaps she had fallen overboard and panicked. He knew how she hated being in deep water and the current was strong in front of the houseboat.

As he held her to him he realized that her shorts and legs were dry. She could not have fallen into the lake.

Something cold and hard pressed into his back. He tried

to lift Briar's arms from around his neck, but her grip was as vice-like as a crocodile's jaws.

Tatton reached behind Pat's back, prized the coffee mug from her fingers and held it up for Pat's inspection. Briar turned her head on Pat's shoulder.

A ray of sunlight caught the bright red and gold flame lilies. They swam in front of her face. Behind them she once again saw the great reptile lying in wait in the silent black water beneath *Gola*.

She screamed and dug her fingers into Pat's back.

'Don't leave me, Pat,' she sobbed. 'Swear that you'll never leave me.'

Pat looked at Tatton gravely. 'I swear, Briar Hanley, that I'll never leave you,' he said.

The words seemed to calm her and her sobs died to shudders, but she still clung to Pat.

Gola G. did not understand what was happening, but he managed to wrap a towel around Pat's waist as he knelt on the decking.

'He was waiting for you,' whispered Briar.

'Who?'

'The mugger. That's why he wasn't on the sandbank this morning. He's under the boat.'

'Whew,' whistled Tatton weakly. 'He was waiting for you to drop into the current. The cunning swine.'

Pat shuddered at the horrific thought of the crocodile hunting him.

'I would never have seen you again,' said Briar and the tears poured down her cheeks.

'There, my love,' said Pat, rocking her gently. 'You have a cry, you'll feel better afterwards.'

'Those eyes, Pat. They were so cold and expressionless.

It was so dark under the boat. If it had submerged I would never have seen it.'

'He was on the lookout for me,' said Pat, still rocking her gently. 'That's why he was floating. Once I dropped into the current he would have gone down and taken me from below.'

'Don't,' begged Briar.

Tatton watched Pat and Briar for a moment then stood up. The sudden hatred he felt for Pat amazed him. He had not realized how much he wanted Briar until he saw her in Pat's arms.

'I'm off to the kitchen. I think coffee and breakfast is what we need.'

Tatton's thoughts raced as he climbed the stairs to the dining deck. He was determined that Briar would leave Kame with him. Pat was too old for her.

Something sneaked in from the darker recesses of his mind. He discounted it, but it hung in his subconscious, motionless and ugly as the crocodile.

Reluctantly he examined it again.

Yes, he thought. It could work, but at first he would have to pretend to accept the love he saw between Pat and Briar. Briar would not be easily fooled.

'Well, Tatton Boyce,' he whispered to himself. 'All is fair in love and war. If I can't get her by fair means then I'll try foul.'

'Did you mean what you said, Briar?' Pat asked. 'I'll understand if it was because you were scared.'

Briar kept her face hidden and her voice was muffled.

'Yes,' she whispered, 'I meant it, Pat.'

Pat uttered a silent prayer of thanks to the mugger lying beneath the *Gola*. He lifted Briar to her feet and kissed her gently.

Tatton studied Pat and Briar as they came to join him for breakfast. Both had showered and changed. Briar's face had all the radiance and beauty of a bride and Pat carried himself with the pride of a bridegroom.

For a moment Tatton felt a pang of conscience for what he was about to do. He dismissed it as he looked at Briar's laughing face. He wanted this woman.

'I have to be back in London by Wednesday,' he said as he cut into the bread which had been soaked in egg and milk before being fried. 'I would like to leave as soon as we return to Kame Two.'

Briar tensed and looked down at her plate.

'Pat, I wish you everything I hoped to find with Briar,' he said.

She looked up at Tatton in surprise.

'You and Pat have everything in common,' Tatton continued, 'but I believe that given time I could have made you love me. You are the only woman I have ever contemplated marrying, Briar. You are very special and I will always cherish the time I spent with you.'

He spooned *marula* jam on to his toast and watched in satisfaction as it dribbled over the edges.

'I would like to speak to you in private after breakfast, Briar,' he said. 'If you have no objection, Pat,' he added.

Pat laughed.

'Not at all. We'll have an hour or so while I check the boat and give Gola G. instructions.'

Now that Tatton had decided what to do, he relaxed. He entertained Pat and Briar with highly exaggerated stories of people he had met on his travels. Breakfast proceeded in a light-hearted mood.

Gola G. put his head around the door at the sound of laughter. He returned to the kitchen, scratching his head. He would never understand those white Africans. Their moods changed as swiftly as the waters in Kariba.

Tatton watched Briar slip lightly down the steps to the lower deck. She had found a blue ribbon and pulled her hair back from her high forehead. Happiness swung like a rainbow-coloured aura around her.

'You look like a schoolgirl who has had her first kiss,' he said as she walked towards him.

Self-consciously Briar put a hand to the ribbon.

'No, leave it on. It matches your eyes.'

She touched him lightly on the arm. She had to talk to him. She now bitterly regretted the night they had spent together at Fig Tree Camp.

He does not deserve to be hurt, she thought as she studied the strong line of his jaw and his dark hair ruffled in the wind. He is a fine man, but I have to make him realize that I intend spending the rest of my life with Pat.

She glanced across to the bank where Pat was loading the old jeep. She did not see a balding man with a fringe of grey hair. She saw a man she had always respected and whose company she enjoyed. She saw a man she loved. Someone who made her feel safe and secure. He was part of her land and she wanted to be part of his life.

Tatton saw her eyes grow soft as she looked at Pat and his resolve hardened. His early love had now turned to a desire to hurt her and destroy her happiness.

'Tatton,' she said hesitantly, 'Nepal and Antarctica sound wonderful and exotic, but they are for people like you. I'm a simple homebody. I love Zimbabwe and want to stay here.'

Tatton remained silent. She could see a nerve twitching in his jaw.

'I'm sorry about Fig Tree Camp,' she continued, her voice barely audible. 'But . . .' she stopped. She could not explain that his tenderness had been a panacea for Kirk Madden's brutal rape.

'Yes, Fig Tree,' said Tatton, leaning against the rail with his back to Pat and Gola G. on the opposite bank.

He studied her face carefully. For a moment he faltered in what he was about to do. Then the image of Briar kneeling on the deck clinging to Pat returned to taunt him. He would not let an older man be the victor. He had to make Briar believe him.

'We should talk about that night,' he said coldly.

The tone of his voice chilled Briar. She had a premonition that something dark and dreadful was about to happen. The crocodile, floating like a slimed log beneath *Gola*, lay in her mind and she shivered.

'It should never have happened, Briar. I am truly sorry.'

Briar felt herself relax. Tatton merely wanted to apologize. Her relief was so great that she scarcely heard what he was saying.

'. . . you remember I said that I could never promise you marriage, only travel, love and laughter.'

Briar nodded. Cold ropes of dread suddenly knotted her muscles tightly.

'I can never marry, Briar. I am HIV positive.'

Blood drained from her face. Tatton thought she would

faint. He underestimated both the woman and her new-found love for Pat.

'You are despicable and a liar, Tatton Boyce,' she said quietly. Her words would have had less impact had she shouted or cried. 'You told me I was safe. You said you had a condom.'

'I had, but I left them at Kame Two,' he answered. 'I didn't expect you to accept me into your bed, Briar. I couldn't help myself. It's the first time I was unprepared. Believe me. Do you really think that I'm the sort of man who would put a woman at risk knowing that I could transmit the virus?'

'You unspeakable swine.'

'Briar, I understand how you feel, truly I do. But . . .' He hesitated. 'I wanted you to be with me always. I found that I wanted to marry you. I have never felt the need for marriage before.'

Briar moved towards him, intent only on ridding herself of the man and his words which had ruined her future.

'How I hate you.'

She seemed unaware of what she was doing. Tatton was totally unprepared for the violent shove. His feet slipped on the wet planks. He clung frantically to the floorboards. His fingers lost purchase as Briar's shoes stamped down on them.

He saw only the fury in her cold blue eyes as the dark water closed over his head.

Feeling the pull of the current he panicked. The croco-dile. He could sense its presence but he could not see it. He remembered Pat saying that it would submerge and attack from the depths.

Pat heard the splash and turned to face the houseboat.

'What happened?' he shouted.

'Tatton and I had an argument. I pushed him. He's in the water,' yelled Briar.

'The mugger!' bellowed Pat as he and Gola G. ran for the small boat.

Tatton's head broke the surface. He tried to draw his legs up to his chest. He could see again the crocodile's teeth, so clear in his camera lens as the courser carefully removed slivers of rotten flesh. He screamed and the image vanished.

Something touched his leg. It was hard and cold. It brought his body to an abrupt halt. He waited to feel the jaws clamp over his leg, as the mugger spiralled down to the depths to drown him.

'The anchor chain,' shouted Pat, as he and Gola G. reached the houseboat. 'The current has washed him up against the chain.'

They reached over and dragged Tatton into the boat.

'Let's go to the jeep,' whispered Tatton. 'I need dry land.'

Pat immediately turned the boat towards the shore. He and Gola G. helped Tatton from the boat. Pat left Tatton sitting in the sun leaning back against the jeep and he returned to the houseboat.

'Briar?' he said as he climbed on board, but one look at her eyes, cold and expressionless as the reptile's, stilled his questions. There would be time for explanations later, he decided.

'Come on, get into the boat,' he said.

On the shore Briar walked beside Pat as if lobotomized. Tatton had his back turned to them, checking his camera equipment. Briar ignored him. She climbed into the front seat of the jeep and waited patiently for Pat to complete his instructions.

Eventually Gola G. nodded, untied the small boat and headed back to the houseboat.

'When they came there was bad blood between the young and the old bull,' he muttered. 'Now they leave, it is between the young bull and Miss Briar.'

Pat decided to respect Briar and Tatton's silence. He waited until they were airborne before he spoke.

'The mugger must have been scared off when Briar glared at him under the *Gola* this morning,' he said lightly. Tatton was still his client and should be gentled.

Silence greeted his attempt. Pat shrugged and studied the topography unfolding below him. He was preparing to land the Cessna at Kame Two before Tatton spoke.

'If it's at all possible I'd like to spend tonight in Harare,' he said.

'Certainly,' answered Pat, secretly relieved that he would not have to sit through a silent dinner with Tatton and Briar. 'Give me an hour to refuel, book your hotel accommodation and check for messages in my office.' He paused for a moment, then added, 'I must apologize for the wet ending to our *Gola* trip. I had hoped to end your visit on a high note.'

Oh you did, thought Tatton, you certainly did. If I can't have Briar you definitely will not. The fury she displayed was because she fell for my story. She realized that there can be no future with you. It was almost worth that swim.

'I enjoyed my stay tremendously,' he said. 'Fig Tree Camp was a special treat.'

Pat felt Briar stiffen in the seat beside him. Fig Tree, Pat thought. So that's what caused this argument. Yet they seemed so happy when they returned. He remembered Tatton's hand resting on Briar's leg. Shrugging away the troubling thoughts he turned his attention to landing the

Cessna. There would be time to discuss the matter with Briar later.

Sheeba whined with delight as she saw the plane land. She licked Rudo's hand frantically, begging to be released, but Rudo kept a firm hold on his collar. It was a rule that Sheeba was only to be released once Pat reached the verandah.

Her excitement at seeing Pat extended to any clients who were with him. They were forced to accept sloppy kisses and scratches as she jumped up to lick their faces and welcome them.

Pat walked into the farmhouse with Sheeba proudly leading the way. He opened the door to his office and Sheeba took the opportunity to lick his hand. Pat ignored her. He was still trying to understand Briar's sudden antagonism to Tatton.

'Rudo,' he shouted. She appeared in the doorway and studied Pat. Something had upset her employer.

'Mr Boyce and I will be leaving for Harare this afternoon. Please see that his luggage is packed and taken to the plane.'

Rudo waited for an explanation, but Pat turned his attention to the pile of letters on his desk. He sorted through them quickly, tossing those which seemed unimportant into a wire tray. One held his attention. He sat down and slit open the envelope.

'Damn,' he said as he read the official document from the Immigration Department.

He folded the letter in half and threw it on the desk, then he picked it up and reread it.

There was a tentative knock on the door.

'Come in,' he called brusquely.

Briar walked into the room.

'Pat, I must talk to you,' she said, nervously twisting the plait which hung over her shoulder.

'Yes. We have a lot to talk about,' he agreed, 'but first read this.' He slid the letter across the desk. Briar picked it up and read it slowly.

'We knew it had to come,' she said. 'Now we must find a solution. We'll have to go up to Tara and Erin.'

'First I must fly Tatton to Harare. We'll leave for New Ganyani at first light tomorrow. Tell Rudo she can come with Buna. Jacob and Shoko will be delighted to see them.'

'Shoko threw Buna into the stream on the last visit, to see if she would float,' said Briar dubiously. 'He's very possessive of Jacob.'

'And has more mischief stored in his small body than a troop of monkeys,' added Pat. 'Briar,' he went on, as she turned to leave. 'I think you should come to the airstrip and say goodbye to Tatton.'

'We have nothing to say to each other, ever,' replied Briar, her expression cold and unforgiving.

Pat nodded.

'It's your choice, but not a very professional one when running a camp.'

She swallowed, then managed a small smile.

'You're right. I'll say goodbye and pray never to see him again.'

'Good girl.'

Sheeba sat on the seat of the Toyota beside Briar. She whimpered softly as the plane circled overhead and then headed towards Harare.

Briar fondled the ridgeback's ears and ran her fingers down the spine of hair standing up on the dog's back.

'He'll be back, Sheeba,' she said. 'You're lucky, he loves you. You have no explaining to do. How am I ever going to explain that I love him but can never live with him? Even if I have an Aids test now and it's negative, I could still have the virus and in five years' time it could be positive. Oh Sheeba . . .'

Tears streamed down her face and Sheeba tried to climb on to her lap to comfort her.

'You silly old girl,' she said between hiccups, 'get back on to your seat.'

Sheeba refused to move. She tried to lick Briar's salty cheeks.

'Oh Sheeba, I love him so much,' sobbed Briar.

She put her arms around the dog's neck and Sheeba's red coat splotched into dark patches as the hair absorbed Briar's tears.

Chapter Twenty-seven

TARA FLUNG back her head and laughed. Her tangled curls danced across her face. She did not seem to feel the wind's cold bite as it whipped across her skin and dried her lips.

'Ganyani could not have been as lovely as New Ganyani,' she said to Erin, seated beside her in the Toyota.

'It was different,' he admitted. 'Here we are near Chete safari area. There we were up near the Victoria Falls. Both areas have their own particular beauty.'

'But you still miss Ganyani and Kame,' she said soberly.

'Yes, Tara, I spent my childhood there. Those memories will always be special and precious.'

Tara could have pinched herself for breaking the joyous mood of the morning. For a moment she had forgotten that Ganyani and Kame meant a life with his twin brothers and his mother.

'Here you will make new memories, Erin,' she said.

Erin nodded and manoeuvred the Toyota around a pothole in the track.

'Today we'll see how you like tracking buffalo,' he said. 'Hopefully we'll build some memories for you to take back to Italy.'

If I return, thought Tara.

She had become a part of New Ganyani very quickly. Every morning early there was a queue outside her clinic. Word of the 'doctor' at New Ganyani had spread with the rapidity of a bush fire. Tara was unable to turn away women who had walked for days to reach the clinic.

Erin warned her that the authorities would hear of the clinic and demand to see her work permit. She had countered that she was not charging for her services therefore it could not be considered work.

Erin merely shrugged. He knew the ways of Africa. He waited daily for a letter or phone call from the Ministry of Immigration demanding to know why his guest was working and stating that her visa had expired.

A soft whistle brought the Toyota to a halt.

Jonas jumped down from the trackers' seat and joined Erin. They squatted over what looked like cattle droppings and cattle hoofprints in the sand.

Erin straightened up and smiled at Tara.

'Your buffalo,' he said. 'The spoor is fresh. It looks as if they are on their way to the spring to drink.'

Tara slung her camera case over her shoulder.

'Take a shot,' said Erin.

She looked around at the grass and deserted road.

'Of what?' she asked.

'Anything. I need to hear how loud the shutter is.'

She focused the Nikon on Jonas and pressed the button. The noise was surprisingly loud in the silence.

'I'd leave the cameras in the Toyota,' he suggested. 'After a few hours of walking they will weigh a ton. You won't be able to use them without alerting the buffalo that we are near.'

As her happy expression hardened into one of intransigence, he quickly added, 'Take your video. It will tuck into your gilet and you won't have it swinging against trees and catching in bushes. Videos are fine. My last client used one and we found that the soft hum doesn't disturb the animals.'

Tara obediently tucked her camera case into the box under the trackers' seat and took out her video.

'Not much room,' she laughed as she wedged it into her gilet. She had to unzip the top of the gilet before the video would remain in place.

Erin blushed as he watched her. He was conscious of her physical attributes. He had come to respect her expertise in the clinic and he appreciated the compassion she showed for the people who consulted her.

'She's a Milanese bush-baby,' he told Pat, when his father phoned to find out if Tara was well and happy. 'I can't believe that this is her first visit to Africa. She now speaks basic Sindebele to the women and children at her clinic.'

'You sound as if you approve of young Tara,' his father had teased.

'I do. She's fun. I enjoy her company,' said Erin, deliberately misunderstanding Pat.

Jonas stood patiently waiting for Tara. He liked her, as did all the staff at New Ganyani.

'You follow Jonas, I'll bring up the rear,' said Erin. 'Don't scream or run. Do as you're told. Remember, buffalo may smell and look like cattle, but all hunters respect and most fear them.'

Tara nodded soberly. 'Don't worry. Jonas's footsteps won't have time to cool before mine take their place.'

Erin looked at her sharply. She had a wicked sense of humour. Her expression was grave but he detected a faint twitch at the corner of her mouth.

Suddenly he wished that he had postponed this expedition until Pat returned with Jacob.

The tracker was spending longer at Kame Two than Erin had anticipated. Apparently Pat had taken Briar and a client down to his houseboat, leaving Rudo and Jacob in charge of Kame Two. Erin was not sure how Tara would behave when faced with her first buffalo. Buffalo were unpredictable. If left alone they were usually as docile as cattle, but if they were wounded or had been harassed they could be fiendishly cunning and dangerous.

He found Tara equally unpredictable. He was never certain whether she was serious or joking, but he admired the enthusiasm with which she embraced life. She had been looking forward to this day of tracking buffalo since her arrival at New Ganyani and Erin could not disappoint her.

He sighed and signalled for Jonas to pick up the spoor. As they walked a faint rustling broke the silence. The dry leaves on the mopane trees moved in the wind like large brown and gold moths opening and closing their wings. Erin groaned. The wind would probably freshen by late afternoon.

Jonas noticed the wind at the same time and looked up at the mare's-tails stretched high across the clear blue of the sky. He turned his eyes back to the ground.

'Not good for buffalo,' he said in Sindebele. Before Erin could answer he heard Tara say, 'Why? Don't buffalo like wind?'

Jonas had heard Tara say the odd word in Sindebele but did not realize how conversant she was with the language. He could not wait to tell Jacob what he had discovered.

When Jacob met Tara in Bulawayo, he returned to New

Ganyani saying that if only Tara understood the language of the country she would be a good wife for Erin. They could then train Erin's sons to hunt, just as he had taught Erin to run on spoor.

'I'm sure the wind doesn't worry buffalo,' replied Erin. 'We don't like it because we don't want the buffalo to scent us. If the wind eddies, it makes tracking more difficult.'

Tara nodded. She added this information to her growing stockpile of facts about Zimbabwe. Jonas slowed his pace. Tara automatically held her breath, uncertain as to why they were now proceeding so cautiously. They were in a stand of second-growth mopane. Probably the result of using Agent Orange during the Bush War, thought Tara, looking at the stunted growth.

She turned round to Erin.

'Was this one of the defoliated areas during the war?' she whispered.

'War?' answered Erin. 'Dad quotes Byron. He calls it "the feast of vultures and the waste of life". I prefer Napoleon's description – "the business of barbarians".' He put his finger across his lips to signal silence, then added, 'Today we are not going to talk about war, only buffalo.'

Tara watched entranced as Jonas puffed ash from a small bag he took from his shirt pocket. The wind caught the grey dust and played with it, swirling it back and forth between the trees.

Jonas stood motionless watching the dust waltzing on the wind. Then he pointed to the right.

Erin nodded. They continued walking forward slowly until they reached a clearing. They stopped and once again consulted the ash bag. Suddenly a crunching of leaves alerted them. A buffalo cow, her eyes wide with fear at the scent of humans, which seemed to cling to her like oxpeckers, tiptoed from the bush.

There was a second of stunned silence as she saw them in the clearing. The cow snorted and pirouetted, her hooves lifted high from the ground. She crashed back into the dry scrub bellowing in alarm.

Immediately every buffalo in the stand of mopane trees behind them stampeded. The wind teased and taunted them, carrying the smell of humans to their flared nostrils.

They milled around blindly, unable to find the source of the hated smell.

'Let's get out of here,' said Erin, 'before one of them tramples us by mistake.'

Soon they left the snorting and crashing behind them and Jonas slowed the pace.

Erin pointed to an anthill rising up high and red ahead of them. A small acacia clung to one side affording light shade.

'We'll stop there for a break,' he said, worried about Tara's possible reaction to the bemused buffalo.

'Well, that was fun,' said Tara, as she flopped in the shade. 'I'll never forget the look of absolute horror on that buffalo's face when it saw us.'

'Here comes more fun,' said Erin, staring at a bank of dust bearing down on the anthill. 'We're downwind from them. They are running from our scent in the mopane stand. Sit still, they'll split and run past the anthill. We're safe up here.'

A faint sound of roaring and snorting reached them.

'Check them as they come past,' he told Jonas. 'See if there are any trophy horns. Our next hunt is for trophy buffalo. It will be good to know what we have in this herd.'

Jonas merely nodded. His eyes were fixed on the massive dark shapes now emerging from the dust. Their hooves beating the hard ground drummed deep as thunder preceding a storm.

The leading animals had galloped past them and were now upwind. The smell of humans again spilled into their wide nostrils. They tried to turn, but were forced on by the stampeding herd. The terrified animals seethed dark and thick as rolling storm clouds around the anthill. The noise was deafening. Erin, Tara and Jonas were marooned in a heaving mass of crazed buffalo.

'The *nyati* must be broken up,' said Jonas. 'It is impossible to find large horns like this.'

Erin was silent for a while, looking down at the roaring sea of black beneath them. He had been relieved by Tara's initial reaction to the buffalo but he did not want to leave her alone now while he and Jonas ran into the herd to break it into smaller groups.

The buffalo would run away from them, faster than ticks scurrying from the body of a dead animal. It was dangerous but exhilarating. Erin had never broken a herd without Jacob. Common sense told him to leave the animals to thunder past them, but some perverse male pride made him want to show off in front of Tara.

'You stay here, Tara, and don't move no matter what happens,' he said.

She nodded mutely. She did not consider a promise binding unless it was made verbally. Erin breathed in deeply, then he and Jonas scrambled down the anthill. Waving their arms and screaming like maniacs they disappeared into the heaving sea of black animals.

Tara screamed and screwed up her eyes, certain that they would be pulped beneath the pounding hooves.

When she opened her eyes again she gasped. The herd seemed to have swallowed Jonas and Erin. She could no longer see Erin's fair head in the dust.

Without thinking, she slithered down the anthill and ran blindly into the boiling, seething press of animals.

The stench of dung, dust and animal sweat was overpowering. Wherever she looked, huge nobbled bosses and curved horns swept past her. She waited for the inevitable thud, as one of them ran into her. Nothing happened. The crazed buffalo parted like tall grass to the body of a lion as they saw her and raced away in another direction.

Eventually the roars, snorts and thundering hooves gave way to a whimper. The storm had passed.

Tara wiped her eyes. They were red and ached with the grit kicked up by the herd. The flash of adrenalin which had sent her racing down the hill and into the herd abated. She felt nauseous and deflated.

'Tara!' Erin was furious. He strode across the open plain to where she was standing. 'I told you to stay on the anthill. Who on earth do you think you are? Superwoman?'

The anger in his voice and fury in his eyes were the starter's gun for Tara's collapse. She sank to the ground and buried her face in her hands.

'I was scared,' she sobbed. 'I couldn't see you. I thought you were dead. There was so much noise and dust. I didn't think I'd see you again.'

Erin looked down at the huddled figure sobbing at his feet. His fury, like the buffalo herd, vanished.

'And that meant so much to you that you ran into that maelstrom of buffalo?'

Erin knelt beside her.

'Yes,' she whispered.

Heedless of Jonas watching, Erin put his arms around Tara and kissed away the tears on her cheeks. His lips moved down and settled gently on hers.

In the dust and stench of buffalo dung and sweat, two young people silently settled their future. Jonas smiled to himself as he led the way back to the Toyota. He had a lot to tell Jacob. He was now certain that they would teach Erin's sons to hunt.

Erin walked behind Tara soberly. He had not intended to kiss her. The sudden depth of his emotions for this woman stunned and frightened him a little. He found that he wanted to taste those soft lips again and keep that dark, curly head cuddled into his shoulder. It was a good feeling. He whistled softly as they walked.

Two old men were squatting on their haunches, like thin brown stick insects, beside the Toyota awaiting their return.

Jonas broke into a torrent of Sindebele when he saw them. They hung their heads.

'Let them speak,' ordered Erin. 'I do not think they came to steal.'

Erin and Jonas listened in silence. The two men gestured as they spoke.

'It looks like a fisherman story to me,' said Tara, looking at one of the men's outstretched arms.

'Almost,' answered Erin. 'He's describing the length of

the horns of the buffalo which has taken over the spring near their village and is terrorizing the women when they go to collect water.'

'Do buffalo do that?' asked Tara.

'Occasionally one finds an evil-tempered old bull who decides to contest an area. He chases anyone who comes near,' explained Erin, listening to Jonas and the two old men.

'Why is he telling you about the buffalo?'

'He wants us to shoot it,' he answered. 'We are allowed to shoot rogue buffalo. They know this. It's amazing how many buffalo become rogues when the villagers want meat.'

Jonas whispered something to Erin.

'Right,' Erin agreed. 'Tell them we'll come tomorrow.'

'Can't we go now?' begged Tara. 'These poor people will have no water and look how thin they are.'

Erin shook his head. The village was an hour's drive away. It would be nearing sunset by the time they tracked and shot the animal. They wouldn't return to New Ganyani until after dark.

'Oh please, Erin. I've never actually hunted buffalo.'

'You won't enjoy seeing the animal shot,' he said.

'I promise I won't do anything silly this time.'

Sensing that the woman was on their side the two old men held out their skeletal hands to Tara and gabbled in Sindebele. Her eyes filled with tears and she looked up at Erin who had turned his back on the men.

'Please,' she said quietly.

'Tell them to climb on the truck,' Erin ordered Jonas.

Jonas grinned. He would take the buffalo liver back to New Ganyani. His family would eat well tonight.

Tara smiled and touched Erin's arm. 'Thank you.'

'If we shoot and wound it, you will do exactly as you're told,' he said. 'No more stunts like today. If you decide to run when we have a wounded buffalo, you'll endanger all of our lives.' Erin looked at her thoughtfully. 'Let me hear you promise to obey my instructions.'

Tara looked at Erin with new respect.

'I promise,' she said.

Erin nodded and reversed the Toyota onto the dirt track. Soon the track dwindled to a single path. Jonas jumped down and walked in front of the Toyota, checking for cavernous antbear holes. Though the bulky, grotesque creature is nocturnal, Jonas hoped to spot one in the open. He enjoyed the flesh of the pig-like creature. It was a rare treat to find one.

Suddenly the two old men in the back started chattering and pointing to the right. Jonas turned and spoke to them.

'If we're to continue at this walking pace, we had better go straight to the spring and find the spoor.'

The men scrambled down from the Toyota. One set off for the village, to alert the people that a hunter was in the area.

The women and children would gather every battered enamel and plastic container they could find and set out for the spring to partake of the spoils.

The other old man joined Jonas. He walked remarkably well, keeping pace easily. Finally the Toyota stopped. With difficulty Tara unclenched her fingers from the handhold on the dashboard. She rubbed her numbed fingers, which ached as blood flowed back into them. She was relieved that the bucketing truck had come to a halt.

'Excuse me,' she said, and ran for the cover afforded by an anthill.

She trampled down the grass and squatted quickly,

almost screaming as a tuft of grass sprang back and tickled her naked flesh.

'There you are,' said Erin. 'We were about to come and look for you.'

He and Jonas had rifles and were ready to move. Tara quickly fell into her appointed place in the file and they walked quietly to the spring.

'Damn,' swore Erin. 'That other old one should enter the Olympics. He must have run all the way.'

'It's the smell of meat in his nostrils that gives him the strength of a young man,' said Jonas.

'If that buff has any sense it'll be miles away by now. We have no chance of surprising it with this hubbub.'

The old man turned his head and looked at Erin and Jonas mournfully.

'My people are afraid of the *nyati* so they make a noise to let it know that they are coming.'

'Wonderful,' said Erin.

The mopane trees thinned to a thickly reeded vlei. A muddy wallow lay to one side of the water and a well used footpath showed where the villagers collected their water.

'I can understand the old bull chasing them,' said Erin sourly. 'Imagine this lot of magpies descending every morning and evening.'

He glowered at the group of people chattering excitedly as they came down the path.

'Tell them to go back up the path out of sight of the spring,' he ordered Jonas. 'Tell them that if I hear one sound from them I'll go back to New Ganyani. They can look for someone else to shoot this buffalo.'

Silence was as instantaneous and complete as the stillness following the retort of a four-sixteen rifle.

Erin rested the butt of his rifle on the top of his shoe as he waited for Jonas to pick up the spoor. Jonas looked up at the sky then across the vlei.

'What's he doing that for?' whispered Tara.

'He's deciding what he'd be doing at this time of day if he was a buffalo,' answered Erin. 'Come,' he said as Jonas whistled. 'He's found spoor.'

To her surprise Tara found that she was shivering.

The thought of one of the massive creatures which had milled round in the crazed herd actually stalking them scared her. Tara Andretti felt the first tremors of respect and fear which buffalo had instilled in African hunters from the time of Selous.

Years of hunting made the old-timers as wise as the bulls themselves. They usually left the old *nyati* alone.

The spoor led them away from the vlei and back into a dense stand of mopane. Every footstep crunched the fallen leaves until they seemed to be walking on firecrackers.

The buffalo has to hear us, thought Tara as she concentrated on placing her feet in the footprints left by Jonas, trying to minimize the crackling. Her eyes roved from left to right, looking for a tree to climb. If the buffalo charged, she wanted to be out of the reach of those sweeping, pointed horns.

She felt vulnerable and insecure without a weapon in her hands. The old mud bull was making no effort to throw them off his trail. The spoor meandered through stand after stand of mopane trees without halting.

'He knows we are behind him,' whispered Jonas, pausing for a moment.

'How? He hasn't seen us and we're downwind to the spoor,' said Tara, airing her new-found knowledge.

'This is the time of day when they walk like old men and graze. We have passed two places with good sweet grass for him to stop at, but still he moves quickly.'

Tara looked around her, expecting to see the huge black shape burst from the bush, but all was quiet, as if the bush was holding its breath, waiting for the outcome of the hunt.

Jonas picked up the spoor again, but Tara noticed that he now glanced around as he walked. His eyes were no longer fixed on the ground. They walked quietly into an area dotted with red clay termitaria. Tara liked to think of these antheaps as turreted fairy castles. It fascinated her to see termite homes which had probably existed in the same form one hundred million years ago, and for a while she forgot the buffalo.

Suddenly she shrieked, jerked roughly from her musing by Jonas. He pushed her behind Erin, then took up his position beside Erin.

Tara gulped. The earth seemed to shake, as part of an antheap they had just passed dislodged itself.

It was the mud bull. He had doubled back on his tracks and stood in ambush waiting for them to approach him as they concentrated on following his spoor.

The four-sixteen rang out. Tara thought her eardrums had exploded.

'Damn,' shouted Erin, 'low. It's in that grass-filled gut.'

Tara could now see the killing rage in the buffalo's eyes. They were mean and crazed. Her ears were ringing. She was deafened. The pounding hoofbeats were muffled, as were the roars and snorts of rage, as the animal crabbed towards them holding its formidable horns high.

Tara squeezed her arms across her chest. She could not stop shivering. Mother Mary save us, she prayed as the second shot ran out. The buffalo staggered as it absorbed the impact. Even as the bullet sped through its vital organs it continued its charge. It seemed as if death itself would not halt the buffalo.

At the third shot the great creature snorted. It dropped its head as if unable to hold up the weight of its broad horns any longer. Slowly its legs crumpled and it sank to its knees, facing them with bowed head as if in prayer. Jonas and Erin did not move. Erin kept his rifle trained on the old bull.

Tara felt the overwhelming sadness which accompanies death. She blinked back the tears, determined not to let the men see her cry, and stared up at the sky.

Slowly and painfully the bull lifted his head. The blood ran from his mouth and trickled across his massive chest. His dying bellow ran out across the silent bush, as forsaken and chilling a sound as the trumpeting of the 'Last Post'.

Tara trembled, but it was not yet over. Once again, his call submitting to death echoed across the land.

She walked away from Erin and Jonas. She stood with her back to them, staring at the glowing sky. Her shoulders shook and her tears, warm and salty as the buffalo's blood, ran down her cheeks.

Erin turned round. She seemed so small and vulnerable. He moved towards her. Jonas put out a restraining hand.

'It is better for her to mourn alone,' he advised.

Erin nodded. 'Let's get the message to the villagers and they can come and hack up the carcass.'

'They have heard,' said Jonas.

Erin was about to argue when the faint sound of laughter and excited talk heralded the arrival of the villagers.

Tara dried her eyes on the sleeve of her shirt when the

women arrived with their pails and knives. Erin and Jonas pretended that they had not noticed her absence.

They slit open the heavy belly. Tara stepped back as foul gases belched out and nauseated her. The men dragged the sack of semi-digested grasses to one side. It was the signal for the women to plunge axes, pangas and knives into the carcass, all hacking and slashing quickly and eagerly. They looked like crazed butchers.

Jonas walked up to one of the men and issued a command. A woman rummaged in her basin under the hunks of meat and held up the large red liver. She wrapped it in leaves and handed it to Jonas.

'We must get back to the Toyota before it's too dark,' said Erin.

Jonas nodded, delighted with the liver, warm and full in his hands.

Tara fell into line. There was no time to talk. Jonas set a gruelling pace. She was determined to prove that she could walk as fast and as far as the men.

The evening star was high and bright as they climbed into the truck.

'They're lucky,' said Erin. 'There's a full moon tonight. There won't be much left for the hyenas or vultures tomorrow.'

'They'll need more than mere moonlight to avoid chopping each other,' said Tara.

Erin was pleased that her voice was firm and steady. She had obviously accepted the death of the old mud bull. Seeing the people's joy at having meat probably helped, he thought.

'They'll light fires to enable them to take all the meat and to keep predators away,' he explained. 'Lions prefer to hunt on dark and rainy nights. The full moon is not friendly to stealth, though as Jacob frequently reminds me, "a lion is a lion is a lion".'

Tara laughed and Erin breathed a silent sigh of relief. She had weathered her first kill. She would be all right in the bush.

He put his hand over hers. Jonas smiled and patted the lump of liver on the seat beside him. Tonight his wife would be grateful for the treat brought home by her hunter husband. He hummed. Tara listened, then picked up the rhythm. Erin listened as the two harmonized.

Italians, like the people of Africa, have an uncanny ability to harmonize and sing effortlessly. Pat had once said Erin sounded like a bull-frog in the mating season when he sang, so Erin wisely left the singing to Tara and Jonas while he tapped on the steering wheel.

Tara's fingers curled around his. She felt as if she had returned from a long and dangerous journey.

Home is with Erin, she thought. All I have to do is convince him and Papa.

Chapter Twenty-eight

PAT HAD brought Jacob and fresh supplies from Kame Two a few hours before and had gone back for Rudo.

Shoko held tightly to Jacob's hand, jerking Jacob's shoulder as he jumped up and down in excitement.

Jacob smiled down at him. The child was still as thin as a mopane twig, though he consumed enough *sadza* and soured milk to feed a dozen children.

'He doesn't grow fat because he never stays still,' said Jonas.

'There will be time for that when he is old,' said Jacob.

'You spoil him. He will never be a good worker.'

'He has only me to call father,' retorted Jacob, 'and he will be a tracker as I am. They are here.' He squinted up at the pale, cloudless sky.

Tara shook her head at Erin and he smiled.

'For once you're wrong, Jacob,' said Tara. 'See, there is nothing.'

She stared into the void above her until she felt light-headed.

'There,' pointed Jacob.

Tara saw a speck, but it seemed to vanish as she stared.

'It's Dad,' agreed Erin.

A few minutes later the faint drone of the Cessna justified Jacob's prediction.

Shoko crowed with delight. Mr Pat always bought Rudo and his new mother never arrived without cakes, sticky toffee and bright pink coconut ice.

The door of the aircraft had just opened when Sheeba came tearing down the strip. Shoko clung to Jacob's legs. The red dog terrified him. Sheeba knew this and growled at him as she skidded to a standstill.

'Stop it,' Erin said to her. 'You should be past the stage of scaring children.'

Sheeba hung her head and sidled up to him. Suddenly she spun round and raced back to meet Briar, Pat, Rudo and Buna. Proudly she escorted them to the Toyota.

Though Pat laughed and chatted, Erin sensed that something was wrong. He knew that he would have to wait until Pat was ready to talk about it.

'Breakfast?' queried Briar as they drove up to the camp and she saw the table set for them.

'I know Dad,' said Erin. 'He's up before birds have fluffed their feathers and doesn't think of things like eating.'

'Cheeky young pup,' said Pat, cuffing Erin playfully on the chin, as they trooped into the dining hut.

After Katoro had filled his mug for a third time with steaming black coffee, Pat sat back in his chair and pulled the letter from his pocket.

'Trouble?' asked Erin, noting the official black letterhead.

Pat nodded. 'Nothing we haven't been expecting. The Immigration Department wish to inform us that Miss Tara Andretti has to leave the country. Her visa has expired.'

They all looked at Tara. She was silent. Her face was white and her lips trembled.

'No,' she whispered. 'No, I can't go.'

'You can always return to Milan and see your family, then come back. You will get another three months as a tourist,' soothed Pat.

'You don't understand, Pat. Once I return, my whole family will close ranks and I'll never be allowed to come back on my own. It's only because you spoke to Papa that I was allowed to come up to New Ganyani.'

Tara turned to Erin and to his dismay tears started welling in her eyes.

'I can't leave my clinic, Erin. What will they do without me? There is nowhere for them to go.'

Erin looked at Pat. 'What can we do, Dad?'

Pat sipped at his coffee thoughtfully, while Briar reached across and covered Tara's hand with her own.

'We obviously can't have her commuting between Italy and Zimbabwe.' Pat blew on his coffee to cool it before taking another sip. 'The only other solution is for Tara to apply for temporary residence here. Once she is granted her TR permit she can work. Eventually she will gain permanent residence in the country.'

Tara pulled at her fingers.

'Papa would never allow me to take up residence in any country other than Italy. I am an Andretti. The Andrettis are Italian.' She thought for a moment, then added, 'Even if Papa weakened, Mamma and my relations would never forgive him. No, that is impossible.'

Pat put down his mug.

'Come, Tara, show us your clinic. Perhaps we'll think of something whilst we are walking around. You had better bring my rifle,' Pat told Jacob, 'and Shoko,' he added as a pair of huge dark eyes stared up at him from behind the tracker.

Jonas appeared carrying Buna on his arm.

'All right, you come too,' he said.

Jonas beamed but Shoko scowled when he saw that his sister was to accompany them. He was certain that she lived on cakes and coconut ice at Kame Two.

'See that Sheeba is tied up,' said Pat. 'I don't want her biting anyone or flushing animals. Let's have a peaceful walk.'

'I closed the clinic for today when we knew that you were coming,' said Tara as they approached the grass building beneath the baobab tree.

'Usually the waiting room is full,' said Erin, pointing to the open-sided section with the rough benches.

Pat walked through the building, studying it carefully.

'You planned and supervised all of this?' he said to Tara.

'Whilst I was in Harare,' said Erin.

'Congratulations, Tara. It's perfect.'

Tara basked in Pat's approval and for a moment her problem was forgotten.

'Let's keep walking,' suggested Pat, linking arms with Tara and Briar. 'I find that I think better on my feet than when sitting on my bottom.'

The girls laughed.

'In that case I'm going to walk with you all day,' said Tara. 'Pat?' she continued, suddenly serious. 'Are those the only options I have?'

'Think, Dad,' said Erin, his face pale. 'We can't let Tara go.'

'Could Tara not go down to Mum's sister in South Africa for a few weeks?' said Briar. 'My aunt lives on a game ranch in the Eastern Transvaal. It's near the famous

Kruger National Park. She's a lovely person and would enjoy your company. My uncle died last year and she's very lonely.'

Pat nodded slowly.

'That would work,' he mused. 'It would give us another three months to persuade Mr Andretti that the temporary residence permit is only to allow Tara to remain and work. It would not mean that she was renouncing her Italian heritage.'

They had turned from the road and were following a twisting path trodden by animals on their way to drink at the stream.

As they approached the water the vegetation became dense. Only faint light filtered through the trees. They spoke in whispers as if in a place of worship. Buna clung to Jonas. She tucked her small hands into the collar of his shirt, pulling it up tight beneath his Adam's apple.

Suddenly she screamed, a thin childish cry of terror. Pat spun round. Jacob was ready to hand him his rifle. The bushes shook and dry leaves crackled as something large broke cover, then slunk away noiselessly. Cautiously Jacob and Pat walked into the undergrowth.

'*Shumba*,' said Jacob, pointing out lion spoor and flicking a tuft of sandy hair from a thorn bush.

'They have eaten and drunk well and were sleeping,' said Jacob, reading the story from the flattened grass.

'If Buna had not screamed we would have walked on them,' added Pat soberly.

'Why did she scream?' asked Briar. 'She could not have seen them, they were completely hidden.'

Jonas spoke to Buna softly and her crying stopped.

'It was Shoko,' he said.

Jacob bent over Shoko and his voice was hard and demanding.

'He was imitating you, Miss Tara,' he said. 'Shoko found a thorn and gave Buna an injection as she bounced on Jonas's back.'

'Tell him if he hurts his sister again, I'll take him to the clinic and use the longest needle I have on him,' threatened Tara.

'This time his mischief worked to our advantage,' said Pat. 'I would not have enjoyed walking on to a sleeping pride of lions.'

'Are they still here?' asked Briar, peering around.

'With full bellies and their thirst satiated, they've probably moved to a more peaceful spot to sleep the day away,' comforted Erin.

'What would have happened if we had walked on top of them?' asked Tara.

'They would probably have run, as they've just done,' answered Pat, checking that his rifle was loaded.

'Or they could have attacked us,' added Erin, 'especially if there were young cubs in the pride.'

Tara shivered though the day was warm. The party proceeded cautiously down to the river bank.

'There,' said Erin. 'Isn't it lovely?'

The stream swirled into clear shallow pools. Blue and apricot commelinas trailed down the banks. Tara broke off a lemon ipomoea flowering beside her. She tucked the flower into Buna's hair.

'There, now you're a pretty girl,' she said and was rewarded with a tearful smile.

The girls took off their shoes and dabbled their feet in the cool water. Shoko sat and moulded strange animals in the wet mud and Buna fell asleep on Jonas's lap sucking her thumb.

'There is a third solution,' said Erin, thoughtfully breaking up a twig and throwing the pieces into the water. He paused and watched the grey sticks swirl slowly around the pool then submerge as the current caught them and deposited them in a pool lower down the river.

They waited, but Erin seemed uncertain as to how to continue.

'Yes?' said Pat eventually.

Erin kept his gaze fixed firmly on the floating twigs.

'Tara could marry me,' he blurted out. 'As Mrs Gifford she could run her clinic.'

A stunned silence greeted his pronouncement. They all looked at Tara.

Jacob and Jonas found it expedient to help Shoko mould animals.

'I told you so,' whispered Jonas.

Jacob frowned. 'Erin has ears like the impala. He hears everything,' he admonished.

'Marriage?' queried Pat, and Erin's neck streaked scarlet as the flame lily.

'It is another solution,' he defended himself.

'A solution or a proposal, Erin?' asked Briar, as Tara studied her toes beneath the water.

'Marriage is a lifelong commitment, son. It's not to be undertaken lightly,' said Pat quietly, when Erin did not answer. 'I can understand you wanting to help Tara, but can you imagine her family's reaction when they learn that the marriage is a sham?'

'I'm sorry, Tara, I didn't mean to blurt it out like this, but I do mean it. Will you marry me? Gifford men have fought and died for this country since the eighteen hundreds and I intend fighting for you, Tara. I've felt like this since we met in Bulawayo, but it's only now that I realize I don't want to live without you.'

Everyone held their breath. Even Shoko seemed to sense that something important was taking place. He stopped splashing in the mud and sat still.

'Let her say yes,' whispered Jonas. For once Jacob did not reprimand him.

Tara looked from Pat to Briar as if trying to read their thoughts, then she turned to Erin.

'If this marriage is our third solution, then I agree. It is the best of all the ideas,' she teased, keeping her face impassive and stern. Erin was horrified.

'A solution,' he stammered. 'Oh no, Tara. I mean it. I want to marry you.'

Tara held out her arms to Erin. 'And I want to marry you and become Mrs Tara Gifford. But ...' she paused. 'Do you think I could have a second proposal, perhaps a little more private?'

They all laughed and crowded round to congratulate the couple as Erin swung Tara off her feet and hugged her.

Jacob and Jonas came to shake hands.

'Your sons will all be great hunters,' they predicted. 'And your daughters will be beautiful and bring much *lobola* when they marry.'

'With the dowry from their husbands we will buy more land,' laughed Erin.

Pat held Tara close.

'I can think of no one I would rather see married to my son. Welcome, daughter.'

Tara stood on tiptoe and kissed Pat.

'Papa?' she said. 'What is Papa going to say?'

'A lot – but we will ignore most of it,' said Erin.

Tara looked at Erin in relief.

Yes, she thought. I have found a man who can stand up to the Andrettis.

Pat turned to catch Briar's attention, but she deliberately stood behind Erin talking to Tara. She was terrified that in the joy of the moment Pat would tell Erin and Tara of their feelings for each other. She had to prevent it.

Pat's shoulders slumped.

Perhaps I misunderstood her, he thought as he watched the love in his son's face when he looked at Tara. It was probably a reaction to the old mugger. That's what I am, old, like the crocodile, an old fool. No young woman would want to be tied to me.

'Dad,' said Erin, moving away from Briar, 'why so sad? We'll still be here on Ganyani. Nothing will change.'

'Oh yes it will,' contradicted Tara. 'You will be a grandfather, Pat. We Italians love children. Erin,' she said 'you do realize that by marrying me, you also marry my family?'

Erin nodded.

'All two hundred of them,' laughed Tara. 'We will be expected to marry in Italy . . .' She paused. 'In a Roman Catholic church.'

Erin was nonplussed at this pronouncement.

'I'll marry you anywhere, Tara. My family are Church of England, but I believe that God is non-denominational. If he is Love, and I believe that he is, then he is there for everyone.'

Tara breathed a sigh of relief. Religion had been worrying her. She knew that unless their marriage was blessed by a Roman Catholic priest she could never marry Erin.

'Thank you,' she said quietly.

Erin laughed and kissed her. They did not see the

stricken look on Briar's face as she glanced up at Pat, but Jacob and Jonas did.

'Tonight the drums will talk of this. Perhaps those in the village of Gola G. will tell us what has taken place between Mr Pat and Briar,' said Jonas hopefully.

'We will hear the drums,' agreed Jacob.

Chapter Twenty-nine

THE NOISE rose to a deafening crescendo at the long table set beneath the thick canopy of vines. Bunches of grapes, black and glossy, hung like chandeliers over the hand-embroidered tablecloth. Andretti family members had been summoned from all over the country to help avert the impending catastrophe.

They were now gathered at Guido's country home overlooking his extensive vineyards. Guido Andretti sat at the head of the table, Maria at his right hand and Tomasina on his left.

'You have done well, Maria,' he said sarcastically. 'I have not seen such a gathering since my father's funeral.'

'Someone has to make you see reason and curb Tara,' replied Maria, popping a fat, green olive into her mouth. 'You have ruined that child. You allowed her to go up to that hunting ranch. It was against my advice, Guido. I told you to bring her home. No, you would not listen. Tara has squeezed and moulded you to her will, like this provolone cheese.'

She stuck her knife into the pear-shaped cheese in front of her as viciously as if stabbing Erin.

'Mamma is right, Papa,' agreed Tomasina. 'What do we know of this man or his family?'

'Tara should be here to marry a good Italian boy and

bear good Italian children,' piped up a voice from the end of the table.

Nods greeted the old woman's words.

'Andrettis always marry Italians. Our blood is pure,' said another. 'The Andrettis are looked up to in Milan. Now they will be mocked. Their daughter has run off with an African.'

'Enough!' bellowed Guido. He thumped the table. Tumblers of red wine spilt their contents over the beautiful cloth. A hush, usually found in vineyards on a hot summer's day, hung over the gathering.

'You cackle like grape-pickers, drunk on the fruit of the vine.'

Maria compressed her lips but said nothing.

Tomasina flicked her hair back over her shoulders. Tara has probably found some *porco* like that Kirk Madden, she thought. No, knowing her, it will be one who talks to trees and wants to save the people of the world. Both poor choices in her view. But like her mother she kept quiet when her father raged.

'Tara has the Andretti spirit. The spirit and force that built our empire. Never forget that.' Guido glared down the table and Marco dropped his eyes to his plate.

If only Tara was my son, the moon and stars would have Andretti written across them, Guido thought.

'Tara has made her choice. I have spoken to the young man and the father. They both seem impressive. The family are financially sound. The son owns his own ranch. Soon you will meet them.' This pronouncement was greeted with a fresh outburst of noise. Guido thumped on the table again. Maria closed her eyes as she saw her treasured cloth stained red.

'Tara wishes the wedding to be here at our country

home. Erin Gifford has agreed to marriage in our church. My grandchildren will therefore be Catholic. What more can I ask? I am a happy man.'

Guido did not feel it necessary to tell the family how Erin had bested him in the argument of where he and Tara would live. Threats, blandishments, the offer of shares in the Andretti business, even the promise of the vineyards as a wedding present, had not swayed the young man's resolve to live on New Ganyani with his bride.

Guido had replaced the phone with a grudging respect for Erin. Now he stared at the members of his family. No, they do not need to know, he thought. But I am happy that Tara has chosen a strong man. He paused for a long moment.

'We will see who mocks the Andretti name when they fight for wedding invitations,' he said. 'Maria, Tomasina, order dresses for the wedding now. No expense will be spared. We have some of the best couturiers in the world in our country. Choose your favourite. Let me be proud of my Andretti women.'

Maria threw her arms around her husband's neck. Nothing brought her out of a bad mood more quickly than the promise of new clothes.

'Now let us eat. I hate cold ravioli,' Guido said, well satisfied with the way he had defused the situation.

A low murmur continued at the end of the long table, but it was now as gentle as the drowsy buzzing of bees. The plentiful food and wine distracted the family members from the adventures of the younger Andretti girl.

'If Guido is satisfied, that is good enough for me,' mumbled an elderly aunt, toothlessly mouthing soft pasta. Red Tiganello from Guido's vineyards washed it down.

'It would not have happened in his father's time,'

muttered her husband. 'The girl would be back here. By the end of the year she would be married to an Italian boy from a good family.'

'Good family,' snorted the aunt. 'Remember that Guido's grandfather made his money dodging between cars, selling cigarettes.' She shovelled another spoonful of pasta into her mouth. 'And other things,' she added.

'Sshh,' warned the relatives sitting near the couple. 'The Andretti empire is a miracle in modern-day Italy. Guido deserves his success.'

They stood with alacrity as Guido rose and proposed a toast to the future happiness of his daughter.

Guido's eyes misted as he sat back in his chair and looked down at his vineyards. They rolled away rich and verdant beneath him. He had hoped that Tara, with her love of nature, would live in the sprawling red-clay-roofed home and run the vineyards. Women were coming to the fore as wine-makers. And he knew she could lead the way in Italy. Guido had dreamed of Tara Tiganello and Tara Frascati.

Now, he knew it would never be. Africa had claimed his favourite child. She would visit Milan, but her heart would remain in the heat and dust of that harsh land. Africa would never let her go.

Chapter Thirty

BEIGE CANVAS director's chairs were placed in a small circle around the fire at the New Ganyani camp. Katoro had put plates of sliced biltong and fried banana chips on the carved wooden chieftain stools which served as side tables.

Briar walked to the fire towelling her hair. The night was cold and she wanted to dry it over the glowing mopane logs. She hesitated as she tossed her hair back from her face, and saw Pat seated in one of the chairs.

I have to face him some time, she thought. It might as well be now.

Sheeba recognized her and bounded away from Pat's side to greet her.

'Sheeba,' called Pat, peering into the dark beyond the circle of firelight.

'It's all right, Pat, she's with me,' said Briar. She let a corner of her towel hang in front of her face as she neared the fire. 'I hope you don't mind if I sit her and dry my hair. It's ice-cold in that open shower.'

Pat stood up and placed a chair closer to his own.

'Good idea,' he said. 'You don't want a cold just before we leave for Milan.'

'I don't know if I'll be going, Pat,' said Briar, studying the flames as they skittered across the wood.

Pat was silent. She could feel both his disappointment and his disapproval.

'You see, Mum and Dad . . .'

'Can well afford the air fare and will be delighted at the news. In fact I'm inviting them to Kame Two for a few days. I'd like them to stay and run the place while we are overseas.'

'Oh, they would love that,' said Briar. 'I think they are lonely without the family at Inyati, especially now that I am not there. Mum would love to spoil your clients and Dad will send them home well versed in present-day party politics. Thank you for thinking of them, Pat.'

Briar put her hand on his leg, then pulled it away as if her fingers had rested on a hot Dover stove.

'I've been thinking about Fred and Blanche a lot, since our time together on *Gola*,' said Pat, idly stroking Sheeba's head. 'I wonder how they would accept Scott's father as your husband.'

The wood popped and sparks splattered like hot oil. Sheeba jumped up and shook her coat. She growled, a deep threatening rumble. Briar took the opportunity to calm her and avoid answering.

Pat leaned across and held her arm, turning her to face him. She tried to pull away, but it was as futile as trying to release a limb from the clamped jaws of a crocodile.

'Briar,' said Pat urgently. 'We must talk. You have to tell me whether you meant what you said on the houseboat.'

She shook her head and droplets of water swung away, glistening like dewdrops in the soft light.

'Don't treat me like this, Briar. You are being cruel and unfair.'

Her bottom lip quivered and Pat was immediately contrite.

319

'I didn't mean to be harsh, little one,' he said. 'Come, talk to me. Tell me what happened at Fig Tree Camp. I'll understand. Talk to me as a friend, as . . .' He stopped himself from adding 'as a father'.

Briar swallowed.

'I'm so ashamed,' she whispered. Pat leaned closer to hear her. He stroked her arm softly and rhythmically.

'Yes?'

Once she started talking Briar could not stop. It was as if Nyaminyami had smashed the coffer dam at Kariba and the waters tumbled and roared across the land. Her words were disjointed and the sequence of events jumbled.

She spoke first of Scott, their innocent love and plans to marry after the war. She then recalled the horror of the rape and shivered as she spoke of Kirk Madden. Her voice was almost inaudible as she described the tenderness of the night she had spent with Tatton and her decision to leave Zimbabwe with him.

She choked and Pat waited patiently for her to continue. Then she spoke of *Gola* and the argument she had had with Tatton, and what he had told her.

'So you see, Pat, I can never marry you.' She waited for a reply, then eventually broke the aching silence. 'Now you will not want to marry me. You cannot and I do understand.'

Katoro padded into the boma with fresh logs for the fire. Pat waved him away. He scurried back to the kitchen and told Jonas to listen at the boma fence as Briar was crying and Mr Pat was grave.

'There is something important taking place,' he said as he stirred the impala stew. 'Go and listen.'

'No,' said Jonas, 'I will lose my job if Mr Pat finds me. You have reason to be there. I do not.'

Katoro shook his head at Jonas's cowardice, picked up a plate of biltong and returned to the boma.

This time he remained a dark shadow as he listened.

Sheeba sensed a presence, lifted her head and growled.

'Quiet, girl,' said Pat. 'It's probably only jackal ferreting around the camp.'

Katoro pressed back hard against the reed fence and willed Sheeba not to investigate. Pat's voice calmed her. She closed her eyes, basking in the warmth of the fire.

Eventually Briar's voice died away and only the crack of logs as they opened to the heat broke the silence. Briar hung her head and stared at the ground. Her still damp hair fell limply over her face. She could not look at Pat. She did not want to see the disgust in his eyes.

Briar felt herself being lifted from her chair, the hands under her arms like steel levers. She was helpless in Pat's grip.

When she was on her feet he smoothed the hair from her face and tucked it behind her ears.

'Look at me, Briar Hanley,' he said softly.

Slowly she raised her head.

'Has it occurred to you that Tatton was lying?' he said.

'No,' she replied. 'I'm sure he used no form of protection.'

'You silly girl,' replied Pat, flicking a stray strand of hair from her forehead. 'Lying about the virus.'

Her eyes opened wide.

'But why?'

'Need you ask? It almost worked. It is one way of making certain that if you didn't leave with him, you certainly wouldn't live with me,' said Pat.

'No. I can't accept that. No one could be that cruel.'

'Love and lust know no boundaries, Briar. A rejected man is as vicious as a rejected woman.'

Pat held Briar to him and she sighed as if she had been on a long lonely journey.

'We will have you tested periodically if it makes you happy,' he said. 'But HIV positive or negative I want you to be my wife, share my bed and know my love.'

Suddenly Briar pulled away from Pat.

'What if it's true and I transmit the virus?'

'Having the virus does not necessarily mean full-blown Aids,' he said. 'Thousands of people are HIV positive and never get Aids.'

Silently Pat promised himself that he would trace Tatton Boyce. He would wring the truth from him if it meant killing the man. He smiled as he felt Briar relax in his arms.

Katoro grinned and tiptoed from the boma to tell Jonas that there would be a wedding at Kame Two as well as at New Ganyani. Jonas raced up to the village to tell Jacob and Rudo the news.

Briar and Pat sprang apart, as quickly as children caught in an act of mischief, when they heard Erin and Tara's laughter.

They were seated together and talking quietly when Tara joined them. Erin had gone to the kitchen to check that Katoro had remembered to put chillies in Pat's portion of the stew.

'You're looking very smug,' said Erin to his cook.

'I am happy about the weddings, Mr Erin,' replied Katoro.

'Wedding, Katoro,' said Erin, picking up the plate of biltong which Katoro had left on the table in his haste to tell Jonas the news. 'Only one wedding.'

Erin joined his father and the two women at the fire.

'Listen,' said Pat.

Softly at first, then growing loud and insistent, the drums started beating.

The wild, shivering fanfare of a kudu horn trumpet broke into the beat and joined the rhythm of the drums.

'That call from the kudu horn is telling everyone of an engagement,' said Pat. Erin nodded.

'It's beautiful. Oh, how I love this country,' said Tara. She crunched a crisp banana chip, licked the crumbs from her lips and said to Erin, 'Could we have a second marriage here in New Ganyani? Please, Erin, I would love it.'

'In traditional dress?' teased Erin and was delighted to see Tara flush.

'Almost,' she said. 'But I couldn't go topless.'

'You could,' laughed Briar. 'In Africa size is considered beautiful. The twig-like bodies of Europeans remind them of the "thin sickness". They like their women well rounded.'

'I definitely meet their requirements,' said Tara.

Pat pushed back his chair and Sheeba jumped up as if ashamed that Pat had caught her sleeping.

'Erin, could I have a word with you?' he said. Erin nodded, put down his whisky and followed Pat from the boma.

'Pat,' called Briar, 'please not now,' but Pat ignored her.

When they were out of hearing Pat draped his arm over his son's shoulders.

'Do you remember a talk we had when I first visited New Ganyani?'

Erin looked puzzled.

'About what, Dad?'

'About employing Briar Hanley to help run Kame Two.'

'Oh that,' said Erin. 'It's worked out well, hasn't it? I do have good ideas at times.'

'Excellent ones,' said Pat, as he started to walk down the dark road. Erin followed, realizing that Pat had something important to say.

'We also spoke of the possibility of my remarrying.'

Erin gasped and stood still. Pat turned to face him.

'At the time I truly believed that I would never want to share my life with another woman.'

'Now you do?' croaked Erin.

No, he wanted to shout. No, you can't do this. How can you forget Mum? But he bit his lip and waited patiently for his father to continue.

'I know, and I think you do too, that no other woman will or could ever take your mother's place. I will always love her and treasure the memories I hold.'

Pat turned and started walking back to the camp. Erin was surprised at how far they had moved away from the boma.

His father seemed unable to continue. When they saw the firelight flickering behind the reeded fence Erin broke the silence.

'If it's Briar, that's not another woman, Dad. She's always been part of our family. Mum loved her.'

Erin's voice caught as he thought of his mother.

'I was the one who suggested that you ask Briar to help at Kame Two. I will accept and love her as I always have.'

Erin put his arms around Pat. In the darkness, son comforted father.

As the two men walked into the dancing light of the fire, Briar's clear blue eyes searched Erin's face for signs of rejection. Finding none, she smiled at him tremulously.

'Welcome to the Gifford family, Briar,' he said as he bent down to kiss her.

Tears of relief welled up in Briar's eyes.

324

'Come on, being a Gifford is not that bad,' he said. 'Stories about us beating our women are untrue. We only do that on Sundays.'

'Pat, Briar!' shrieked Tara as she realized what had happened.

'Women!' said Erin, shaking his head as he watched Briar and Tara weeping, enfolded in each other's arms. 'If this means they are happy what do they do when they're sad?'

'Katoro,' he shouted. 'Bring the champagne.'

'Champagne, in a bush camp?' queried Pat.

'I keep a bottle in case a client shoots a trophy animal. It's happened twice. They feel very special being toasted with champagne in a dusty boma.'

Briar and Tara accepted glasses from a beaming Katoro.

'To our women,' said Pat and they drank.

'To Africa and the people who make it special,' said Briar.

'To happiness and peace on our ranches,' said Erin.

'To a double wedding at New Ganyani,' said Tara.

Pat, Erin and Briar stared at her.

'Isn't it a wonderful idea?' she asked.

'Magnificent,' said Pat, draining his glass. 'Let's have the biggest bush wedding of the century.'

As if in response to Pat's words, the kudu horn trumpeted loud and wild, urging the drummers to pick up a faster beat. The wind lifted wisps of singing from the village and swirled the words around the boma.

Pat raised his eyes to the winter sky where the stars seemed to jostle for space.

Thank you, he said silently. Thank you.

Chapter Thirty-one

TSVAKAI TIGERA snatched the flimsy sheet of fax paper from his secretary. She had skim-read the message before handing it to him, something they were forbidden to do, but Matamba paid well.

'Fax machines,' he grumbled. 'They are the curse of the modern world. A man can never find peace. The paper messages are always waiting.'

He glanced down at the signature at the foot of the page and straightened in his chair. It was from the American billionaire.

'I thought we were free of him for a few years,' mumbled Tigera as he removed his glasses, polished them and replaced them on his nose. Slowly he began to read and his fingers tightened on the paper. His secretary waited to hear it tear, but Tigera restrained himself.

'Visit. Hunt. Check on progress,' he said quietly. 'Very well, American, all can be arranged. Get Mr Kumirai Matamba on the phone,' he ordered. His secretary hurried to obey.

Matamba groaned as he lifted the phone.

'What does he want?' he said softly, as he recognized the secretary's voice.

'I am sorry you are not well today, Mr Matamba,' she

326

said clearly, 'but I think it is important that you accept this call. It is from Mr Tsvakai Tigera.'

'Trouble?' he queried.

'Yes, Mr Matamba. I am putting you through now.'

Matamba heard the click, then silence. Tigera enjoyed making people wait.

'My friend.'

Ah, thought Matamba, he wants a favour. One is always his friend at such times.

'It is good to speak again,' he answered mildly.

He had avoided going to Harare. He was trying to distance himself from Tigera.

'I am sorry to hear that you are ill.'

'Ill?' said Matamba in surprise, then he remembered the secretary's voice over the phone. 'It's nothing serious. Too much rich food.'

Tigera smiled. Good. Matamba's appetite would be his coffin, he thought happily.

'Can you contact your friend Fred Hanley?' he asked, placing special emphasis on the word friend.

'Yes,' said Matamba cautiously. 'Why?'

'We need him to persuade that arrogant young Gifford to arrange a hunt for our American, the one with the money.'

'I thought he was back in the States,' said Matamba.

'He was, but like most men with too much money, he cannot sit still. He must find new ways to spend it.'

Matamba nodded. The American was not a fool, he was coming to check that his money was still in the country.

'He is cunning. He gives us one time for his return and then comes at another.'

'But he will not catch us out,' gloated Tigera, scrabbling

in the wooden box for a fresh cigar. 'Our plan to give land to the Giffords was a good one. It makes us safe.'

Matamba grunted his assent. So it's our plan now, he thought. If it wasn't for me, you would be leaving the country on urgent business, to avoid meeting this American.

'Make Gifford understand that this is to be a "free" hunt. A favour to the government. I will accompany the American.'

'You?' said Matamba, his voice echoing his surprise. 'You hate the bush.'

'Correct, my friend, but one of us has to be with the American. We cannot afford to leave him alone with the Giffords. Imagine what they could tell him.'

'He would probably believe them,' said Matamba softly.

Tigera drew in his breath sharply. He hoped that Matamba was jesting. Matamba picked up a pad and pen and started writing as he spoke.

'I agree it is better for you to go on the hunt. I'm not fit enough.'

Tigera chewed on his cigar. 'Let me know when you have contacted your friend and set up the hunt.'

Tigera's secretary stretched out her hand to take the phone, when he added, 'Oh, the American wants to visit Pat Gifford's photographic ranch as well. Ask Hanley to set up visits for both areas.' Tigera dropped his voice. It was low and menacing. 'Make it clear that I expect first class treatment. The best of everything. They will of course meet all costs.'

'Goodbye, my friend,' said Matamba almost inaudibly.

Taunting and giving commands to the Giffords is like poking a thorn branch at an adder. The adder's strike is fast and deadly. I fear that theirs will be the same, thought Matamba as his pen moved slowly across the page.

Matamba completed his letter to Fred Hanley and fed the paper into his fax machine.

'Done,' he said. 'Now I wait to hear from Fred.'

His great stomach gurgled. The acid which burned deep inside told of fear and worry. He had a presentiment of danger.

Chapter Thirty-two

ERIN SPOKE quietly to Tara, seated beside him in the Toyota. He was taking her to shoot an impala. To his amazement she had decided that she could not sit in judgement on hunters until she had actually shot an animal. They needed meat for the camps and Erin suggested that she should do the shooting after seeing how upset she was over the death of the buffalo. Although he did not believe that she would actually kill the antelope when she saw it, he had arranged a hunt for her.

Their low voices carried clearly to Jacob and Jonas on the trackers' seat.

'Will this American's arrival mean that we have to delay our wedding?' asked Tara, as the Toyota jarred into a pothole. 'The Milan ceremony?'

'Yes, it will,' said Erin. 'By four or five weeks, perhaps two months, Tara. But it is important that we do this hunt.'

Tara nodded. 'I understand, but my family will think that you are trying to back out of marrying me.'

'I may be brave, but I'm not stupid,' said Erin with a wide grin. 'If you didn't get me for breach of promise, your family would. No, Tara, I'm afraid that you are doomed to be Mrs Gifford.'

Tara put her small hand over his on the steering wheel.

'Why does this American want to see Kame Two, as well as hunt on New Ganyani?' she asked, stroking his fingers lightly.

'Fred says he put up money for the Department of National Parks to buy the land from the government. I understand he has spent years in Africa, so he is accustomed to money going astray. He is making certain that the two areas are actually being utilized.' Erin chuckled. 'I'd love to be there when Tigera explains why I have the title deeds to New Ganyani.'

The name Tigera electrified the two trackers. They had been sitting back comfortably on the seat, not needing to look for spoor until they reached the spring. Jacob stared at Jonas for long moments. They leaned forward to hear the conversation.

'We must speak and plan for the visit of that *bere* Tigera,' Jonas whispered.

'We will. He will have a hunt he will recount to his ancestors,' answered Jacob, 'as he will not be alive to tell anyone else.'

'Tigera can hardly expect the American to understand or condone the slaughter which took place on Ganyani,' said Erin. 'Kame Two will be easy to explain. Dad is merely a concessionaire.'

'When this billionaire sees what Pat has done he'll probably demand that they extend the concession,' mused Tara.

'Dad and I intend working on him,' said Erin, 'but I'm sure that's why Tigera is accompanying him on the hunt. He'll probably stick to the man like buffalo dung to the soles of shoes.'

Tara laughed.

'Let's not talk of the American and Tigera now,' said

Erin. 'We are here to find an impala and see if you can drop it as well as you can knock over tin cans.'

Tara grew quiet and put her hand back in her lap. Erin glanced at her, but she had turned her head away and was studying the bush. Now that the time had come to shoot an impala, she was no longer certain that she wanted to kill an animal.

She sighed. She was committed. It'll make me more a part of Erin's life, she decided, but her fingers danced nervously in her lap.

All too soon they drew up at the spring. Wavelets of mud ringed the water, telling of game which had been drinking.

Jacob and Jonas circled the spring, pointing at marks in the mud and conversing in low voices. Eventually Jacob gave a soft whistle.

Tara bent down to pick up the two-seven-five Rigby which Erin had given her.

'I'll take that,' said Erin. 'It gets heavy after a while.'

They seemed to wander in circles, with Jacob and Jonas pausing frequently to discuss the small tracks with the pointed tips.

'They look like mopane leaves,' said Tara as she stood beside Jacob studying the ground.

'Not quite,' disagreed Erin.

'Well, new, narrow mopane leaves then,' said Tara, not to be bested.

At one stage a herd of buffalo had milled in the area. The ground was pounded into a thousand ridges and indentations.

'Well, that's that,' said Tara, lifting the damp curls which clung to her neck. 'Now we've lost the impala.'

'They'll pick them up,' contradicted Erin.

Tara was about to disagree when Jacob pointed with

his stick. He's just guessing, she thought. It's impossible to differentiate spoor in a buffalo mêlée.

To Tara's amazement, the dainty prints appeared again on a narrow path meandering away from the scuffed arena.

Jacob moved forward slowly with frequent pauses. Erin had explained that game enjoyed grazing with impala, as the wary antelope had superb eyesight, hearing and sense of smell. The graceful animal warned the game well in advance of impending danger.

Secretly Tara hoped that the impala would scent them and bolt before she had to use the Rigby. She was trying to find an excuse to call off the hunt when Jacob dropped to the ground. They followed, dropping down like dominoes.

One behind the other, they crawled to a mopane thicket. No one said a word. Jacob held out his hand. Jonas placed two sticks tied together in the middle with a piece of rubber tubing into his sandy-pink palms.

Jacob set up the X-shaped gun rest and Erin handed him the rifle. He rested the polished wooden stock on the tripod and motioned to Tara to crawl forward. Erin joined her. Tara had still not seen any impala. Now Erin lifted his head slowly and she followed suit.

She stifled a gasp. A group of impala were browsing fifty yards away. They were all males and held their lyre-shaped horns proudly. Their rufous backs shaded to ochre on their slim flanks. Their abdomens were creamy. The colours made her think of the striped chocolate sticks they used to eat as children in Milan. She did not want to kill one of these gentle creatures. A voice warm and soft filled her ear.

'The one closest to you. Remember, aim behind the shoulder. Keep your eye on the sights. Squeeze the trigger. Don't jerk.' Erin kissed her on the cheek. She was alone.

She curled her finger around the trigger and peered through the telescopic sights. The antelope seemed to be in her lap. She could hear Erin's voice. The Rigby's sights moved to the impala's shoulder then dropped to a perfect position behind it.

Tara squeezed the trigger, but she anticipated the retort and flinched. The bullet struck the leg just below the shoulder, shattering the bone. The impala spun around. It fell in the dust, then like a man on crutches tried to join the fleeing herd.

Tara stared at its dangling leg in horror.

'No,' she screamed. 'Look at what I've done.'

She threw the Rigby on the ground and tried to run after the gazelle. Erin raced to stop and calm her, whilst Jacob lifted and examined the discarded rifle.

Reverently he wiped the dust from the barrel and checked the sights. Jonas joined him to mourn the mishandling of a beautifully crafted weapon.

'I think Nsimba will bear children and work to heal people at the clinic,' said Jacob, stroking the barrel of the Rigby.

Jonas nodded sadly. 'She will not hunt with Erin. She does not have the wish to kill,' he said.

'Let us hurry. We must find and kill the *mpala*. Until it is dead her heart will tear and she will hate everyone,' said Jacob.

The trackers set off after Erin and Tara.

'We must follow the *mpala* before the blood trail dries,' said Jacob.

His words ripped apart the web of self-pity Tara had begun spinning around herself. She knuckled the last of the tears from her eyes.

'I'm ready.'

'Good girl. Let's go,' said Erin, shouldering his rifle, leaving the Rigby in Jacob's gentle care.

Tracking the wounded impala was like following a paper-trail. Blood spots were splattered on the dry leaves and twigs, marking its hobbling progress.

'The bullet must have hit an artery,' said Erin to Jacob.

'There should not be so much blood,' agreed Jacob. 'But it is good. Soon it will weaken and lie down.'

Jacob was wrong. The gazelle kept going. Shock and adrenalin urged it on. Tara refused to rest. She drank a mouthful of water and continued to search for spots of dark blood. Each splash of blood deepened her guilt.

I'll never touch a gun again, she vowed as she stumbled over the rough ground and fallen branches.

Erin did not try to reason with her. This was something she would have to accept.

It was late afternoon when Jacob came to a halt in a small clearing. He stood in front of Tara trying to shield her, but she pushed him aside.

'I'm so sorry. So very sorry,' she whispered. The ram lay on his side, his graceful lyre horns covered with dust and his flanks heaving.

As he sensed their presence he lifted his head. The effort was too much. It fell back to the ground with a sickening thud. His eyes were now dull and glazed with pain. There was no fear, he was too close to death. Tara's shoulders shook as if she was in the grip of a fever.

'Shoot him, please, Erin. Don't let him suffer any more.'

The shot rang out before she finished speaking. The impala shuddered and lay still. Tara knelt beside the animal and stroked its neck.

'Please forgive me,' she whispered, 'I didn't mean to cause you this pain.'

Erin walked up to where she knelt talking to the dead animal.

'Come, Tara, soon it'll be dark. It's a long way back to the truck.'

'We have to bury him, Erin,' she said, not standing up.

'Tara,' Erin pleaded, 'it's meat. We have people at Kame Two who have to be fed.'

'Please, Erin,' she pleaded. 'Not with this impala. Please bury him.'

She started crying again. The sobs were obscenely loud in the hush which had fallen over the bush after the shot. Jacob and Jonas shrugged and unstrapped the collapsible spades from the pack on Jonas's back.

Erin turned at the sound of metal striking hard clay.

'The buck belongs to the hunter,' said Jacob softly.

Erin nodded. He broke off a handful of grass and placed it in the impala's mouth.

'For the journey,' he said.

Tara looked up at him gratefully.

'Thank you,' she said.

Jacob and Jonas patted the mound of earth into shape with their spades and stood back.

'The *bere* will feast well tonight when they dig up this good meat,' said Jonas.

Jacob nodded and stepped forward to help Tara arrange a bunch of flame lilies on the gazelle's grave.

Tara glanced back over her shoulder as they left the clearing. The soft rays of sunlight found and touched the crinkled red and yellow petals. They seemed to flicker like tongues of fire on the simple grave.

Chapter Thirty-three

FRED HANLEY ran his fingers through his mop of silver hair. Blanche reached up and flicked a strand away from his eyes.

'I wish you'd let me cut it short,' she said.

'My hair is better than a hat, it keeps my head warm on these winter mornings,' he replied, smiling down fondly at his wife.

'What time will Briar and Pat be here?' she asked for the third time in thirty minutes. 'I miss her so much. It'll be good to see Pat again. Do you realize that we haven't heard from them since they phoned to tell us of Erin and Tara Andretti's engagement?' Blanche touched Fred's arm. 'I do hope that they are all right and that nothing dreadful has happened on Kame Two.'

'Stop worrying. Pat would have contacted us if there was a problem. Briar could not be safer than in his care.'

Blanche smiled. 'I'm sure you're right. What time is your meeting with Matamba?'

When Fred had received the message from Matamba, he decided to apply a little more pressure. He insisted that they hold a joint meeting during which Matamba would put the request to Pat Gifford personally.

'I cannot ask someone who has been uprooted from

all he loves to tell his son to arrange a free hunt for the man who was the cause of him losing his land,' argued Fred.

'But Pat Gifford has Kame Two,' said Matamba miserably. He had no wish to face Pat Gifford.

'No, my friend. He owned Kame, now he merely leases Kame Two,' replied Fred coldly. 'And you and I well know that such agreements can be toppled.'

Matamba acquiesced and a meeting was arranged for the following week.

Now Fred and Blanche waited at their home in Bulawayo for Pat and Briar to arrive. The sound of a car alerted them and Blanche ran down the steps to the gravel driveway.

'There's Mother,' said Briar, clutching Pat's hand.

'Having second thoughts, Briar?' said Pat gently. 'If so tell me now and we'll say nothing to your parents.'

'Oh no, Pat. It's not that. It's just . . .'

'I understand. Don't worry. Let me tell them.'

Fred followed his wife down the stairs but more slowly. From his vantage point he could look into the car. He saw Briar untangle her fingers from Pat's and he frowned.

Perhaps Blanche is right and there is trouble at Kame Two, he thought. Pat is obviously comforting Briar. He shrugged and joined Blanche. We'll soon know, he decided and he fixed a smile of welcome on his face.

Blanche flew into Briar's arms.

'Oh, I have missed you so much. Let me look at you.' She studied her daughter in silence. 'You're a little thinner but looking happy and contented. Kame Two obviously suits you.' She kissed Briar again and keeping her arm around her waist she turned to Pat.

'Pat, it's good to see you. We don't see enough of you now that you're in the Chizarira area.'

Pat kissed her and shook hands with Fred.

'Hopefully that will change in the near future,' he said.

Blanche felt her daughter stiffen. She looked at Briar. Her face was white and her eyes showed fear and uncertainty. Blanche held out her hand to Fred. He clasped it and held it between his own.

'What has happened? Tell us,' she said quietly.

'Come inside,' said Fred, conscious of the two gardeners watching them curiously. 'We have time for tea before our meeting with Matamba.'

Blanche rang for tea. They exchanged idle gossip until it was poured and they were alone.

'Fred, Blanche,' said Pat, 'we have been friends for more years than I care to count. I respect and love you both and value your friendship.'

Blanche held on to Fred's arm tightly. Pat looked at Briar, who smiled at him tremulously and nodded.

'I want to marry Briar.'

There was a stunned silence. Fred sank back into the floral cushions and Blanche stared at Pat with her mouth open.

'Marry?' she said at last.

'Yes, Mummy. I love Pat and I've agreed to be his wife.'

Briar held up her hand to stall her mother's outburst.

'I know that there is a difference in our ages, but we are both mature and know what we want.'

Seeing her mother's face set into lines of rejection, Briar hurried on.

'You were only seventeen when you married Dad. You were a child and look how happy you've been. I'm almost twice that age. Give me a chance to enjoy some of the happiness you have had with Dad.'

Briar turned to her father. He held out his hands to her.

Like a child who runs to its parent for comfort, Briar nestled into his arms.

'Do you realize that you are asking me to accept my best friend as a son-in-law?' he whispered into her ear.

Briar laughed.

'I hadn't thought of that, Dad,' she said.

'Blanche?' queried Pat. 'Does this meet with your approval? It's very important to both of us that we have your and Fred's blessing.'

'Of course you do,' said Fred.

Blanche burst into tears.

Briar stared at her mother aghast. 'Mother,' she said, 'I am going to marry Pat Gifford. Even though I'm not a young girl, I still need and want my mother at my side on my wedding day.'

'It's a shock.' Blanche wiped her eyes. 'After Scott, I . . .'

'Scott is dead, Mother. I am not going to live on memories for the rest of my life.'

'Drink your tea, my love,' said Fred. 'We have to leave for our meeting.'

Dutifully Blanche sipped the hot, sweet liquid.

'Where will the wedding take place?' she asked, returning her empty cup to the tray.

The tea has worked, thought Briar. Mother is all right.

'Erin and Tara want to have a wedding at New Ganyani when we return from the society one in Milan,' answered Pat. 'They want us to be married at the same time.'

'Wonderful idea. A good old-timers' bash,' said Fred. 'You can start inviting people, Blanche.'

'Everyone we know,' laughed Briar.

'And even some we don't,' added Pat.

'Erin will have to shoot enough animals to feed an army. Do you realize how many villagers will arrive?' said Fred.

340

'The drums will send the invitations across the country. People will go on arriving for months after the ceremony.'

'We'll make certain that the drums beat out the day and date clearly,' answered Pat. He could imagine Erin's dismay at having to feed a never-ending stream of villagers who had walked for weeks to attend the great feast.

'This time the drums can beat out happiness and I will be able to listen to them,' said Blanche.

Fred stood up and pulled his wife to her feet. 'Let's congratulate the couple,' he said. 'Then we must go.'

Blanche smiled as Pat bent down to kiss her. 'I am sorry for my tears,' she said. 'It's just that . . .'

'I understand, Blanche,' he answered and enfolded her in a bear hug.

A few minutes later, Fred's car roared down the driveway, scattering the freshly raked gravel.

The gardeners watched it go through the gates and shook their heads.

Matamba was in his garden, warming himself in the winter sun. He was bending low over a rose bush which had recently been pruned.

His back was facing the driveway and his dark grey trousers seemed about to split at the seams.

'He looks like an old elephant bull from behind,' whispered Briar.

'He seems even fatter than he did at our meeting in Harare,' said Fred. He saw Pat's expression in the rearview mirror and was sorry that he had reminded him of the occasion.

Matamba walked slowly towards them. He shook hands all round and invited them inside for tea.

'We've just had . . .' said Blanche.

'Tea would be most welcome, Kumgirai,' interposed Fred. He used Matamba's Christian name only when they met in private.

Matamba ushered them into his study and rang a small copper bell on his desk.

'Arrange for tea,' he commanded the woman who appeared in the doorway. 'And cake,' he added as she turned to leave.

'But the doctor?'

'Is a fool,' said Matamba. 'A stomach like mine needs to be fed. Dieting will shrink and kill it. It needs food. Bring cake. And *kapenta*,' he added defiantly.

Fred rose to his feet and Pat followed suit as Matamba's wife bustled from the room. Briar and Blanche exchanged glances but kept quiet.

'Fred,' said Matamba. 'You understand my predicament.'

'I understand Mr Tigera's predicament,' answered Fred. 'He has a wealthy American patron to placate and convince that the money which was given for conservation is being well utilized.' He paused for breath. He studied Matamba's sweating face, as if peering at a beetle through a magnifying glass. 'You want me to persuade my friend Pat Gifford and his son Erin to allay this American's fears. You, or should I say Tsvakai Tigera, want a free safari trip?'

Fred paused and let the silence grow. A carved cuckoo clock on the wall ticked monotonously.

'Times are hard, Kumgirai,' he continued meaningfully. 'The sort of photographic safari he is asking for is very expensive. The camp will have to be closed to other clients for the duration. It will be a great loss in earnings.'

'But—' blustered Matamba.

'I will need something in return,' pressed Fred. Pat

listened to his friend and understood why he had been a respected member of the Senate. The man was both hard and clever.

'What would that be?' queried Matamba, his lips barely moving. 'You do realize,' he added quickly, 'that Tigera has to approve.'

'Indeed I do,' said Fred. 'I also know that you have information which can help him decide in our favour.'

Matamba gulped and tea splattered across his shirt. How could Hanley possibly know of the plans to utilize the protected area around the Falls? It is not possible, he comforted himself. He obviously means something else.

'I assure you . . .' Matamba began.

'Kumgirai, we understand each other,' said Fred shortly. 'We both have sources of information and sometimes they overlap. Let me tell you what Tsvakai Tigera will agree to.'

He fixed his unblinking gaze on Matamba who was nervously crunching fried *kapenta*.

'The money which is to be paid to Pat Gifford for the purchase, the forced purchase, of Kame will be used to buy Kame Two,' he continued.

Matamba choked on the small fish. Fred waited patiently until he regained his breath. He turned to Pat, who was trying to hide his astonishment.

'I presume you would rather have Kame Two and forge new memories, Pat?' said Fred, turning to his friend. 'You have also moved all your villagers and their livestock from Kame.'

'Yes,' whispered Briar. 'Please, Pat.'

Pat nodded and Fred continued.

'Although Mr Gifford has lost his home and all he loves in Kame and Ganyani, he is prepared to be reasonable and accept in exchange a piece of untamed wilderness. It will take years before he shows any profit from the photographic safaris.'

'Tigera will never agree,' blustered Matamba, leaning forward over his desk. 'Never.'

'Never is not a word in my vocabulary, Kumgirai,' answered Fred. 'Mr Gifford has been treated very badly. I need not tell you what the American's reaction will be to the story of Ganyani and the forced removal of a family who for generations have been committed to conservation and the good of the country. Americans believe in liberty and they hold strong views on human rights.'

Matamba fell back in his chair. His open mouth gasped for air, like a *kapenta* dangling in a net high above the water.

'My friend, remember that very wealthy men are able to buy the ears of those in power. An international scandal involving you and Tigera would be most unfortunate and unwelcome.'

Fred smiled at Matamba. It was the long fixed smile of a Zambezi shark.

'Kame Two could be a wedding present to Pat and Briar. The wealthy American will be most impressed when he sees proof of how well you manage the funds, and how wisely you choose people to have the land. He may even donate more money to your department.'

Pat spoke for the first time. 'It could still be called a reserve. Very few people would know that I and not the government own the land.'

Matamba shook his head and his jowls wobbled like a baying bloodhound.

'You drive a hard bargain, Fred,' he said. 'This is not a good time to talk to Tigera. You have heard of the outbreak of poaching near Chizaria?' He continued before Fred could reply. 'Our president wants it stopped. It is damaging our tourist industry.'

Fred nodded sympathetically. 'I understand his concern. Tourists do not enjoy being shot at.'

Matamba looked at Blanche, Pat and Briar. 'Could I speak to you in private, Fred?' he asked.

Fred nodded. Matamba rang the bell and his wife arrived to entertain Pat and the women in another room.

'It seems that these poachers are trained and sent in by a European, a man who knows the countryside. There is talk of a small army he has recruited. Our rangers are unable to contain or control the situation. The poachers are armed and seem to take as much pleasure in shooting our rangers as in killing elephant and rhino.'

'All the more reason for giving Kame Two to Pat Gifford,' said Fred. 'He will patrol his area and keep it free of poachers just as his son does at New Ganyani. Do you not understand, Kumgirai? These men are necessary. You need men like the Giffords. We are surrounded by countries who will welcome men of their experience. Keep them here. Give Pat Kame Two. Make certain he has something to fight for. No poachers will remain on his property.'

Matamba picked up a *kapenta* by its tail and dropped it into his mouth. His stomach had settled as he listened to Fred. Fred was a wise man; he would have made a good induna, he thought. He has given me spears with which to impale Tigera.

'I presume you mean that the leader of the poachers is a white man?' Fred asked.

'Yes,' said Matamba, uncomfortable with any talk which could be termed racist.

'Have you and Tigera gone through the list of hunters,

345

rangers and dispossessed land-owners and concession holders whom you have thrown out of the country in the past
year?' asked Fred. 'It's probably someone who has a
grievance. If he knows the country and the poachers are
successful, then I'd suggest that you look for a hunter or
ranger.'

'Thank you, Fred,' said Matamba, genuinely grateful
for the suggestion.

At the door Fred turned back and bumped into
Matamba who was close behind him.

'What happened to that Madden who had the concession near New Ganyani? I hear people are now fighting
for it.'

'Madden?' said Matamba guilelessly.

'Yes. Kirk Madden, the one who helped you during the
war,' snapped Fred, suddenly tired of playing politics.

'Ah,' said Matamba, recognizing signs of Fred's temper.
'I believe that he has a post in Kenya. It certainly is not
him.'

Tigera had contacted Matamba a few months ago to
say that Madden had disappeared from his remote outpost
on the Kenyan border with Somalia. There were signs of a
scuffle in the house. It seemed that Madden had been
surprised at night and taken by the *shufta*. He was certain
to be dead as the Somali guerrillas dealt with Kenyan
rangers swiftly and cruelly.

Fred wondered why Matamba dismissed Madden so
lightly. He shrugged. It was not important and was certainly not the reason for his visit.

Pat looked up as Fred and Matamba entered the back
room where Briar and Blanche were admiring the latest
Matamba baby. Fred winked at Pat, as Matamba held out
his hands for his son.

'Thank you for your hospitality, Mr and Mrs Matamba,' said Pat. 'Please inform Mr Tigera that I look forward to welcoming him at Kame Two in a fortnight's time. My son will run a three-week safari for him on New Ganyani.'

'Two weeks. That is too soon,' said Matamba, handing the child back to his wife.

He knew that Tigera wanted the poachers' ring broken and the leader caught before he ventured into the bush. The man hated wild animals. He preferred to hunt in cities.

'Much as I would like to oblige Mr Tigera and his guest, it will not be possible to delay,' said Pat. 'We are all leaving to attend my son's wedding in Italy at the end of the month. Everything has been arranged. It will be a large society wedding and the dates cannot be changed.'

'This is also the best time to hunt,' said Fred. 'The jesse bush is almost bare, as are the mopanes. It's too cold for mosquitoes. The rains have not created dozens of new pans which scatter the game. Now they all drink at the main pans.'

'Fred is right,' said Pat. 'We can offer Mr Tigera and his friend an excellent hunt now. He need have no fear of poachers on Kame Two, the terrain is too difficult for easy access and escape. They are not able to move quickly in the hills and gorges, especially if they try to carry ivory tusks.'

'New Ganyani, where the American will hunt, is of course near the Chete area, but Erin Gifford and his trackers will look after him and Mr Tigera. They'll be in more danger from an old evil-tempered buffalo than from poachers,' added Fred as he held the front door open for Blanche, Briar and Pat to leave. 'I will be at my home in Bulawayo until the end of the week, Kumgirai. Contact me by Friday.'

Matamba's jowls seemed to droop even lower, as he listlessly waved farewell to Fred.

'Tigera is afraid and the actions of cowards are unpredictable,' he muttered as he stomped into the house to arrange a meeting with his colleague. As he closed the front door his wife handed him a flimsy piece of fax paper. Matamba read it as he walked to his study. His wife watched him crumple it into a tight ball and hurl it across the room.

'I warned him,' roared Matamba to the empty room. 'I told Tigera not to blacklist the white officials in the Department of National Parks. Did he listen? No. Now we have an inquiry into the number of resignations. Questions are being asked as to why so many good men are losing their jobs and having their reputations ruined.'

Matamba crossed the room and grunted as he bent to pick up the balled paper. He unravelled it and reread the message. 'Tigera is a fool. I warned him. Inquiries are like worms. Once they are in your entrails they spread out, eating everything. You grow thin and weak as they multiply,' he said quietly. He was now more in control of himself.

He sank into his chair, which creaked as it accepted his weight. Mentally he itemized the misdeeds a commission of inquiry could uncover. His head dropped on to his arms and he lay sprawled on his desk as if awaiting the executioner's axe.

Chapter Thirty-four

KIRK MADDEN crouched over the small fire. It was cold in Chizarira and he shivered as the evening breeze strengthened. He could not risk making a larger fire. The rocks guarding the entrance to the cave, deep in the mountains, were no guarantee that the glow would not be noticed by a passing ranger. He was wary, even though he knew that the authorities did not have the funds to pay for anti-poaching units to patrol this wild and rugged area.

Poachers usually chose places with fairly easy access. That was one of the reasons he based his operation in the north of Chizarira, where Mount Tundazi reared up almost one and a half thousand metres. The rocky valleys and deep gorges choked with riverine vegetation were perfect for his needs. There were sufficient antelope in the well-watered area to feed his men, and elephant and black rhinoceros were there, waiting to be taken.

The ivory and horn would be unearthed from the caches when he moved his group to another area, where they would attract attention away from Chizarira. The trophies would be carried out at night, in easy stages.

His partner, Tip, would oversee that part of the operation. Tip squatted opposite Madden and warmed his hands over the fire. He coughed. It was a harsh, rasping sound and it irritated Kirk.

'That trumpeting of yours will bring any ranger in the area straight to us,' Kirk said angrily.

'It's this damn awful place you've chosen,' Tip retorted. He was short and wiry with protruding front teeth. As the firelight flickered across his drawn features, Kirk thought that he looked like a ferret. His hair was streaked with grey and his scalp, pink with cold, showed through. 'There are no rangers in this forsaken hole. They would have to be brain-damaged to come up here.'

Just as you are, he thought, looking at Kirk Madden with hatred.

Tip had met Kirk on the Somali border. He was born in Somalia and ran with a band of *shufta*. He had stopped them from killing Kirk when they ransacked the rangers' outpost, looking for rifles and ammunition. He had liked the anger in Kirk's eyes as the *shufta* surrounded him and prodded him with their spears.

Suddenly the idea of talking English again appealed to him. He ordered his men to keep Kirk alive. For a while Kirk lived a precarious life with the guerrillas, but he was uneasy and disliked taking orders.

He worked on the Somali-born Tip, feeding him stories of ivory waiting to be taken in Zimbabwe and fuelling his fears of the war being waged along the Somali border by the Kenyan authorities. He made Zimbabwe sound like a utopia for poachers.

Tip and Kirk were like twins, fathered by greed and born amoral. Tip decided that Kirk was right and he left his *shufta* friends. The war being waged against them was becoming uncomfortable. He joined Kirk and they moved their poaching business to Zimbabwe. The rewards were good, but Tip found that once they entered Zimbabwe,

Kirk became dictatorial and his mood swings were frightening.

Tip decided that once the cache of ivory and horn in the Chizarira area was safely out of the country, he would return to Kenya. He rubbed his hands together over the flames. His knuckles were red and cracked and his skin was as rough as sandpaper.

'We move to the Chete area in a few days,' said Kirk abruptly.

'But we haven't finished here,' Tip argued.

'We finish when I say so,' replied Kirk. 'Besides, I won't need you in Chete. I know the area well.' His eyes narrowed, as dark thoughts crowded his mind. 'I once ran a concession there.'

Tip looked up in surprise, but the questions remained unasked as Kirk's yellow eyes held him in their merciless glow.

'Remember, Tip,' Kirk said, 'you are taking out the ivory, but don't try to disappear with my share. This world is too small to hide you.'

Tip shivered and nodded.

'Isn't it dangerous to go to a hunting area?' he asked to change the subject.

'A little more risky, yes. But I hear one of the government's big boys will be hunting near there with a wealthy Yank.'

'Why get mixed up with guys from the government and Yanks who are full of ideals?' persisted Tip.

Kirk stared into the flames before answering and when he did his voice was as sharp and hard as steel tempered in the heat of the fire.

'Because the government official is the one who had my

licence revoked and ruined the good life I was leading. He is about to become the prey. My prey. The hunter is the brother of someone I hated.'

'You'll blow our whole operation,' protested Tip, between bouts of coughing. 'It's not worth it.'

'I'll decide what is worthwhile and what is not,' snapped Kirk.

I should have let my *shufta* kill you the night we raided your outpost, thought Tip grimly.

'If you mess with government groups in Africa, you'll have the whole damn army on our heels,' he warned. He coughed again and spat a ball of phlegm into the fire. He watched the flames sizzle until they dried and consumed the wet mucus, before he spoke again.

'I'll need most of the men to carry the tusks. If we are to move at night and bury them before daybreak I'm going to need our best.'

'The best will be with me. You only need muscle. It does not take brains and tracking skills to carry loads and dig holes,' Kirk argued, pulling up the collar of his jacket.

Tip was silent. He was even more determined now to move out of Zimbabwe as soon as possible.

The two men settled themselves beside the fire, pulling their tattered sleeping bags up around their shoulders. The porters were already asleep on the floor in the back of the cave.

The fire flickered and spluttered. Tip coughed and whimpered in his fitful sleep.

At New Ganyani, Jacob and Jonas sat near a much larger fire. The greatcoats they wore kept out the winter chill. They were well fed and warm. They conversed in low voices, glancing round to make sure that none could overhear them.

'It is certain,' said Jacob. 'I heard Erin talk to Mr Pat on the radio. They go first to Kame Two, then here, to hunt with us.'

Jonas stuck his hands deep into the pockets of his heavy coat.

'Tigera,' he said at last. 'It is Tigera.'

'Yes.'

The two men were silent, each engaged in his own thoughts.

'It must be done. Never again will we have this opportunity,' said Jacob.

Jonas nodded. 'Our ancestors have sent him to us, but we must be careful. It must be an accident.'

'No man will be able to prove otherwise,' said Jacob quietly. 'Neither Erin nor Mr Pat. They will attend the funeral in true innocence.'

'But they know of Rudo,' whispered Jonas.

'They have the silence of forgetfulness about that,' Jacob replied with authority. 'Remember, only you and I were there, to hear the name of the one who sent those *bere* to my wife. Only we know it was Tsvakai Tigera who paid them. Only we will know why Tigera will die. We ...' Jacob broke off as a skinny young boy came scampering to the fire and flung himself into his lap.

'Shoko!' Jonas's wife called the child.

'It is all right, he is with us,' answered Jacob. 'I'll bring him to the hut to sleep. You go to bed. Don't worry about Shoko.' Turning back to Jonas, he sad, 'We will speak more of this matter tomorrow.'

They did not want the child to hear them talk of murder. The two men sat up late into the night talking of hunting while silently making and discarding plans. Shoko grunted softly as he sat on the ground beside Jacob.

At last Jacob stood up and stretched.

'It is time to leave our brains for our ancestors to talk to,' he said to Jonas. 'A plan will come while we sleep.'

Jonas nodded and wrapped his coat closer around himself. Jacob lifted Shoko and carried him to share the sleeping mats with his sons in his hut.

Chapter Thirty-five

TIGERA HAD complained and found fault with everything from the day he arrived at Kame Two with the American, though he was careful to be polite when the American was within earshot.

Briar had lost patience with Tigera and she looked at the large torn blister on his heel with secret glee. He would not be able to walk on that foot for a few days.

Tsvakai Tigera winced and gasped as he eased his foot into the bowl of warm salt water which Rudo placed on the floor in front of him. His hands grasped the arms of the chair and he groaned.

'Keep it in the water as long as you can,' said Briar, watching him. 'Salt is an excellent disinfectant and will clean that blister.' She turned to Rudo, who was standing in the doorway. 'Bring me the bottle of methylated spirits and some cottonwool,' she said, with a wink.

Rudo smiled and left the room.

'Now this may hurt a little,' said Briar, 'but if you are going to hunt with Erin we need your feet toughened.'

She took the bottle of mauve liquid from Rudo and splashed some liberally on to the wad of cottonwool. Rudo held Tigera's foot up, so that Briar could administer the spirits.

Tigera stifled a scream. His face screwed up in a

grimace of pain. Briar poured more spirits on to the wet pad.

'This will dry it up,' she soothed, as he writhed at the sting of the liquid. 'You must not put a shoe on that foot for at least two days. It's a bad blister.'

Tigera's face hardened as he realized that Pat and Briar would be alone with the American.

'I'll walk,' he snarled.

'If you do, you will not be able to take part in the hunt on New Ganyani,' warned Briar, 'and your friend can't wait for the hunt to start. He is very excited at the prospect of shooting an African buffalo.'

The threat worked.

'I'll rest tomorrow, but only for one day,' agreed Tigera reluctantly.

'Rudo and the staff will take good care of you,' said Briar. 'Now I must go and serve tea. You lie down and have an hour's sleep.'

Rudo's face dropped and her expression was woeful as the door closed behind them.

'I do not like or trust that man,' she whispered.

Briar squeezed her hand. 'Neither do I, Rudo, but we must be nice to him. He gives out the concessions. If we want to keep Kame Two we must pretend to like him.'

Briar joined Pat and the American on the verandah for tea.

'Mr Tigera will not be going with us tomorrow,' she said. 'He has a bad blister on his heel and can't walk.'

'Good,' said Pat unwittingly, 'then we can try that gorge where we found the Taita falcon for Tatton.'

He saw Briar's expression change and bit his tongue.

'That will be a first for me,' said the American, 'and I'll

enjoy a hard climb. I spend too much time on jets and in boardrooms.'

Briar looked at him carefully. He ducked when he walked through doorways and it seemed to her that his shoulders would brush the sides. He was hefty with the slight suggestion of a belly, but he walked easily in the bush. She and Pat spoke lightly of Zimbabwe and its wildlife, conscious that Tigera might be listening in his bedroom.

As the sun lost its heat and sank in a sudden burst of splendour, Pat took out a bottle of malt whisky and poured a liberal tot for the American. After dinner Pat suggested an early night as the climb would be long and arduous the following day.

Tigera spent a restless night cursing the blister and trying to forget Matamba's suggestion that Kame Two should be sold to Pat Gifford. He was uncomfortable in Pat's presence. Those ice blue eyes seemed to burn into the secrets of his soul. Pat had also managed to win the American's admiration. The two men were easy in each other's company.

I'll have to walk carefully, thought Tigera, as sleep finally calmed his tumbling and troubled thoughts.

The next morning he scowled as he watched the jeep jolt down the track without him. He would not be able to direct the conversation that day. His presence would not deter Pat's tongue.

Talk to the American of Ganyani, he threatened silently, and this concession will end before you have spent five years on Kame Two.

He turned from the railing and shouted for someone to bring him a telephone. Rudo hurried to obey, unwinding the long black extension cord behind her.

He grabbed the phone and waved her away. She paused behind the door, hearing him start talking to someone called Matamba, then hurried to the kitchen. She did not want anyone to see her eavesdropping. Tigera was still talking when Rudo carried a tray of tea out to him.

'I do not like it, but I will think on your suggestion,' she heard him say.

He glared at her and she scurried away.

'Pour your own tea,' she hissed as she closed the door sharply behind her. 'I do not need to hear your conversation. It will be as bad as the evil which hides behind those thick glasses.'

Pat and Briar were like children released early from school. They laughed and joked as they drove the American benefactor to Taita Gorge. He had asked them to call him Mel, but in private they still referred to him as 'the American'.

Pat led the way up the steep gorge with Briar bringing up the rear. All three were out of breath when they reached the rim, as Pat had set a punishing pace.

'Whew, that was something,' said Mel as he sank back against a rock.

Pat handed him the water bottle and he drank deeply. Briar shook her head. She would drink only when they reached the bottom again.

'Man, what a view,' enthused Mel, wiping his mouth with the back of his hand.

'There,' shouted Briar. 'There it is. Oh, you are lucky. Even though the Taita nests here, we don't often see it.'

Mel tried to focus the binoculars on the fast flight of the bird.

'He's a little fellow, but those eyes are sharp and mean. He looks as if someone owes him money.'

Pat and Briar laughed at Mel's description.

'Now tell me,' said Mel. 'If your family were early pioneers, why do you not own any property? You seem like the sort of guy who would want his own ranch. I don't slot you in as a manager.'

Briar looked at Pat and then stared down into the gorge.

'Circumstances,' answered Pat laconically.

Sensing more behind the single word, Mel persisted with his questioning. Realizing that the American was not going to be satisfied until he knew the facts, Pat recounted the whole story.

Mel's face seemed to grow as hard as the rock he leaned against.

'So you only have a concession for Kame Two,' he said.

'It's a good life,' Pat answered, 'and Erin owns New Ganyani. He is young and capable and is turning it into an excellent hunting ranch.'

'Rudo, your housekeeper, tells me that you are to be married soon,' said Mel. Briar flushed and put up her binoculars to save answering.

'Nothing is secret in Africa,' said Pat. 'The drums have been beating for days. Everyone will know of the wedding, the hunt, plus your visit with Tigera.'

'Yes. Tigera,' said Mel.

With the two words Briar felt as if a cobra had hissed near her. The American's genial expression had vanished. This is what he probably looks like in one of his boardrooms, she thought. I would not like to cross him in business.

359

She glanced at Pat and he smiled at her.

'Penny?'

'I was thinking how lucky we are to be in Taita Gorge instead of a boardroom,' replied Briar quickly.

'A few of my executives should come up here. It would change their lateral and linear thinking patterns,' growled Mel, still musing over what Pat had told him.

Briar was suddenly worried about what the American would say to Tigera and wished that they had kept quiet. But the American was a good listener and inspired confidence.

'Mel?' she said tentatively. 'Please don't mention our conversation to anyone.'

'Our conversations are no business of Mr Tigera or any other member of the board which deals with hunting rights and concessions,' said Mel.

He paused and scanned the gorge, again trying to find the Taita.

'I have a meeting scheduled with Mr Tigera after the hunt. If you have no objection, Pat, I'd like the use of your office tomorrow. The meeting will be brought forward owing to pressing matters which necessitate my departure immediately after the hunt. You do have a fax machine, don't you?'

When Pat nodded, Mel smiled. It was a thin triumphant lifting of the corners of his mouth. 'Good, then I can have the papers signed.' He patted Briar's arm. 'Don't worry, Briar, it's amazing how money puts pens to papers.'

'I'm so afraid that we'll lose the concession to Kame Two,' she said. 'We have such wonderful plans for the future here.'

'You are running a tight operation now, Pat and Briar. I look forward to my next visit. Then you can show me what new camps and trails have been made. I'm not easily impressed, but with more people of your calibre, this country could head the list for tourist destinations.'

'Thanks, Mel, we appreciate that,' said Pat. 'Now let's start the scramble down. It always seems to take longer going down than climbing up.'

'Because everyone has wobbly knees,' laughed Briar.

Tigera heard them, long before the jeep rounded the bend in the road. They were singing loudly and out of tune. Pat beat out the rhythm on the hooter.

The staff ran down the road in consternation. Pat hooted only when he needed them urgently. They lined the road and stood amazed to see Mr Pat and the American singing and laughing.

'Stop,' said Briar. 'The staff will think we're mad.'

Tigera scowled. Something had happened. This was the first time Pat had brought the American back to Kame Two in such a good mood. He watched closely, hidden by the dense bougainvillaea, as the American put his arm around Pat's shoulders and kissed Briar on the cheek.

All three laughed and walked towards the verandah. Tigera scurried back to his room and settled himself on a chair with his foot resting on a pillow. He looked as if he had been there all day as they walked in.

'Mr Tigera,' said Briar, 'I do hope my staff looked after you well today.'

Tigera merely nodded. He was studying the American. The man stood over him like a menacing buffalo bull. There was a hidden threat in his stance and Tigera recalled the conversation he had had that morning with Matamba. Perhaps it would be wise to give some consideration to his words, he thought. Mel's greeting confirmed his decision.

'The meeting we have planned for after the hunt will take place tomorrow morning,' he said.

'But,' blustered Tigera, 'my secretaries? Mr Matamba?'

'We have a telephone, a fax and a plane on standby if necessary,' said Mel curtly. 'I wish to conclude a business deal tomorrow.'

'But of course,' said Tigera ingratiatingly. 'I merely wished to make it easier.'

'Thanks,' said Mel. 'What I want is simple and the deal is very easy to set out.'

Tigera pleaded a headache due to his blistered foot and remained in his room for dinner. Rudo served him in icy silence. She was pleased to see him look so discomfited.

After dinner he once again asked for the phone. Rudo left when she heard the name Matamba.

When he replaced the receiver Tigera sat staring at the Baines print of the Victoria Falls which hung over his bed. Eventually he sighed and hobbled to the bathroom. He brushed his teeth in time to Matamba's words.

'If you want more money from the American you must sell Kame Two to Gifford. No one will question the sale, especially when you show them the new donation. If he likes Pat Gifford, you can be sure that he will give more money to conservation.'

Tigera was now certain that Pat and the American had discussed the forced sale of Ganyani and Kame. He was not looking forward to the meeting the following day.

As he closed his eyes he reached a decision. I will tell the American that I am so impressed with the way that Gifford is running Kame Two that I am thinking of letting him buy the land. Should Gifford leave the country it will revert to the Department of Natural Parks, he comforted himself. There are ways of getting him to leave Zimbabwe should I want the land.

His head sank into the soft pillow. In the moonlight which rested on the bedside table, his glasses gleamed like predatory eyes.

Tigera entered Pat's office to find the American already seated behind the heavy *mukwa* desk. He compressed his fleshy lips. The man had put him at a disadvantage before they even started talking.

He hid his annoyance behind a smile and sat down on the small upright chair opposite Mel.

'I've been making some enquiries,' said Mel, gesticulating to the phone which he had not used. 'I find that Pat Gifford has Kame Two on a concession basis.'

'A very generous one,' broke in Tigera. 'We don't usually give out concessions which can be renewed by the same person. They go to the highest bidder. It's all a matter of money,' he said. He shrugged and smiled at Mel, as if they were part of a conspiracy.

Mel wanted to shake Tsvakai Tigera until the insincere little man cried for mercy, but he returned the smile. Many a man has been betrayed by his tongue, he thought. Let's hear what this sycophant has to say.

'Why have you and your board made an exception in Pat Gifford's case?' he asked innocently. 'Has it not aroused a lot of envy?'

'No one questions us,' boasted Tigera, then, seeing something unpleasant lurking in the depths of Mel's eyes, he added hurriedly, 'They all know that we are above suspicion.'

Mel nodded his head slowly, then he hit the desk with the flat of his hand.

'Above suspicion?' he said incredulously. 'Are you telling me that in a small African country, members of the government are above suspicion? Where I come from and, man, is that some place, even our President's motives and movements are watched and queried. I'm beginning to regret that I ever invested in this country.'

Tigera trembled. He saw his safe empire crumbling.

'No, no. I did not mean that at all,' he protested desperately. 'What I meant was that we would never do anything illegal. People know this and trust us. Please don't misunderstand me.'

'Well,' said Mel, popping a stick of gum into his mouth. 'Perhaps I got the wrong idea. Perhaps it is worth investing a little more towards conservation. With people of your integrity I'm sure my money will be put to good use.'

Tigera was nauseous with relief.

'I swear there is no safer place to invest your money. For a man like yourself, who invests in the future of the world, its animals and their habitat, Zimbabwe is the only place.'

Mel congratulated himself. It had been easier than he imagined. Hit now, while he is running scared, he thought.

'I'm sure glad to hear that, Mr Tigera. Before I sign another cheque I have a proposition. No, not a proposition, a condition.'

'Anything,' said Tigera.

'Pat Gifford is to be allowed to buy Kame Two. Not the concession rights. He is to have title deeds to the land.'

Swine, thought Tigera, they did get to him yesterday. Eventually they will pay for this.

To the American's amazement, Tigera's face broke into a huge smile.

'We are brothers at heart,' he said.

Like hell, thought Mel, I'd rather have the devil as my sibling.

'I have been so impressed with what Gifford has done on Kame Two that I spent most of yesterday phoning members of the board. I'm happy to be able to tell you that Mr Matamba feels it is within our power to sell Kame Two to Pat Gifford. I was going to suggest this to you today, as you donated the money to buy the land.'

'Great,' said Mel, rolling the gum into a ball with his tongue. 'I'm sure that Mr Matamba also agreed to sell it for the same price the government is paying Gifford for his previous ranch, Kame.'

'This is a much larger piece of land. The eventual income will—' Tigera broke off as Mel stood up.

'In that case I have a meeting to attend in Natal. They need land for an elephant corridor.'

Tigera swallowed. 'I'll put the matter to Mr Matamba,' he said.

Once the American was out of the country they could renege on any deals.

'Now,' answered Mel, crossing his legs on the desk and folding his arms behind his head. 'Tell Matamba to fax through the papers, complete with the necessary signatures. We'll sign here.' He peered at Tigera. Tigera had only seen pictures of icebergs, but the American's eyes seemed as cold and hard as those islands of ice.

'I presume signed facsimiles are legal,' Mel went on. 'If not we'll fly to Harare or Bulawayo immediately. I want this matter completed before my hunt.'

He grinned at Tigera. His perfectly capped teeth shone like a crocodile's.

'I dislike combining business and pleasure. Tomorrow the hunt starts. This business must be wrapped up before then.'

'The signed facsimiles will be honoured,' Tigera replied.

Briar was in her bedroom packing for the hunt on New Ganyani when Pat burst into her room waving a handful of papers.

'He's done it,' he said. 'He's done it. Look, these are signed by both Matamba and Tigera.'

He swung Briar into his arms and waltzed her around the room.

'What is signed?' she asked breathlessly.

'The title to Kame Two. We now own Kame Two and I'm giving it to you as a wedding present.'

'Pat, you can't!'

'Oh yes I can and I have. Apart from the fact that I love you and want you to have Kame Two, it's the sensible thing to do, Briar.'

Pat sat on the edge of the bed and lifted her on to his lap.

'I'm older than you and therefore likely to go before you.'

'Don't,' said Briar and placed her fingers across his lips. He felt them tremble, but continued.

'It will make me happy to know that whatever happens, I have provided for you. Make me happy, Briar.'

Mel looked in as he passed Briar's room to see her reaction to the news. He continued down the corridor with a jaunty lilt to his stride.

Tigera remained seated on the hard chair in Pat's study. The little man disliked being bested. He stared at the desk which Mel had recently vacated.

'That is one snake which I will milk until its fangs are harmless,' he muttered. 'Anyone who makes that much money must have secrets. I'll find them and then, Mr American, you will smile when you sign cheques for me.'

Chapter Thirty-six

TARA STOOD with her hands on her hips in the centre of the boma. She could detect not a single grass head on the freshly swept ground. She had driven the staff hard.

When the camp staff heard that Tsvakai Tigera was arriving with the wealthy American who had bought land to be set aside for safaris, they had happily worked long hours. The camp was perfect. Tara was satisfied.

Katoro perspired as he stood over his prized Dover stove. The aroma of freshly baked bread mingled with the odour of popcorn. Tara decided that if her version of popcorn pleased the Texans then it would probably be a success with the American billionaire.

Erin, Jacob and Jonas had checked the area around the camp for game spoor. Erin hoped to pick up a large antelope that afternoon and make biltong.

'All Americans like jerky,' he told Tara, 'so we'll have some dried venison for him before he leaves. In this cold weather it'll dry quickly. It'll also give me the opportunity to see how well he shoots before we go for a buffalo.'

Resplendent in new khaki uniforms and beige veldskoen, Erin, Jacob and Jonas left for the airstrip to greet Tigera and the American.

Shoko had been confined to the village for the duration of the American's hunt, but Tara was dubious of the villagers' ability to restrain the child.

Jacob was unusually quiet on the drive.

'What's wrong?' Erin asked him. 'Don't tell me you're nervous of meeting the great Tigera and his American benefactor.'

'Tigera is but a Shona in a position of power,' said Jacob quietly. 'It is not fear I have for him.'

Erin understood the threat in Jacob's voice, but chose to ignore it. The plane was taxiing towards them and they turned their faces from the dust.

'Is it the footprints?' Jonas whispered.

Jacob nodded. Whilst searching for game spoor near the camp Jacob had seen what appeared to be the imprint of a shoe, but something had been dragged over it to disguise the print. He and Jonas decided not to alarm Erin before they were certain that it had not been made by one of the villagers. They knew how important the hunt was to Erin. They checked the shoes of all the men in the village, but none showed the deep, wavy lines near the toe.

It was now too late to track the prints. The hunt would start at daybreak. Jacob was worried. The drums had told too many people of the hunt with the important American and Tigera. They had also warned of poachers in the Chizarira area, poachers whose guns spoke before they did.

But last night the drums told of silence in the mountains of Chizarira and fears that the men had moved elsewhere. The message beaten out on the night winds was one of danger to all villagers. They also spoke of two men who were worse than the men they led.

Jacob knew that he had to warn Erin about the poachers.

369

He wanted Tigera. No poacher was going to give the ma
an easy death.

They turned their attention to unloading the plane.

Tara flicked an imaginary speck of dust from one of th
canvas chairs set around a freshly started fire.

'Mother Mary, let this hunt go well,' she said softly
'This American can send us so many hunters. I know tha
Erin hates Tigera but I will make him like us.'

She looked up at the sky but could not see the yellov
Cessna.

'It must have landed,' she said. She crossed to the mirro
hanging on the reed wall above the basin beside her hut
She fluffed up her curls and tucked her shirt into her khak
shorts.

Chapter Thirty-seven

KIRK MADDEN twiddled the focus ring on his binoculars and the Zeiss lenses filled with Tara's ample breasts as she smoothed down her shirt.

'So young Gifford has found that nice piece of pasta,' he said, as he studied her petite body. 'Wouldn't mind a few mouthfuls of it myself.'

Kirk and his men were hidden on a rocky hilltop within binocular range of the camp. He had studied the layout and the movement of the staff carefully. Now he awaited the arrival of Tigera with Erin. He could have killed Gifford a dozen times that morning as he lay on his belly training his rifle sights on the young man, but he wanted Erin to know who was handling the gun. He wanted to see fear in both Tigera and Erin's eyes as they looked at him: their executioner.

He felt the same thrill of excitement which had pounded blood into his brain and tingled his nerves during the war. A low hum alerted Madden to the arrival of the Cessna. He burrowed even lower beneath the bush which afforded him concealment.

'Don't let him fly over the camp,' he said.

As if the devil was guarding one of his own, the plane merely circled the landing strip and disappeared from view.

Pat had decided to drop Mel and Tigera and return to Kame Two for Briar, Rudo and Buna.

'I'll let Erin collect Tigera and Mel at the strip and settle them into New Ganyani,' he said to Briar. 'This is supposed to be a hunt, not a family outing.'

'I know, Pat,' she replied, 'but Tara and I have so much to discuss about the weddings and Rudo is longing to see Jacob, though I don't think Shoko will be pleased to have his sister at the camp.'

Pat laughed. 'It's just as well that Mel likes you, or he'd object to this family reunion during his hunt.'

'Oh, we'll keep out of his way. We'll stay in camp when you men hunt,' said Briar.

Erin and Tara stood to one side of the boma as Mel with Tigera at his heels inspected the camp.

'This is what I call a real African hunting camp,' said Mel, a little later, falling back into one of the canvas chairs and stretching out his long legs.

Tara breathed a sigh of relief and signalled to Katoro to bring refreshments.

'Coke, beer or tea?' said Katoro proudly.

'Coke would be great. In the can,' he called as Katoro scurried away.

'I never drink when I'm shooting. Over the years I've been out with too many idiots nursing hangovers. I'm too old to enjoy brush shots and accidental discharges, especially when they come from four-sixty Wetherbys.'

Erin grinned. 'I know what you mean. The more guns they carry the safer they feel, until they press the trigger. After the retort and recoil they are too terrified to use the rifle again.'

Both men laughed and a bond of understanding and companionship was formed. Tigera perched on the edge of

s chair, disliking the American's instant approval of Erin
d the camp.

Jacob and Jonas were still standing to attention beside
e Toyota. Erin noticed them and called across the boma.

'I won't be needing you until after lunch. Please see that
e Toyota is ready. We will be looking for plains game
is afternoon. Tomorrow we go for the buffalo.'

They nodded and left the boma. On their way out of
e enclosure Tigera looked up at them, but the trackers'
es were inscrutable.

'They will not finish lunch before three o'clock,' Jacob
edicted. 'Let us look for more of the prints I found.'

'Our *sadza* will be waiting on the fire,' said Jonas,
nging to sit back in the sun with a full belly.

'Go to the village and sit with the women and children,'
unted Jacob. 'I will go alone to find the men who tried to
ver their marks in the sand.'

Jonas capitulated, as Jacob knew he would.

'Let us go,' he said.

irk Madden was tense. He had not relaxed since his men
d found a skinny child scampering down the hill with a
r of chocolate taken from Kirk's pack which was wedged
neath a rock.

Though Kirk slapped the child's face until its head
cked like a metronome, the boy only pointed into the far
stance when asked where he came from.

Eventually Kirk decided that the child was simple and
uld not talk. He told his men to let him go.

The boy vanished, running in the opposite direction to
e camp. The men soon lost interest in him and turned
eir attention back to New Ganyani.

Kirk froze as he saw Erin's two trackers leave the boma. Like pebbles tossed into still water, they walked in ever widening circles away from the cluster of huts.

'Damn,' he swore, as Jacob suddenly bent down on one knee to scrutinize the ground.

'They have found something,' he said to one of his men lying near him. 'I told you to run branches across our tracks.'

'We did.'

'Obviously not well enough,' Kirk snarled, as he watched Jacob signal for Jonas to join him.

'Move back,' ordered Kirk. 'We can't stay here. Those two are like *bere*, nothing turns them when they find spoor.'

Silently Kirk cursed his band of hand-picked poachers. He should have checked that the leafy branches dragged behind them had obliterated all footprints. Now, he would not be able to keep the camp under close surveillance. He would have to rely on gossip among the women in the village – and luck.

Jonas looked at the scuffed print and nodded in agreement.

'They have tried to cover their tracks,' he paused. 'The drums spoke of poachers.'

'Poachers do not come close to hunting camps. They are wise in the ways of the bush,' Jacob answered slowly as he stood up. 'No. I think these are here for another reason. It is not animals they seek.'

Jonas shivered. Jacob was seldom wrong.

'Tigera?' he whispered.

'Tsvakai Tigera is mine,' said Jacob. 'I will kill the man who tries to take him first. I will see Tigera's eyes roll

374

ith fear. He will know that Rudo is my wife before he
es.'

Jonas silently asked his ancestors to give him protection
he was with Jacob when they found Tigera alone. His
iend's eyes were as hard and expressionless as his voice.
e recalled the night he and Jacob had run on the spoor of
e men who mutilated Rudo. It had been easy to avenge
er injuries. But everyone knew of Tigera. He was a
owerful man in the country. His death would not pass
nnoticed.

'He is yours,' said Jonas, showing no outward sign of
s disquiet.

'Good. Let us find who these men are and what they
ant so close to our camp,' said Jacob.

The trackers searched for new prints until they heard
e hooter of the Toyota. They broke into a run and
rrived in the boma just as Tigera and the American
merged from their huts, ready to go out into the bush and
ke an antelope.

Katoro whistled and signalled to Jacob. Jacob glanced
Erin and went to the kitchen.

'Shoko!" he gasped.

The child was sitting on a stool with a basin of bloody
ater beside him. Katoro held a cloth in his hand. Shoko's
ce was swollen and one eye was closed.

'Call Tara,' commanded Jacob. 'Tell her it's urgent.'

Alone with the child, Jacob held him in his arms.

'Who did this?' he whispered.

Blood seeped from a cut in Shoko's lip as he spoke and
acob dabbed at it softly.

'The white man with red hair,' he lisped.

Jacob was cold with killing rage but he rocked the child
ently.

'Can you show me where you saw this man?' he asked.
Shoko nodded.

'Can you take me now, or are you in too much pain?'

'Now,' Shoko whispered, nestling close to Jacob.

'You are brave and you are my son,' said Jacob.

Tara hurried into the kitchen. It had been an excellent
lunch and everyone was in a good mood. Even Tigera had
relaxed and been pleasant. It boded well for the safari.

'Jacob,' she said, 'Erin is waiting for you. They are all
ready to leave for the hunt. Why have you called me?'

She drew in her breath sharply as Jacob turned round
and she saw the bloodstains on his khaki uniform and
Shoko in his arms.

'What's happened?'

'Please call Erin. It's very important,' said Jacob. He
had decided to tell Erin about the footprints he had found.

'But I must take Shoko to the clinic,' argued Tara.

'Later. First I must speak to Erin. Alone.'

Tara looked from Shoko to Jacob and ran from the
kitchen.

'Do not let the others see that you are upset,' warned
Jacob.

Tara heard him and walked back to the boma.

'Erin,' she said calmly. 'Please come to the kitchen.'

'Tara, we are about to leave. It will be too late to find
an antelope if I stay and listen to Katoro.'

'Excuse me,' Tara said, with a sweet smile to Mel and
Tigera. She walked up to Erin and pretended to hug him.
Her fingers dug into the soft flesh inside his elbow and he
winced.

'Come,' she whispered flatly.

'Please excuse me,' said Erin. 'Jonas, see that everyone

on the Toyota. I'll sort this out in a minute. It's just one
f the daily problems we face when running a bush camp.'

The American grinned and climbed into the seat beside
rin's. Tigera looked at Jonas, but there was nowhere for
im to sit except up on the trackers' bench. Jonas checked
ae first-aid box which he knew was in perfect order and
ft Tigera to scramble up on his own. He watched as
igera favoured his blistered foot.

That blister may work for us, he thought. He will not
e able to keep up with Erin and the American. One of us
ill have to stay back and help him.

Jonas smiled. Jacob would like the idea. He looked back
ver his shoulder. Where was Jacob? he wondered. He
ever kept clients waiting. Jonas longed to jump down and
un to see what had happened, but he was not about to
icur Erin's wrath by disobeying his instructions.

Briar strolled up to the hunting vehicle and chatted to
1el and Tigera. It was unlike Erin to be late. She crossed
er fingers, hoping that nothing would upset the smooth
peration of this important safari.

What is it, Tara?' said Erin sharply as soon as they were
ut of earshot of Mel and Tigera.

'Trouble,' she answered and her face was white. Erin
:ormed into the kitchen, expecting to deal with a person-
lity clash among his staff.

'Damn,' he swore, as he saw Shoko. The child tried to
ury his face on Jacob's shoulder and fresh blood dripped
n to Jacob's shirt.

'Who has he been fighting now?' asked Erin, his voice
ard and exasperated.

'He has been beaten,' said Jacob.

Erin listened carefully.

'The child is in pain and needs attention,' said Tara.

'No,' contradicted Erin. 'Jacob is right. We must find out who these men are and why they are watching our camp. We also need an excuse to call off the hunt for this afternoon.'

He dropped his face into his hands.

'That's easy,' said Tara. 'Tell them Shoko fell and has fractured his cheekbone. It needs setting. Jacob and Jona have to help me with him as he won't let anyone else touch him. Americans are always sensitive to the needs of children and Tigera is a man of Africa. Children and cattle are important to him.' She paused for breath. 'Let Jacob carry him past the Toyota. I don't believe that they will want to go on the hunt and leave the child like this.'

'It is a good plan,' said Jacob.

'We can carry Shoko to where he saw the men, then Miss Tara can look after him in the clinic.'

'Briar can take the American and Tigera on a walk. She walks like a man and will tire them. They will also hear of many birds as Briar knows the names of all our birds.'

Erin lifted his face from his hands.

'What would I do without the two of you?' he said.

They trooped out of the kitchen. The laughter stopped at the Toyota when they saw Jacob with Shoko in his arms.

Tigera and Mel believed Erin's story. 'Let's fly him to Harare,' Mel suggested. Erin and Jacob stiffened. They had not considered this possibility.

Tara stepped in front of the group.

'The child needs to recover from the shock first. It would be most unwise to fly him out now. I'd like to xamine him in the clinic. If I feel he needs hospitalization, hen we can fly him to the city.'

Erin and Jacob breathed a sigh of relief.

'I'll need Jacob and Jonas to help me,' added Tara. 'The hild trusts them and will lie still if they are near.'

Jonas was amazed. What had happened to Shoko? Tara new that Jacob was the only person to whom Shoko istened. He had no control over the little monkey, but he limbed down from the vehicle obediently.

As soon as Briar was out of sight, closely followed by Mel and Tigera, the two trackers and Erin set off with hoko.

Shoko pointed out the rocky hill in the distance and hivers ran through his little body. Jacob held him tightly, elling him how clever and brave he was to pretend he ould not talk. He promised the little boy that he, Jonas nd Erin would punish the man who had beaten him.

'I took chocolate from his bag,' Shoko confessed in a mall voice.

'It is bad to steal,' said Jacob, 'but by finding the men you have done a very good thing and we are proud of you.'

Shoko tried to smile, but whimpered as his swollen lip plit open.

'Come, little one. Let me make your lip better,' said Tara. 'You have been very brave, now show me how trong you are.'

To everyone's amazement Shoko loosened his grip around Jacob's neck. He held Tara's hand tightly and walked away with her.

'He is afraid that the men are still on that hill,' said Erin.

'I hope they are,' answered Jacob and Jonas nodded.

The three men approached the hill cautiously, moving

from tree to tree, but nothing moved and no one contested their right of way.

'Shoko did not speak yet these men left in a hurry,' said Jacob. They were now standing on top of the hill and had a perfect view of the camp.

'But not in so much of a hurry that they did not brush over their tracks,' said Jonas.

Jacob's eyes narrowed. 'They were watching when we found that print,' he said.

Jonas whistled softly. 'From here they could easily have shot any one of us.'

Erin squatted beside the bush beneath which Kirk had been concealed.

'What do they want?' he asked, chewing a dry piece of grass. 'Why watch our camp and then leave?'

'The man who leads them is cunning,' said Jacob. 'He was afraid that when Shoko returned to his home he would lead someone here. They will be a long way from New Ganyani now.'

Erin took the chewed straw from his mouth and tossed it away. He glanced at where it fell then jumped up, as if stung by a wasp, and ran to the bush.

He went down on his hands and knees.

'Here,' he called. 'This is where the leader lay. Look at the hollow he made in the ground for his hip. It commands an ideal view of New Ganyani.' He lifted his rifle and peered through the scope. 'I wonder who he is after?' Erin turned to Jacob and Jonas. 'Find the other hiding places. Find out how many men he has with him.'

'He is worried,' whispered Jonas as they climbed back up the hill.

'Do not mention Tigera,' warned Jacob.

'Your silence is mine,' said Jonas.

Both trackers sat down beside Erin.

'Four,' they said. 'He has four with him.'

'You found nothing else?'

'No,' answered Jacob. 'This time they have been careful, but we could break their spoor if we searched tomorrow.'

There was a long silence as the men looked across at the camp.

'Tomorrow we hunt,' said Erin. 'We cannot afford to upset the American or Tigera. Tigera!' he repeated. 'I wonder if that is who they are after. That swine must have a million enemies. I have to treat him well on this hunt, but I know that he ordered the slaughter on Ganyani.'

Erin suddenly grinned. 'If it's Tigera they want, I certainly won't shield him.'

Jacob and Jonas lowered their eyes and said nothing.

Erin returned with the trackers in time for supper.

Rudo crumbled pieces of coconut ice and carefully fed Shoko, as she listened to Jacob's account of the men who had been watching New Ganyani. She stroked Shoko's head softly as she gave him titbits. At the end of the story she pursed her lips.

'I do not like this, Jacob. There is trouble for all in camp. Be careful when you hunt tomorrow.'

'I will.'

'Do not keep your eyes on the ground, search around you. You will need the eyes of an eagle.'

Jacob had not told her that Tigera was the man who had ordered her mutilation. Now, seeing her distress over the men who had hidden on the hill, he was pleased that he had not shared the information with her. She would probably have told the Old One and Pat would not have allowed him to go on the hunt or be near Tigera. Jacob knew he would never have another opportunity as wonderful as this hunt in which to avenge his wife. In the city, Tigera was always closely guarded. But as he did not want the American to think that he had enemies and needed protection, he had reluctantly ordered his bodyguards to remain in Harare.

Tara and Erin forced themselves to laugh and tell stories at dinner, though each wrestled with disquieting thoughts.

Tara was confused. Erin would not tell her what had happened to Shoko. Shoko would not speak. She had seen Erin, Jacob and Jonas run back into camp just before Briar returned with Tigera and Mel.

She had a feeling that Erin was keeping something from her, something important. Years of living with her father had taught her that when questioned, men usually told implausible tales or lied. Patience was what brought answers.

Pat and Erin walked Mel and Tigera to their respective huts after dinner.

'Get a good night's sleep, as we'll be up early tomorrow,' said Erin.

Satisfied that their guests were comfortable, father and son returned to the camp fire, but instead of sitting down Erin kept on walking.

Once they were out of the boma and on the road Pat broke the silence.

'What is it, son? Having second thoughts about the wedding?'

'Oh no, that's not the problem. Tara is wonderful. Everything is fine. But ...' He paused and kicked at a stone. He did not want to worry Pat. He needed to prove that he could manage New Ganyani on his own.

'Tell me,' said Pat.

When he had finished, Pat walked on, rubbing his bald dome.

'I have heard something I didn't tell you,' said Pat. 'It didn't seem important at the time, but Tigera has news of a band of poachers led by a white man who are creating fear and mayhem in the Game Department. Tigera wanted to delay the hunt until they were caught.' Pat thrust his hands deep into the side pockets of his gilet.

'Perhaps this is the gang,' said Erin. 'We can't call off the hunt, Dad. It'll only prove that we are inept.'

'Tigera probably wouldn't allow us to cancel now. He would lose face in front of his American billionaire and I'm sure he knows there is a lot of cream left in that cow,' said Pat soberly. 'Tomorrow, see that both Jacob and Jonas have rifles and tell them they may shoot to kill if we come across the poachers.'

Erin nodded.

'Hopefully that little monkey Shoko has moved them right out of the district,' said Pat. 'For once his mischief worked to our advantage.'

'They certainly left the hill in a hurry. Poor kid was badly beaten, but he is clever and tough,' added Erin.

Pat and Erin turned and walked back slowly, pausing to listen to the night sounds.

'Where they have gone depends on what, or maybe who, they want,' said Pat. 'If you don't mind I'd like to join the hunt tomorrow.'

'It will be great to have you, Dad. Please don't tell Briar about the poachers, as she'll tell Tara and I'll have Tara demanding to come as well, to look after me.'

'I heard about her rescuing you from the herd of buffaloes,' Pat teased.

'We'll say nothing to the girls or clients. But get Jacob to alert the villagers and Katoro. They must not wander around in the bush until we are certain that this gang have really left the area.'

The night passed slowly for Pat and Erin and they were standing at the camp fire sipping coffee long before the camp awakened.

Sheeba slunk up to join them, as if ashamed that she had overslept on the foot of Pat's bed.

'And you call yourself a watchdog?' said Pat as he saw her pad softly towards the fire. Her ears drooped and her tail stuck to her belly as she stood as close to him as she could.

'A lion could have taken me and you would have slept through it. You're getting old, Sheeba.'

The ridgeback squirmed as if in embarrassment.

'Forgive her, Dad,' said Erin. 'I can't bear to watch her humble act, she does it so well.'

Both men laughed and Sheeba's tail immediately stood up over her back, swinging like a windmill's sail.

'It's a good day that starts with laughter,' a deep voice boomed. Mel walked out of his hut, stretched his arms high above his head, then scratched his chest.

'What happened to you, Erin? Wet your bed?'

Erin grinned. He liked the big American.

'It's Dad, he has to be up before sunrise every day, winter and summer.'

'The hour before the sun rises is my quiet time,' said Pat. 'Everyone needs a time to listen to their soul.'

'That's a neat idea,' said Mel, going into a series of knee-bends. 'I must try it some time.'

'You try my quiet time and I'll try your exercise regime. My belly would benefit from it,' retorted Pat, throwing a log on to the fire.

Tigera pulled the blankets up under his chin as he lay listening to the banter at the fire. He wished that he was back in Harare in the comfort of his home, not here shivering in a grass hut.

Turning on his side, he pulled up his knees into the foetal position. As his heel rubbed across the sheet he winced. The blister had felt better until Briar took them on that walk yesterday. Now it was raw and aching. Tigera wondered why they had cancelled the antelope hunt, merely because a child had been hurt. Children hurt themselves all the time, running around like unguided missiles.

He was certain that there was another story, but no one was talking. The fear of poachers still lurked in his mind, but he decided he would keep close to Erin and the protection offered by his rifle. He was drifting off to sleep again, when Briar's voice startled him.

'Mr Tigera, when you are ready I would like to take another look at that blister. You may have a long walk today and I would like to be sure that you are comfortable.'

'If not you can stay in camp with us,' said Tara. 'We would enjoy your company.' Briar screwed up her face as if she had eaten a lemon. Tara merely smiled and winked at her.

Tigera glared. He was definitely going on the hunt. The last time he had left the American alone with Pat and Briar he had lost control of Kame Two. He was not prepared to lose any more land or have his authority undermined. No, today he would walk with the men.

'The blister is fine, thank you,' he called.

Tara nudged Briar in the ribs.

'Blisters can be tricky things, Mr Tigera,' Briar answered. 'They look dry and healed, but after a few hours the skin softens again. I would really like to put a light padding over it. Just for comfort.'

Would this woman never stop nagging, thought Tigera as he slowly eased his legs over the edge of the bed.

'Briar is right,' called Erin from the camp fire. 'You need to be fit today, Mr Tigera. If that blister opens, we will have to leave you in the bush and collect you on our way back to the Toyota.'

The thought of spending hours alone, seated under a tree with wild animals and poachers wandering around, decided Tigera.

'I will call as soon as I have washed and dressed,' he said.

'Good, Mr Tigera,' answered Briar. 'Breakfast will be on the table in half an hour.'

Tigera groaned quietly. Not even for the American will I go on another hunt, he thought.

He completed his ablutions and glanced at his watch.

'Miss Hanley,' he called.

Briar and Tara hurried into Tigera's hut. 'Oh dear,' said Briar, looking at the blister, which had burst. 'The quickest way to cure this is for me to dab it again with spirits to dry it.'

'No,' replied Tigera emphatically. 'You can put a plaster or something over it.'

Tara shrugged. 'Briar is right, Mr Tigera, but we'll do whatever you wish. First a little antiseptic cream, then a gauze pad and we'll hold it in place with a wide strip of plaster. There you are,' she said, standing back to survey her handiwork. 'Now we'll help you put on your sock and shoe.'

Tigera pulled his foot away. He felt that beneath their outward concern they were mocking him.

'I can manage,' he said curtly.

'If it's not done correctly the plaster will curl in at the sides and rub against the raw flesh,' warned Tara.

When Tigera did not deign to reply but busied himself with his sock and shoe, the girls gathered up the bowl of water, plaster and bandages and left him alone.

Jacob watched Tigera walk from his hut to the call of the *mbira*. His sharp eyes noted how Tigera favoured his left foot, though he straightened up and walked normally when he saw the girls at the breakfast table.

'Good morning. I hope you slept well,' said Erin as Katoro pulled out a chair for Tigera.

'As well as can be expected in the circumstances,' answered Tsvakai Tigera ungraciously.

'Best night's sleep I've had in years,' said Mel jovially.

The two women bustled around Tigera, pretending that he needed special attention because of his injury. It made him feel important and he managed a forced smile with his coffee at the end of the meal.

Chapter Thirty-eight

KIRK MADDEN'S stomach growled and rumbled, a reminder that he had eaten only dried meat and drunk water from the stream since the previous afternoon, when they had fled from the hill overlooking New Ganyani.

His mood was as sour as his stomach. The night had been cold and he was unable to make a fire for fear of detection. His men had curled up against the bank of a dry river bed, while he sat counting the long hours to dawn.

One of his men returned just before sunrise with the information he needed.

'They go to hunt buffalo,' he said, as he squatted beside Kirk. 'They drive first to Tenga Spring to look for spoor.'

'You are sure of this?' asked Kirk sharply.

'Yes. The old woman did not lie before she died. I found her at the stream washing clothes. She also told me that everyone had been warned not to leave the village as there were poachers in the area.'

Kirk smashed his fist into the palm of his hand.

'So they know we were on the hill. That child,' he said, 'I should have killed him.'

The poacher looked at Kirk thoughtfully. The man was a good leader. He was ruthless and did not know the word pity.

'You still can,' he said. 'The child is in the village and will be there all day.'

Kirk's eyes glittered, then deadened to a cold yellow stare.

'No,' he said. 'We must be at Tenga Spring before they arrive. This time we will make sure that we leave no sign of our presence. Wake the others.'

Suddenly he spun round and caught the man by his collar, jerking him off his feet.

'The woman?' he snarled. 'Where is the woman?'

'Her body is folded into a *dikita*'s hole,' he said. 'She was small and fitted easily.'

'Good,' answered Kirk and pushed the man away. The antbears can dig holes twelve feet deep, he thought. It's unlikely that anyone will find her. If the hyena smell the rotting flesh and drag her out, it will look as if they killed and ate her.

His band were soon in single file trotting behind him. Kirk knew the Tenga Spring area well as he had often used it as a starting point for a buffalo hunt. As they neared the spring Kirk swung away in a wide circle. He was determined that Erin's trackers would see nothing to alert or alarm them.

He positioned his men on a termitarium which rose up thirty feet and was topped by a huge mahogany tree. Dense scrub covered the side facing the spring. His men burrowed under the bushes on the opposite side and lay silent and patient as hungry felines. Kirk checked that they were hidden to his satisfaction then swung himself into the tree. Immediately the dark green leaves closed behind him and he vanished.

*

Tigera's mood had definitely improved by the time they reached Tenga Spring. In deference to his injured foot he was given the seat beside Erin. Mel sat on the trackers seat. This small victory over the American made Tigera smile.

Perhaps all is not lost, he thought. Once the American leaves I can arrange to make life very difficult for Gifford on Kame Two. Soon he will beg me to buy the land from him.

These thoughts warmed Tigera and kept him happy until the Toyota jerked to a halt. Erin bumped off the track and parked in the shade of some acacia trees.

'It'll be warm walking so leave any extra clothing in the truck,' he said.

Tigera looked up at the sky. It shone a pure, azure blue through the branches of the acacias. He unzipped his sleeveless gilet, and rolled it into a tight bundle. He opened the cubby-hole and peered in. It was empty save for a rather grimy roll of crepe bandage. He wedged his gilet into the space, pushing the pressure bandage to the back.

He relaxed in his seat as the men scurried around the vehicle, like ants invading a termite nest. He felt that his injured foot allowed him to sit back and let the others work.

'We're ready,' called Erin, moving round to Tigera's side of the Toyota. He held out his arm and Tigera made a show of leaning on it as he climbed down.

'Sure you don't want to stay in the truck?' asked Mel, with thinly veiled sarcasm in his voice. 'You seem to be in real pain with that foot.'

'No. Once I start walking it will ease,' said Tigera quickly. He chastised himself for over-playing the invalid.

Erin left him in the care of Jacob and Jonas and did a

quick mental check. His gaze skimmed over the vehicle, making certain that nothing important had been left.

He turned away to join the group of men, then leaned across the passenger seat and opened the cubby-hole. Erin recognized Tigera's gilet. He did not want Tigera to turn round and see him rummaging in his clothes. We've never needed the bandage, he thought. He slammed the cubby-hole shut, shouldered his rifle and told Jacob and Jonas to pick up spoor. The men waited at the spring while the trackers scouted for buffalo spoor in the trampled mud.

Jonas veered away from the spring. He gave a low whistle and pointed with his stick. Jacob joined him. The two men conversed in low tones. Jacob shrugged then nodded.

'We have spoor,' he said to Erin.

'Dad,' said Erin, standing back for Pat to move in behind Jacob.

Pat shook his head. 'It's your hunt, son. I'll bring up the rear.'

It was still cool when the men entered the mopane scrub, but soon they were sweating lightly and the first mopane flies homed in on them.

Erin noticed that Jacob and Jonas kept glancing around as they walked. Good, he thought, they have not forgotten the poachers.

Tigera was keeping up. The padding over his blister was keeping his heel comfortable. He felt safe walking with Mel in front and Pat behind him.

'The *nyati* is going to the river bed with the tall reeds,' said Jacob over his shoulder to Erin.

'Damn him,' swore Erin. 'Could he not have given us an easy hunt and gone to the grassy plain near the mud wallow?'

'A lion . . .'

'Yes, I know,' said Erin, 'is a lion is a lion.'

'Well, we can't trail six people down into the reed bed
We'll probably stumble over some other *nyati* lying chew
ing the cud.'

The trackers and Erin squatted in a tight circle. 'Tigera
is not hunting. He is so short we would lose him in the
reeds,' said Erin. 'He can stay up on the bank.'

Jacob's expression darkened. He wanted to remain close
to Mr Tigera that day.

'Why do we three not go down and flush out the *nyati*?'
asked Jacob. 'Leave the American and Mr Pat up here with
Tigera. Once we have the *nyati* out of the reed bed, they
can join us again.'

'It's a good suggestion, Jacob. Thank you,' said Erin.
Pat agreed and watched as Jacob, Erin and Jonas climbed
down the bank and waded into the reeds holding their
rifles high above their heads. The thick reeds slapped at
their faces, like waves on an uneasy sea, as they forced
their way through the seemingly impenetrable ocean of
green.

Jacob and Jonas had no time to look around for
poachers. Their attention was focused on forging through
the reeds and flushing out the buffalo. It was a dangerous
operation, for if the buffalo heard them or caught their
scent, it could run over them in its panic to escape.

Pat ran his binoculars down the reeded valley. There
were open patches where the buffalo had trampled the
reeds flat as they rested after grazing, but he could see
no sign of the buffalo Jacob had tracked into the river
bed.

Tigera sat on the bank and dangled his legs over the
edge. He was not concerned whether they found the animal

or not. He wished that the day was over and they were back in camp.

'There,' shouted Mel and raised his gun. Tigera jumped and cracked his sore heel on the hard clay of the bank.

'Look, they are going to walk right on the damn thing. It's lying down in front of them and they can't see it. The reeds are too high.'

'Don't shoot!' shouted Pat, but he was too late. The retort deafened Tigera. The river banks picked up and played with the echo, bouncing it from side to side like a ball.

The trackers and Erin looked up at the men on the bank. They stood frozen, their rifles ready in their hands, as the earth seemed to open up in front of them.

Instead of one, three buffalo broke cover and crashed through the reeds. The animals had been sleeping and ran away from the men down the river bed.

Pat looked at Mel and swallowed his words of anger. The American was ashen and seemed about to faint.

'Sit down,' Pat ordered, taking his gun from him. Mel sank to his knees.

'Hell, I'm sorry,' he said. 'That was a damn fool thing to do. I could have killed them.'

'Yes,' agreed Pat soberly. 'They are fortunate that the animals ran away and not on to them. You could, of course, have wounded one of the beasts. It's an acute and difficult angle when shooting down at an animal. We could have a wounded buffalo on our hands.'

Tigera grinned. Not only was the American discomfited and humbled, but the hunt would now be called off and they could return to New Ganyani. His heel throbbed where his foot had hit the bank and he did not relish the idea of stumbling over rocks and shrubs.

Suddenly Pat stood up and whistled. The three men in the river bed looked up at him. He pointed to the opposite bank, standing sideways on to them and holding out his arm like a signpost.

'It's our *nyati*,' whispered Jacob. 'Mr Pat has seen it break cover. It must have waited for the noise to stop and now it has climbed from the reeds.'

'It will move fast, until it is sure that there is no one following,' added Jonas.

'We'll move out of here as well, in the direction Dad has given us,' Erin decided. 'You can pick up spoor on the opposite bank.'

'The others?' queried Jacob.

'Dad can bring them round the top of the reed bed,' said Erin. 'They need not climb down here. We will meet up on the other side.'

Jacob threw back his head and gave the wild cry of the great fish eagle. Pat focused his binoculars on them and watched as they told him of their plan in sign language. Pat clenched his fist above his head and answered the whistle.

'Come,' he said to Mel and Tigera, 'we'll meet them on the other side.'

'But the buffaloes have gone,' Tigera protested.

'Those were the wrong ones. They were another group sleeping in the reed bed. Ours is more wily. He has left the reeds quietly and is running away on the other side.'

'Then how do we catch up with him? We'll have to let him go,' persisted Tigera.

'No. Once he calms down and hears no sounds of pursuit he'll slow to a walk again. Jacob and Jonas will pick up his tracks. Don't worry.'

My only worry is that they will find the beast, thought Tigera.

As he climbed to his feet Tigera realized that his blister was no longer comfortably padded. With each step he took there was now a slow burning sensation.

He gritted his teeth, determined to remain with the American. But by the time they rounded the end of the valley and started walking to where Erin and the trackers were waiting, his limp was pronounced.

Jacob and Jonas watched Tigera like lions selecting a weak animal from the herd.

'He limps,' said Jonas.

'It will get worse,' added Jacob. He turned to Erin.

'Mr Tigera is not walking well with that foot. If your American is to shoot his buffalo, then you and Mr Pat should go ahead. Jonas and I will follow you with Mr Tigera.'

Erin hesitated.

'You will never catch up to the *nyati* at the speed Mr Tigera is walking. Look at him.'

'And he will get slower as the sock rubs the blister,' added Jonas.

Erin studied Tigera. They are right, he thought. It's important to keep Mel happy. That way Tigera will be happy too, as the little swine will get more money out of Mel.

Every time Erin looked at Tigera, he saw his sable antelope scattered across the hilltop in Ganyani and rage burned red and hot in his body. But the man was his guest, he was inviolate.

There will be another time, he promised himself. The little coward will be safe with Jacob and Jonas, he decided. They are both armed and well able to protect him.

Erin drew Pat aside and outlined the new plan.

'Excellent,' said Pat. 'Tell them.'

'Mr Tigera,' said Erin, 'I have decided that Jacob and Jonas can stay with you. You can then favour your foot and follow us more slowly.'

Tigera's face darkened.

'Jacob and Jonas are the best trackers and hunters I have ever known,' said Pat, 'and it will be safer to keep your distance from the buffalo. After all,' he smiled, 'it is Mel who wants to face an African buffalo.'

It worked. Tigera had no desire to be close to one of the massive creatures. One of the Parks rangers had been impaled on a buffalo's horn. Tigera had seen the gaping hole where the man's rectum had been, as the beast had swung the ranger round its head, trying to dislodge him.

Tigera swallowed and looked at Jacob and Jonas, but both trackers were studying the ground.

'All right, Jacob?' asked Erin. He was a little concerned. Jacob had been unusually quiet all day.

'We will not be far behind you,' said Jacob. 'Mr Tigera will be able to enjoy the kill.'

'Are you boasting about your tracking skills?' teased Pat. 'Remember you will have to move fast to catch up with us.'

'We will hear you and cut across to where you are. We will not have to walk in the footsteps of the *nyati* as you must,' Jacob said smiling.

'As you will be walking a little slower, look for any snares or trap lines,' said Erin.

Jacob and Jonas nodded. They understood that he was warning them to be on guard.

Tigera watched Mel leave with Erin and Pat. They'll be too busy tracking the buffalo to speak of land concessions, he comforted himself. I'll see that those trackers keep me close to them.

Imperiously Tigera waved Jacob and Jonas on. Their faces were impassive and their sharp eyes veiled as they fell into single file, Jacob in front and Jonas bringing up the rear.

They climbed the hill slowly and the red stones rolled beneath their shoes. Jacob held out his 'pointing stick' for Tigera to hold to make the climb easier.

'I do not need help from an N'debele,' spat Tigera.

Jacob tucked the stick back into his belt and ignored the slithering and stumbling he heard behind him. He had formulated no plan for Tigera. He knew that he had to die, but was content to wait. He had the patience of those born in Africa. Something would happen.

Jonas whistled softly and Jacob stopped.

'What is it?' asked Tigera apprehensively.

Jacob and Jonas studied the wire looped across a narrow game path.

'Poachers' snares,' Jacob said, as he started unravelling it.

'We must go on and meet the others,' said Tigera.

'We were given orders to look for traps and snare lines. You heard Mr Erin,' said Jonas.

The trackers followed the line of snares which led into a shallow dry donga. During the rains the water would rush down the small ravine. Now it held mounds of dry brown, black and gold winter leaves cupped and captive.

The snares led to the head of the ravine and down into it. Animals used it as an easy path up the hill and the poachers had capitalized on an excellent place to set their lines.

Jacob rolled the snare wire into a small loop and hung

it on his belt. Tigera sat beside him, taking every opportunity to rest his foot. It now ached with each step he took. Jonas stepped into the ravine, beautiful in its river of leaves.

Suddenly Jacob saw Jonas leap into the air as if pulled up on puppet strings. He jumped up on to the bank breathing heavily, then walked back slowly to Jacob and Tigera.

'There is a new snare. One I have not seen before,' he said calmly. 'Come and see it before I unwind it.'

Tigera placed his hand on the ground to push himself up.

'No,' said Jacob. He had read something in Jonas's eyes which alerted him. 'You rest here. It is not worth using that foot to see a snare. I will check it and return.'

Tigera watched the trackers walk beside the ravine.

'See,' said Jonas triumphantly and pointed his stick at the leaves. He tightened his grip as the stick was almost knocked from his grasp. Straw-coloured venom ran like mucus down the stick.

The puff-adder drew back its broad, subtriangular head to strike again.

'He is large,' said Jacob, noting the long pointed tip to its tail.

'And angry,' added Jonas as the snake inflated itself and let out the air in a warning hiss.

Both men turned to look at Tigera, who was polishing his glasses and paying little attention to what he considered to be a waste of time.

'Our ancestors have sent us an *iBululu*,' said Jonas.

'It will be a painful death and that is good,' added Jacob.

They left the snake angry at being disturbed. It had

398

come out of semi-hibernation and was basking in the
wintry sun when Jonas crackled the dry leaves behind it.

Its warning hiss had saved Jonas and he leapt for the
bank. In spite of being sluggish, and having the reputation
of not moving until stepped on, the snake strikes at one
hundredth of a second and can hit its prey three to five
times in rapid succession.

The puff-adder held its flattened head jerked back in the
defensive position, ready to strike again if necessary. Its
silvery-grey eyes watched Jacob and Jonas as they retreated
back up the dry stream bed.

It closed its wide open mouth and the recurved fangs
returned to their sheath of skin in the roof of the mouth.

'What did you find?' asked Tigera with little interest as
the trackers returned to him.

'They seem to have set a line of snares down the dry
stream bed,' said Jacob. 'It will be softer for your heel if
we walk on the leaves. The stones on the banks cause your
ankle to turn as you walk and it applies pressure to your
foot.'

'Which rubs that blister raw,' finished Jonas.

Tigera nodded.

'I'll lead the way,' said Jacob. 'If you see me go up on
to the bank, ignore it. I'll only be checking that they have
not laid a double line of snares.'

'Keep walking on the leaves,' said Jonas. 'It's a short
cut to where the American is.'

A light breeze lifted a handful of leaves and let them
rest softly on the pale yellow and brown snake with the
dark brown chevron bands across its back and tail. Snake
and leaves were woven into a symphony of golds and
browns. The camouflage was perfect.

Jacob had judged the male puff-adder to be at least

three feet long. He knew it could throw itself forward the full length of its body when striking, so about five feet away from the snake he stepped up on to the bank and gesticulated for Tigera to go on.

The snake heard the leaves crunching. As the sounds grew closer it opened its mouth and rotated its needle-sharp fangs through ninety degrees to the forward position at the front of its mouth, ready to strike.

Tigera's hearing was not tuned to noises in the bush and the crunching of the thick bed of dry leaves muffled the snake's warning hiss.

He was enjoying the cushion the leaves gave to his sore foot when the snake hit him. It was so fast that Jacob and Jonas were not sure that it had struck. It seemed merely to jerk its head back with its mouth stretched wide open.

Tigera felt no pain with the first strike and he stepped forward onto the angry snake. As he felt the soft writhing beneath his feet he looked down.

He screamed, a high-pitched call of unimaginable terror. Like many people born in Africa, his fear of snakes was almost pathological.

He could see the long fangs with the venom dripping from the orifice at the tip. In the pale sunlight it looked as if the snake had dipped its fangs into raw egg-white.

Tigera's weight was crushing the snake. It struck and struck again.

Its fangs penetrated the popliteal vein behind his knee, injecting the venom deep inside.

The puff-adder's venom is as toxic as that of the mamba or the cobra, but is usually slower. Tigera sank to his knees on the leaves beside the snake. Jacob and Jonas immediately collected rocks and stoned the *iBululu*. It coiled and twisted as the rocks and stones sank into and bloodied its colourful body. Its strongly keeled scales rubbed against Tigera in its death throes. But Tigera was in the grip of a terror so pure that he neither saw nor felt the puff-adder.

Jacob was distraught. The solution which seemed so perfect was not going to work. He could not avenge Rudo's mutilation or the Giffords' loss of Ganyani and Kame. The snake had not bitten Tigera.

He was about to step on to the leaf bed and lift Tigera out, when Tigera screamed.

The cytotoxic venom was working. It was killing the living cells in his body and the pain was intense. Jacob remembered Erin saying that only morphine could kill the pain caused by the strike of an angry puff-adder when it held back none of its store of venom. The morphine was in the truck and that was at least a two-hour walk away from the dry stream.

Tigera will have time to contemplate the agony of those he has sent to their deaths, thought Jacob, as he watched Tigera flail wildly in the leaves and claw at his leg.

What Jacob could not foretell was that, instead of acting slowly, the venom was racing to the heart in the bloodstream.

'We must get Erin and Mr Pat here,' said Jonas, looking away from where the dead snake and Tigera were lying.

'No,' answered Jacob. 'Let it be.'

'They have the American with them. It will seem strange to him that we did nothing to try and save the man,' reasoned Jonas.

Jacob listened to Tigera's screams.

'Fire twice,' he ordered. 'They will call off the hunt and come.'

Jacob had not completed his sentence when Jonas lifted the thirty-six Springfield and fired into the air.

Pat, Erin and Mel were closer than the trackers realized. The buffalo had taken them in a wide circle and seemed to be returning to the reed bed.

'Trouble,' said Erin as they listened to the two retorts.

The men set off at a trot in the direction of the retorts.

'How will we find them?' panted Mel.

'They'll fire two shots at five-minute intervals until we reach them,' said Erin.

'Five minutes is up,' said Pat. 'Stop and listen.'

'There,' said Erin as a double retort rang out just in front of them.

Chapter Thirty-nine

KIRK MADDEN scanned the reed bed carefully. 'They are not there,' he said.

'That single rifle shot came from this direction,' argued one of his band of poachers. Kirk and his men had heard the retort from Mel's four-sixty Wetherby a few miles away. The hills held and threw the echo across the scrub and mopane to where they were cautiously tracking the hunters.

'See,' said the poacher, bending down and scrabbling in a tuft of short grass. He opened his palm and the sun gave credence to his claim. The casing gleamed like a tiny gold ingot in his hand.

Kirk took it and read the imprint stamped on the empty bullet casing.

'Wetherby,' he said. 'It must be the American who shot.'

'And missed,' said the poacher, proud of finding the casing. 'They are still on its spoor.'

'That means we can walk faster,' said Kirk. 'They'll have to move to catch up with the buffalo. Their attention will be focused on the spoor. We can afford to close the gap between us.' He pointed to the head of the reed bed. 'We'll go round the top of the bank. It's longer than cutting straight across, but we will be able to move more easily up here than down in that sea of reeds.'

As Kirk spoke, two shots rang out in quick succession. The poachers paused.

'Keep moving,' ordered Kirk. 'They seem to be in trouble.' He smiled and the poachers broke into a jog.

Jonas fired a second time. Kirk Madden and his men sank to the ground. If Jonas had not fired they would have walked right on to them. The trackers were bending down in a dry gully with their backs to Madden.

Kirk motioned to his men to remain where they were while he belly-crawled forward. He had to see what the trackers were looking at. Damn, he cursed silently as he recognized the body writhing on the leaves. The bloody fools have shot Tigera. Rage filled him and threw out reason.

Tigera was mine, you idiots. He was mine to kill. Kirk lifted himself on to his knees. The trackers still had their backs to him. They seemed to be trying to hold Tigera down and were paying no attention to anything around them.

Kirk's finger tightened around the trigger. The stock pressed into his cheek. He knew that his first shot had to be perfect. He needed to get the second tracker before he recovered from the shock of the retort and turned to return fire.

'Madden!' Pat's voice froze Kirk's finger on the trigger. 'Drop that gun!'

Pat, Erin and Mel had approached cautiously. The rifle shots warned them of trouble and they were prepared. They crept up behind Kirk just as he was about to shoot Jacob. They thought he had already shot Tigera.

Pat heard Briar's soft voice say, 'I am so ashamed.' Pat's hand shook on his rifle as he looked at Kirk.

'Stand up,' Erin ordered.

The sound of Erin's voice drove Kirk into a fierce desire to kill. Young Gifford's trackers had taken his prize, Tigera - now he would take the last of the Gifford boys.

Jacob and Jonas had turned and stood with their rifles trained on Kirk.

Slowly Kirk straightened, then like a top he spun round, firing at the same time.

Pat heard Erin grunt as the bullet struck. Without thinking, he fired.

Kirk stood and stared at them.

'Damn you Giffords,' he whispered. The words bubbled through the blood which streamed from his mouth.

Jacob and Jonas were at his side as his knees buckled. But Pat's aim had been true. Kirk Madden's yellow eyes glared up at the sun high above him, but death had taken away the light in them.

His men saw him fall. Sinuously as snakes, they coiled out of their hiding places. Using the monotonous descending notes of the emerald-spotted wood dove to keep in touch, they slithered away from the place where Kirk lay. By nightfall they would have dispersed and there would be nothing to connect them with Kirk Madden.

The call of the dove faded away. The sickening silence was broken by a scream from Tigera. Pat ignored it and turned to his son. A red stain was spreading across Erin's shirt and his face was pale.

'Dear God, don't take my son,' whispered Pat, as he gestured to Jacob and Jonas to help him. Jacob unstrapped his hunting knife and ripped Erin's shirt open. They used the shirt to wipe away the blood. Then Pat wadded the shirt into a pad and strapped it to Erin's shoulder with his belt.

'It looks like a flesh wound, son,' Pat comforted. 'The

bullet seems to have gone through your shoulder. Madden did not have time to aim. It doesn't seem to have touched bone. We'll clean it up back at the Toyota, then put you in Tara's tender care.'

Erin managed a small smile. 'Thanks, Dad. That will be fun.'

Tigera screamed again. Pat and Mel raced to where he lay. 'Where did Madden get him?' asked Pat, then he saw the fat, bloodied body of the puff-adder lying over Tigera's arm.

They lifted Tigera on to the bank. Pat had no need to ask where the snake had bitten him – his leg had swollen to double its size.

Pat turned him over. He and Jacob squeezed three sets of fang marks. Blood and lymph oozed from two sets, but when they saw the marks deep in the popliteal vein they shook their heads.

'He is a dead man,' said Jacob and Jonas nodded.

'Can we do nothing for him?' asked Mel, pointing to Tigera. He did not like the man, but he felt sympathy for a fellow being in torment.

'We could try Erin's pressure bandage,' said Pat.

Erin shook his head. 'It's in the Toyota behind Tigera's gilet,' he said.

Jonas smiled. Erin had forgotten the bandage which cured snake bites. The ancestors were smiling on them.

'In any case, once the venom is injected into a vein nothing will help, certainly not my bandage. It only slows the movement of venom until the victim can be treated.'

Tigera was still conscious, but his screams were fainter now. The cytotoxin was poisoning the cells in his brain.

Jacob bent over him as if to comfort him. 'Remember the slaughter you ordered on Ganyani. Remember, too, the *bere* you sent to mutilate my wife Rudo. I, Jacob, have had my revenge. Die slowly, Tigera.'

Tigera looked up into Jacob's dark eyes, almost touching his face. He tried to speak, but fell back. His head cracked loudly on the brown stones.

'It is over,' said Jacob, standing up. Pat glanced at Jacob then seated Erin in the shade of a tree, ignoring his protests.

'Jacob and Jonas will bring the Toyota as close to us as they can,' said Pat.

'But I'm capable of walking, Dad. It's only a flesh wound. You said so yourself,' reasoned his son.

'You may be capable of walking back to the Toyota, my boy, but we have to carry these bodies,' said Pat, pointing to Tigera and Madden. Jacob and Jonas looked at each other. Their eyes smiled though their faces remained grave. Mel looked down at the dead men then stepped forward and pulled the eyelids over Kirk's yellow eyes.

'That's better,' he said. But nothing changed the rictus of hatred and anger on the dead man's mouth.

Mel looked around and when no one stepped forward to do the same for Tigera, he leaned over and closed his eyes. A glint caught his attention and he started. The snake. Had it moved? He approached the bed of leaves cautiously. Lying deep in the coils of the thick snake were Tigera's pebble glasses. The sun played on the lenses, sending out flickering signals of gold and silver.

Mel felt nauseous. He saw the little man assiduously polishing his glasses and placing them neatly on his nose. Suddenly the dead body seemed alive again. He picked up the glasses and flinched as his fingers touched the warm body of the puff-adder.

'Don't mess around with the snake,' warned Pat,

watching Mel tidy the corpses. 'There can be flecks of venom on it. Get some of that stuff on your hands and you'll be a sick man.'

Mel nodded and unconsciously wiped his hands on his trousers. He then folded the glasses and placed them deep into the pocket on Tigera's shirt. As he buttoned down the flap keeping the glasses in place, he sensed the men studying him. But when he looked up, Jacob and Jonas were conversing in low tones with their heads turned away, and Pat seemed intent on checking Erin's makeshift dressing.

Mel wiped his hands again and turned to Pat.

'The venom is haemotoxic, isn't it?' he asked.

'Originally it was thought to be,' answered Pat. 'It was believed that extensive haemorrhaging and internal bleeding were the cause of death. But research has now proved that the venom is cytotoxic. It kills living cells. The same sort of poison they use for leukaemia and other cancers.'

Mel shuddered. He left the bodies and threw himself down on the ground beside Erin.

Pat turned to his trackers. 'Try not to drive into any antbear holes on the way back, Jacob.'

The two trackers nodded. They stood up and without glancing back broke into a loping run. As they ran they sang. The hum sounded like a swarm of angry bees. Jacob took the lead and his voice rose loud and clear. Jonas joined in the refrain. Their voices were deep and resonant.

Pat closed his eyes. He could see the impi lifting their legs up high and stamping their feet down as they hit their ox-hide shields. Nature itself stood still and listened when the impi sang.

'Is that song to mourn the death of Tigera and this

other man?' asked Mel as Jacob and Jonas melted into the bush.

'It is certainly about death,' replied Pat diplomatically.

'Who is he?' asked Mel, pointing to Kirk. 'Or should I say, who was he?'

'One of Tigera's henchmen,' said Erin.

'An ex-hunter who had his licence revoked and was kicked out of the country,' said Pat.

'He certainly looks a tough character,' mused Mel, flicking at an ant on his forearm. The three men lounged in the shade and waited for the familiar grinding which would tell of the Toyota's approach.

'What do we do now, Dad?' asked Erin, pressing the bloody shirt tightly against his shoulder. It was beginning to ache and he felt nauseous.

'I'll have to fly the bodies to Harare and report the deaths,' said Pat, his face grim and lines of worry furrowing his forehead.

Erin looked at Mel. He could not take charge of a buffalo hunt now, as the bullet had penetrated his right shoulder.

'I'll come with you,' said Mel.

Pat shook his head, but Mel continued as if he had not seen the gesture.

'I was a witness. I believe that my testimony will bear weight with the officials in Harare.'

'But your hunt, your buffalo?'

Mel smiled at Erin. 'Nothing could keep me away from New Ganyani. I'll be back to hunt with a married man. No,' he corrected himself, looking at Pat. 'With two married men.'

The first fat bluebottle flies arrived to buzz eagerly over

the mangled body of the puff-adder. Soon they found the blood on Kirk and settled on his chest.

Mel and Pat stood up and broke branches from the mopane scrub. These they latticed over Kirk.

The mournful yet haunting call of an emerald-spotted wood dove rang out once again close to them.

The last of Kirk's band of poachers left the area, whistling to his friends.

'A beautiful call,' said Pat. 'In it is all the harshness and beauty of Zimbabwe.'

Softly he imitated the bird's song, then whispered the words:

> 'My mother is dead
> My father is dead
> All my family is dead
> And my heart goes dum, dum, dum.'